UNIVERSITY O...
HARLAXTO...
HARLAX...
GRA...

HARLAXTON COLLEGE

R0143

D0352347

THE PLEASURES OF PEACE

by the same author

The Culture Club: Crisis in the Arts

Richard Rogers: A Biography

The Pleasures of Peace

Art and imagination in post-war Britain

BRYAN APPLEYARD

UNIVERSITY OF EVANSVILLE
HARLAXTON COLLEGE LIBRARY
HARLAXTON MANOR
GRANTHAM, LINCS.

012010

faber and faber

LONDON · BOSTON

First published in 1989
by Faber and Faber Limited
3 Queen Square London WC1N 3AU

This paperback edition first
published in 1990

Typeset by Input Typesetting Ltd, London
Printed in Great Britain by
Cox & Wyman Ltd, Reading, Berkshire

All rights reserved

© Bryan Appleyard, 1989

Bryan Appleyard is hereby identified as author of this work
in accordance with Section 77 of the Copyright, Designs
and Patents Act 1988.

*This book is sold subject to the condition that it shall not, by way of trade
or otherwise, be lent, resold, hired out or otherwise circulated without the
publisher's prior consent in any form of binding or cover other than that
in which it is published and without a similar condition including
this condition being imposed on the subsequent purchaser.*

A CIP record of this book is available from the British Library

ISBN 0-571-16185-5

For Charlotte

So now I must devote my days to The Pleasures of Peace –
To my contemporaries I'll leave the Horrors of War
                              Kenneth Koch, *The Pleasures of Peace*

Contents

Acknowledgements

As well as published sources, there have been many conversations over the past few years that have helped me formulate the ideas in this book. In some cases these conversations have arisen from my journalism. I have, therefore, frequently picked brains under slightly false pretences. In acknowledgement of those and of many other debts, I would like to thank the following: Peter Ackroyd, Will Alsop, Kingsley Amis, Nigel Andrew, John Bodley, Melvyn Bragg, Michael Moorcock, Iris Murdoch, Harold Pinter, Dennis Potter, Richard Rogers, Friedl Weinert.

I would also like to thank my wife, Christena Appleyard, for convincing me of the simple truth that, if I did not sit down and write *The Pleasures of Peace*, it would not get written.

For permission to include prose quotations and extracts from poems grateful acknowledgement is made to the following:

Cambridge University Press for Dorothea Krook, *Three Traditions of Moral Thought*.
The Carcanet Press for C. H. Sisson, *Collected Poems* and *God Bless Karl Marx*.
Century Hutchinson Ltd for Kingsley Amis, *Collected Poems 1944–1979*.
André Deutsch Ltd for Geoffrey Hill, *Collected Poems*.
Faber and Faber Ltd for W. H. Auden, *Collected Poems* and *The English Auden*; T. S. Eliot, *Collected Poems 1909–1962* and *Notes Towards the Definition of Culture*; Ted Hughes, *Selected Poems 1957–1981*; Seamus Heaney, *Death of a Naturalist* and *North*; David Jones, *The Anathemata*; Philip Larkin, *The Whitsun Weddings* and *High Windows*.
Faber and Faber Ltd and the Ezra Pound Literary Property Trust for *The Cantos*.
Anthony Sheil Associates for Peter Ackroyd, *The Diversions of Purley*.

Olwyn Hughes and the Estate of Sylvia Plath for *The Colossus* and *Ariel*.

The Marvell Press for Philip Larkin's 'Church Going', from *The Less Deceived*.

John Murray Ltd for John Betjeman, *Collected Poems* and Kenneth Clark, *Landscape Into Art* and *Civilization*.

Douglas Oliver for quotations from 'In the Cave of Suicession', Street Editions, Cambridge, 1974, published in his collected poems *Kind*, Allardyce, Barnett; London, Lewes, Berkeley, 1987, copyright and all rights reserved by the author.

Oxford University Press for Craig Raine, *A Martian Sends a Postcard Home*.

Peters Fraser & Dunlop Group Ltd for Arthur Marwick, *British Society Since 1945*, published by Penguin Books.

J. H. Prynne for quotations from *Poems*, Agneau 2, Edinburgh and London, 1982. © J. H. Prynne 1969, 1979, 1982.

Routledge and Kegan Paul Ltd for Peter Redgrove, *Dr Faustus's Sea-Spiral Spirit*.

Iain Sinclair for quotations from *Lud Heat*, Albion Village Press, 1975.

Thames and Hudson Ltd for Frances Spalding, *British Art Since 1900*.

Vision Press Ltd, London; Barnes and Noble Books, New York, 1976, for Peter Ackroyd, *Notes for a New Culture*.

The author and the publishers apologize for any errors or omissions in the above list and would be grateful to be notified of any corrections that should be incorporated in future reprints.

Introduction

In time, the years that have passed since the Second World War will be reduced by certainties. Some names and works will survive, others will vanish according to a logic whose nature we cannot know. Yet it will seem inevitable to those who construct it, just as the rough justice of our version of preceding periods appears to us to represent a kind of absolute. Dickens and George Eliot are 'great' novelists of the nineteenth century, Browning and Tennyson two of its great poets. It did not seem so simple to readers of the time.

Nowadays it is much worse. There is far more 'art' clamouring for our attention as well as far more criticism attempting to explain its nature and even, occasionally, trying to predict what will last. In addition, there is no agreement on what constitutes greatness. Art is continually being redefined and tradition subverted. The future is thus made doubly unknowable: not only do we not know what will survive, we cannot even guess why it should, or even whether the 'tradition' – our own certainties about Dickens and Browning – will persist.

We are obliged to live in our period and to accept its terms. That means accepting a bewildering plurality, acknowledging that no one style dominates our age and that there are no universally applicable standards to which we can refer. It also means that we have become accustomed to a high degree of specialization. We have long accepted that understanding quantum mechanics or genetic engineering in detail probably precludes a grasp of modernist aesthetics, but also, increasingly, we do not expect anybody to be an authority on both painting and theatre or even on two opposing tendencies within the same art form. The idea of art is claimed by a multiplicity of voices. This may represent a healthy plurality, but the danger is that the ensuing creative and intellectual babble will make us strangers in our own time.

It is possible, however, to speculate about what actually has happened in the forty-four years since the war. Some themes are, even now, clear. There has been the long struggle with the formidable artistic legacy of the first half of the century, with the knowledge that we live in the shadow of a period comparable in greatness to the Renaissance; the attempt to cope with the imaginative power of science, which has seemed to usurp the role of art as the central creative force of its day; the ambiguity and uncertainty of the national identity: do we have a distinctive national culture that can survive American ascendancy or our accelerating integration with Europe? There has been history itself, and the search for a coherent basis for art in a socially fragmented and irreligious world.

Any one of these themes, as well as a number of others, could be convincingly traced through the period and presented as the single, defining characteristic of the age. Indeed, the cultural histories of the future may do just that. But, from today's perspective, no single explanation would feel quite true. There is only the babble.

This book is therefore a speculation. It aims to illuminate those works and ideas which appear today to be the most important of the period. Inevitably it is a personal view and its limitations are those of the time at which it has been written. The immediate past can frequently seem very distant and very alien; that strangeness can be perceived only through the medium of the present. I am fully aware that some connections I may make could not have been made at the time; but this is not history – it is an explanation of the present, not the past.

So, from this present, the book speculates about the significant, the lasting works of the imagination. Of course we can never be sure such judgements will last more than a moment. We can only assert that, from this temporary and makeshift perspective, the best of these works cannot be reduced.

The book is divided into four parts covering, roughly, the periods 1945–51, 1952–63, 1964–73 and 1974 to the present day. I break out of this chronology when I find it necessary. The individual sections within the four parts are thematic, and again, this is only a rough arrangement. Some sections cover a single artist, some a single issue, others many artists or many issues. In addition, the themes are often deliberately broad. My intention has been to try to avoid making either works or artists too simply representative. By its nature any cultural history will tend to do this; at worst this turns each work of art into a symptom or an expression of fashion. To do this is to deny the complexity of art.

There are two serious omissions. I have not written about music. This is the purest incompetence. I am unable to discuss music convincingly and I decided at an early stage that any attempt to do so would seem incongruous. I have also not covered popular culture. In part this is because it has been so extensively covered elsewhere but, more important, I believe it lies outside my subject. Its primary concerns are neither with art and its identity nor with the ideas associated with those concerns. The claims of, for example, popular music to importance in either area tend to be incidental to its intentions. There are, I know, many more omissions, conscious and probably unconscious. But something, many things, had to go if this book were not to be an impenetrable thicket of names and dates.

Bryan Appleyard
February 1989

PART ONE

Strange Light

Wildflowers had spread over the bomb sites: rose-bay willowherb, coltsfoot, groundsel, Oxford ragwort, Canadian fleabane and Thanet cress.[1]

At 10.20 p.m. on 1 May 1945 German radio announced that Hitler had died 'fighting to his last breath against Bolshevism'. But, strangely, his destruction did not provoke the obvious response, that we could return to our normal lives, that day had at last broken and a nightmare was over. Instead there was a sense that he had changed everything, exposed our weaknesses and misconceptions. Some line of communication with the past had been severed.

'Napoleon set the final seal upon an era of human history [*The Times* wrote of his death]. Hitler has no less certainly brought its successor to a close. The liberalism and *laissez-faire* of the nineteenth century are gone beyond recall. So has the policy of the balance of power and all that it entailed. He has compelled mankind not indeed to think with him, but to think again. But those remoter consequences have still to unfold themselves in their full force. For the moment it is more than enough to know that the world is rid of its most dangerous malefactor.'[2]

On Monday 7 May Germany's unconditional surrender was agreed at Reims to be ratified at Berlin the next day. On Tuesday, VE-Day, a service of thanksgiving at St Paul's began with the hymn 'Now thank we all our God'. Winston Churchill addressed the crowds in Whitehall just before 6 p.m.: 'When shall the reputation and faith of this generation of English men and women fail?' he asked.

'Reprieved from total ruin,' *The Times* wrote under the heading 'Into the Light', 'men may begin to breathe again and indulge in visions . . .'[3]

In Berlin, at sixteen minutes past midnight on Wednesday morning in a brilliantly lit room, Field Marshal Keitel murmured, 'I am

3

prepared to sign it', took off his right glove, placed a monocle in his left eye and put his name to the surrender terms.

Another service at St Paul's on the Sunday began with the hymn 'All people that on earth do dwell'. A continuity was being celebrated, of a nation and its people. Dawn had broken and the sleeper had opened his eyes to be startled by how much seemed to have survived the night. His first reaction was a natural relief – relief that, among other things, the lights could shine again.

At the opening of Charles Williams's novel *All Hallows Eve*, published in 1945, his heroine stands on Westminster Bridge. It is twilight but the city is not as dark as usual. Lights are on, yet shutters, blinds and curtains have not been closed. The blackout is over. 'Those were the lights of peace. It was true that formal peace was not yet in being; all that had happened was that fighting had ceased. The enemy, as enemy, no longer existed and one more crisis of agony was done. Labour, intelligence, patience – much need for these; and much certainty of boredom and suffering and misery, but no longer the sick vigils and daily despair.'[4]

Yet Williams's heroine was dead, a ghost wandering through London in her afterlife for whom the city becomes the field of a battle between good and evil. The simple, happy relief at the onset of peace is instantly replaced by a chilling oddness, a horrible literalness in the way the visions of the spirit world are realized. For Williams, like William Blake before him, *saw* his demons. In any event, his evocation of peace was the purest imagining: he died before hostilities ended.

But peace *was* an event in the imagination. Its physical reality took place far away as vast armies laid down their arms on battlegrounds across Europe. Meanwhile, at home, the paraphernalia of war had long begun to recede into the past. The final peace terms simply locked them away for ever.

'In the last days of April [Corelli Barnett was to write forty years later] and the first days of May the light of peace began to glow strangely on the familiar Britain of sirens and tin-hats, battledress and sandbags, stirrup-pumps and air-raid shelters. It transmuted at a touch all such apparatus of recent survival into historical relics, at one with the medieval battlements of England's castles and the pikes and halberds in the Tower Armoury.'[5]

The war had become heritage: odd, distant and sentimentally cherishable. Its tools, deprived of function, became ornaments, *aides-mémoire*, like snapshots or souvenirs. But its more lasting legacy – the physical ruin of the cities – could not be so easily subsumed into a soothing, domestic iconography. Wild flowers may have colonized and softened the bomb sites but their connotations of pastoral harmony were set against disturbing discontinuities. Muriel Spark recalled them almost twenty years later at the beginning of her 1963 novel *The Girls of Slender Means*:

'Long ago in 1945 all the nice people in England were poor, allowing for exceptions. The streets of the cities were lined with buildings in bad repair or in no repair at all, bomb-sites piled with stony rubble, houses like giant teeth in which decay had been drilled out, leaving only the cavity. Some bomb-ripped buildings looked like the ruins of ancient castles until, at a closer view, the wall-papers of various quite normal rooms would be visible, room above room, exposed, as on a stage, with one wall missing; sometimes a lavatory chain would dangle over nothing from a fourth- or fifth-floor ceiling; most of all the staircases survived, like a new art-form, leading up and up to an unspecified destination that made unusual demands on the mind's eye. All the nice people were poor; at least, that was a general axiom, the best of the rich being poor in spirit.'[6]

Peace was a shock in every respect: the shock of seeing cities at peace yet still torn and surreally plundered by war; the shock of rejoicing. In spite of the years since the tide had turned against Germany, people encountered victory almost with disbelief. The myth of England, evoked over and over again in Churchill's oratory, seemed to be true after all. The hymns in St Paul's, even the wild flowers, spoke of the unbroken continuity of the national will, character and landscape. Britain had prevailed as she had before against her European and Imperial enemies. The sandbags and the stirrup-pumps really were the descendants of the armour and heraldry that had, yet again, overcome the French in 1944 in Laurence Olivier's film of Shakespeare's *Henry V*.

Also in 1944 there was Michael Powell's and Emeric Pressburger's film *A Canterbury Tale*. It is a fable, a film with a message. Modern pilgrims are on their way to Canterbury, unconsciously retracing the 600–year-old steps of Chaucer's characters. Along the route a Land Girl, an American sergeant and an English sergeant meet near a perfect English village. There they find the local girls are being terrorized by the Glueman, a mysterious figure who leaps out at them in the dark and pours glue on their hair. The villain is exposed as the local magistrate; he attacks the girls to discourage them from going out at night and thus forces the men to stay indoors and listen to his otherwise unpopular lectures on English history. The case solved, the pilgrims finally reach Canterbury where, as tradition demanded, each is granted a blessing: the girl hears her boyfriend is not dead, the American receives his girlfriend's letters and the Englishman is given a chance to play the cathedral organ. Beneath all the strange, sun-drenched and theatrical pastoralism is the clear message that a mystical English unity exists to confer blessings and insight. The wartime cast of Land Girls and soldiers only serves to emphasize the permanence of that unity, embedded as it is in the stones of the cathedral and the village.

There was also the shock of being faced with a future without the system of meanings, values and directions provided by the existence of a common enemy. For Charles Williams the forces of darkness had been real enough, with or without the war; peace would simply be a different type of struggle. But for H. G. Wells, the old rationalist, the old atheist, finding a purpose in history, in life, was more of a problem. In 1945 Wells was dying of cancer and the collapse of his liver functions in his 'coldly elegant'[7] house overlooking Regent's Park. Playing the role of the optimistic Edwardian, he had written in *The Happy Turning*: 'The human mind may be in a phase of transition to a new, fearless, clear-headed way of living in which understanding will be the supreme interest in life and beauty a mere smile of approval.'[8]

With the defeat of Hitler, the 'most dangerous malefactor', such a belief may have had a certain glib attraction. But in Wells's dying heart the war between the Edwardian and the despairing, embittered

6

old man was also coming to an end. The real victor emerged in *Mind at the end of its tether*: 'Our universe is not merely bankrupt; there remains no dividend at all; it has not simply liquidated; it is going clean out of existence, leaving not a wrack behind. The attempt to trace a pattern of any sort is absolutely futile.'[9]

Symbolically, Wells's laboured imagery of commerce – bankrupt, dividend, liquidated – fails to contain his dismay. He settles for a Shakespearian evocation of nothingness and an impatient dismissal of reason itself. Typically his two sides – the old Edwardian Utopian with a longing for clear, Hegelian patterns in history and the cantankerous nihilist in despair at the palpable vacuity of it all – embodied the ambiguity of the war's end. A terrible episode had ended but the programme for the next phase had not been written and, meanwhile, the stain of the past's crimes seemed ineradicable. In spite of the sense of a new beginning, the age remained somehow late, devoid of energy or reason to continue. Its severance from the past left it at a beginning certainly, but a beginning of nothing. The great, inexplicable evil of the concentration camps was repeatedly driven home by newspapers and newsreels in 1945, suggesting that centuries of European civilization had constructed little more than a charnel house. In Hitler our age had produced a man who seemed to reduce all history's previous malefactors to minor mutations from the norm – 'The greed and ruthlessness of others who have sought to conquer Europe appear compared with his the excesses of normal albeit brutal men.'[10]

Meanwhile the atom bombs that ended the Japanese war in August provided visions of tremendous foreboding. Human conflict had finally refined its mechanisms to the point where it could offer extinction, Wells's universal cessation. The imagination struggled to subdue these portents.

'All that can be said with certainty [wrote *The Times* after Hiroshima had been bombed and the world was still waiting for the clouds of debris to clear to allow reconnaissance aircraft to photograph the devastation], is that the world stands in the presence of a revolution in earthly affairs at least as big with potentialities of good and evil as when the forces of steam or electricity were harnessed for the first time to the purposes of war . . . Science itself is neutral, like the blind forces of nature that it studies and aspires to control.'[11]

The Bomb, in this argument, was like any other product of the union of neutral science and blind nature. But the effort is unconvincing. The dread of chaos and disintegration lies behind the leader-writer's prose and the affirmation of the free, rational objectivity of the efforts of post-Renaissance science rings desperately hollow. The bodies may have indulged but the imaginations held back from the crude rejoicings in the Mall, Trafalgar Square and at St Paul's, sensing that there had been a breakage; something had been severed, not rejoined.

There was an even crueller twist to all this for it was not just a disconnection from the past by a simple historic barrier. That had happened many times before: some great event had changed things, but the old world could still be retrieved in reminiscence. This time, however, that world seemed to have been corrupted. We could not look back wistfully to the past because it could be seen to be gestating Hitler and the Bomb. How could history be so pure and calming when all its efforts could produce only such destruction, such suffering?

The end of the First World War saw the first triumphant appearance of P. G. Wodehouse's perfect fictional vision of human stability and judgement, the eternal butler, in his 1919 novel *My Man Jeeves*. Jeeves had brought tea for the awakening Bertie Wooster in a sunlit land that knew nothing of the trenches. At the end of the Second World War Wodehouse was living in a flat in Paris, bewildered by the anger he had caused at home with his few harmless broadcasts from Germany while interned for the duration. Jeeves, Wooster and the sunlit land were to survive intact, but they had become the letters home of an exile, dispatches from a foreign country.

Yet, in spite of the dismay and the multiple shocks of peace, the idea of reconstruction was potent. Life, after all, showed every sign of going on. Some mechanism, politics or vision would be necessary for its conduct and the very fact that we were beginning again offered a kind of framework. The Great War of 1914–18 has always been seen as the century's most effective disillusioning force, when the old dispensations seemed to founder, but it was the war of 1939–45 which, above all, signalled that the old order could not be left to its own devices. General Haig and his trench warfare had blighted the notion of authority; but a lost empire, the rise of the USA and the USSR and the exposure of the evil heart of Europe now threatened Britain's entire historic identity. The threat was expressed most spectacularly by the 1945 general election result when Churchill's Tories were discarded in favour of Clement Attlee's Socialists.

'It was not a vote about queues or housing,' Cyril Connolly wrote in *Horizon*, 'but a vote of censure on Munich and Spain and Abyssinia . . . Talk of it as a vote against the religion of money and the millionaire hoodlums.'[12] Like Wells, Connolly appeared somehow to want to link a social climacteric with the idea of commerce: the 'millionaire hoodlums' evoked the black marketeers who had done well out of the war. For post-war humanists like Connolly the contrast between the wartime sacrifices of the fighting men and the people, and the self-enrichment of the capitalists and the spivs had become intolerable. Edwardian optimism may have been replaced by despair, but that, in turn, was replaced by a new, undeceived, secular determination to get things done. Jeeves was all very well in his context as a fixer to the ruling classes, but less cultivated heroes were needed now.

The heroes were to be the bureaucrats of equal treatment for all. A health service, pensions and schools represented 'a monumental expression of the principle of universality'[13] whereby society was to be unified by vast welfare networks which aimed to eradicate social injustice. It was about reason, planning and the conviction that it was the only way we could escape from the blighted past.

Even so, that past lay all about. The rubble on which the bureaucrats wished to build everywhere revealed fragments of the old world, dispersed and forced into grotesque conjunctions, but legible none the less. The artists were similarly dispersed by the years of war. In 1945 Aldous Huxley, the precociously brilliant cynic of the literary society of the 1920s, was in Llano del Rio in the Mojave Desert, meditating on the impending triumph of technology. W. H. Auden was living in a womb of domestic squalor in New York, having abandoned his 1930s belief in the social function of poetry. T. S. Eliot published *Four Quartets* in 1944 and came to the view that European civilization as a whole was threatened by the rise of the USA and a

Labour government. Francis Bacon, meanwhile, after a false start in the 1930s, had rediscovered his role as a painter and exhibited *Three Studies for Figures at the Base of a Crucifixion* in 1945.

The culture seemed dispersed over vast intellectual and physical distances. This produced a type of imaginative agoraphobia. The years immediately after the war were marked by the appearance of a series of more or less popular works which attempted grand syntheses intended to restore a sense of wholeness to the world, to reduce its immense and threatening spaces. The ideology of reconstruction alone was too parochial to account for everything: Britain herself seemed too hemmed in for her local preoccupations to amount to much. There were new and incomprehensible forces as well as the privations of rationing and successive economic crises brought on by the accumulation of wartime debt.

The impulse to transcend the particular, to attempt to assemble the big picture, inspired Humphrey Jennings. He was a film-maker, born in 1907 into a liberal arts-and-crafts family background; his father was an architect and his mother an artist. During the war he had made films like *Listen to Britain* and *Fires Were Started*, strange, poetic collages of national life, but from 1937 until his death in 1950, he was also assembling a literary anthology entitled *Pandaemonium* in which he chronicled 'the coming of the machine age as seen by contemporary observers'. It began with Milton and ended with William Morris. Throughout, it contrasted 'the means of vision' with 'the means of production' - the transformation of the world by the imagination with the brute transformation of matter by labour.

In his introduction Jennings wrote:

'Unless we are prepared to claim special attributes for the poet – the attribute of vision – and unless we are prepared to admit the work of the artist (that is to say the function of "imagination") as an essential part of the modern world there is no real reason for our continuing to bother with any of the arts any more, or with any imaginary activity. No reasons except money, snobbery, propaganda or escapism. In this book however it is assumed that the poet's vision does exist, that the imagination is a part of life, that the exercise of the imagination is an indispensable function of man like work, eating, sleeping, loving. I do not propose to ask the obvious next question: "What then is the place of the imagination in the world of today?" I prefer to inquire what may have *been* the place of the imagination in the making of the modern world.'[14]

Jennings's short 1945 film, *A Diary for Timothy*, was scripted by E. M. Forster. It is in the form of an address to a baby, supposedly born in 1944, about the kind of world he may expect to inhabit. Timothy's face is superimposed upon the flames of war. We are shown a warm, optimistic portfolio of images of people at work: the Welsh miner Goronwy, the engine driver Bill, the farmer Alan, and Peter, a wounded pilot. A European culture is evoked – wholesome, continuous and enfolding. John Gielgud is seen playing Hamlet at the Haymarket Theatre and Dame Myra Hess playing Beethoven at a wartime concert in the National Gallery. The music is very beautiful, the narrative points out with a distant, wistful helplessness, but it was written by a German. Timothy, the heir of old, broken Europe, must think about that as he grows up through the long years of peace.

For Jennings the opposition that lay at the heart of the 'modern world' was that between production and vision, the machine and the imagination, but mechanization was not simply an enemy of poetry: it was a new force the poet had to encompass. His book and his films provided no argument on the issue, but a collage in which extracts drew meaning from their proximity to others. This method lies at the heart of all film – in montage lies the truth – but, in addition, it suggested the confused legacy of the war, the apparently random rubble of the culture on which wild flowers had, unnervingly, begun to grow.

Modest Windows

In the imagination there was still this green, legendary land beyond the ruined cities. It hung like a mirage behind the victory celebrations, just as it had once lived in the minds of those poets who found themselves fighting in the grey sterility of the trenches: the land of 'England', a name which, left to its own devices, evokes always a rural, never an urban, landscape. In this land soft, rolling hills and dales enfolded villages, with their pubs and parish churches whose infinitely various spires provided the only vertical accents in an otherwise horizontal world. Spitfires and Hurricanes had wheeled gallantly over these hills and fields; small and outnumbered, they had taken on the forces of an urban, industrialized nation and won. The landscape of the small and the green with its ancient weathered buildings and local eccentrics had produced another generation of reluctant but undefeatable warriors. It was a moral force, but it was also the standard by which all beauty was judged. 'Almost every Englishman', Kenneth Clark wrote in 1949, 'if asked what he meant by "beauty", would begin to describe a landscape – perhaps a lake and mountain, perhaps a cottage garden, perhaps a wood with bluebells and silver birches, perhaps a little harbour with red sails and white-washed cottages; but, at all events, a landscape.'[1]

In his 1941 novel *The Aerodrome* Rex Warner, a close friend of W. H. Auden during his politically engaged phase in the 1930s, set this landscape against the ideologies that threatened its moral stature, its very existence. On the one hand there is the village with the rector, the church and the pub; on the other there is the aerodrome with its Fascist aspirations towards order, large-scale organizations and efficiency. The novel is a harsh parable of the irreconcilable differences between the two, a rare excursion in English fiction into an entirely symbolic mode. It was inspired in part by the fashionable and portentous preoccupations of the 1930s but, equally, by the sense that, for all the moral dangers of Fascism, England was in danger of

12

being trapped in a paralysed past. 'That you are still tied to the immense and dreary procession of past time is true,' the Air Vice-Marshal explains to the hero, a man in search of his identity and trapped between the worlds of aerodrome and village, 'it is the business of a man, and particularly of an airman, to rid himself, so far as he can of this bond.'[2]

There was another landscape of the more distant past, known as 'Britain'. This was a wilder land of marshes, forests and mists inhabited by earlier, more intractable races. It had become the popular playground of tweedy, academic whimsy with J. R. R. Tolkien's *The Hobbit* (1937) and his *Lord of the Rings* cycle of the mid-1950s. It also emerged, surprisingly, in Evelyn Waugh's 1950 religious tale, *Helena*, the story of the saint who discovered the True Cross: *she* was from Britain. 'Once, very long ago, before ever the flowers were named which struggled and fluttered below the rain-swept wall there sat at an upper window a princess and a slave reading a story which even then was old.'[3]

But this more remote, more difficult land inhabited by 'folk' and subject to great conflicts and mythologies was too universal and too similar to the folk-landscapes of other nations. Waugh felt uncertain there; his own post-war persona was strictly English and of the type that saw only destruction resulting from the onslaught of the new. 'It has been', he wrote, 'the experience of a middle-aged Englishman to be born into one of the most beautiful countries in the world and watch it change year by year into one of the ugliest.'[4]

The point was that, although the war to defend the landscape of England from the mechanized threat had been won, there were other dangers. In reality, these dated back almost two hundred years to the beginning of modern industry and of the long process that transformed the rural poor into an urban proletariat. The spiritual dangers of this process had been chronicled by the English literary classes to the point where they became an artistic convention, but never before had the old English landscape been so closely linked to the national identity. Industry and Empire once provided national causes as potent as any parish church, but now, with the Empire in decline and industry tainted by two mechanized European orgies of destruction, 'England' came into its own.

The modest windows palely glazed with green,
The smooth slate floor, the rounded wooden roof,
The Norman arch, the cable-moulded font –
All have a humble and West Country look.[5]

That was John Betjeman in a collection of poems published in
1945. The architectural details are listed precisely and with technical
expertise in a seamless rhythm suggesting the weathered, worn-in
quality of the objects themselves. But two adjectives – 'modest' and
'humble' – carry the real rhetorical charge. These details make no
grand claims: instead they have a stature of their own, far removed,
and implicitly superior to, any pre-war artistic or political heroics.
This is not T. S. Eliot's 'Waste Land', or the Spain of W. H. Auden:
it is England.

Yet it was not quite clear precisely what was at stake. Sure enough,
Waugh simply saw an ideal of aristocratic rural life being routed by
democratic urban change, but in 1945 the legendary landscape of
England was as easily found as the bomb sites in the cities. And, from
Wordsworth onwards, mourning its despoliation had been a national
pastime. In short, little had changed but, at the same time, it was the
very threatened, hemmed-in quality, its fragility, which created much
of the defensive fear and intensified the old longings, from the
trenches of 1914–1918 to the perfect young men in their fighter
cockpits over Kent. The act of its preservation and conservation was
a means of nourishing the national character.

But Betjeman's arch, roof and font are being looked at by a modern
man and through the distanced gaze of an architectural expert. They
are there, but they do not mean to him what they meant to their
makers. His loving litanies of detail suggest a spiritual completeness
for the observer in sadness and nostalgia, but the very fact that the
details are being cherished for themselves gives the game away. This
is a dream of the countryside and its rituals as self-justifying, closed
spiritual circuits. The life that had formed them had long gone.
Betjeman's was a dream of 'England' in which its culture had been
frozen in an ideal past. It was not a means of shoring up something
for fear it would be lost, but a celebration of that loss.

Remove, however, the explicit nostalgia and the self-conscious

observer and you have the truly self-contained artistic world of Wodehouse. His endlessly various ploys demand no external reference and
no rhetoric of national salvation. Their meaning lies in the delicate
equilibrium whereby aunts are forever fearsome creatures and trade
is an activity both inherently comic and remote, while lovers and other
enthusiasts pursue their own ends through a miasma of embarrassment, obligation and coincidence. *Full Moon* was published in 1947
as though internment and national rejection had never happened to
its author. Set in Blandings Castle, where the prize pig the Empress
of Blandings continues to fatten under the obsessed eye of Lord
Emsworth, it runs with the usual clockwork precision, isolated and
immune from Wodehouse's own problems and those of the world.
The town and the country form the customary poles of the narrative;
some survive and thrive in the former, but Lord Emsworth, in particular, can function only in the latter. 'London, with its roar and bustle
and people who bumped into you and omnibuses which seemed to
chase you like stoats after a rabbit, always had a disintegrating effect
on the master of Blandings Castle, reducing his mental powers to a
level even below that of the jellyfish to which his brother had compared
him.'[6]

The artistry of Wodehouse lay in the way he would elaborately
balance such conflicts effectively to neutralize the novel as a whole.
No attitude, posture or opinion triumphs. The world goes on troubled
only from within by containable, understandable crises. Even yearning
for the existence of such a place appears grotesque since its very
seamlessness almost precludes any such emotion. But somehow it
seemed to be there, sun-drenched and perfect, if not in this village,
then in the next.

The rhetorical force of the little world of England, with its firm
belief in the virtues of the neighbourhood and the moral significance
of the quotidian, was too good for the film industry to miss. It was
turned, with remarkable precision, into serious drama in David Lean's
1945 film *Brief Encounter*. A doctor and a housewife fall in love and
conduct their affair through meetings at a local railway station. The
imagery is urban but there is no mistaking the Little English banality
of the tea rooms, the impatient waitress and the insistent narrative
importance of the train timetable. Nor can we miss the cataclysmic

significance with which the idea of adultery is endowed. And it is this significance – the grand passion – which must ultimately lose out to the life-sustaining rituals of domestic banality. The film derives its style from that of the well-made West End play. Its content is the conflict between overpowering feeling and the necessary forms of daily life. In the rejection of the demands of passion, English continuity is sustained.

But cinema habitually identifies its role as public and proselytizing in a more direct fashion than this. It tends to require a programme to justify its cost and complexity. The apparent triumph of Englishness in the war provided just such a programme.

It was a posture that had been anticipated in Walter Forde's 1939 film *Cheer Boys Cheer*, in which a small local brewery, Greenleaf, fights off a big city competitor, Ironside, in an assertion of the eccentric virtues of village life.[7] Black limousines confront ivy-clad cottages and machines are pitted against craftsmanship: a confrontation to be staged again and again by the movies that came out of Ealing Studios under Michael Balcon. He believed that British life should be used as a specifically propagandist weapon – it was, he appeared to be saying, so obviously attractive. Although this frequently meant using the same imagery as Wodehouse, the effect was entirely different. Wodehouse novels end not with resolution but with the assurance that the world with all its contained conflicts would continue: there is no lesson to be learned, no nod of approval on the last page. But Balcon's polemical posture required his plots to resolve with a victory for the virtues of Little England. It was a formula that started to go wrong when more difficult talents – like that of Robert Hamer – emerged from the studios.

In Hamer's section of the multi-director film *Dead of Night* (1945) a wealthy couple are to be married. She gives him an antique mirror in which he begins to see visions that drive him to the edge of insanity. Dark forces threaten his stability, just as adultery had once threatened society in *Brief Encounter*. The woman smashes the mirror, having discovered that in 1830 it had reflected a murder. With this perfunctory explanation normality is restored, though unconvincingly. What remains in the mind, rather than the conventional plot and its resolution, is the hard, brittle, un-Ealing quality of the style. With

Kind Hearts and Coronets in 1949, this brittleness seems to force its way completely out of the Ealing mode. Here there is something of Wodehouse's self-contained quality combined with a hard, though comic, amorality entirely foreign to the world of Wooster and Emsworth. A Wildean decadence and self-consciousness have penetrated the sunlit village landscape. The film celebrates a defiant, selfish indulgence, which the all too honourable little ambitions of Ealing threatened. The closing shot of the memoirs of the callous murdering hero effectively seals off the work from the proselytizing aspirations of Balcon. It says: this is a film, the underlying reality is no longer.

Charles Barr wrote that the shot 'is the image of the film itself, since these memoirs, prologue and epilogue apart, constitute the film. To the question of how we finally take it all, what we make of it, the answer we are left with is this: the memoirs, the film, the total artefact. The memoir is the message, the meaning is the film.'[8]

The movie was virtually a rogue. Barr summarizes the true tradition of Ealing thus:

'Ealing never loses its allegiance to the ideal community described in *Passport to Pimlico* and *The Blue Lamp*: stable, gentle, innocent, already consciously backward-looking and based on the elaborate set of loyalties and renunciations that will by now be familiar. This community recedes inexorably into the past. Partly, the specific processes of postwar history leave it behind; partly its own internal frailty, its lack of dynamism, renders it vulnerable to the passage of time as such, like a preserved mummy crumbling when exposed to the air.'[9]

In fact the history of Ealing was to demonstrate the failure of the myth of England as a practical, if not an aesthetic, programme. This is how Balcon described his purpose in 1945:

'Every shade of opinion should be represented, and the scope of the films should go far beyond the purview of the Government documentary. Fiction films which portray contemporary life in Britain in different sections of our society, films with an outdoor background of the British scene, screen adaptations of our literary classics, films reflecting the postwar aspiration not of governments or parties, but of individuals – these are the films that America, Russia and the Continent of Europe should be seeing now and at the first opportunity.'[10]

It was a startling affirmation of the meaning that had become attached to victory. Yet again, at the heart of the national life was perceived a core of values – linked to our countryside and our characters – which needed to be demonstrated to the world, as though to replace the more pragmatic and increasingly discredited systems of empire.

By 1956 Ealing had closed and the company had moved to a corner of the Metro-Goldwyn-Mayer (MGM) lot at Elstree, becoming a colony of the USA. From there Balcon wrote: 'We shall go on making dramas with a documentary background and comedies about ordinary people with the stray eccentric among them – films about day-dreamers, mild anarchists, little men who long to kick the boss in the teeth.'[11]

The diminution of ambition is painful to contemplate. The heroic individuals, whose activities once dwarfed those of governments, have become 'day-dreamers, mild anarchists, little men' or, most deadening of all to the imagination, 'ordinary people'.

Apart from the obvious business mistake of believing that British films could be self-supporting in a world overwhelmingly dominated by the American industry, Balcon made a more serious error. He believed that in his imaginary Britain there was an exportable, transmissible moral force – you had merely to show the little people and their lives and the message would be clear enough. The war seemed to have reinforced this conviction beyond reasonable doubt. It appeared to have shown that there was practical, physical power in Little England that could overcome any amount of efficiency or political theory. The 'little' boats of Dunkirk – a drama filmed by Balcon on a curiously small scale under the aegis of MGM in 1958 – and Churchill's notion of 'the few' who won the Battle of Britain implied that right, however outnumbered, could actually triumph over might: the rolling hills and the churches had a core of resilience denied to the enemy. But by 1956 Balcon was obliged to devalue this myth; the war had been won on American money, the moral force of the landscape was mere propaganda, a fabrication devised to catch the mood of victory. The world might be prepared to see our ways as eccentric or cute, but by 1956 – the year of Suez – it was not prepared to listen to our homilies. The Empire and the landscape had gone and, as Lionel Esher was to ask, 'the Commonwealth could replace the former but what the latter?'[12]

The green and pleasant land was flawed. The connection with the past, apparently affirmed by victory, was an illusion. Significance drained from it leaving the imaginary land pale and insubstantial. Perhaps the cause was simply the realization that it *was* imaginary, for, above all else, the post-war period rediscovered the aesthetic of realism which, layer by layer, stripped away the deceptions of a continuous national identity.

Lost deceptions lie behind the drained, bloodless feeling that pervades Philip Larkin's 1947 novel *A Girl in Winter*. In 1943 Larkin emerged from Oxford – where he had befriended and been overawed by Kingsley Amis – to become a librarian. He had published two collections of poetry – *Poetry from Oxford in Wartime* and *The North Ship* – in 1944 and 1945. His first novel, *Jill*, appeared in 1946; *A Girl in Winter* was his second and last. It concerns Katherine Lind, a foreigner of unspecified nationality, who works in a small-town library in England during the war. A message from an old English pen-friend and almost-lover, Robin Fennel, takes her back to her first visit to the country six years before, and this episode occupies most of the novel. At one point Robin imagines England through Katherine's eyes: 'Small fields, mainly pasture. Telegraph wires and a garage. That Empire Tea placard. And you know, don't you, that Britain is small country, once agricultural but now highly industrialised, relying a good deal for food on a large empire. You see, it all links up.'[13]

It is the familiar landscape, brought somewhat up to date by the placard, a detail that could have come from *Brief Encounter*, but the point is precisely that it does not link up. The perspective is empty, painful and the summary glib. Robin's very remoteness suggests that his words have no substance and, towards the end of her visit, Katherine has finally grasped the point: 'She had come expecting to solve a mystery, and she had found at the end that there was no mystery to solve.'[14] Later her own sad insight into the effects of ageing is cast in the form of a landscape image, but one that is a bitter recasting of the usual rural spectacle:

'Life ceased to be a confused stumbling from one illumination to another, a series of unconnected clearings in a tropical forest, and became a flat landscape, wry and rather small, with a few unforgettable landmarks somewhat resembling a stretch of fen-land where an occasional dyke or broken fence shows up for miles, and the sails of a mill turn all day long in the steady wind.'[15]

Nothing happens – things just go on. The turning sails are not a pretty rural feature, they are interminable, dull, pointless, a reminder only of passing time. As a novel *A Girl in Winter* is a willed dead end; only in his poetry was Larkin to find a satisfactory way of dealing with the blank inconclusiveness of his vision. But its tone, passive and mournful, and its content, a passionless despair, mark a kind of beginning, albeit of a retreat. They show an impatience with all the postures of the past. From that comes the awful, constricting revelation that the world just happens day by petty day. The English artist is again hemmed in by his landscape, but no longer in a tight, wholesome community, strong enough to withstand external threats. Now he is trapped in his own sense of absence. Betjeman delighted in loss, pretending it was a gain; Larkin cannot take pleasure even in that. There was simply nothing there to start with. Our age was obliged to face the fact: the grand movements of history would simply have to pass us by. As Larkin's friend and literary kindred spirit Kingsley Amis wrote in his 1944 poem 'Belgian Winter':

> Then if history had a choice, he would point his cameras
> Oh yes anywhere but here, any time but now;[16]

This was the beginning of the powerful orthodoxy of provincial realism which was to reign in the 1950s. More precisely, it was foreshadowed in a slightly more self-conscious, more literary version of the same approach in William Cooper's 1950 novel *Scenes from Provincial Life*. Cooper is the pseudonym of Harry Summerfield Hoff, and as a teacher in Leicester before the war he had published novels under his own name. His book does not share Larkin's air of finality and there is a more novelish feel – Larkin repeatedly veers off in the

MODEST WINDOWS

direction of a prose poem. But there is the same sense of wan helplessness, of incomprehension at the posturings of the world:

'When you go to the theatre you see a number of characters caught in a dramatic situation. What happens next? They have a scene. From the scene springs action, such as somebody pooping off a revolver. And then everything is changed.

'My life is different. Sometimes observant friends point out to me that I am actually in a dramatic situation. What happens next? I do not have the scene; or if I do, it is small and discouragingly undramatic. Practically no action arises. And nothing whatsoever is changed. My life is not as good as a play. Nothing like it.'[17]

Even the war between the little world of home and the big world of passion of *Brief Encounter* has now given way to something smaller. Real life does not even have that, apparently realistic, conflict. The stakes are so much smaller, the choices so much more trivial. In an introduction to the novel Malcolm Bradbury later wrote:

'By the postwar period the root-conditions of modernism were more or less exhausted in English society, and the cultural dominance of Bloomsbury was certainly coming to an end; it was hard for the new generation of English writers to take up the modernist mode for the exploration of their culture. Cooper later placed himself in the context of an explicit revolt against the "Thirties" novel in its mannerist and experimental guise, and against the French *anti-roman*. Art, he said in an essay of 1959, depended not on a series of attacks on the powers and place of the human mind, but an assertion of mind.'[18]

The undeceived gaze of the new realism was turning away from many things – from the frailties of post-war reconstruction, from religion, from culture, from modernism and from the world. Yet there were others equally intent on those objects. The dream of a unified national culture, for example, was busily being shored against its ruin by the appearance in 1948 of F. R. Leavis's *The Great Tradition*. Leavis, the cantankerous academic outsider, had fought from Cambridge for over twenty years for the establishment of a new, tough critical orthodoxy for English literature which gazed exclusively and relentlessly at the text, almost to the exclusion of all else. In a literary continuity Leavis believed he could discern the heart of the culture as well as its secular roots in an ancient form of organic community. *The Great Tradition* was his attempt to trace this orthodoxy along the fictional line running from Jane Austen through Eliot, James and Conrad.

A more tortuous, less prescriptive assault on the idea of a sustainable and continuous culture appeared in 1948 – T. S. Eliot's *Notes Towards the Definition of Culture*. Eliot had been engaged on this work for some time, but the intrinsic abstraction and obscurity of his ideas had prevented him reaching any kind of satisfactory form. His project was to relate a nation's culture to its religion and on this basis the book aspired to define a form of unified, ideal society. This impulse, and the real tension in the book, derives from the fear of imminent social and political disintegration which obsessed Eliot in the post-war period. The obsession produced a demand for a new European unity of purpose. An appendix to the essay consists of a transcript of some broadcasts he had made to Germany entitled *The Unity of European Culture*. It concludes:

'My last appeal is to the men of letters of Europe, who have a special responsibility for the preservation and transmission of our common culture. We may hold very different political views: our common responsibility is to preserve our common culture uncontaminated by political influences. It is not a question of sentiment; it does not matter so much whether we like each other, or praise each other's writings. What matters is that we should recognise our relationship and mutual dependence upon each other. What matters is our inability, without each other, to produce those excellent works which mark a superior civilisation. We cannot, at present, hold much communication with each other. We cannot visit each other as private individuals; if we travel at all, it can only be through government agencies and with official duties. But we can at least try to save something of those goods of which we are the common trustees; the legacy of Greece, Rome and Israel, and the legacy of Europe throughout the last 2,000 years. In a world which has seen such material devastation as ours, these spiritual possessions are also in imminent peril.'[19]

The prose barely conceals the rising panic at the suspicion that all that remained of the culture was broken concrete. That collapse was the vision of Ezra Pound's *Cantos*, poems that were still being written, their moments of greatness increasingly buried beneath mountains of incoherence. Eliot took no pleasure from the ending of hostilities, finding the noise of the fireworks after the surrender of the Japanese more disturbing that the bombs of the Blitz. He believed the post-war world was less moral than that of the 1930s.

Peter Ackroyd described his state of mind:

'There was a prospect ahead of centuries of barbarism which, in an interview the year before, he had already related to the coming dominance of technology. The barbarians did not arrive in his lifetime, but there is no doubt that Eliot was aware that he was witnessing the end of the culture which, more than thirty years before, he had travelled to Europe to find.'[20]

Late, religiously converted Eliot turned from the hard, glittering modernism he had once created with *The Waste Land*, to replace it not with his nervy, invocatory prose but with *Four Quartets*, published as a whole in 1944, in which 'we see the outlines of a tradition beautifully limned but shimmering like an hallucination before it disappears'.[21]

In those poems the effort to hold the idea of the nation together as an imaginative unity found its most moving and complete artistic expression. They were a bridge constructed between the pre-war and post-war worlds. In a mighty effort of will Eliot composed his mournful, unforgettable music in praise of a culture of perfect spiritual equilibrium where landscape and history – neither of them tainted by the encroaching fragmentation of the present – would interpenetrate to suggest the model of salvation.

> A people without history
> Is not redeemed from time, for history is a pattern
> Of timeless moments. So, while the light fails
> On a winter's afternoon, in a secluded chapel
> History is now and England.[22]

School Building

The huge shift from *The Waste Land* to *Four Quartets* made Eliot's role ambiguous. The first – published in 1922 – stood unchallengeable as one of the literary peaks of the first half of the century. With James Joyce's *Ulysses*, it was likely to be the first title evoked by any mention of the word 'modernism' and, as such, took on associations of decadence and artiness quite foreign to Eliot's character. In Evelyn Waugh's *Brideshead Revisited*, published in 1945, Anthony Blanche, the aesthete *par excellence*, is even glimpsed at Oxford reciting passages 'in languishing tones' through a megaphone: ' "*I, Tiresias, have fore-suffered all*," he sobbed to them from the Venetian arches . . .'[1]

But, since Eliot's reception into the Church of England in 1927 and his own painstaking intellectual effort to rejoin his writing to a single, continuous, European tradition, his literary function had been transformed. Where once he had seemed to be the representative of a supreme modernity, the first man to construct something that was convincingly poetry in the complete absence of any vestige of Truth, now he seemed to be striving heroically to reconstruct that Truth. Primarily, of course, the Truth was religious, but its incarnation was the fabric of European civilization. *Four Quartets* was a religious meditation, but also an assertion of unity and timelessness. Thus Eliot, whose modernism had once threatened to detonate the academies, became the great defender of the academic faith. Constantly he spoke of the intercourse of the cultured classes and, as he laboured at his desk as a publisher at Faber and Faber, he became to the public the very emblem of the idea of 'literature' – serious, learned and conservative.

Yet he was also seen as the great and most productively surviving reminder that giants seemed to have walked the earth in the pre-war years. The early twentieth century had seen an efflorescence of genius comparable to that of the Renaissance. The fact of modernism weighed heavily on the artists of the immediate post-war period;

succeeding generations seemed obliged to live in the shadow of its grand claims and ambitions.

The Larkin–Cooper response, which became one of the central and most paralysing orthodoxies of the entire post-war period, was that there had been something fatuous about the whole exercise. Their reaction found virtues in the idea of the 'ordinary' and the mundane in opposition to the modernists' flamboyant displays of learning and cosmopolitanism. In 1945 one image seemed to validate this view of the whole enterprise as somehow cranky and pointlessly arrogant. Ezra Pound – the dedicatee of *The Waste Land* and modernism's noisiest evangelist – had been captured in Italy by the Americans and imprisoned as a traitor for his pro-Fascist broadcasts during the war. From 24 May Pound was locked in a wire cage at Pisa, news of which was greeted with some delight in London: 'Altogether a repellent person,' snarled the *Spectator*, 'who seems likely now to receive part, at any rate, of his desert.'[2]

The point was clear enough: Pound's treachery was an affirmation of the associations of the 'difficult' and arrogant art of the early twentieth century with Fascism and the war itself. The war had been won by the ordinary continuities of Little English life, not by men who wrote incomprehensible poetry and painted distorted, garish pictures.

Modernism was, in any case, distanced from British sensibility by more than just the war. Most of its great names were foreign, even if the Americans Eliot and Pound seemed to have annexed the whole corpus of English culture for their own purposes. In addition, the 1930s had intervened with a concerted local reaction against the manners and the politics of the High Modernists. Their haughty disconnection from anything but their art and their largely right-wing postures were replaced by the 'engaged' poets, who sprang up under the tutelage of Auden and were inspired by the one great cause of the decade – the struggle against Fascism.

Spain – 'that arid square ... soldered so crudely to inventive Europe'[3] – and its civil war provided a cause for the new left-wing intellectuals to rally around. It offered a sense of urgency, which was used specifically to reject the obsessive cultural contemplations of the modernists. Auden's 'Spain 1937' caught the point with absolute and characteristic precision:

Yesterday the belief in the absolute value of Greek;
The fall of the curtain upon the death of the hero;
Yesterday the prayer to the sunset,
And the adoration of madmen. But today the struggle.[4]

More popularly, the 1930s seemed like an extension of an Edwardian summer – but this time a new, expanding middle class could afford some of the good life previously available only to the gentry. Cities spread amiably into the countryside to form suburbs, landscapes soothingly balanced between the urban and the rural. Betjeman glorified the life in these enclaves in his Metroland pastorals and they created the popular image of the 1930s as an English idyll to which the world – large scale, vainglorious and uncomprehending – had no access.

The formal concerns of modernism thus seemed remote both from the politically committed intellectuals and the newly affluent suburban gentry. Moreover, they were easily lampooned. In 1928 Evelyn Waugh created the chilling architectural modernist, Professor Otto Friedrich Silenus: 'The only perfect building must be the factory, because that is built to house machines, not men. I do not think it is possible for domestic architecture to be beautiful but I am doing my best ... man is never beautiful, he is never happy except when he becomes the channel for the distribution of mechanical forces.'[5] The modernist is satirized in terms of his fascination with the machine and his antipathy to the domestic – the first the enemy and the second the foundation of all that was Little England.

By 1945 the prevailing orthodoxy was that the radicals of the 1920s had either been rejected or, like Eliot, subsumed into the establishment. F. R. Leavis, the eternal reconstructor of orthodoxy, wrote a new ending in 1950 for his 1932 work *New Bearings in English Poetry*. It explained the process thus: 'The particular piece of history in question illustrates how, when resistance to the new thing collapses, the readjustment is effected, orthodoxy reconsolidated, and the world made safe again.'[6]

But modernism was not a unitary force to be contained and subdued. More than anything else it was simply a period. Many and complex were the connections between the different achievements of that period, but almost equally numerous were the differences. In literature modernism was politically right wing, mandarin in tone and cared little for social issues; its purpose was the imaginative grasp of the entire culture. Across the spectrum of the visual arts the whole tone was softer. In painting, the British modernism of the 1930s was positively pastoral, the artists characteristically clustered in rural communities such as St Ives. The furthest extreme from the literary posture was to be found in architecture: there, modernism was politically left, demagogic in tone and convinced it was the one art that could achieve social transformation. Its purpose was the reconstruction of the world.

Before the war, its reception in Britain had been about as warm as that accorded to other forms of modern art. There had been sporadic acceptance: houses by the New Zealander Amyas Connell and the Highpoint One block of flats in Highgate by Lubetkin and Tecton won admiration in the continental ateliers where the original forms and ideologies had been conceived. Equally, however, there had been a ferocious backlash. Sir Reginald Blomfield, a strict adherent to the lore and formal vocabulary of Beaux Arts classicism, called the movement 'modernismus' and dismissed it as an invention of the Germans and the Jews. Indeed, so complete were the divisions that, during the war, two precisely opposed plans – Beaux Arts and modern – for the reconstruction of London ran side by side as equally viable contenders.

But in this one area the idea of the modern prevailed. There was the obvious need for new building to fill the bomb sites and sweep away the slums. Such a project brought with it the acceptance of the necessity to start again as if from scratch. The Labour election victory signalled a determination to clear away the debris of the past and to construct anew. Specifically, there was the problem of the legacy of Victorian building, which accounted for most of the fabric of our cities. Lionel Esher has pointed out how even the preservationists of the 1940s saw most of this Victorian urban landscape as expendable, a mess due to be cleared away: 'Where the dingy terraces still stood rotting sandbags oozed on to the pavement, rats infested the cellars, summers of uncut grass choked the back gardens, and black tape or dirty plastic lined the windows. Britain could take it but on the clear understanding that all this mess would be swept away.'[7]

Yet, equally, the soft-left, Fabian tendencies of the Government and of British taste in general would be unlikely to tolerate the full, brutal radicalism of architectural modernism's ideological scaffolding. One Labour minister expressed a wish 'to re-create the classless villages of the seventeenth and eighteenth centuries'.[8] Nevertheless, the idea of the modern had been broadly accepted. A Labour Party document on housing and town planning after the war had said: 'The architect of today is as competent as at any period in our history to design buildings which, while serving their purpose in the most efficient way, are beautiful and reflect the culture, outlook and spirit of the times.'[9]

What was needed to satisfy this mildly herbivorous and muted acceptance of the new was a modification of the full-blooded visionary proselytizing of the carnivorous originators of modernism most typically found in the writings of the Swiss architect Le Corbusier. Maxwell Fry, himself the designer of the purist, Corbusier-style Sun House (1935) in Hampstead, tried to soften the blow in an article in *Horizon* in 1946: 'The vocabulary of modern architecture is capable of enrichment though it lacks the service of an organised and deeply-felt religion,'[10] he wrote, echoing the constant complaint from *Horizon*'s editor, Cyril Connolly, and half its contributors about society's lack of a 'prevailing myth'. Fry went on to play down the significance of the modern movement's frequently hysterical loathing of ornament and then proceeded to fit the whole idea into a genially optimistic view of the culture in general.

'I should point to the interest in architecture and town planning among the general public; the generous and imaginative interpretation of school building programmes by the educational authorities, the growth of the National Trust not entirely because of taxation; the popularity of Puffin and King Penguin books; the rapid absorption of an expensive monograph on a living English sculptor: Henry Moore; the well-filled concert halls; British Arts Council; the current brand of humour to be found in say *Lilliput* or *Punch* . . .'[11]

This idiosyncratic list suggests the sort of recipe the mild-mannered, liberal reconstructionists wished to put together. It was an attempt to present modern art as being at one with the egalitarian mood of the day, and it fitted neatly into the type of cultural public service sensibility which had produced the BBCs classical music Third Programme in September 1946.

Connolly's *Horizon* was an appropriate place to attempt to resolve the conflict between the humane and the modern. Connolly himself was prone to alternating bouts of cataclysmic gloom and buoyant optimism; the first mood generally arose from a conviction that Europe and its civilization were coming to an end, the second from the certainty that precisely the opposite was the case. The conflict mirrored that between modernism and humanism and was deeply embedded in both the readership and editorial policy of his magazine – in which it surfaced in an architectural context in relation to a block of flats, again in Hampstead, built in 1933 by Wells Coates. Known as the Isokon Flats, the block had been the standard bearer of hard modernism. It was described by the historian John Summerson as the most memorable British building of the 1930s; but in 1946 the readers of the otherwise devotedly modernist *Horizon* awarded it second prize in a competition to find the ugliest building, and in 1947 Connolly wrote: 'Since we have no idea what are the values of our present civilisation we cannot get an architecture which embodies them.'[12]

Architecture seemed to bring out a kind of squeamishness among the intellectuals. The feeling was that, more than any other art, it needed a theoretical programme, based either on belief or on a vision of society, which would inform its execution at every stage. In the fragmentation they perceived all around them, the intellectuals were all too ready to believe that no such programme or synthesis was possible; but this underestimated the radical convictions behind the political and popular reconstructive energies. The old picture of Britain after the industrial revolution was to be redrawn. The eighteenth-century transformation of the rural peasantry into the urban proletariat could not perhaps be reversed, but at least the lot of its victims' descendants could be improved. Light and air, the qualities of the countryside, could be brought into the cities.

The models at hand for this process were the visionary cities of European modernism – most spectacularly Le Corbusier's *Ville*

Radieuse, full of *'espace, verdure et soleil'*. With Powell and Moya's Churchill Gardens estate in Pimlico, started in 1946, the process began. The estate consisted of slab-shaped blocks mixed with lower-rise development, all arranged in communal gardens. It was followed by so many similar projects that, today, it may seem entirely unremarkable, but at the time it was the apotheosis of the modern, a statement about urban life drawn from the continental theorizing of the pre-war years. Such buildings were to rise from the slums and bomb sites like rational phoenixes from the ashes of chaos. They were to banish darkness. Light was their inspiration. Low Victorian terraces or even high, cramped tenements darkened each neighbour's aspect, but now housing could reach into the skies from the city below like jungle trees searching for the sun. Horizontal England, with its church spires as lonely vertical accents, had once been transported to the cities as fields of low, blackened terraces, but in the new welfare world light was health. Light penetrated the dark mysteries of the family structure and revealed us all as part of the same community. Light was atheist, unambiguous – a 'prevailing myth' to replace the religion whose passing Connolly could only compulsively mourn.

Somewhat modified, this modern architectural vision became the orthodoxy at the Festival of Britain in 1951. The temperature was modified; much of the visionary heat was removed from the plans and designs of the buildings on the South Bank of the Thames. It was replaced by a sort of cajoling warmth in deference to the Festival's attempt to lead the masses gently into the future. The buildings had a contemporary rather than an aggressively modern feel, and the layout was pure English picturesque; on the whole grand gestures were avoided. The one exception came again from Powell and Moya: the Skylon, a slender needle tapering to points at both ends and suspended by steel cables. As a form it signalled neither the rhetoric of pre-war modernism nor the persuasion of the more domesticated post-war version. It suggested instead the type of thrill associated with science fiction, that of the pure clean gleam of technology. It implied some unspecified function, possibly space travel or communication over vast distances, which was far removed from the bricks and mortar of reconstruction or even from Labour's social engineering. Just as surely as the friendly forms of the other structures, it had its descendants in later years.

Either way the significance of the modern was established. New people thinking new thoughts could do things better than in the past. What was being celebrated at the Festival was not Imperial pomp but British ingenuity and humanity, the wonders of science and the sheer lightness of the world to come. It was an attempt to will into existence a prevailing myth, humanist and reasonable, which would sweep away the darknesses of the past and replace them with towns as picturesque as the countryside. Work on Harlow New Town began in 1949, though Peterlee was held up due to subsidence worries; these were the big, visible steps towards the New Jerusalem, which was to replace the rapidly shrinking Empire. Four years before the Festival, at midnight on 14 August 1947, power had formally been transferred from Britain to the new Dominions of India and Pakistan. Just before that moment the Indian Constituent Assembly met and began their proceedings by singing the hymn 'Vanda Mataram'. Pandit Nehru, independent India's first Prime Minister, told the delegates: 'At the stroke of midnight, while the world sleeps, India will awake to life and freedom.'

Back in Britain the event was interpreted as an assertion of the wisdom and experience we could still offer the world, at the very moment of the dissolution of our Imperial might.

'We pass to the two Dominion Governments [Sir Stanley Reed MP wrote] an administration of high efficiency, perhaps over-elaborate, perhaps too expensive, but one embracing all the functions of modern government; with it the framework and tradition of a civil service without superior in integrity and the true spirit of service. We leave an India free from the threat of aggression, with its boundaries intact, without external debt and with substantial overseas resources. We bequeath to India a superb system of public works.'[13]

The end of the Empire was an assertion of the virtues of empire, of the virtues of Britain. The Festival of Britain was similarly an assertion of our benign power to progress into a new role. We would embrace the modern in forms carefully softened to suit the national taste.

31

This softening is demonstrated by the hesitancy of Maxwell Fry's remarks about the new architecture as well as by the Festival's picturesque layout, for British modernism was diluted in execution. The national version made many more concessions to the irrational and the picturesque than anything seen on the continent. Nevertheless, the ideas behind it were responsible over the next thirty years for a radical change in Britain's self-perception. Ruthless urban development in the name of the modern provided ready-made imagery for a more knowing, cruder sense of alienation than that felt by Larkin. It suggested a penetration of British lives, not only by European collectivist ideals in the big city housing developments, but also by American ideals of mobility in the way motorways lanced through the countryside, making the landscape both visible and inaccessible. The parish church and the cottages in their folds of hills became ever more hemmed in, ever more beleaguered.

The later doubts and the conservation backlash, which emerged in the late 1960s, were evidently related to the literary anti-modernism which was already well established by 1945 – indeed John Betjeman was to be one of the heroes of the later reactions against modernism in both poetry and architecture. But the combination of the British and the modern began to inspire a new and more complex feeling of unease long before modern buildings became unpopular. This was a specifically post-war phenomenon in that it did not spring from entrenched positions of the 1930s. It emerged in *The Wrong Set*, Angus Wilson's first collection of short stories, published in 1949.

Wilson was born in South Africa and educated at Westminster and Oxford. He worked in the Foreign Office and then the Reading Room of the British Museum, a background that provided his fiction with a rare awareness of the life and psychology of bureaucratic organizations and of the complex relationship between learning and life. In *The Wrong Set* the characters possess a sort of listless cruelty and a wry, decadent insight into their own increasing ineffectualities. One character sums up their plight: 'Well, we've reached the point of fantasy. Vitiate the minds or what passes for the minds of people with education, teach them to read and write, feed their imagination with sexual and criminal fantasies known as films, and then starve them in order to pay for these delightful erotic celluloids. *Circenses* without *panem* it seems.'[14]

Things do not quite work. People are trapped in their petty cruelties and misconceptions in a world they do not understand. Behaviour becomes disjointed. In 'Raspberry Jam', Wilson's first published short story, two old ladies murder a bullfinch, an image of bizarre horror and chilling infantilism which found echoes throughout the fiction of the next forty years. In his next collection, *Such Darling Dodos* (1950), he tightened the focus on this empty, directionless middle class, deracinated by forces they could not begin to understand and baffled by the prospect of whatever lay ahead.

Graceful Attitudes

In the late 1940s the deracination of the middle class was most frequently attributed to the lack of a Cyril Connolly 'prevailing myth'. The analysis behind the explanation was simple enough. Once, religion had provided a common reference: not only did its terms permeate the language, but its injunctions provided an absolute morality to which all conduct would ultimately be answerable. Through whatever tribulations or divisions, society was cemented together by this system: but the adhesive had failed. The reason would provided an intellectual playground for years to come but, broadly, could be summarized under two headings: the rise of science and social fragmentation.

The first was clear enough: since the Renaissance religion had implicitly been retreating before the progress of reason; in the nineteenth century the retreat became explicit in the face of Darwinian evolution and other scientific advances. By the middle of the twentieth century science seemed, at least to the layman, to be adequately equipped to answer all outstanding questions about the universe, given time. The social fragmentation argument suggested that religion had survived in what had been a largely rural society contained within fairly rigid hierarchies. The rise of the cities, the transformation of old systems of authority and the dissemination of learning all made the claims of a single authority with unique access to the truth less credible.

The dismay at the spectacle of a ravaged Europe and the blank feeling of indirection expressed by many at the end of the war were attributed to the lack of a common purpose, which only religion could provide. Reconstruction was precisely such a purpose; it simply seemed too small and too local to be a complete answer. Its claims were purely relative and appeared insignificant when confronted with the catastrophic absolutes of Belsen and Hiroshima. Nevertheless, the Labour Government and its many supporters were committed to progress towards a humanist Utopia based on welfare provision and the availability of a common culture.

But if 'the romantic utopian abolishes heaven and the devil, and then invents a new heaven and a new devil, more flattering to himself'[1] there were still those for whom the old heaven was paradise enough. The religious artists, confronted with triumphant humanism, were free to take on the proud intensity of the outsider. Evelyn Waugh's *Brideshead Revisited* was published in 1945 with a uniquely cautionary blurb on the dust jacket of the first edition: 'It is ambitious, perhaps intolerably presumptuous; nothing less than an attempt to trace the workings of the divine purpose in a pagan world, in the lives of an English Catholic family, half paganized themselves, in the world of 1923–39.'[2]

Waugh was forty-two in 1945 and he had been educated at Lancing College and Oxford. His initial literary reputation was made with his first novel, *Decline and Fall*, in 1928. After a divorce from his first wife, he was received into the Catholic Church in 1930. His output of brilliant, cynical comic novels continued through the 1930s as did his travel journalism. His systematic attempt to incorporate the faith into a novel was, therefore, essentially a new development.

Ambitious *Brideshead* may have been, but it was also exotic. Catholicism was not the national religion and such a precise fictional examination of its operation rebelled against the more sprawling, empirical traditions associated with the family saga in the English novel. Waugh enjoyed the dissident quality of his religion.

'I, personally, [he wrote] do not believe that there will be universal peace and goodwill until the world is converted to Christianity and brought under Christ's Vicar; whether that will ever come about is not ordained, but depends on human free-will. It may well be that the Church will remain for ever an underground movement and that the Second Coming will find it still in a minority.'[3]

Perhaps it was its very un-Englishness and systematic quality, the sheer, hard, rational nature of the mechanism of salvation, which made *Brideshead* such a success; it was a bestseller on both sides of the Atlantic. With its romantic high style and lofty, aristocratic Catholicism, Waugh discovered he had found his range as well as a popular market. The sharp brilliance of his pre-war fiction had never attracted anything like his new audience. He became a literary celebrity whose opinions were sought, especially by the relentless Americans. Success suited his new, haughty posture and he found himself free to publicize a solid, anti-modernist aesthetic. 'The failure of modern novelists since and including Joyce is one of presumption and exorbitance. They are not content with the artificial figures which hitherto passed so gracefully as men and women. They try to represent the whole human mind and soul and yet omit its determining character – that of being God's creatures with a defined purpose.'[4]

High Catholicism permitted Waugh a far more ferocious tone with which to assault the pre-war titans than that of Larkin: it provided him with cold certainty. If Joyce and others were mistaken in this one key respect, they were mistaken in every respect, their whole enterprise was the most ludicrous folly. Their effrontery lay in their pride, in the satanic belief in their own powers of reconstituting culture and individuals through the medium of their own genius. But they could not reproduce the workings of grace. The sacred and cabalistic over-tones of the aesthetic attached by its admirers to Joyce's last and most impenetrable work, *Finnegans Wake*, stank of diabolic rituals, of seeking on earth absolutes which could be found only in heaven.

Above all, Joyce and others were signalling what had already been said – that language was a formal absolute, that the limits of our being were to be found in the forms of our discourse. For Waugh this was '*la trahison des clercs*', the heresy of the over-subtle, a sin to which he knew himself to be prone. In his 1950 novel *Helena* he writes of the Christian tutor Lactantius:

'Lactantius had been able to bring nothing with him save his own manuscripts and was thus left, with all his unrivalled powers of expression, rather vague about what to express; with, more than that, the ever-present fear of falling into error. He delighted in writing, in the joinery and embellishments of his sentences, in the consciousness of high rare virtue when every word had been used in its purest most precise sense, in the kitten games of syntax and rhetoric. Words could do anything except generate their own meaning.'[5]

The very activity of the writer – especially of the great stylist, which

Waugh unquestionably was – is an invitation to sin. Potentially it elevated the intricacies of art, the 'kitten games', above the simple imperatives of salvation. Predictably therefore, *Helena* fails as a novel because Waugh's absolutes went too far. The drama of salvation and the operation of grace which kept *Brideshead* moving – albeit at times uncertainly – are missing and nothing but a tract remains. It does, however, show a contemporary literary rarity: entirely distinctive passages of fine, modern devotional prose: 'For His sake who did not reject your curious gifts, pray always for the learned, the oblique, the delicate. Let them not be quite forgotten at the Throne of God when the simple come into their kingdom.'[6]

The oddity of *Helena* apart, Waugh dealt with the aesthetic problem of religion and the modern English novel through his adoption of rigorous Catholic obedience. The faith was a rock, still and unchanging, upon which human dramas were enacted. These dramas occurred because of free will which allowed individuals to turn from God by choice. Society as an issue barely concerned him; he would not, for example, share Eliot's Christian pessimism about the possible fate of European civilization, since, he would argue, such matters were in the hands of God and indecipherable to the individual, whose proper business lay in working out his own salvation. He was, of course, an implacable enemy of the herbivorous left-wing mentality that lay behind the Labour Government and the 1951 Festival. This left Waugh's novels free to play the traditional role of dramatizing human conflict and emotion and left the language free to attain the precision and purity towards which it had historically striven before modernist doubts intervened.

It was a baroque conception. The elaborate artistry derived pleasure from its own execution, producing variations of increasing ingenuity to the point where the original meaning, the rock of the faith, was almost concealed, a process that mimicked the concealment of the Truth in real human affairs. It was the polar opposite of the method pursued by the other major Catholic novelist of the time – Graham Greene.

Greene was an almost exact contemporary of Waugh – he was forty-one in 1945 – and was also a Catholic convert, having been received into the Church in 1926. His first book of verse, *Babbling*

April, had been published while he was still a student at Oxford but, again like Waugh, his wider reputation was established during the 1930s. He confronted the same problem of unifying the aesthetic demands of the novel with the transcendent ones of religion. For Greene the novel was a means of examining the implications and coherence of doctrine; where Waugh would say truth is truth, take it or leave it, Greene would feel obliged to push the whole issue of taking or leaving to the limit. His conception of the power of the Church is far more ambiguous and shot through with doubt. Where Waugh could dismiss Joyce's conception of character as hopelessly flawed, Father Rank in Greene's *Heart of the Matter* (1948) suggests that even the supreme authority on earth can go only so far: 'The Church knows all the rules. But it doesn't know what goes on in a single heart.'[7]

This inclusion of the nature of the faith itself in the drama of the novel moves the entire work into a wider arena and denies Greene the possibility of anything like Waugh's baroque devotions. He cannot perform arabesques, secure in the knowledge of the faith; he is obliged to confront the faith itself rather than simply its working in the world. This produces the characteristic Greenian sense of a continuing, bewildering, unresolvable puzzle: 'If this book of mine fails to take a straight course,' says the narrator in *The End of the Affair* (1951), 'it is because I am lost in a strange region: I have no map.'[8] The words have a distinctively modern ring, anticipating the interminable variations of cultivated alienation that echoed down the 1950s and 1960s. But that was to be the alienation of atheism: this is the alienation of a believer who is obliged for ever to fence with his faith.

It was a quality that aroused the suspicion of George Orwell. For him such fencing suggested that only the aesthetic demands of the novel were being satisfied, not those of doctrine. 'The cult of the sanctified sinner', he wrote in a review of *The Heart of the Matter*, 'seems to me to be frivolous and underneath it there probably lies a weakening of belief, for when people really believed in Hell, they were not so fond of striking graceful attitudes on its brink.'[9]

Perversely, however, Greene's Catholic fiction was to prove more static than Waugh's. His prose was, in any event, a less flexible vehicle and the very open-endedness of his version of doubt allowed him simply to wander the world to find new backdrops against which to play out his dramas.

Greene's topicality remained his strength so far as his public was concerned. Not only did his locations seem to bring with them something of the remoteness and immediacy of a news report, but his tone – spare, narrative-driven and pointedly bleak – came to match the disillusioned, anguished note of the 1950s, first glimpsed in Larkin and Cooper and rapidly to become a desolate orthodoxy.

Dangerous Citizens

Science was one orthodoxy that seemed still fertile, full of new growth and energy, threatening to enter our lives at every point through the medium of technology. The bewildering theoretical claims of pre-war science matched in strangeness and difficulty those of the modernist artist; but they were not so easily dismissed. Hiroshima came as a hard endorsement of their significance. Faustian man, inheritor of the divine, restless discontent of the Renaissance, had pursued knowledge to its logical, apocalyptic conclusion.

'The race is now on between the atomic bomb and its desire to explode,'[1] murmured Cyril Connolly drily in his sad-smart mode, anticipating the curious process through which the Bomb was to take on a wholly autonomous personality. The *Spectator* simply said that the weapon took us from one stage of civilization to another,[2] while the *New Statesman* adopted the more optimistic view that it would in time result in world government and perpetual peace.[3] More convincing, however, was a report in August 1945 in the *New Statesman* of a Mass Observation survey of public feelings about the Bomb. This quoted 'one middle-aged working man' as saying: 'It's too much, we're going too fast. I'm on the same sort of thing in the foodline so I know what it is. We're a generation too early. We're not fit to handle such things.'[4] In July 1947 the *New Statesman* reported another survey, which showed that most people expected an atomic war.

The 'working man', alarmed at the rate of scientific progress and convinced that, somehow, his generation was not fit to handle it, is a potent image. In part he echoed the quandary of the Angus Wilson characters who seemed to lack the cultural equipment to cope with a new kind of world. Arising from that, he also exemplified the general sense of the age that the modern, in both its optimistic and apocalyptic forms, was being imposed on a society not radically different from that of fifty years earlier. At the Festival of Britain the bright exercises in modernism and the worship of technology were viewed by men and women dressed in cloth caps, suits and dresses identical to those of their parents. There was a discontinuity between the modernity of the intellectuals and the sensibility of the masses. In the case of the Festival this simply made the masses that much more difficult to lead. In the case of the Bomb, it endowed the scientists with demonic attributes.

The most influential novel of the period to incorporate this discontinuity as well as the apocalyptic pessimism that was abroad was George Orwell's *Nineteen Eighty-Four*, published in 1949. It was, broadly, a development of Orwell's anti-totalitarian tract, *Animal Farm*, which had been published in 1945. But, where that book had used the form of an allegorical fairy tale directed at the specific target of the corruption of the Russian Revolution, the later novel broadened its assault to include a variety of authoritarian crimes and adopted the much more significant form of science fiction.

It was a development of 'sci-fi' that moved the technology away from the centre of the stage. Earlier examples of the genre had tended to be based on the excitement of technological prediction. Orwell, however, included technology – such as his two-way telescreens – only as a symptom of the political changes that had turned Britain into Airstrip One and produced the dictatorship of Big Brother. The point was that Orwell did not see science and technology as a blind, neutral force in the manner of *The Times* after Hiroshima, but rather as another politically determined development. They were at one with the reorganization of the world into ever larger units – in the novel there are only three states: Oceania, Eastasia and Eurasia – and they served the interests of such units by providing the means of communication and surveillance.

The success of the novel springs from the precision with which it captures a wide range of anxieties about the future and the direction of technological and political change. In his story of a rebel against Big Brother who is finally brought to heel, having betrayed everything he believed to be of value, Orwell created a modern myth, an expression of communal anxiety far more effective than the simply political analysis that lay behind *Animal Farm*.

The Bomb, however, was not specifically at the heart of Orwell's novel and, apart from the odd imaginative excursion into a post-holocaust world as in Aldous Huxley's 1949 novel *Ape and Essence*, the weapon did not seem at once to conjure up the associations of instant apocalypse it was later to acquire. It appeared as one more big question in an age when big questions were positively voguish. Books such as Lewis Mumford's *The Condition of Man* and Erwin Schrödinger's *What is Life?* led a fashion for large-scale syntheses, presumably in response to the grumbling about the lack of a prevailing myth.

But, pre-eminently, the Bomb represented the issue of science. Specifically it threatened the cosier, optimistic view of science, which regarded it as a wholesome stripping away of illusions about the world, a process that would be politically liberating.

'Now this political ignorance [wrote George Bernard Shaw] and delusion is curable by simple instruction as to the facts without any increase of political capacity . . . I cannot change their minds; but I can increase their knowledge. A little knowledge is a dangerous thing; but we must take that risk because a little is as much as our biggest heads can hold; and a citizen who knows that the earth is round and older than six thousand years is less dangerous than one of equal capacity who believes it is a flat ground floor between a first floor heaven and a basement hell.'[5]

This was science as a faith in the facts as opposed to religion - a faith in an arbitrary and dangerous authority – but its real power was far greater than simply an ability to correct popular misconceptions, for science could potentially lay claim to becoming the primary imaginative enterprise of the race. This meant that it was a threat for the postwar cultural synthesists. The attempt of, for example, Leavis to centre the whole of Western culture on the corpus of English literature looked a little pallid next to the distressingly real claims of twentieth-century science. A dim awareness of this embarrassment may have explained the bitterness of the 'Two Cultures' row, a donnish dispute that achieved national notoriety in 1959. C. P. Snow, the novelist and physicist, advanced the view that our culture had bifurcated – there now existed two mutually uncomprehending camps, the sciences and the humanities. It was a view that drew maddened refutations from Leavis.

The problem was that in the first half of the twentieth century science had detached itself, even in the popular mind, from mere technology and its imaginative realizations in, say, the science fiction of H. G. Wells or Jules Verne. Instead it seemed to be intruding in the domain of more mainstream philosophical and literary activity; so, where Darwin may have been seen to challenge the narrative truth of religion, Einstein and Freud seemed to be threatening to supplant its functions.

Science threatened to provide the unity the world was seeking. L. L. Whyte, writing in *Horizon* in 1948[6] on the likely progress of scientific thought in the ensuing decade, predicted the appearance of a single, unified science which would incorporate sociology and psychology. There would be new conceptions of natural processes and, in a prediction of quite breathtaking inaccuracy, he forecast that fundamental physics would become a completed subject. This, he claimed, would lead to a wave of theoretical clarification. At that point unified science would constitute the 'only moral authority'. Marxism and religion would wither away. The only real extremism in this view was the automatic linkage between a unified science and moral authority. As for the rest, it would have seemed natural enough to a culture that regarded, indeed almost defined, science as an inevitable and relentless progress in a single direction.

Indeed, such a view – expressed in rather gentler forms – lay behind the whole reconstructive impulse. The Festival of Britain had friendly, technological wonders on display, while its Dome of Discovery and the Skylon suggested a domesticated science, a wholesome wonder at one with the Festival's encouraging noises about art and the masses.

The great apostle of 'advanced' thought in this area was Bertrand Russell. He was seventy-three in 1945 and about to embark on his post-war career as popular educator and campaigner, a curious role for a logician and philosopher. In 1949 he delivered a series of lectures entitled *The Impact of Science on Society*, which anatomized the liberal-optimistic view of science, in particular as realized in technology. First he gave an encouraging list of the real improvements in material well-being, a list that would have been intended to have some salutary significance for a nation suffering under the privations of austerity for far longer than it might reasonably have expected.

43

'Most people have warmth in winter and adequate light after sunset. The streets, except in time of war, are not pitch dark at night. All children go to school. Everyone can get medical attention. Life and property are much more secure (in peacetime) than they were in the eighteenth century. A much smaller percentage of the population lives in slums. Travel is vastly easier, and many more amusements are available than in former times. The improvement in health would in itself be sufficient to make this age preferable to those earlier times for which some people feel nostalgic. On the whole, I think, this age is an improvement on all its predecessors except for the rich and privileged.'[7]

For Russell, the analytical philosopher, much of this improvement had been created by a change in the definition of science: 'Science used to be valued as a means of getting to *know* the world; now, owing to the triumph of technique, it is conceived as showing how to *change* the world.'[8]

Most significantly, the success of science had induced a conceptual change which had direct political significance:

'The triumphs of science are due to the substitutions of observation and inference for authority. Every attempt to revive authority in intellectual matters is a retrograde step. And it is part of the scientific attitude that the pronouncements of science do not claim to be certain, but only the most probable on present evidence. One of the greatest benefits that science confers upon those who understand its spirit is that it enables them to live without the delusive support of subjective certainty. That is why science cannot favour persecution.'[9]

This is extraordinarily flabby stuff from the author of *Principia Mathematica*. The penultimate sentence, for example, appears to be saying that once you can live without subjective certainty, then you can live without subjective certainty – which does not take us very far. And, in general, Russell's apparently clear, commonsense style works to conceal the extravagant assumptions and spectacular leaps of faith behind much that he says. But the point was that science had been enlisted in the anti-religious cause. Its dissident pedigree stretched back to Galileo's defiance of papal power, and its claim to moral and political significance lay in the belief that correct observation dwarfed abstract authority as a means of understanding the world. Scientific man, free of illusions, the offspring of the Renaissance, was the measure of all things. Whether viewed pessimistically, as the cancer that would destroy the humane or religious fabric of the culture, or optimistically, as the bringer of steady material improvements, this was the one ideology sufficiently potent and widespread to qualify as a 'prevailing myth'. It had usurped religion as the unquestioned framework of experience. It was even codified by its accompanying philosophy: positivism.

Originally positivism had been defined by the nineteenth-century French philosopher Auguste Comte as the third and final phase of human knowledge, which succeeded the theological and metaphysical phases. It was the scientific phase in which the futile pursuit of absolutes was abandoned and humanity surrendered itself to the dominance of the processes of science. This was a characteristically French rationalist formulation for which twentieth-century British analytical philosophy would have little time, but, through the medium of logical positivism, the idea of a philosophy that conclusively endorsed what were perceived to be the scientific forms of knowledge took root.

It was outlined for a generation by the publication in 1936 of A. J. Ayer's book *Language, Truth and Logic*. This was republished in 1950 with an apologetic note from Ayer about the young-man's tone in which it was written. But the tone was an integral part of the book – it was proselytizing, impatient and convinced. Above all, it was spectacularly and persuasively lucid, a quality that made it one of the most widely influential of the age's philosophical works.

Ayer may have shared Comte's respect for science, but he could share none of his rationalism for Ayer is an English philosopher *par excellence*, an inheritor of the long and distinctly anti-continental tradition of empiricism. For the rationalist, truth can be generated by the mind alone; for the empiricist, everything derives ultimately from sense experience.

Language, Truth and Logic is an outline of what Ayer called radical empiricism. In later years he was to explain its method as 'a blending of the extreme empiricism of Hume with the modern logical techniques developed by people like Bertrand Russell'. Sense impressions are all we have. A priori truths such as those of mathematics and logic are systems of tautologies which tell us nothing of the world. Rationalism and idealism are misuses of language. So what does philosophy do? First, it withdraws from the high ground; it can explain neither our behaviour nor the existence of the world, nor can it prescribe the manner in which we should live. Its sole remaining obligation is 'the explication of concepts'. It can only clarify, it cannot produce its own propositions.

Ayer's book concludes:

'It is indeed misleading to draw a sharp distinction, as we have been doing, between philosophy and science. What we should rather do is to distinguish between the speculative and the logical aspects of science, and assert that philosophy must develop into the logic of science. That is to say, we must distinguish between the activity of formulating hypotheses and defining the symbols which occur in them. It is of no importance whether we call one who is engaged in the latter activity a philosopher or a scientist. What we must recognise is that it is necessary for a philosopher to become a scientist, in this sense, if he is to make any substantial contribution towards the growth of knowledge.'[10]

This elision of philosophical and scientific processes had profound implications. For the professional philosopher it may have been an interesting technicality, heavily foreshadowed by one interpretation of Ludwig Wittgenstein's *Tractatus Logico-Philosophicus* and familiar enough from the positivists of the Vienna Circle. *Language, Truth and Logic* merely happened to be its first British exposition. But Ayer's book was read widely outside specialist circles and, as a result, it broadcast the message for the first time to an all-purpose intelligentsia and to the artists.

'This is a delightful book,' commented Bertrand Russell, somewhat capriciously. More to the point, it was a book that attempted to annex for science a huge part of the territory formerly claimed by the arts. It did so by dismissing metaphysical discourse as meaningless, and thus appeared to remove the artistic and literary overtones from philosophy and to relegate the discipline to a new, somewhat humbler role as the handmaiden of science. For some this could be heady stuff. It appealed quite clearly to a no-nonsense, rather xenophobic tradition of British thought which had culminated in the empiricism of the eighteenth century: it would therefore attract a certain type of Little Englander as well as anybody impatient with the grander, more airy claims of Victorian idealism. It also echoed anti-totalitarian sentiments: Communism and Fascism, for example, were primarily rationalist exercises. The anti-totalitarian hero of Orwell's *Nineteen Eighty-Four* can be seen as essentially a defender of familiar British empiricism against Big Brother's army of rationalists. During his interrogation by O'Brien in the Ministry of Love, Winston Smith struggles to hold on to the empirical:

' "Do you remember," he went on, "writing in your diary, 'Freedom is the freedom to say that two plus two make four'?"

"Yes," said Winston.

O'Brien held up his left hand, its back towards Winston, with the thumb hidden and the four fingers extended.

"How many fingers am I holding up, Winston?"

"Four."

"And if the Party says that it is not four but five – then how many?"

"Four."

The word ended in a gasp of pain.'[11]

This is a fictional image of Russell's condemnation of arbitrary authority and his endorsement of the political value of objectivity, of disinterested and clear observation. Where a philosopher like Ayer would go only so far as to say the claims of his opponents are nonsensical, a novelist like Orwell can demonstrate that they might be dangerous nonsense. Yet Ayer is defending the scientist whereas for Orwell science is the servant of O'Brien. British empiricism is by no means a one-way street.

Ayer's anti-metaphysical polemic also validated the familiar mistrust and loathing of many 1950s writers of anything resembling cant or pretentious generalization. It created a language in which the difficult, seemingly perverse questions which challenged any hint of vagueness became respectable, a part of intelligent discourse. This was the hard, sceptical mode, the weapon that was at hand for the assault on the old illusions to be conducted by a generation in the 1950 and 1960s.

It also represented an awkward challenge to the metaphysical ideal of culture behind the tradition of the liberal-humanist critique in Britain. The very mention of the word 'values' was now likely to attract a deluge of positivist scorn.

In literary terms Ayer's role was thus profoundly anti-romantic. He would have no time for Connolly's grumbling about a 'prevailing myth' or for Leavis's organic society, both of which were in essence variations of the romantic longing for a lost Utopia. Ayer, in contrast, belonged to a cooler tradition of English classicism. He was the purveyor of the hard scientific view, a codifier of the most potent doctrinal system of our age.

Nightmare Shapes

The variety of cultural responses and aesthetic postures, in the face of victory, austerity, the legacies of modernism and of apocalyptic foreboding was impressive. There was neither orthodoxy nor dominant artistic fashion, but there was one quality which appeared to be common to most: the tendency to justify a position as being distinctively British. Confronted by a broken and ravaged Europe, a vast and sinister USSR and an industrially supreme USA, understandably we needed to assert the national identity, be it Little England, Great Britain or the home of a transcendent religious unity.

Evelyn Waugh's Catholicism appealed to a pre-Reformation model of Englishness. This was the legacy of the ancient families who turned up for the funeral of Guy Crouchback's father in *Unconditional Surrender*, the final part of his war trilogy, published in 1961. 'Tresham, Bigod, Englefield, Arundell, Hornyold, Plessington, Jerningham and Dacre'[1] the loving litany ran. Waugh himself was provocatively to adopt the manners of an English gentleman; when in London he was pleased to point out that he rarely strayed outside St James's. Eliot, meanwhile, with all the enthusiasm of an American converted to Englishness, was creating a visionary Anglican unity. Ayer was reviving British empiricism, Betjeman was celebrating the old built fabric of the nation and Ealing Studios were selling the virtues of Little England. The progressive, modernist reconstructors even devised a species of modern architecture softened in the name of the English picturesque.

Nevertheless, the *idea* of the foreign presented them all with a complex problem. Six years of war, during most of which the continent had been enemy territory, had strengthened the sense of isolation from Europe. In addition, the massive infusion of their military personnel over the last two years of war had exaggerated the awareness of the Americans as deeply alien. In spite of their presence here, they retained their legendary identity as the inhabitants of a cinematic landscape of big cars and tall buildings.

Suddenly to be confronted with peace and renewed contact with Europe was worrying enough, but there was the additionally traumatic sense that the old pre-war relationships could never be re-established. Two power blocs now dominated the world, implying a larger scale of organization than that prevailing in the 1930s as well as the dwarfing of the once mighty European nation states. And, of course, there had been the very nature of the war itself: it seemed to represent a terrifying and almost intolerable loss of innocence.

For a start there were the concentration camps. Rumours of the extent of the Nazis' Final Solution to the Jewish Problem had been circulating for some time, but by April 1945, with the American liberation of Belsen, Nordhausen and Buchenwald, doubt, disbelief or refusal to face the facts had gone. 'The Allies appear to be confronted with a nation the vast majority of whom are destitute of any public conscience whatsoever,'[2] the *Spectator* said. Also in the *Spectator* an MP wrote: 'There is indubitably a deep streak of evil and sadism in the German race.'[3]

Isolating the evil as a particular quality of the German race was the most reassuring response. It could be taken as external reinforcement of the Balcon view that there was something fundamentally wholesome embedded in the British way of life that was denied to other nations. Or, less nationalistically, it could be argued that this was simply a more appalling version of the message of the First World War – that the old order was morally bereft, corrupt beyond hope of redemption.

'The Captains and the Kings', the *New Statesman* wrote in affirmation of this second view, 'have made between them a century of greed, aggression, hatred and blood. They may now depart.'[4] Even more generally, it could be taken as a further symptom of the decline of the West. From this perspective the images of the camps, being seen increasingly on newsreel films, suggested something even more terminal than the unthinking carnage of 1914–18. This was planned, industrialized restructuring of the human race in the name of an ideology that had specifically defined as its enemy the softness and decadence of the West and its liberal longings.

Furthermore, this evil had been rooted out of old Europe only thanks to American might and money. The continent itself had proved helpless in the face of its own depravity. It was the perfect inspiration for one of Cyril Connolly's bouts of epic despair:

'Morally and economically Europe has lost the last war [he wrote in *Horizon*]. The great marquee of European civilization in whose yellow light we all grew up and read or wrote or loved or travelled has fallen down, the side-ropes are frayed, the centre pole is broken, the chairs and tables are all in pieces, the tea urns empty, the roses are withered in their stands, and the prize marrows, the grass is dead.'5

Even Connolly's francophilia, the posture from which he had once lambasted the philistinism of the British, had been replaced by a sense of 'the moral apathy and physical slowness of France'.

The novelist and critic V. S. Pritchett was less willing to be carried away by the rhetoric of languid despair. Writing in the *New Statesman* in January 1945, he anticipated the problems that the intellectuals, cosmopolitan by ambition, would face. 'To imagine Europe – that is the hardest thing we have to do. The picture comes to us in fragments and to piece it together and above all hold it in the mind is like trying to hold a dissolving dream and to preserve it from the obstinate platitude of our waking life.' He added: 'To imagine France again, to know that it cannot be the France we remember . . .'6

Pritchett was being less of a journalist and more of an artist than Connolly. He saw the important sense in which 'Europe' was a product of the imagination, a once-coherent entity of history and association which, for six years, had been possessed by demons. Pritchett was willing Europe back into existence, clothing it with the imaginative unity with which it had once been endowed.

Unfortunately Europe was not to prove easily reduced to any such unity. It had become exotic in the interim – strange and unpalatable growths had appeared.

'Existentialism is upon us [Rayner Heppenstall wrote in *Horizon*]. It dominated the thought of continental Europe before the war. We caught whiffs of it in the work of Berdyaev, Unamuno, Shetsov and the Protestant theologians. The names of the German existentialist philosophers Heidegger and Jaspers had been distantly heard. Kierkegaard, the fons et origo, was being issued under quiet, Anglican auspices by the Oxford University Press. Now the lid is off Europe, and we are appalled by the nightmare shapes which existentialism has assumed in our absence . . .

A philosophy which originated in Christian faith has become, in France, a philosophic *Danse Macabre* whose first assumptions are atheistic, nihilistic and desperate.'[7]

This was a curious view of the doctrine. Certainly it sprang from Kierkegaard and Protestant theology, but its manifestations were varied and seldom quite as diabolic as Heppenstall suggested. Broadly, existentialism emphasized the individual's role in the construction of his own destiny. It rejected as 'bad faith' any behaviour that sprang from the belief that the individual was forced to act in particular ways by, say, patriotism, religion or whatever. The existentialist creates himself anew every day. In the hands of Jean-Paul Sartre this became the ideology of the self, which has been, in many respects, a common-place of the post-war artistic consciousness. Man is a lonely figure in a godless world. He is given nothing but himself, no rules, no auth-ority, no predetermined model of existence. Heroically he must strive for the one condition worth having – that of liberty.

For Heppenstall, though, the whole of existentialist thought was simply a rationale for pessimism, a glorification of futility and despair. He was swiftly followed by A. J. Ayer, who compared the logic of Sartre to that of *Alice in Wonderland* and concluded that the French-man's problem lay in the misuse of the verb 'to be'.[8] Another reviewer of a summary of existentialism associated it directly with the war sufferings endured by the people of occupied Europe: 'It might be argued that such people scarcely "exist" and it may well be that men and women on the continent, who have had to make, during the last ten years, more desperate choices than we are used to making, will find in existentialism an echo of their own experience.'[9]

The tenor of all these criticisms was that existentialism was foreign, wilfully 'difficult' and unwholesomely posturing. For Ayer, its empha-sis on the 'traditional' philosophical problems of human choice and conduct and on the significance of existence itself was anathema. These were precisely the areas he believed logical positivism had established as being beyond the realm of 'real' philosophy. The fury of the reaction was, at least in part, explained by the scale of the existentialist invasion. Sartre's trilogy *Les Chemins de la Liberté* was published in Britain as *Roads to Freedom* between 1947 and 1950. His first novel, *Nausea*, was published in Britain in 1949. Albert Camus's *The Outsider* appeared in 1946 and *The Plague* in 1948. Guido de Ruggiero's *L'Esistenzialismo* appeared in 1945 as the first explication of the latest developments in the philosophy.

Existentialism fell on barren analytical and suspicious literary ground after the war. Its rhetorical impact, none the less, was enormous for it provided a heroic mode, a framework of grand gestures in which the blossoming sense of absence and failure could be indulged. Where the hero of a William Cooper novel lived with a nagging sense of provincial unease, a Sartre hero would be grappling with the nature of his existence and with the growing sense that he could find liberation only in his awareness that he was responsible for his own being. A tragic heroism became the imaginative property of France in the minds of the young British immediately after the war. The very fact of the Occupation seemed to endorse the grand and attractive pessimism in which the French had chosen to clothe themselves. A Paris of black-clad, wraith-like, self-determined creatures contrasted with a Britain of provincial automata to whom nothing much ever happened. France was also seen as a society into which the intellectual was integrated, accepted and admired for his efforts. 'Literature is enormously important there,' Cyril Connolly wrote after a trip to Paris, 'and one sees how pervasive, though impalpable, have become the irritable lassitude, brain-fatigue, apathy and hum-drummery of English writers.'[10] It was a view helpfully endorsed by Sartre in his *What is Literature?*, translated in 1950, in which he gave his own view of the literary world that had found him so alien:

'In England, the intellectuals are less integrated into the collectivity than we are; they form an eccentric and slightly cantankerous caste which does not have much contact with the rest of the population . . . The English writers make a virtue of necessity and by aggrandizing the oddness of their ways attempt to claim as a free choice the isolation which has been imposed upon them by the structure of their society.'[11]

Outside the literary world, of course, the centrality of Paris was more familiar. In the visual arts Parisian dominance had been accepted as a matter of course in British thinking ever since the defences of French modernism by the Bloomsbury Group art critic Roger Fry in his collections of essays *Vision and Design* of 1920 and *Transformations* of 1928. Fry's successor as the continental conscience of British art was Herbert Read. Fifty-two in 1945, Read was a Yorkshireman who had worked as a fine art academic and as editor of the *Burlington Magazine*. He had also produced a substantial body of poetry and literary criticism as well as a stream of books on the visual arts. To him, Paris and existentialism made perfect sense. 'It is not without significance that it is precisely in Paris, where the revolutionary attitude in art has prevailed so long, that this new philosophy has arisen.'[12]

For Read, the lonely existential hero, inventing himself daily, was the very type of our age. He had immediate aesthetic implications.

'We have now reached a stage of relativism in philosophy just where it is possible to affirm that reality is in fact subjectivity, which means that the individual has no choice but to construct his own reality, however arbitrary and even "absurd" that may seem. This is the position reached by the Existentialists, and to it corresponds a position in the world of art that requires a similar decision.'[13]

The immense gulf between this view of art and philosophy and that of Read's literary opposite numbers is revealing. It illustrates the profound differences between modernism in the visual arts and modernism in literature. Both viewed the age as some kind of intellectual climacteric. But the literary response to this was a type of extreme classicism – the anti-romantic ideals of 'hard dryness' – which, in Eliot, became radical conservatism, a belief in the need to struggle to offset the fragmenting effects of the twentieth century. In the visual arts, in contrast, there had not been the same determination to extirpate the nineteenth century. Romanticism was not rejected, rather it was embraced. Surrealism, a movement for which Read had been the most important British apologist, indeed regarded itself, in André Breton's phrase, as 'the prehensile tail of romanticism'.

Existentialism provided the intellectual backdrop for the romantic image of the individual as alone and self-justifying. Read's gleeful embracing of the philosophy as 'subjectivity' is the romantic opposite of Ayer's classicism. In fact, Read associated the very idea of classicism with some kind of basic moral blemish: 'Wherever the blood of martyrs stains the ground, there you will find a doric column or perhaps a statue of Minerva.'[14]

In Read there is a variety of radicalism, a determination to keep the excitement of modernism intact as a permanent revolutionary movement in art. This inspired an international imaginative impulse in contrast to the specific local attempts at cultural synthesis of Leavis or Eliot. The calm, mutually reinforcing network of the world's intelligentsia to which Eliot and Leavis appealed for the salvation of Europe was also dreamed of by Read, but to him it was a revolutionary core. Writing of the International Surrealist Exhibition in London in 1936, he spoke of this group as visionary outsiders: 'When the foam and froth of society and the press had subsided, we were left with a serious public of scientists, artists, philosophers and socialists. Fifteen years have now passed by, bringing with them death, destruction and diaspora of another world war; but that serious public still remains.'[15]

Read's romantic acceptance of art as an absolute, of the permanent role of the artist, insulated him from the kind of pessimism felt by others. He took delight rather than misery from the upheavals of the day because they validated his belief in the radical changes in the nature of reality and of the self that were taking place. He exemplified the belief in the international as opposed to the merely British. In painting and sculpture such a belief was more prevalent than in literature: a withdrawal back into island Britain was largely avoided, the modernist legacy of Picasso and Matisse was sustained.

In this context the end of the war signalled the joyous reopening of the great masters; a reopening symbolized at the end of 1945 by a Picasso and Matisse exhibition at the Victoria and Albert Museum. Yet in spite of the relative success of the continuity of modernism in painting, the exhibition provoked more horror and outrage at the spectacle of the modern than any other comparable event. This ability of the visual arts to shock and dismay proved one of the most enduring and familiar characteristics of the arts as popularly perceived in the post-war period. The exhibition had many successors.

Almost the first and certainly the most eloquent expression of disgust came in a letter to *The Times* from Evelyn Waugh.

'Senor Picasso's paintings cannot be intelligently discussed in the terms used of the civilized masters. Our confusion is due to his admirers' constant use of an irrelevant aesthetic vocabulary. He can only be treated as crooners are treated by their devotees. In the United States the adolescents, speaking of music do not ask; "What do you think of So-and-so?" They say; "Does So-and-so *send* you?" Modern art, whether it is Nazi oratory, band leadership, or painting, aims at a mesmeric trick and achieves either total success or total failure. The large number of otherwise cultivated and intelligent people who fall victim to Picasso are not posers. It may seem preposterous to those of us who are immune, but the process is apparently harmless. They emerge from their ecstasy as cultured and intelligent as ever. We may even envy them their experience. But do not let us confuse it with the sober and elevating happiness which we derive from the great masters.'[16]

The words make every necessary point about the terms of the conflict: Picasso is associated with a dangerous loss of control under the effects of hypnotism or Nazi oratory. Shrewdly, rather than confronting the works and their admirers head-on, Waugh addresses himself over their heads to an imaginary audience of civilized lovers of the old masters who are immune to such trickery. He then patronizes the modernists by saying that no lasting damage is being done to them. Modernism is Nazism, the crude mindlessness of popular music, a kind of illness, but, above all, it is *not* about real art.

In the *New Statesman* Roger Marvell reported Waugh's letter as having 'gravely assured readers of *The Times* that admirers of Picasso were not necessarily, in other respects, stupid' and Marvell had gone on to comment that 'the painful truth is that we live in an incomparably specialised age'.[17] For *Apollo*, the art magazine, the columnist 'Perspex' agreed with Waugh.

'I confess that for me this stuff means precisely nothing, and I refuse to be bludgeoned into dishonesty by the vogue for it. Picasso and Matisse have both been, and presumably are, leaders; but so were the more enterprising of the Gadarene Swine . . . To some of us, perhaps to an increasing number amid the turmoil and lack of absolute standards of the contemporary world, the solid craftsmanship of the past drives us to getting our aesthetic pleasures from work definitely historic.'[18]

Like Mass Observation's 'working man', Perspex believed we were going too fast, we did not yet know how to handle these things. Best to stick with the 'definitely historic'.

Poignant Key

The painter Victor Pasmore also went to the Victoria and Albert Museum's exhibition. Aged thirty-seven in 1945, Pasmore had been one of the leading figures of the Euston Road School. This centred on the teaching of Pasmore, William Coldstream, Claude Rogers and Graham Bell and it aimed to provide a realist response to surrealism, placing humble observation before imaginative flourishes at the heart of the painter's craft. It tended to reject the modernist tradition of Picasso and Matisse in favour of one that paid more attention to artists like Sickert, Degas and Cézanne. Pasmore had been through an experimental abstract phase in the 1930s, but had abandoned these attempts in 1936 just before the foundation of the Euston Road School in 1937.

Pasmore, however, did not share the political and social enthusiasms of the other members. He was less convinced of the realist creed. Indeed the waverings of his career between the twin poles of realism and abstraction seem now to make him a representative figure of the uncertainties of British art as a whole. 'Here, displayed in riotous profusion,' he said of the exhibition, 'was the furniture of the Renaissance naturalist tradition, but distorted, fragmented, lampooned and transformed by a colossal expressionism.'[1] Once again the tone is one of awe – the Englishman confronted with the heroic scale of foreign innovation. The very word 'colossal' suggests a confidence that Pasmore seemed to feel he lacked. After the exhibition and a series of discussions with close friends, Pasmore returned to abstraction with the works *Abstract in Black and White* and *Abstract in Five Colours*, exhibited in May 1948.

However, in spite of the overpowering awareness of continental modernism during the 1930s, Britain had emerged at the centre of the issues. In part this was due to a slightly delayed reaction to the innovations of the 1920s. In that decade Britain had seemed relatively isolated from the continent, a state of affairs whose end began with the Tate Gallery's decision to exhibit contemporary European art from 1926. This new acceptance was accelerated by the number of foreign artists who came to live in Britain as a result of persecution by the Nazis in Germany and the Communists in the USSR. The Bauhaus, for example, had been forcibly closed in 1933, the year of Hitler's accession to power. Walter Gropius, Marcel Breuer, Naum Gabo, Moholy-Nagy, Piet Mondrian and Eric Mendelsohn arrived in Britain, unexpectedly establishing the country as at least the geographical home of a substantial part of the modern movement.

The word 'movement', however, proved somewhat misleading. It is a term of art rather than literary history, which tends to prefer the term 'modernism' and to be less prone to broad categorizations into schools and 'isms'. In the propagandist atmosphere of the 1930s, there were a number of attempts to form a modern programme based on a fixed coterie of members. In architecture MARS (Modern Architectural Research Group) attempted to mimic the success of its European equivalent – the CIAM organization. In painting, Unit One came into existence in 1933 in support of what Paul Nash described as 'a truly contemporary spirit'.[2] Its members included Ben Nicholson, Henry Moore, Barbara Hepworth and the architect Wells Coates. The group lasted two years, its fragmentation beginning as soon as it became clear that there was no way of unifying the variety of different artistic intentions under a single heading. This was in spite of Herbert Read's brave attempt to claim that, however different the members might be, they were united by their social role as artists.

Nicholson, meanwhile, had embarked on a course of full-blooded abstraction. He had been chairman of yet another group, the Seven and Five Society, and now wished to change its name to the Seven and Five Abstract Group. Unfortunately this, too, foundered after the first entirely abstract exhibition held in 1935. Non-abstract members had been upset and the society fell apart. In terms of art, as opposed to mere organization, however, this period saw Nicholson produce his relief pictures, which were among the finest and clearest expressions of 1930s British art's aspiration towards ideal forms, unified and legible. Mingled with constructivist influences from Russian *émigrés* like Naum Gabo, this aspiration produced yet another attempt to draw modernism together in the form of the book *Circle* (published in 1937 and edited by J. L. Martin, Ben Nicholson and Naum Gabo) which placed rather greater emphasis on architecture and design. In addition, of course, there was surrealism, the most enthusiastically organizing of all the movements, which found its primary group expression in the 1936 exhibition.

Against this background, the Euston Roaders appeared as a group determined to reconnect art to a wider public with social and political intent and realistic form. As such it was painting's correlative of the similarly anti-modernist and politically engaged posts of the 1930s.

The 1930s, in painting, represented a period full of conflicting impulses and inhabited by potent, influential figures. The desire to proselytize, to organize, however, tends partly to conceal the significance of some individual work. The career of Paul Nash, for example, displayed a steady movement from his landscapes of the 1920s to more complex effects under the influence of the modernist invasion in the 1930s. His combination of a specifically English sense of landscape with surrealism's sense of disquiet and foreboding found its most celebrated expression in *Totes Meer* (*Dead Sea*) of 1940–1 in which a sliver of hills and trees in the distance is dwarfed by a pit full of the tangled wreckage of German war planes. The wreckage was broken and faceted, evoking a cubist restructuring of the visible world as though war had miraculously begun to imitate art.

Echoing the memories and associations of Muriel Spark's re-creation of the post-war urban landscape, in *The Girls of Slender Means*, the art critic Adrian Stokes commented on his connection between Cubism and destruction after the war:

'A collapsed room displays many more facets than a room intact: after a bombing in the last war, we were able to look at elongated, piled-up displays of what had been exterior, mingled with what had been interior, materializations of the serene Analytic Cubism that Picasso and Braque invented before the first war: usually, as in some of these paintings, we saw the poignant key provided by some untouched, undamaged object that had miraculously escaped.'[3]

Where the trauma of the First World War had seemed to defeat innovative modern art movements such as futurism or vorticism by showing the kind of terminal logic that could be seen to lie behind their machine fantasies, the Second World War appeared as a cruel, dreamlike validation of much that was modern. In the Flanders trenches former advocates of the new machine age frequently found that their extreme condition forced them to retreat to a kind of muted pastoralism – a direction followed precisely by the artist Christopher Nevinson. But the horror of the Second World War was more spacious, less static and the very fact of the large-scale bombing of cities seemed to open the world up to new ways of seeing. Most obviously, of course, there had been that great precursor of the visions to come: Picasso's *Guernica*.

But there was something about Nash's paintings that represented a unique type of British synthesis. His idea of the 'metaphysical landscape' evoked the legacy of Samuel Palmer and this connection, this Englishness, drew from Herbert Read, on Nash's death in July 1946, one of his more noticeably felt, less programmed passages of criticism:

'One returns, for a final emphasis, to Nash's fidelity to a certain nativeness, a quality representing the historic English tradition in English art. I had often characterised this as "lyricism": it is a quality which we find in the delicate stone tracery of an English cathedral, in the linear lightness and fantasy of English illuminated manuscripts, in the silvery radiance of stained glass. It returns, after an eclipse, in our interpretation of classicism – in our domestic architecture, in our furniture and silver, in Chippendale and Wedgwood. The same quality is expressed, distinctly, in our poetry and music. It is not a conscious tradition, as inevitable and as everlastingly vernal as an English meadow.'[4]

A more conscious and direct evocation of Englishness had been pursued by John Piper. He too had been an abstract artist but, in 1936, in the magazine *Axis* he had written an article rebelling against abstraction and surrealism and reasserting the value of the English tradition of Constable, Blake and Turner. In 1937 Piper began work on the first *Shell Guide to England*, to be edited by himself and John Betjeman; it was an exploitation of Piper's own lifelong fascination with English churches. Like Betjeman's poetry, Piper's painting became a precise and loving celebration of the threatened and decaying fabric of England. He created a complex and sombre visual style to produce the perfect contemporary image of the romantic, decaying ruin. And, as with Betjeman, it was never precisely nostalgia, since the love of the condition of loss and decay was always too great.

Piper's initial rebellion against the modernist orthodoxies had made clear his concern at the loss of the subject of painting itself. He wished to see objects in their context, neither surrealistically juxtaposed nor cubistically shattered. Perhaps this same concern lay behind the development of Graham Sutherland's work in the 1930s. Again the spirit of Samuel Palmer walked: Sutherland's landscapes were imbued with the same notion of 'significance' but, in the 1930s, they also began to include distorted and mysterious natural forms. These were isolated within the canvas, an implicit rejection of the apparently random edges of the frame of landscape naturalism.

The dark and forbidding mood of these canvases reflected Sutherland's own liberal disquiet about international developments, a sensation that reached its full expression in the Northampton Crucifixion completed in 1946. The isolation within the canvas places the Christ figure in dynamic, ambiguous space riven with suggestions of a hard, unforgiving geometry. The suffering appears through the tight, agonized concavities derived explicitly from the images of the concentration camps. 'So in the agony of Christ's martyrdom on the Cross,' wrote one critic of the painting, 'Sutherland voices the present crisis in civilisation.'[5]

In Sutherland, the critic Kenneth Clark could discern a new efflorescence of an expressionist tradition, which he defined in terms of his own romantic, at times sentimental, version of art history.

'They are what we now call "expressionist" artists, a term which is not as worthless as it sounds, because, in fact, the symbols of expressionism are remarkably consistent, and we find in the work of these early sixteenth century landscape painters not only the same spirit but the same shapes and iconographical motives which recur in the work of such recent expressionists as van Gogh, Max Ernst, Graham Sutherland and Walt Disney. Expressionist art is fundamentally a northern and an anti-classical form, and prolongs, both in its imagery and its complex rhythms the restless organic art of the folk-wandering period.'[6]

Sutherland's later reputation rested on his portraits as well as on his vast tapestry of Christ enthroned in glory for Coventry Cathedral. But, artistically, his most profound impact arose from the mood of ambiguous unease and expressive energy that emanated from his works of the 1930s and 1940s. He combined Piper's longing for a return to a 'real' subject with a determination to make the painting effective externally, rather than as a self-referring system. He reacted against the Platonic purity of forms beloved of 1930s modernists and against the apparent inwardness, an artistic hermeticism, that seemed to lie behind the entire modernist effort. It was a framework of reaction that found its must ruthless expression in the work of Francis Bacon.

From the beginning Bacon was an oddity. Untrained as an artist, he had worked in the late 1920s and early 1930s as an interior decorator and furniture designer. A few of his paintings from this period survived his compulsive need to destroy large numbers of his canvases. From 1936 to 1944 there is a gap and then, suddenly, his *Three Studies for Figures at the Base of a Crucifixion* appeared. They were shown at the Lefevre Gallery in 1945 alongside work by Sutherland and Frances Hodgkins.

Where Sutherland had provided the means of contemplating suffering and pain, Bacon appeared to be offering the ordeal itself. In sketched-in room perspectives, reminiscent of Sutherland's fragmentary geometry, each painting shows a figure, the outer two cropped by the outermost edges of the canvases. One is distantly human, though horribly distorted, one is reminiscent of a large bird, though balanced on an ungainly tripod, and one is doglike. All are in some way perched – on a table, on some kind of furniture base and on a fragment of grass. All are engaged in a private expression of suffering and horror – the crucifixion of the title provides one explanation, but there seems no prospect of a resurrection in this world. Above all, there is no chink of humanity; our sympathy is not enlisted; the figures are too vile and too isolated within their own violence to allow us access. Nor is there any narrative development to be deduced from studying the paintings: they are related in basic compositional terms by the inward movement of the two outer figures and by the forward snarl or grimace of the central figure. In addition they all appear to be in some form of interior. Beyond that, they just seem to be arbitrary assaults on our nervous system. At what is the doglike man howling? Most horrifically, it seems to be at the moment of realization of his own condition.

Within the forms themselves, the influence of Picasso is detectable; but, that aside, they seem to spring from an imagination fundamentally at odds with the mainstream of post-Fry modernist history. Above all, they reject the landscape and all its associations. In that tradition lay an artistic self that was in essence passive, accepting the exigencies of the occasion of the painting. The implication of the landscape, however modified by style or expression, is that there is, in some sense, nothing there. The idea of the metaphysical eye penetrating to the mystery of things that ran from Palmer to Nash and Sutherland suggests the discovery of a hidden meaning by the act of seeing and of painting. But is this merely sentimentality, might there not be *only* a barren nothingness? 'Also, I think that man now realises that he is an accident,' Bacon said later, 'that he is a completely futile being, that he has to play out the game without reason. You see all art has now become completely a game by which man distracts himself.' And, he added, the artist 'must really deepen the game to be any good at all'.[7]

Three Studies announced the resurgence of a self-conscious and aggressive expressionism, though perhaps a bleaker version than the one to which Clark had referred. There *was* henceforth to be a subject for the artist, the precise nature of which may be a matter of chance – 'I want a very ordered image but I want it to come about by chance,' said Bacon[8] – but its obligation is to act as directly as possible on the nervous system of the observer. Bacon made the point in a description of his method of working:

'Then the next day I tried to take it further and tried to make it more poignant, more near, and I lost the image completely. Because this image is a kind of tightrope walk between what is called figurative painting and abstraction. It will go right out from abstraction but will really have nothing to do with it. It's an attempt to bring the figurative thing up to the nervous system more violently and more poignantly.'[9]

Bacon was associated with yet another school, somewhat tenuously known as the School of London – the other principal members being Lucian Freud, Frank Auerbach, Leon Kossoff and Michael Andrews. The notion of a school in this case is perhaps just a general heading for post-war expressionism. As a group they eschewed abstraction and their conviction of the importance of the activity and technique of painting itself put them out of step with later developments of the avant-garde. They were to retain their faith in the figurative throughout the 1950s and 1960s when the forces of American abstract expressionism must have seemed overwhelming. Eventually they found themselves champions of the figuration that emerged in the 1970s and 1980s.

The nature of Bacon's work and of that of most of the other expressionists is pessimistic and profoundly antipathetic to the romantic optimistic strain dominant in the mainstream of British modernism. Bacon's world has lost God, and humanism has failed to fill the void. From the same inspiration, his response is the polar opposite to Larkin's. The Baconian public pose with its gambling and drinking is closer to that of some hard-boiled American writer on a self-destructive quest to unite life and art or of an 1890s decadent than to that of the average daily victim of petty defeats who was appearing in realistic fiction. Bacon's figures represented isolation and abandonment on a heroic scale, comparable to that of the existentialist heroes who had chilled and irritated the British intelligentsia.

Reclining Figures

It was Henry Moore who in 1945 came to represent the entire spirit of English modernism in the visual arts. After the war he became an official, representative artist, holding a series of public offices and always in demand as a committee figure. This level of acceptance rapidly became international. In 1946 an important retrospective of his work was held at the Museum of Modern Art in New York and, in 1948, he was awarded the Grand Prize for Sculpture at the Twenty-fourth Venice Biennale. By then he was widely accepted in the critical and the popular imagination as 'the greatest sculptor in the world', a post he occupied, more or less unchallenged, until his death on 31 August 1986.

It is important to emphasize Moore's public stature because it is unique in British art of the post-war period, indeed almost of any period. In the visual arts the British tradition has generally been perceived merely as an afterthought. Full of local oddities and the occasional under-appreciated genius, it has been seen as a kind of insular commentary on the great achievements of the continent and, in later years, of the USA. British architecture, in particular, suffered from its role as an eccentric offspring of European parents: Vanbrugh's and Hawksmoor's English baroque or Soane's classicism is never adequately included in architectural histories – both remain too irre-deemably strange.

Modernism intensified the isolation. Roger Fry's criticism estab-lished the ascendancy of continental innovations at the expense of the British. In the 1930s, however, some modernist territory was reclaimed and Moore emerged from this process as the British artist who, above all, was perceived as an equal of Picasso, Matisse or Brancusi.

Moore was born in 1898 in Castleford, Yorkshire, the son of a fiercely self-improving miner, into a close-knit, large and apparently happy family. He went from local school to the Leeds School of Art and, after serving in the First World War and returning to teach at

66

Leeds, he won a scholarship to the Royal College of Art in 1921 where Sir William Rothenstein had just taken over as principal. Rothenstein turned the college's emphasis away from the academic tradition towards a more practical approach. He was also responsible for introducing his students not only to new art but to the great artistic figures of the day. The effect was to induce a sense both of confidence and internationalism. It was an obvious reaction against the parochial stubbornness that had so often characterized English art teaching.

Single-minded and energetic, Moore established almost at once the nature of the problems and influences that were to feed his work for the rest of his life. He used the college to learn to draw and the African and South American works in the British Museum as a vast pool of sculptural forms, a source of inspiration unnoticed by most of his contemporaries. His plundering of non-European work was partly inspired by Fry, who had drawn attention to the power of African and Mexican sculpture, and partly by Moore's own desire to escape from the legacy of the Renaissance. Sculpture, more than any other art, seemed to have been unable fully to free itself from the burden of the achievements of the Italians. To the modernists it was an art that appeared to have been in suspension since Donatello.

The statuesque, monumental primitivism towards which Moore was drawn had also become the inspiration of the modernists in Paris. Moore travelled there in 1922, the year of the publication of *Ulysses* and *The Waste Land* and one year after the appearance of Picasso's *Three Musicians*. In later years Moore said that he had really ever needed only two sources of inspiration: Picasso and the British Museum.[1]

Finally, Jacob Epstein and Eric Gill provided a precedent for Moore's own mistrust of the sculptural techniques of the immediate past. They had championed direct carving as opposed to casting and in this idea Moore found the ideology of 'truth to materials', which dominated his work of the 1920s and 1930s. Indeed, so powerful was this inspiration that many of his earliest works are held back imaginatively by an apparent reluctance to disturb the natural condition of the stone beyond the most minimal carving. His awe at the nature of the material was at war with his need to sculpt.

Moore, therefore, stood at a crossroads. In the work of Rodin,

Brancusi and Epstein sculpture seemed to be coming of age and to be calling on a range of influences in a way that promised a massive opening out of its repertoire. Primitive forms suggested an escape from the Renaissance and suited the modernist impulse towards mythic, impersonal statement, a movement away for portraiture and towards the creation of universal forms. This movement was of immense significance to sculpture, whose role as a public art had dominated its recent history and had frequently made it seem subservient to its occasion – as memorial, monument or whatever. Modernist ambition could accept no such role. Art was free-standing, self-justifying or it was nothing. Its responsibilities lay far beyond those of society. A new public sculpture would consequently demand more from and give less to its audience.

In the 1930s many others stood at this same crossroads. The world of images seemed to be opening up almost too rapidly – one possible reason for the mania for 'isms', groups and manifestos noted earlier; they were ways of controlling the seemingly infinite number of possibilities. Moore played his part in these factions – notably surrealism – but none ever quite contained everything he wished to do. His talent was like that of Picasso or Le Corbusier: capable of an almost infinite series of variations once its basic themes had been established. Thanks possibly to his background and his education under Rothenstein, he seemed to have few conceptual worries about his work. He discovered his forms in the process of drawing or carving rather than in thought.

The one form that proved most potent both in his own work and in that of others was the reclining figure. Beginning with the *Reclining Figure* of 1929 in Hornton stone, Moore turned the form into his own trademark as well as a sculptural problem that haunted the next generation. The idea sprang most directly from ancient Mexican sculpture, in particular the reclining image of Chacmool, the Rain Spirit from Chichen Itzá. There were European antecedents, notably in baroque sculpture, but they had nothing of the primitive power which Moore intended. The real point was that the reclining figure represented a reaction against the Renaissance ideal of the upright, standing image. Behind that ideal lay the aspiration towards equilibrium, human perfection and towards man's freedom from the restraints of the earth. The reclining figure, in contrast, stressed, above all, the human relationship to the ground. Its geometry was created by gravity and its pull on the living forces within the body. Of the sculptor it demanded a wholly new expressive repertoire to cope with the complexities of the relationship between figure and base; but equally, it offered Moore an entirely distinctive and almost infinitely variable image. It provided him with a way of avoiding completely the problems of the conceptual. It was a liberation of which he was fully aware.

'I want to be quite free of having to find a "reason" for doing the Reclining Figures and free still of having to find a "meaning" for them. The vital thing for an artist is to have a subject that allows him to try out all kinds of formal ideas – things that he doesn't yet know for certain but wants to experiment with, as Cézanne did in his "Bathers" series. In my case the reclining figure provides chances of that sort. The subject-matter is *given*. It's settled for you, and you know it and like it, so that within it, within the subject that you've done a dozen times before, you are free to invent a completely new form-idea.'[2]

This is an important statement as it reveals the way Moore dealt with what, in many ways, is the central problem of modern art – that of meaning. The idea of the modern is always accompanied by the sense of a severance from the codes, systems and values of the past. This implies that there is no accumulated system of references or of beliefs that can complete the experience of a work of art with a 'meaning'. The connection between, say, the image of a mother and baby and the birth of the saviour of the world is revealed as arbitrary. The truth value of the connection evaporates.

For the Renaissance sculptor, whatever his actual beliefs, the form of a Virgin and Child or a pietà are given. Moore had no such forms and, as the passage quoted above shows, he felt their absence. In discovering his own and investing them, arbitrarily perhaps, with something of the same hieratic significance, he freed his gift from the uncertainties that plagued most of his contemporaries.

This creative freedom and the scale of his gift made Moore an astonishingly productive artist throughout his career. In addition, his stylistic range is so vast that generalization about his work is almost impossible. But his obsession with the natural forms of landscape is unavoidable. The form of the reclining figure in itself permitted him to find landscape analogies in the human body. At times this takes on a gentle, pastoral quality, but more frequently the effect is of massive, dramatic power evocative of the landscape of Stonehenge – of 'Britain' rather than of 'England'.

The Second World War deprived Moore of the material to continue sculpting and he turned to drawing, to produce his series of sketches of life in the underground shelters during bombing raids and of miners at work. They were immensely successful – they seemed accessible and directly emotional – and established Moore in the popular mind as a modern artist who was also at one with the way Britain wished to feel about herself. He bridged, as it were, the gap between Evelyn Waugh and Picasso.

The drawings are perhaps most remarkable for the way in which the figures, huddled together in the shelters, or the miners, hewing at the coal face, are turned into Moore sculptures. They are stylized in the extreme – devoid of individual character and representative as much of formal variation as of the crowded contortions of the shelters or of the physical effort of coalmining. Just as he had once discovered the reclining figure as a *given*, an answer to the question of content which freed his sculpture, so now he was using drawings from life as an excuse for invention and variation rather than as the specific emotional hook they were popularly taken to be.

The idea of an accessible form of the modern was endorsed by Moore's *Madonna and Child*, which was unveiled in 1944. This had been commissioned by Walter Hussey, the vicar of St Matthew's, Northampton, a relentless enthusiast when it came to modern art who, at the unveiling ceremony, promptly commissioned Graham Sutherland to produce a crucifixion. Moore's work is calm, simple and naturalistic: his figures exude a scale and monumentality, recognizable from his earlier work, but without any overt 'modernity'. In fact, formally, it displayed a startling number of the preoccupations of his more abstract work, but they had all been controlled by the specific requirements of this sculpture. And, far from Moore having somehow abandoned the modern, in the post-war years he pursued an even greater range of formal preoccupations than he had in the

1930s – torsos, helmets, internal and external forms, warriors and, in the mid-1950s, a sudden and spectacular leap into upright forms with the series of 'Motives'.

The continued variety of his invention as well as the seminal power of his pre-war work ensured that British sculpture could henceforth be seen only as for or against Moore, it could not ignore him. The direct, unexplained style of his creativity and the thoroughness with which he pursued every possible variation of his own themes make him a difficult influence but a useful enemy. In the event his own rejections of the Renaissance heritage brought him firmly back into the fold. His sudden discovery of drapery as an expressive device in the post-war period signalled a return to one kind of classicism as did his increasing acceptance of casting. In the event the next generation dealt with him precisely by identifying him with that tradition – of Renaissance classicism – which they, in turn, wished to reject.

In 1951 a young sculptor, bored with his work at the Royal Academy Schools, considered who might be the greatest living sculptor. Deciding it was Moore, he went and knocked at his door at his home in Perry Green, Hertfordshire. Moore complained that he should have made an appointment; nevertheless, he invited him in for tea and examined some of his work. Six months later Anthony Caro began work as Moore's assistant. He stayed for two years. 'The Henry Moore attitudes stayed a long time in the work, and in the way I conducted my studio and my life,'[3] Caro said later. Thus, even the one man who would rival him in critical estimation as the leading modern British sculptor had no choice but to start from Moore.

A Mouth

The USA was on the way: huge, indecipherable in her many aspects, energetic and powerful. She represented a threat both imprecise and real. Her industry and wealth had won the war in Europe just as her technology had defeated Japan. In 1945 the USA alone possessed the atom bomb, the final tool of the Faustian imagination, yet, equally, she alone of the nations who had inherited the civilization of the West seemed to have come through the war unscathed. When Europe lay in ruins, America, her offspring, was still building and growing.

Even the left-wing Bertrand Russell was seduced; he associated the USA with a heady radicalism: 'T. S. Eliot, whose acquaintance I made when he was my pupil at Harvard, turned his back upon America, his somewhat reactionary opinions are, no doubt, all due to revolt against the ideas of his native country.'[1]

Meanwhile, with impressive clairvoyance, Denys Sutton, an art critic, wrote in October 1949 in *Horizon* that we should look to New York as we had once looked to Paris as the centre of the creative West. A determined quest for meaning, wrote Sutton, had placed the USA in the vanguard of modern art. 'Yet though the majority of painters are still of secondary importance it is difficult to resist the feeling that the artist in America is filled with confidence and is about to scale the heights.'[2]

Sutton had anticipated the overwhelming impact in the 1950s of the abstract expressionists – Rothko, Pollock, Baziotes and Rheinhardt – and the significance of their 'quest for meaning'.

The imagery of size was irresistible when talking of the USA. For a start, nobody any longer doubted that the move towards a two-power world was now well under way. The complex and still unresolved quarrels of a gaggle of little European states were dwarfed by the one epic confrontation between capitalism and Communism as embodied in the USA and the USSR. The latter, however, had lost much of its appeal. 'The last great political tragedy of our world', wrote Philip Toynbee, reviewing Arthur Koestler's *The Yogi and the Commissar*, 'may well be the deposition of the Soviet myth a decade too late.' [3] George Orwell added: 'There can be no question about the poisonous effects of the Russian *mythos* on English intellectual life.'[4]

The USSR had once been the home of the one great social and political experiment of the century. It seemed to embody the left-wing aspirations of the British intelligentsia. It was a nation that had embarked on the radical road to social justice, and any shortcomings detectable in Russian society after the revolution could be accepted as inevitable problems on that long and unprecedented journey. But Stalin's pact with Hitler could not; it was an event of such traumatic implications that the subsequent alliance with Stalin against Hitler could do nothing to dispel its bitter memory. The pact meant that Stalin, unlike his sympathizers in the West, did not value some distant ideal of a perfect and just society. Rather he believed in expediency and power – he was, in short, no better than Hitler. The anti-capitalist road to a new, fairer world turned out to have been mined.

By the time of the outbreak of the Korean War in 1950 there was no question that Communism had come to represent an evil equivalent to that of Nazism. Clement Attlee, the Labour Prime Minister, had no hesitation in defining the threat in a broadcast on 30 July. 'We all have vivid memories of what war means,' he acknowledged. But he went on: 'For, make no mistake about it, the evil forces which are now attacking South Korea are part of a world-wide conspiracy against the way of life of the free democracies ... They are ruthless and unscrupulous hypocrites who pretend to virtues which their philosophy rejects.'

So the USA was our undisputed ally, with her hard, heroic dream to be set against the parochial realism of the British of the 1940s and 1950s. She was wholeheartedly capitalist so would have no truck with the egalitarian aspirations of the socialist intellectuals before the war and of the voting majority afterwards. The USA had soaring, danger-ous cities which seemed possessed of some hubristic ambition to create a divine metropolis on earth, and her landscape was typically a vast, open prairie, the landscape of epics as opposed to the lyrics of church spires and villages. But, most of all, the USA was a land of dreams, whether in the form of the silk stockings peddled by the GIs, or in the dark, urban tensions of her gangster movies and the rural epics of her cowboy films.

The USA was irreparably other, and yet she had now twice intervened in British history, on both occasions presenting herself as our deliverer from the clutches of the Evil One. That it had been done twice seemed to reinforce the sense of the provinciality of our quarrels in Europe – these days we were to be sorted out like a recalcitrant western town by a US Marshal or like a knotty problem in the big city by Philip Marlowe.

W. H. Auden and Christopher Isherwood arrived in the USA on 26 January 1939 on the liner *Champlain*, having been seen off from Southampton by E. M. Forster. In that same month W. B. Yeats died, an event that drew from Auden one of his finest poems, in which he confessed the momentous change in his thinking about the real power and significance of poetry.

> For poetry makes nothing happen: it survives
> In the valley of its making where executives
> Would never want to tamper, flows on south
> From ranches of isolation and the busy griefs,
> Raw towns that we believe and die in; it survives,
> A way of happening, a mouth.[5]

Auden was born on 21 February 1907 in York. He had startlingly pale hair and skin and large, fleshy hands. His father, a doctor with amateur interests in Saxon and Norse antiquities, christened him Wystan after St Wystan, a prince murdered in 849. When Auden was still an infant, the family moved to Birmingham. From there he went to Gresham's School and Christ Church, Oxford. At Oxford in 1926 Tom Driberg showed him a back issue of T. S. Eliot's magazine *The Criterion* containing *The Waste Land*. Soon afterwards he announced that he had torn up all his juvenile poems and his undergraduate style veered suddenly towards the Eliotic.

In 1927 he sent some of his work to Eliot at Faber and Gwyer (later Faber and Faber). Three months later he received the guarded reply: 'I am very slow to make up my mind. I do not feel that any of the enclosed is quite right, but I should be interested to follow your work.'[6] Nevertheless, in 1929 Eliot published Auden's *Paid on Both Sides* – described as 'a charade' in *The Criterion* – and in 1930 he accepted, for Faber, Auden's *Poems*.

From that point onward Auden's reputation in poetry paralleled that of Moore in sculpture. Like Moore, he developed a spectacular technical mastery of his art, shifting effortlessly through a variety of complex and arcane verse forms as well as creating a tone and dramatic context for his verse that were unique and, for his own and a succeeding generation, extremely difficult to shake off. Where Eliot seemed inimitable, wrapped in some private struggle which periodically produced verse of inexplicable grandeur, Auden was everywhere, cajoling and explaining, immersed in the issues of his day. Technically he could produce dazzling cinematic elisions of imagery combined with a strange, disruptive urgency:

> The clouds rift suddenly – look there
> At cigarette-end smouldering on a border
> At the first garden party of the year.
> Pass on, admire the view of the massif
> Through plate glass windows of the Sport Hotel.[7]

His political poems, with their exhortations to the working class or rallying cries to the anti-Franco cause in the Spanish Civil War, were explicit reactions to the remoteness of literary modernism. They proclaimed the urgency of the poet's task in engaging with the world at all costs. By 1939 his stature was unquestioned by a generation to whom his topical immediacy had come as a relief after the difficulties of the 1920s modernists.

Geoffrey Grigson had founded the magazine *New Verse* in 1933. It closed in May 1939, and in his final issue Grigson wrote a valedictory on the supremacy of Auden:

'*New Verse* came into existence because of Auden. It has published more poems by Auden than by anyone else; and there are many people who might quote of Auden: "To you I owe the first development of my imagination; to you I owe the withdrawing of my mind from the low brutal part of my nature to the lofty, the pure and the perpetual." Auden is now clear, absolutely clear of foolish journalists, Cambridge detractors and envious creepers and crawlers of party and Catholic reaction and the new crop of loony and eccentric small magazines in England and America. He is something good and creative in European life in a time of the greatest evil.'[8]

As the Yeats poem demonstrated, however, Auden's arrival in the USA coincided with the abandonment of the political games of the 1930s. He began to leave behind the attitudinizing, the posturing and the youthful exhilaration of socialism and the envisioned birth of a new world order, in which Auden had once distantly dreamed that the poet could be reunited with the society from which he had been severed by the industrial revolution. But by 1939 he ceased to believe in this Utopia. Poetry was becoming a private activity, a 'way of happening, a mouth'. It was not answerable to the great world of politics and the demands of nations, only to itself and to the language. Europe and her quarrels were distractions. Auden and Isherwood knew they could make livings as writers in the USA, far from the impending storms of the old continent, so they left.

They left as old friends, a familiar literary double act, but thereafter their careers diverged. Auden exchanged his socialism for an existential Protestantism, discovered through the writings of Reinhold Niebuhr. Isherwood left him behind in New York in favour of California, mysticism and yoga. The USA, huge and protean, was, above all, what you imagined it to be.

Auden was reborn in New York into the life of the man lost in the great city, whose social obligations are minimized and for whom art became the self-contained, hermetically sealed interstices in a life otherwise riven with inconclusiveness, irritation and failure. He began the process of childish dependence on habit that was to descend into wilful infantilism in his later years. Slippered and eccentric, he began to incarnate the idea of a private, dissociated art. In the mornings he would kick himself into wakefulness with benzedrine and at night he would rock himself to sleep with seconal – the ritual meals of his 'chemical life'. He was embracing the artificiality required by his art and exuding an unprecedented degree of self-containment, enhanced by his new-found love of Chester Kallman.

Around the time war broke out in September 1939, Auden met

Benjamin Britten and Peter Pears. They had been in the USA for the summer, intending to return to England at the end of August. With the advent of war, they decided to stay in New York for the time being. Auden and Britten collaborated on the opera *Paul Bunyan* and they lived together in Brooklyn Heights, but Britten could not embrace the USA with Auden's enthusiasm: 'Whereas Auden in America welcomed an alienation and impersonality which was, he believed, the salutary destiny of the modern artist, living disconnected from community and prizing his rootlessness as a sign of existential freedom, Britten's brief period in America only convinced him of his ineradicable Englishness.'[9]

In California in 1941 Britten picked up a copy of the *Listener* magazine dated 29 May. It included an article by E. M. Forster on George Crabbe, the poet born in 1754 in Aldeburgh, Suffolk, who had written *The Village*, a precise, unromantic description of rural life. The evocation of home was too much and Britten returned to England in March 1942. For Auden, though, the USA provided the freedom in which his art could exist, disconnected from the exigencies of life. John Bayley contrasted this later position with that of Yeats:

'Whereas Yeats identifies himself and his poetry completely with one another, Auden sets up – most illuminatingly – a barrier between the man who is subject to the laws and limitations of being in the world, and the poet who is not . . . As poet, "playing God with words", he is free; as a human being he must live with and for other human beings; and he must never confuse his two roles.'[10]

F. R. Leavis was to take a characteristically less charitable view of Auden's version of the role of poetry: 'Mr Auden's honesty,' he wrote in *The Common Pursuit* (1952). 'there is no need to question; it may perhaps be said to manifest itself in the openness with which his poetry admits that it doesn't know how serious it supposes itself to be.' [11] Exactly.

The first large-scale expression of the American Auden was *New Year Letter* of 1940. It is a long argument in short, strict couplets which frequently crystallize into the quotable Auden with which a generation had become familiar:

Art is not life and cannot be
A midwife to society.[12]

This is explicatory, moral Auden, setting the record straight and preparing for the remainder of his poetic life.

For the Time Being: A Christmas Oratorio was published in 1944, although written between October 1941 and July 1942. It is dedicated to Auden's mother, who died in 1941: – 'When mother dies,' he wrote to a friend, 'one is, for the first time, really alone in the world, and that is hard.'[13] The poem was intended to be set to music by Britten and it is Auden's only explicitly religious work. His usual attitude was that poetry was secular and therefore separated from religion, rather as it was from life.

In the character of Herod, the rationalist, the humanist, Auden dissected the optimistic view of the world without God. He speaks in prose: 'Barges are unloading soil fertilizer at the river wharves. Soft drinks and sandwiches may be had in the inns at reasonable prices. Allotment gardening has become popular, the highway to the coast goes straight up over the mountains and the truck drivers no longer carry guns . . .'[14] Against this steady progress, this landscape of sensible comforts, the new child is an impossible threat:

'Reason will be replaced by Revelation. Instead of the Rational Law, objective truths perceptible to any who will undergo the necessary intellectual discipline, and the same for all, Knowledge will degenerate into a riot of subjective visions – feelings in the solar plexus induced by undernourishment . . .

'I've tried to be good. I brush my teeth every night. I haven't had sex for a month. I object. I'm a liberal. I want everyone to be happy. I wish I had never been born.'[15]

Auden was always a poet of ideas, at his worst. His phenomenal technical ability in adapting almost any verse form to his needs allowed him to slip into a jaunty, argumentative tone made acceptable by the quality of the verse and the occasional flashes of his finest style, in which he evaded the formulaic nets of his admirers. *For the Time Being* suffers from its need both to be set to music and to move through the process of the Nativity, but the 'Flight to Egypt' sequence brings the authentic Auden tension, in which his dramatic sense takes him fully into his repertoire of alien voices and away from argument. Childhood has become a desecrated kingdom, the Voices of the Desert speak in snide, weary cadences.

> Come to our jolly desert
> Where even the dolls go whoring;
> Where cigarette-ends
> Become intimate friends,
> And it's always three in the morning.[16]

The desert is the barren, corrupted world of the city. At three in the morning, all experience is past, lived out. Behind the Narrator's closing words lurks the rationalist, murdering Herod. We are returning, he says, to the 'Aristotelian city', packing up the decorations, half accepting the significance of the Christmas festivities, though not really caring. But:

> For the innocent children who whispered so excitedly
> Outside the locked door where they knew the presents to be
> Grew up when it opened.[17]

The menacing ambiguity of childhood also opens Auden's next long work, *The Sea and the Mirror*.

> and O
> How the dear little children laugh
> When the drums roll and the lovely
> Lady is sawn in half.[18]

The work is inspired by *The Tempest*, a useful literary precedent for Auden's own attempt to place the activity of art within his new framework of Christian beliefs. The attempt may fail but in section III, 'Caliban to the Audience', it produces something spectacularly new from Auden: a pastiche of the prose of Henry James, a device Auden justified by the fact that Caliban, being inarticulate, had to borrow from Ariel the most artificial and literary language possible.[19] Its effect is to express the supreme artificiality of the entire artistic effort which, platonically, can only reflect the divine order:

'that Wholly Other Life from which we are separated by an essential

emphatic gulf of which our contrived fissures of mirror and pro-
scenium arch – we understand them at last – are feebly figurative
signs, so that all our meanings are reversed and it is precisely in its
negative image of Judgement that we can positively envisage Mercy;
it is just here, among the ruins and the bones, that we may rejoice in
the perfected Work which is not ours.'[20]

That Auden discovered a style in pastiche is significant. He had
always many voices and the ability to take on many forms, but his
incessant productivity could not conceal that the very act of poetry
had always seemed, even in his most banally political phases, to be a
kind of ritualized removal from the quotidian self. The willed, driven
rhetoric of the pre-war 'Spain 1937' says more about the needs of
Auden the poet than about the Civil War. Confronted with the literary
playground which his post-war ordering of priorities has created, the
danger was that there would be nothing at all to do. He could have
been silenced, having lost the imaginary meanings of the past and
having denied himself the literary exploitation of the real – that is
Christian - ones of the present. Art would have to happen in spite of
life, somewhere in the spaces in between. That, however, offered
neither content nor form; pastiche provided both. The form was that
of another, the content was self-generating – an infolding meditation
on what could be said or done:

'Confronted by a straight and snubbing stare to which mythology is
bosh, surrounded by an infinite passivity and purely arithmetical dis-
order which is only open to perception, and with nowhere to go on
to, your existence is indeed free at last to choose its own meaning,
that is, to plunge headlong into despair and fall through silence
fathomless and dry, all fact your single drop, all value your pure alas.'[21]

Late in April 1945 Auden flew to England, bizarrely clad in the
uniform of a US Army major. He had managed to find himself a
position in the Strategic Bombing Survey, whose task was to visit
Germany and assess the effects of air raids. He stopped in England
and dismayed old friends by his vicious attacks on the English way of
life and his eulogies on the superiority of American culture. His
posturing proved of little significance. Auden's England was too potent

a creation to be eradicated even by its author. Far removed from the
lovably rural snapshots of Betjeman or the organic fantasies of Little
Englanders and New Critics alike, it was a complex, worn and marked
landscape of history and of childhood portent.

In May 1948 Auden completed his poem 'In Praise of Limestone'.
He travelled to England again that year with his lover, Chester Kallman. In May they moved on to Paris and Italy. The poem ends:

> Dear, I know nothing of
> Either, but when I try to imagine a faultless love
> Or the life to come, what I hear is the murmur
> Of underground streams, what I see is a limestone landscape.[22]

Unseen Lights

H. G. Wells was born into the lower middle classes of Bromley in Kent in 1866. He died on 13 August 1946. Energetic and argumentative, he had been a socialist, a science-fiction writer, a comic novelist, a creator of intellectual and fictional potboilers, an autobiographer and, finally, a pessimistic visionary and prophet. 'We should hazard a guess', Kingsley Martin wrote after Wells's death, 'that no writer in this century has so deeply influenced his generation.' He was a man popularly and politically associated with 'that tradition of self-confidence and belief in progress which was the real religion of the Victorian and even of the Edwardian epoch'.[1]

Wells was cremated; a year later his son Anthony West and his half-brother George Philip Wells chartered a boat, the *Deirdre*. They planned to scatter the ashes at a point in the sea between Alum Bay on the Isle of Wight and St Alban's Head on the Dorset shore – an idea inspired by a passage from Wells's 1909 novel *Tono-Bungay*. At the end of the book the narrator sails down the Thames from Hammersmith in an experimental new destroyer called X2 – 'To run down the Thames so is to run one's hand over the pages in the book of England from end to end.'[2]

The narrator is struck by the connection between the progress of the boat and of his book. The analogy expands to encompass the whole of London and the nation as he passes the docks, Essex, Kent and finally into the open sea:

'And now behind us is blue mystery and the phantom flash of unseen lights, and presently even these are gone, and I and my destroyer tear out to the unknown across a great gray space. We tear into the great spaces of the future and the turbines fall to talking in unfamiliar tongues. Out to the open we go, to windy freedom and trackless ways. Light after light goes down, England and the Kingdom, Britain and the Empire, the old prides and the old devotions, glide abeam, astern, sink down upon the horizon, pass – pass. The river passes, London passes, England passes . . .'[3]

When Wells and West sailed out in the *Deirdre*, they found themselves facing a freshening wind and a tide running the wrong way, and were unable to reach the spot they had chosen. The ashes were cast into the sea before the boat reached the open Solent: 'The wind took them off as a long veil that struck the very pale green water with a hiss.'[4]

The Festival of Britain opened on 3 May 1951 with a service at St Paul's. The opening hymn was 'Ye servants of God, your master proclaim'. Strikes and appalling spring weather had blighted the preparations, and six years of austerity had weakened the proud, popular national certainties of the war's end. *The Times*'s leader writer welcomed the festivities with some hesitancy: 'The consequences of lack of unity among creative artists and their public are by no means wholly bad. Absence of certainty has bred a friendly spirit that invites visitors to enjoy themselves and not to be bored by lectures. The harshest critic of the exhibition should admit that it is great fun to go round it and that, after doing so, the impression is left of a nation proud of its accomplishment and still zestful.'[5]

The next day's leader on the Festival was more specific about the new uncertainty. The belief in progress, the death of which had foreshadowed the physical death of H. G. Wells, was now slowly perishing in the popular imagination. There was a painful contrast between the 1951 Festival and its predecessor, 100 years before.

'It was staunch resolution that Britain should offer her best to the world in spite of everything she has suffered and the troubles she may still have in store. The creators of the 1851 exhibition were, as the King said, "far-sighted men who looked forward to a world in which the spectacular advances of art and science would uplift civilization to enduring peace and prosperity". It would be as unprofitable to dwell on the contrast between that vision and the uncertainties of to-day as it would be false to affect the optimism which mid-Victorian England sincerely felt.'[6]

Wyndham Lewis was born in the USA in 1882, though he came to England as a child. He became the leader of the vorticist movement and, with Ezra Pound, a vital, polemical defender of modernism. But with time his loathing of twentieth-century civilization drove him to ever more savage rhetoric and to a lonely position on the extreme right of politics. As a painter he could be precise and unforgettable; as a writer he swung between the wordy, the banal and the magnificent.

On 19 May 1951, a couple of weeks after the opening of the Festival, he published an article in the *Listener* entitled 'The Sea-Mists of the Winter'. It described how, in summer 1949, he had been painting his second portrait of T. S. Eliot: 'I had to draw up very closely to the sitter to see exactly how the hair sprouted out of the forehead, and how the curl of the nostril wound up into the dark interior of the nose.' Lewis was suffering from cranial pharyngeoma; he was going blind. 'And meanwhile I gaze backwards over the centuries at my fellow condamnés. Homer heads the list, but there are surprisingly few. I see John Milton sitting with his three daughters (the origin of this image is, to my shame, it seems to me, a Royal Academy picture) the fearful blow at his still youthful pride distorting his face with frustration ... Well, Milton had his daughters, I have my dictaphone.'

Lewis concluded the article: 'And finally, which is the main reason for this unseemly autobiographical outburst, my articles on contemporary art exhibitions necessarily end, for I can no longer see a picture.'[7]

Ezra Pound wrote in Canto CXV:

> Wyndham Lewis chose blindness
> rather than have his mind stop
>
> [...]
>
> When one's friends hate each other
> how can there be peace in the world
> Their asperities diverted me in my green time.
>
> A blown husk that is finished
> but the light sings eternal
> a pale flare over marshes[8]

The long veil of Wells's ashes over the Solent was an age's valedictory as were the new Festival's diminished and compromised aspirations. The strange light of peace had proved equivocal, fragile and, for blind Lewis and poor, mad Pound, barely distinguishable amid the debris.

PART TWO

Late Times

In a collection of essays published in 1959 the Roman Catholic poet and artist David Jones included a piece about the Victorian writer George Borrow, the author of *The Romany Rye* and *Lavengro*, who died in 1881. 'Thus, this man', wrote Jones, 'who died fourteen years only before I who wrote this introduction was born, had, so he tells us, talked with a man who, long years before, had known a person who in infancy had been lifted on to a stile in order to have a look at some armoured horsemen moving in the direction of Naseby on a summer morning in 1645.'[1]

Jones was and remains an oddity: a writer, painter, illustrator and calligrapher possessed of a visionary religious conviction as well as a modernist ambition to find a form of art that would encompass all history and all civilization. It was a post-war correlative of the task Eliot, Joyce and Pound had once set themselves. He was born in 1895 in Kent, the son of a Welshman and, through his early art training, he became obsessed with the mythic and historical themes of Wales. He fought in the trenches in the First World War for over two years, an experience that resulted in an epic mixture of poetry and prose entitled *In Parenthesis*, begun in 1927 but not published until 1937. It was a long, dense account of the experiences of a Private John Ball from his training camp to a battle in the trenches where he is wounded. Its technique of concentration, imagistic narrative and allusion derives directly from the innovations of the modernists and, indeed, both T. S. Eliot and Herbert Read were to single out the book as a major work of its day.

His second book, *The Anathemata*, was published in 1952. Again it is a vast, epic mound of material, obsessively assembled with one overriding ambition: somehow to include everything. In his preface Jones wrote:

'What is this writing about? I answer that it is about one's own "thing",

89

which *res* is unavoidably part and parcel of the Western Christian *res*, as inherited by a person whose perceptions are totally conditioned and limited by and dependent upon his being indigenous to this island. In this it is necessarily insular; within which insularity there are the further conditionings contingent upon his being a Londoner, of Welsh and English parentage, of Protestant upbringing, of Catholic subscription. While such biographical accidents are not in themselves any concern of, or interest to, the reader, they are noted here because they are responsible for most of the content and have had an overruling effect upon the form of this writing.'[2]

This is not an excuse for explicit autobiography, rather a way of explaining the one centre, the one point of anchorage, in the whole work – Jones himself. He is a product of a language and a history. His is the perspective from which their infinite associative complexities are to be observed:

> The adaptations, the fusions
> the transmogrifications
>   but always
> the inward continuities
>   of the site
>   of place
> From the tomb of the strife-years the
> new-born shapes begin already to look uncommonly like the
> brats of mother Europa.
> We begin already to discern our own.
> Are the proto-forms already ours?
> Is that the West-wind on our cheek-bones?[3]

The Anathemata is the story of Britain seen through the compressed, complex forms of a particular variety of modernism. Pound, Eliot and Joyce echo through its pages but, though Jones may share their technique, his intentions are quite different. He is using their focus on the language itself to discover not a new, imaginative unity but a unity which his faith assures him is already there. This unity is, however, concealed by our age. 'The period in which we live now', he wrote, 'is alien to sign, sacrament and sacramental acts and not

one of us can totally escape that alienation.'[4] This is an insight comparable to the anti-modern disgust of Waugh and it echoes a remark at
the beginning of Kenneth Clark's book, published in 1949, *Landscape
into Art*: 'We who are heirs to three centuries of science', wrote Clark,
'can hardly realise a state of mind in which all material objects were
thought of as symbols of spiritual truths or episodes in sacred history.'[5]

Jones shared with Clark this sense that science has destroyed our
ability to detect transcendent meaning in the world:

'The times are late and get later [he wrote in the preface to *The
Anathemata*], not by decades but by years and months. This tempo of
change, which in the world of affairs and in the physical sciences
makes schemes and data out-moded and irrelevant overnight, presents
peculiar and phenomenal difficulties in the making of works, and
almost insuperable difficulties in the making of certain kinds of works;
as when, for one reason or another, the making of those works has
been spread over a number of years. The reason is not far to seek.
The artist deals wholly in signs. His signs must be valid, that is valid
for him and, normally, for the culture that has made him. But there
is a time factor affecting these signs. If a requisite now-ness is not
present, the sign, valid in itself, is apt to suffer a kind of invalidation.'[6]

At some time in the recent past some severance occurred – Jones
recalled that, in the 1920s, he and his contemporaries knew it as 'the
Break'. We fell from the world of significance into an alien land in
which signs had neither value nor permanence. But the artist cannot
retreat from this insight into a dream of the past; he must forge new
significance with the tools of the present, with the radical techniques
of modernism. So Jones's remark about Borrow is not touristic wonder
at the fact of the past, but an awestruck attempt to affirm our direct
attachment to it. In that attachment is meaning, which can be regained
only by an effort of reconnection. In that fragment Jones is attempting
in one breathless sweep to move us from the now of his writing to
the then of the stile on the summer morning. The demonstration
should renew us; endow our experience with a depth we had forgotten.

'While the riddle element has always existed in poetry,' Auden
wrote in a review of *The Anathemata*, 'the disappearance of a homogeneous society with a common cult, a common myth, common in

terms of reference, has created difficulties in communication for the poet which are historically new and quite outside his control.'⁷

Auden's own response was the subtle and complex construction of a special space for his art, sealed off from life and religion on Prospero's island, a glittering landscape of mirrors. Jones is more direct; he wants his art to work upon the things of the world and make them sacred once again. By doing so he will restore the language to its former density and richness: 'The arts abhor any loppings off of meanings or emptyings out, any lessening of the totality of connotation, any loss of recession and thickness through.'⁸ Thus the anathemata themselves are 'the blessed things that have taken on what is cursed and the profane things that somehow are redeemed.'⁹ They are the things of the world given absolute and irreducible meaning.

Jones's enemy is that rootless primitivist, the man without a past, incapable of raising his eyes from the hard, shallow meaningless facts of the world – the scientist. 'Technocracy draws us away from the sign world,'¹⁰ he wrote. But Jones too is a primitivist, a believer in a lost wholeness, a vanished organic community. It is a familiar theme from the anguished writings of Leavis, Read, Connolly or Lewis, but Jones did not share the sense of impotence in the face of bleak technology. His poetry did not stand on the sidelines providing a commentary on the sense of loss, it tried to create a new language which would rediscover the sign. He did not wish to produce an idea about anything, he wished to produce the thing itself.

In the event failure was perhaps inevitable. As his often pointlessly contorted prose shows, Jones tended to lose control of the number of ways in which a relatively simple idea could be expressed. The resulting jumble of associations is not, therefore, an organic, artistic whole so much as a random mound, bonded by willed and imposed correspondences and concealing a kind of polemic. But his importance as something more than a passive artist, awash in the enigma of the present, remains, as does the significance of his imaginative attempt to reformulate the past. This attempt, shorn of its forced mythologies and sentimental accretions, resurfaced in British fiction thirty years later. But in the 1950s the failings of the immediate past and the production of symptomatically broken art dominated British culture.

History, for that age, was an accumulation of signs, certainly, but other artists were to find them merely illegible. 'As a poet of the historic consciousness,' wrote Lawrence Durrell in his 1957 novel *Justine*, 'I suppose I am bound to see landscape as a field dominated by the human wish – tortured in farms and hamlets, ploughed into cities. A landscape scribbled with the signatures of men and epochs.'[11] But this 'suppose' can only produce wistful longing:

'In the harbour of Alexandria the sirens whoop and wail. The screws of ships crush and crunch the green oil-coated waters of the inner bar. Oddly bending and inclining, effortlessly breathing as if in the rhythm of the earth's own systole and diastole, the yachts turn their spars against the sky. Somewhere in the heart of experience there is an order and coherence which we might surprise if we were attentive enough, loving enough or patient enough. Will there be time?'[12]

In effect, the 1950s saw the emergence of British artists who could be said to be wholly post-war. There had been a tiredness in the late 1940s that seemed to overwhelm any new creativity. On the one hand the Festival of Britain had represented an uncertain, hedged modernist optimism, on the other there was outright despair that both Edwardian rationalism and Victorian idealism were no longer at hand to write the programme for the future. And what had replaced them seemed either arid or exotic. There was analytical philosophy with its nagging insistence on eradicating every last trace of metaphysics and there was existentialism – bleak, foreign and apparently terminal.

To an artist such as Jones this was consistent with his primitivist contrast between the world of machines and the world of holy signs, leaving him with the difficult task of recreating or, at any rate, postulating the latter. But at least it gave him a task; for the unbelievers the problem came earlier: where to start.

Small, Clear

There was at least one spectacular public assertion that a new beginning could be made: Elizabeth II was crowned in June 1953. A new Elizabethan age was to be born in a new climate. 'The Queen's face looks at us from French newspapers', wrote the *Spectator*, 'as well as from our own, and in America, where strait-laced, puritanical, anti-monarchist traditions are still alive, the advertisers offer "Coronation" cosmetics, jewellery and clothes to a public which sees nothing incongruous in the situation.'[1]

The monarchy was discovering its modern role as a kind of national talisman, a system of images and rituals sustained, to a large extent, for the benefit of foreigners. Yet the nation still had its native ingenuity and courage. 'A nation that can still produce men who climb to the top of Everest, who give one example after another in Korea of the highest military virtue, and who invent and fly the best passenger aircraft in the world, is certainly not lacking in imagination and flair.'[2] This is, of course, the over-stimulated rhetoric of the moment; but it summarizes the defiantly defensive quality of contemporary national pride. The Empire being dissolved and our military might hopelessly overshadowed, there was a need still to shake our tiny fists. This view was lampooned by the journalist in John Osborne's play *Under Plain Cover*: 'Happy is the land where the desire for symbols and display is expressed so harmlessly and yet so richly. Truly, an orb in the minster is worth a monster in orbit.'[3]

Meanwhile, there was still the great task of reconstruction, but its ideology had been enfeebled by the doubts of its own practitioners. In addition to the ambiguity of the war's end and the, at best, tentative embracing of the future by the intellectuals, the tribunes of the new equality were unsure. They had spoken of a British 'poverty of aspiration': certainly the Labour Government had provided the promised welfare measures, but the fragility of the post-war economy meant that austerity clung to Britain like a particularly bad winter. The new world was a long time coming.

A Conservative Government was returned in 1951, something of an anomaly. At the 1945 election Labour had taken 47.8 per cent of the vote and the Tories 39.8 per cent. In 1950, again a Labour victory, the figures were 46.1 and 43.5. In 1951 Labour actually took its highest ever share of the votes at 48.8 per cent, 0.8 per cent ahead of the Tories, but the constituency system produced a Conservative majority. While Labour support was as strong as ever, political reality uprooted the frail growth of post-war, socialist idealism.

The rationing and the developing bureaucracy required to run a more socialist state had, in any case, inspired a degree of popular impatience and disillusion. The welfare state was not being rejected, it had simply been revealed as not quite the instant panacea that had been advertised. It was evidently a good thing but it did not immediately suggest the next step. Iris Murdoch observed in 1961 that its creation had brought with it a certain 'lassitude about fundamentals'[4] and Kingsley Amis noted that 'the welfare state, indeed, is notoriously unpopular with intellectuals.'[5] Nevertheless, there was some persistence of the old idealism, even in Amis: 'I feel that unless something very unexpected happens I shall vote Labour to the end of my days, however depraved the Labour candidate may be and however virtuous his opponent.'[6]

The very idea of Murdoch's 'fundamentals' would have had an alien, possibly continental ring. The Coronation aside, greatness or significance were not only missing, they did not appear to be wanted. In *British Society Since 1945* Arthur Marwick wrote:

'In all spheres there was a sense of dominance by established in-groups, a feeling of following the current cult. In all spheres British thought and artistic endeavour were inward-looking, seemingly unconcerned with the great issues which racked continental intellectuals: existentialism and social commitment, the challenge to Marxist faith presented by Stalinist tyranny, the possibilities of a Catholicism attuned to the needs of the modern world. The many British literary works which bring in the Second World War seem somehow to treat it as a little local affair, without epochal significance, when compared, say, with American novels dealing with the same war, or the British literary reaction to the First World War.'[7]

Yet this very lassitude, this unconcern, provided a kind of conviction for a new generation of artists in the 1950s, and brought with it the resurrection of realism as a means of rejecting the tortured doubts about form and content of the modernists and their disciples. The most celebrated vehicle of this rejection was the Movement, a loose agglomeration of novelists and poets united by a more or less consistent ideology of common sense and an impatient desire to get on with playing their part in the supposedly 'real' literary tradition that predated the contortions of modernity. There were also the consciously working-class novels from less obviously literary figures such as Stan Barstow and Alan Sillitoe. As a form of social critique, however, realism was nothing new; only in the cultivatedly philistine sensibilities of the Movement was a genuinely original tone emerging.

Behind this tone lay a mistrust of the idea of art itself. Typical Movement figures such as Kingsley Amis, John Wain or Philip Larkin loathed the effete, salon mannerisms of Stephen Spender or Edith Sitwell as well as all the cultural paraphernalia and pretension with which they were associated. Eliot was, of course, implicated and Pound was, all too evidently, a charlatan. Indeed the article which christened the Movement conducted the ritual with the aid of a catalogue of rejection; it appeared in the *Spectator*: 'Who do you take with you on the long weekends in Sussex cottages, Kafka and Kierkegaard, Proust and Henry James? Dylan Thomas, *The Confidential Clerk*, *The Age of Anxiety* and *The Golden Horizon*? You belong to an age that is passing.'[8]

It was a catalogue possessing all the neat finality of an injunction from a Paris couturier. It summarized all that had previously been accepted as 'artistic' – the provinces of the 'established in-groups' noted by Marwick. All continental mannerisms were 'out' as was the hermetic London society which had embraced them. Instead there was the 'reality' of provincial life – though a less poetic version than William Cooper's – and a determination not to allow theory or speculation to distract the uncompromising, undeceived realistic eye.

There were, as always, inconsistencies that defied any manifesto of the Movement's intentions. The self-conscious worship of the cultural past, for example, was heavily lampooned in Amis's *Lucky Jim* in the character of Professor Welch: a man with a laughable belief in the cultural potency of madrigals and all the marginalia of a distant age. But at the same time the myth of a better past lurked behind the entire anti-modernist posture of the Movement. The poet D. J. Enright, in particular, was in thrall to Leavis with his sense of an organic community, a wholesome society which had at some stage been fragmented. In addition, the wholesale rejection of the more shamelessly artistic recent past was rhetorical rather than actual. Auden hovers over the early poetry of Amis and of many other adherents of the Movement. The truth was that his range and the sheer effectiveness of his variations of tone made him unavoidable.

What was clear was that this new realism represented an attempt to set art within a more manageable context. The critical baggage of literary society – 'Kafka and Kierkegaard' – seemed to have become too heavy and too remote. Indeed, the entire symbolist and modernist modes were perceived to be too portentous, too insistent that they be accepted only on their own difficult terms. In their place was the 'real', the actual perspective of experience with its limited horizons and its complete absence of the grand, heroic style.

In John Wain's 1953 novel *Hurry on Down* the hero, Charles Lumley, sticks pins into a map to decide where to go when he leaves university. There is no hierarchy of attractions or significance to be found on the map. London, once the obvious choice, has been over-turned as a centre of meaning; his destination may as well be randomly determined. Meanwhile, Lumley feels nothing but distaste for the typically avant-garde novel being written by his friend Froulish and he regards with morbid objectivity his own decline into drug-running, a moral abandonment justified only by his pursuit of a girl. The very thinness of the book's texture arises from its certainty that there is no culture, no context, which can provide depth and context. But if there is no culture there does at least seem to be a community of sensibility. Wain's plot, for example, in which a disaffected young man from a provincial university pursues a seemingly unattainable girl, almost startlingly foreshadows Amis's *Lucky Jim* (1954).

Kingsley Amis was born in south London in 1922. He took an English degree at Oxford, his course being interrupted by the war.

As an undergraduate he met, among others, Larkin and Wain, and he wrote a novel called *The Legacy* with a hero called Kingsley Amis. Although not published it had the effect, Amis later explained, of getting 'my modernism out of the way'.[9] He published poetry – *Bright November* in 1947 and *A Frame of Mind* in 1953 – but, with *Lucky Jim*, he became the Movement figure most instantly recognizable to the public, the representative of all clear-eyed 1950s, no-nonsense realists.

His novel is a much more complex and important achievement than Wain's as it does actually seem to forge a new posture, a positive new mode for the novel, out of the Movement's manifold rejections. It does so, in part, by being deceptively comprehensive: where Wain's hero seemed to see little more than the same cultural and spiritual vacuum whichever way he turned, Amis's Jim Dixon sees a plenitude of possibilities. The world could be right, fair and rewarding, but such possibilities only act as fuel for Dixon's wounded introspection and his horror that so much of what seems so palpably wrong should be so materially successful. Most obviously there is the figure of Professor Welch's son, 'the pacifist painting Bertrand', the posturing, hypocritical London artist: 'The only action he required from Bertrand was an apology, humbly offered, for his personal appearance . . .'[10] But Bertrand has the girl – 'the sight of her seemed an irresistible attack on his own habits, standards, and ambitions, something designed to put him in his place for good'. [11]

Dixon is obsessed, both with his own loathing and with the success of others. The fact that Bertrand has the girl brings the two into conflict. Behind the passage lies a curious moral atavism – he loathes Bertrand but Bertrand has the girl and that calls into question the rightness of his own loathing. Perhaps Bertrand deserves the girl and has been rewarded by some system of justice that operates in spite of Jim.

From such spectacles Dixon recoils into his repertoire of grotesque facial expressions and a glum acceptance of his own failures, but the acceptance does not modify his loathing. The energy of his distaste is undiminished by a world that seems to be telling him that he is wrong. The novel's movement is in any case towards the revelation that he is neither wrong nor alone. In the futile society that he observes, there are more sophisticated, if less effective, souls who see through the patterns of relationships, the very patterns Dixon finds merely confirm his worst suspicions. 'Don't worry,' says Carol to Dixon when dancing with him, 'it's all connected, all connected.'[12]

The connection turns out to be the vacuity and hypocrisy of those very people Dixon suspects are vacuous and hypocritical. His guilt about his clinging girl friend, Margaret Peel, is dispelled; she is revealed as a dangerous neurotic, something he had long suspected but had been afraid to act on. Meanwhile his suspicions about the fallibility of Bertrand are all confirmed and he wins the girl. So the novel makes a point: its hero is a real hero who is proved right. It is a morality tale in which the good man, the one endowed with common sense and an undeceived gaze, is rewarded. The world of responses inside his head is validated by experience. The forces of pretension, dishonesty and dull sobriety are defeated. The pact with the reader, established by our enlistment in Dixon's cause, is triumphant.

The simplicity of this, combined with the clarity and accuracy with which Amis knows his enemies, should not conceal the heart of the novel: its complete acceptance of Dixon's horizons. The comedy and the commentary both arise from the fact that we are, without apology, entirely inside Dixon's head. From this vantage point we may occasionally catch distant glimpses of another world that introduce a jarring rhapsodic note:

'As he stood in the badly-lit jakes, he was visited again, and unbearably, by the visual image that had haunted him ever since he took on this job. He seemed to be looking from a darkened room across a deserted back street to where, against a dimly-glowing evening sky, a line of chimney pots stood out as if carved from tin. A small double cloud moved slowly from right to left. The image wasn't purely visual, because he had a feeling that some soft unidentifiable noise was in his ears, and he felt with a dreamer's baseless conviction that somebody was going to come into the room where he seemed to be, somebody he knew in the image but not in reality.'[13]

More often, though, we simply see the real world as defective, not living up to some unspecified standard of Dixon's. From that comes the enduring discontent, the constant irritation that emerged in all of Amis's subsequent novels. It is a sense that the age has failed his heroes, that in some way the time was lacking in substance, sense or conviction. The feeling was expressed more specifically by Doris Lessing in her contribution to an odd 1957 collection of essays, intended by its editors as a kind of waving of the disgruntled flag, called *Declaration*: 'We are not living in an exciting literary period,' she wrote, 'but a dull one. We are not producing masterpieces, but large numbers of small, quite lively intelligent novels.'[14] Combined with that smallness was the curious suspicion that some sort of confidence trick had been perpetrated, a swindle in which even science was not blameless. An essay by John Wain, also in *Declaration*, caught this somewhat paranoiac note:

'Where were all the things my parents and their friends used to prophesy when I was a nipper? Nowhere it seemed except in the pages of early Wells, mouldering on the shelves. Strangest of all was the attitude of people who had been young in the twenties, and were now getting into middle age. In their youth, it had seemed that the rigid crust of conventional life was cracking from top to bottom; a few more holes punched in it, and it would be nothing but a heap of crumbs. And behold! everything had somehow drifted back into something like old shape; things like marriage, and private property, and war, and the division of the world into nations, and the church, and the public schools – there they all were, the same as ever. To such people the twentieth century must seem like one long tragic swindle.'[15]

Yet again the feeling is that something is missing. But Amis, Lessing and Wain are not dreaming of David Jones's sacramental forms, rather of a world that had meaning in the most elementary sense – where progress was possible, where the good, sane chap could triumph. Dixon's discovery in *Lucky Jim* is that meaning can be imposed on the world by strong, self-made men. Gore-Urquhart, the man who finally employs him and frees him from provincial bondage, explains why he puts up with the boredom of mediocrities: 'I want to influence people so they'll do what I think it's important they should do. I can't get 'em to do that unless I let 'em bore me first, you understand. Then just as they're delighting in having got me punch-drunk with talk I come back at 'em and make 'em do what I've got lined up for 'em.'[16]

Dixon finally abandons introspection and acts; he grabs the girl and goes to London. Doubts are dispelled in a flagrantly unmodernist way. The hero, his perceptions now justified, becomes the avenger. His consciousness, his tone, has become the measure of all things and, in doing so, it creates a fictional voice which was borrowed by novelists for the next thirty years: a voice of limitation and defeat, which triumphs because the rest of the world is discovered to be just as limited and defeated.

But *Lucky Jim* is a moral tale that puts forward two views of the world and allows one to triumph. It possesses a strict comic structure in which an awry and unjust world is eventually righted. The issue it does not raise, at least not successfully, is how far the point of view, the position of the observer, conditions the perceptions. This is a structural issue for which Amis, publicly at least, would have little patience. It reeks too much of the kind of modernist self-involvement from which he believed he was escaping – remember the 'Kingsley Amis' character in his unpublished first novel *The Legacy*. But in the work of his Oxford contemporary, Philip Larkin, the issue had become more urgent. Clearly, in one sense, Larkin entirely abandoned the technical problem of a fictional point of view when he abandoned the novel in favour of poetry. In doing so, however, he was obliged to confront the somewhat more elusive problem of a poetic persona. But his own statements of his intentions were always carefully evasive: 'I write poems to preserve things I have seen/thought/felt (if I may so indicate a composite and complex experience) both for myself and for others, though I feel that my primary responsibility is the experience itself, which I am trying to keep from oblivion for its own sake. Why I should do this I have no idea, though I think the impulse to preserve lies at the bottom of all art.'[17]

Whether from unwillingness or ignorance there is a great deal that Larkin is carefully not saying in this statement, much of it concealed behind words like 'it's own sake' and 'I have no idea.' Even in this apparently simple statement the tension can be felt between the experience as something *out there* and the poet *in here*. For all Larkin's careful rejection of the antics of modernism, he is obliged to accept its awareness of the position of the observer; only by doing so can he arrive at a distinctive poetic voice. He may claim Thomas Hardy as his precursor, but Eliot's 'impotent consciousness' also lies behind his poetry, even if it is heavily modified by an essentially prose mentality. For Larkin's poetry is always tight, complete and contained; its images make points, its rhythms enhance prosaic meaning. Its uncertainties, its elements of a genuinely modern poetic consciousness are always suppressed by the old treadmill of old meanings.

'Church Going', published in 1955 in the collection *The Less Deceived* is the Movement poem *par excellence*. The poet wanders into a country church, his persona of the provincial hick intact:

> Once I am sure there's nothing going on
> I step inside, letting the door thus shut.
> Another church; matting, seats and stone,
> And little books; sprawlings of flowers, cut
> For Sunday, brownish now; some brass and stuff
> Up at the holy end; the small neat organ;
> And a tense, musty, unignorable silence,
> Brewed God knows how long. Hatless, I take off
> My cycle-clips in awkward reverence,

There are then two stanzas describing the small drama of his visit, followed by four of introspection, progressing from why he stopped at the church in the first place to what on earth such a place could possibly mean any more. The final stanza essays a statement:

> A serious house on serious earth it is,
> In whose blent air all our compulsions meet,
> Are recognised, and robed as destinies.
> And that much never can be obsolete,
> Since someone will forever be surprising
> A hunger in himself to be more serious,
> And gravitating with it to this ground,
> Which, he once heard, was proper to grow wise in,
> If only that so many dead lie round.[18]

The last line acknowledges the frail support of all this seriousness, accepting the loss of the superstructure of faith and the absurdity of the poet's own awe. There is an argument for the sanctity of this place but it is an 'if only that' argument; it is a last line of retreat. All that replaces faith is a humble contemplation of oblivion.

The poem goes a long way towards actually dissecting the deeper significance of the Movement's limitation of vision. It shows the artist considering a world that has lost its meaning: both its undeniable otherness and what might be left of imaginative importance. But this does not inspire him to a new language, a new synthesis; rather it evokes passive contemplation, an experience to be retained in rhythmic, rhyming lines. History cannot be denied; the ceremonies that have taken place in the church may be an accumulation of fictions, but they provide the means for our needs to be 'robed as destinies'. Yet, equally, this is only a history of habit, not of the grand imperial tragedies of Eliot or the political, cultural and aesthetic imperatives of Auden. It is not, above all, a history to be re-imagined.

Indeed the fact of habit, the nervous tic of the poet, sends him into empty churches, and virtually undermines the careful balancing of the final stanza. The poem could almost end with the last line of the previous verse, 'It pleases me to stand in silence here', but, in reality the final verse was the real literary project. As Frank Kermode put it: 'Here, as elsewhere, the project is to make possible the large and otherwise impossible statement, the kind of things all modern poets have to work for, as, for example, Mr Larkin works for the last stanza of "Church Going".'[19]

David Wright, reviewing *The Less Deceived* and other Movement works,[20] said they were possessed of a 'frightened, welfare-state mentality', the point being that a certain matter-of-factness, a shoulder-shrugging air of 'what can we do?' seemed a desperately feeble posture for a new wave in English writing. Of course this underestimates the achievement of both Larkin and Amis in evolving a language of limitation, a style forged from their awareness of the impossibility of the grand artistic gesture or synthesis, but, at the same time, Wright did spot a depressing tendency for artists to adopt a marginal role – as commentators rather than initiators.

In the long term this became associated with a certain view of the whole of British culture as isolated, limited in ambition and of little interest to the rest of the world. Even the idea of wandering into parish churches has a Little England quality about it. Indeed, this made it an exemplary activity to inspire Larkin's poem.

The truth was that, in spite of the undeceived posture, the Movement was still deeply involved with the idea of the significant British landscape. In their insularity its practitioners implicitly believed in the possibility of the restoration of a native Britishness: a feeling that could be traced back to Gavin Bone, Amis's and Larkin's tutor at Oxford, who sowed the seeds of their anti-modernism and stressed the value of the native English stock.[21] More generally, it was a mood that could be associated with a kind of tub-thumping literary empiricism that emerges from time to time as a critical rather than creative posture.

Outside the Movement itself, Robert Graves was thumping the same tub. In a series of lectures in 1955 he conducted an onslaught on the pantheon of Pound, Eliot, Yeats, Auden and Dylan Thomas: 'Are you men and women of culture?' he asked in a curious echo of the tone of the *Spectator* article. 'Then you are expected not only to regard these five as the most "significant" modern writers but to have read all the "significant" literature that has grown up about them.'[22] Graves went on to appeal to the perennially attractive idea that, concealed somewhere by all this other stuff, the pure, clear tradition of real writing persisted: 'Despite the spate of commercial jazz, there has always been a small, clear stream of living jazz music; despite the great outpouring of abstract or semi-abstract art (the more abstract, the more imitative and academic) there has likewise been a thin trickle of admirable painting and sculpture. The same is true of poetry.'[23]

The members of the Movement would by and large have endorsed every word of that, but the thin trickle and the small, clear stream were to prove elusive. All the Movement's impatience could not quite find an outlet in the Englishness of Piper or Betjeman - that entire effort was too effete. The reality of their situation was that, though they were appealing to ideals of clarity and ordinariness in literature, they were using those ideals to express the severance, the dissolution of the very tradition from which they claimed that clarity sprang. For them the countryside and the landscape had lost their drama of meaning. Jim Dixon yearned for the city: 'While he explained, he pronounced the names to himself: Bayswater, Knightsbridge, Notting

Hill Gate, Pimlico, Belgrave Square, Wapping, Chelsea. Not, not Chelsea.'[24] Meanwhile Larkin's pastoralism is regimented and urban:

> I thought of London spread out in the sun,
> Its postal districts packed like squares of wheat.[25]

The Movement was trying to see significance in limitation as though such a vision were somehow timeless and joined to the art of the past. But the images of Britain – churches in rural landscapes, or libraries in provincial towns – were no more real than the broken concrete of a shattered European culture; they were merely chosen to appear so, paraded before our eyes to be endowed with the appropriate topical significance. Angus Wilson had spotted the danger: 'I have also suggested that mere topography has been made to bear a ludicrously heavy load of significance, that inevitably this confinement of the most serious moral values to terms of English geography has increased the natural insularity of our culture.'[26]

There was, however, an optimistic version of all this. Intellectual common sense and increasing affluence could be seen as invigorating rather than depressing; perhaps the nation really was bound for a new, bourgeois paradise. Edward Shils, writing in 1955, summarized:

'Continental holidays, the connoisseurship of wine and food, the knowledge of wild flowers and birds, acquaintance with the writings of Jane Austen, a knowing indulgence for the virtues of the English past, an appreciation of "more leisurely epochs", doing one's job dutifully and reliably, the cultivation of personal relations – these are the elements in the ethos of the newly emerging British intellectual class.'[27]

Very Nice

The Movement continued to contemplate the landscape. Confined and airless, it was none the less Britain: sombre, grey and undoubtedly significant. It was, however, undramatic. Indeed, a dramatic past had been rejected in favour of something devoid of histrionics, of the violent assertion.

Yet the immediate past of the theatre was, above all else, well mannered and quite containable within the confines of Little England. Theatre was integral to the official view of culture, it was a local treasure less violently disturbed by the twentieth century than poetry, painting or the novel. John Gielgud and Laurence Olivier seemed part of a tradition stretching back to Shakespeare's Globe Theatre, while Terence Rattigan wrote plays that were 'well made' and dealt with the narrow crises of English life. In addition, the later plays of T. S. Eliot adopted the modes of history or drawing room dramas, recognizable and identifiable with the stage mannerisms of the day.

A reaction to the immediate past in the theatre, therefore, demanded a more expansive rhetoric than that of the Movement. John Osborne's *Look Back in Anger* was first produced at the Royal Court Theatre in 1956. Its impact was lasting. It came to represent the supreme expression of 1950s dissent, a social critique that appeared to provide an artistic embodiment of the implications of Britain's withdrawal from the Empire and the Suez Crisis of the same year.

The truth is, however, that *Look Back in Anger* represents primarily the discovery of a theatrical mode. The popular historical view that lumps it together with the Movement and working-class realism as part of some topical reaction makes little sense: the play is too vehement and egotistical for the Movement, while neither its context nor its form bears anything more than a superficial relation to 1950s realism. Osborne had actually alighted upon a way of filling the stage with words while resorting neither to the moral or historical clutter of Rattigan nor the symbolic portentousness of, for example, John

Whiting. It was an innovation on the plane of theatrical language. Take, for example, part of a speech from Whiting's *Marching Song* (1952): 'A man is an army, a striking offensive force. Each one of us has the line of communication stretching out. With some of us it is weak and with some of us it is strong according to our courage. The line goes back to other people, places and ideas.'[1]

And, from *Look Back in Anger*:

'I suppose people of our generation aren't able to die for good causes any longer. We had all that done for us, in the thirties and forties, when we were still kids. There aren't any good brave causes left. If the big bang does come, and we all get killed off it won't be in aid of the old-fashioned grand design. It'll just be for the Brave New-nothing-very-much-thank-you. About as pointless and inglorious as stepping in front of a bus. No, there's nothing left for it, me boy, but to let yourself be butchered by the women.'[2]

The sheer, rhetorical noise of Jimmy Porter's speech derives from the fact that he so triumphantly has nothing to say. Osborne was fully aware of the paradox; in his opening stage directions he commented on Jimmy's personality: 'to be as vehement as he is is to be almost non-committal'. [3] Where Whiting's abstraction was intended to fill the stage with implication, with resonances derived from a moral direction, Osborne fills the same space with a rhetoric, a celebration of anguish for its own sake. The point was that the conventional forms of drama, even more than those of fiction, could not function in a fragmented society. Osborne elaborated eleven years later:

'We live in a society of such lurching flexibility that it is no longer possible to construct a dramatic method based on a shared social and ethical system. The inexorable process of fragmentation is inimical to all public assumptions to indeed ultimately to anything shared at all. A theatre audience is no longer linked by anything but the climate of dissociation in which it tries to live its baffled lives. A dramatist can no longer expect to draw many common references, be they social, sexual or emotional. He can't generalize in the old way. He must be specific to himself and his own particular, concrete experience.'[4]

The passion with which Osborne identifies social fragmentation as the destroyer of old artistic categories is quite different from Larkin's mournful contemplation of a church, and he is not one to conclude with the same 'if only' argument. His fragmentation is real, conclusive and not amenable to the compromise of a weakened, if still viable, unity. His conclusion, however, is vague and indecisive: 'his own particular, concrete experience' neither defines his own plays nor provides a meaningful programme for anybody else's. In fact, Osborne's innovations with the play were rhetorical rather than formal; as a play, it is supremely and conventionally theatrical, a fact he subsequently pointed out himself. What Osborne had been looking for and had discovered was a way of being theatrical with new words: Jimmy Porter's grand speeches, his vehemence, presuppose wider audience than the other characters on the stage. *Look Back in Anger* was simply Osborne's way of making recognizable drama out of nothing – a kind of circus of disbelief. This fact probably prompted Stephen Spender's remark in *Encounter* that the play 'with its beautiful rhetoric, is the nearest thing to poetic drama we have had on the stage for many years'.[5]

What was important about Osborne's drama was neither the anger nor the disaffection, but the centrality of dramatic language. Throughout his plays he uses energetic, passionate language as vivid colouring. Confrontations, dilemmas and struggles are excuses for outpourings of the words which hold Osborne in thrall. The words themselves are stable; society may be in question, but *they* are not – characters speak with belief and commitment. With Harold Pinter's *The Birthday Party* (1958) the real implications of a theatre of the word become more apparent.

Pinter was born in 1930 to a Jewish family from the East End of London. He had acted and written poetry before his first play, *The Room*, was produced in 1957; but with *The Birthday Party* he found his form and his audience.

Pinter's awareness of language is profoundly different from Osborne's. Where Osborne needed to formulate a new occasion for grand eloquence, Pinter discovered a means of filling the stage with words that were subject to a much more intense, inward pressure. His is not the language of polemic, rather that of uncertainty. His words appear to admit of the infinite possibilities of alternative meanings even as they are spoken. This has extended to his own statement about his dramatic method. He invariably declines to commit himself to any clear intention and presents his own imaginative processes as almost entirely devoid of analysis beyond the need to make a play out of his initial image.

Pinter could not 'aim' words in the way that Osborne did. He is too aware of the problems of any statement: fragmentation has infected the language. Osborne was drunk on words as weapons in the world, Pinter can see nothing but the words, a strange, alien interconnected fabric which only ever *seems* to possess meaning. In this Pinter is a rarity among British literary artists of the 1950s in that his preoccupations link him directly to modernism. His doubts about the possibility of statement are those of a modernist sensibility. Equally, however, he is suffering from the trauma of late modernism – or possibly post-modernism as it was called – which produces a kind of shrinkage of the art away from the large, cultural designs of the past. The modernist awareness of form in Pinter, as in Samuel Beckett, produces a reduction of the possibilities of expression.

In *The Birthday Party* the stage directions are pared down to a minimum, characters are not specified beyond 'Petey, a man in his sixties' and the location is 'the living-room of a house in a seaside town'. The point is that the words alone will bear the burden of the play. Where Osborne could not bring himself to throw out the dramatist's conventional notation of control, Pinter finds he has no choice. The dialogue itself announces a wholly new form of theatrical language:

MEG: Are they nice?
PETEY: Very nice.
MEG: I thought they'd be nice. You got your paper?
PETEY: Yes.[6]

We are at a far greater fictional remove than with Osborne. There is an unsettling combination of strangeness and familiarity. Of course, the obsessive rhythms of banality owe much to Samuel Beckett – the English version of his play *Waiting for Godot* had appeared in 1955. But Pinter adopts a more 'realistic' mode; his speech patterns are closely derived from life. In the words of Andrew Kennedy, they are 'saturated with idioms'.[7] Pinter, however, twists these patterns into increasingly mannered contortions that fight against the underlying naturalism of the seaside setting, the fried bread and the corn flakes about which Meg is so concerned. The effect is so characteristic of Pinter – dislocation and recognition.

The struggle within the language and the uncertainty of meaning are then realized in the actual drama of the play. The seeming gentility of the speech forms is used to conceal the mounting threat from Goldberg and McCann, the two visitors to the house who stage the birthday party itself. The trappings of realism are undercut by the ambiguity of the language. There are lies everywhere, realism itself seems to be a wilful turning away from the sinister truth. When the intruders take away the wrecked, incoherent Stanley only Petey raises a mild objection. 'Stan don't let them tell you what to do!' he cries, the horror being the triumph of the language as coercive, destructive of the self. But he is swamped by Meg's compulsive acceptance of the reality of the drama, the birthday party:

MEG: I was the belle of the ball.
PETEY: Were you?
MEG: Oh, it's true. I was. (Pause) I know I was.[8]

The word 'know' takes on a poignant, helpless resonance. The play mixes the language of realism and stylized absurdity. Throughout, except for Petey's cry, the words dominate the action, both concealing and creating it. In Pinter's 1960 play *The Caretaker*, the effect of hypnotic overpowering language becomes more direct:

MICK: No strings attached, open and above board, untarnished record; twenty per cent interest, fifty per cent deposit; down payments, back payments, family allowances, bonus schemes, remission of terms for good behaviour, six months lease, yearly examination of the relevant archives, tea laid on, disposal of shares, benefit extension, compensation on cessation, comprehensive indemnity against Riot, Civil Commotion, Labour Disturbance, Storm, Tempest, Thunderbolt . . .[9]

Forms of language are being fabricated into self-generating nets from which the victim cannot escape. Mick's speech uses the new language of bureaucracy which, even in its normal context, is a kind of trap, an impersonal means of summarizing and systematizing a life. Removed from that context, the words take on echoing, empty, threatening resonances to form a chilly membrane of sound. It is as though 'Church Going' had stuck at the mention of the bicycle clips – one maddening detail inspires a vacant litany from which there is no escape.

The overall gloom of Pinter, the evident pessimism of his tone, has perhaps proved his most fecund legacy. Later playwrights, lacking his verbal and intellectual control, have adopted the portentousness and the empty haunted quality for directly political ends. They have attempted to link the emptiness to a precise flaw in the organization of society.

Pinter's mannerism and his heightening and deforming of naturalistic speech patterns represent his most important innovation. At one level this was a way of pulling the rug from under realism by demonstrating that realism itself was a form of concealment, of evasion of the real pattern of influence, coercion, memory and imagination. In this sense Pinter represents the appearance of a kind of expressionism in drama. Just as Bacon used the conventions of the room, the portrait, even of the crucifixion, as the starting point for his repertoire of distortions, so Pinter used the conventions of the language of a dramatic 'reality' for his. In his work the shabby, gloomy iconography of the 1950s takes on the status of a myth of futility and of alienation within the net of words.

Instantly Elated

In 1956 the Tate Gallery mounted an exhibition drably entitled *Modern Art in the United States*. A variety of developments were covered, but the most important, the most shocking, was to be found in the final gallery. There the British were exposed for the first time to yet another huge, uncontainable foreign development that, like existentialism, seemed to have grown unnoticed to a dangerous and threatening size: abstract expressionism. The final gallery contained works by Kline, Gorky, de Kooning, Motherwell, Pollock and Rothko. Their canvases were big, uncompromisingly abstract and suffused with a passion and confidence that mocked smaller British aspirations. 'I was instantly elated by the size, energy, originality, economy and inventive daring of many of the paintings,' Patrick Heron wrote of the exhibition. 'Their creative emptiness represented a radical discovery, I felt, as did their flatness, or rather their spatial shallowness . . .'[1]

The paintings had a rawness which appeared to be expressive of a culture that had advanced beyond ours, while retaining and suddenly reviving its closeness to a more primitive past. They were both infinitely more sophisticated and yet simpler than the British art of the day. Christopher Isherwood, in his novel *The World in the Evening*, published in 1954, saw this potent contradiction in some undefined frontier in a Philadelphia landscape:

'These woods seemed wilder and more tangled than the woods of England, and they reminded you that this country was only so recently snug and suburban; that this used to be an outpost of the world, a front-line of fanatically humourless, drably heroic men and women, entrenched behind their Bibles and prejudices, their dark stuffy clothes and their stone farmhouse walls, grimly confronting the pagan wilderness.'[2]

The USA was powerful and energetic yet only just civilized. Her sophistication and wealth were a recently applied veneer; beneath lay the wilderness.

The straightforward meaning of the exhibition in terms of the politics and geography of art was that Paris had been usurped by New York. Abstract expressionism represented an international transfer of power across the Atlantic. Modernism in painting was no longer simply the tradition of Picasso and Matisse. Now it was in the hands of Pollock and Rothko. And it *was* modern. The New Yorkers had evolved an entire critical posture – codified in Clement Greenberg's collection of essays published in 1961 under the title *Art and Culture* – quite unlike anything that had gone before and seemingly disconnected, liberated, from the complexities of the European past. The keys to this aesthetic were those identified by Heron as creative emptiness and shallowness, though his words have a somewhat deliberately sensational air about them. More precisely, abstract expressionism redefined the role of the painter and the act of painting.

Jackson Pollock, the great precursor of all the developments of the movement, had, some years before, begun to treat the painted canvas as an event in itself. His particular marks on the canvas referred to no external occasion. His paintings were not windows on the world, or expressive organizations of colour and form: they were neither more nor less than canvases with marks on them. These marks were simply the physical notations of the artist's interaction with the canvas, an interaction sometimes described as 'existentialist' because of the extent to which each event was entirely self-created without the demands of representation.

It was a method that offered to sweep away the problems of the past and its impact was unavoidably moral. These painters were telling the truth: there was nothing there but paint and canvas. The ideal Platonic forms of Nicholson's abstractions or the lush interiors and calm odalisques of Matisse and his followers became part of the old system of deception. The American painters were intent upon the true modernist enterprise: the investigation and exposure of form itself. They seemed pure, upright, innocent. In the anguished personalities of Pollock and Rothko were discovered new models of the heroic, romantic artist.

For British art this came at a crucial moment. Bacon and Freud had brought a new energy to figuration and to heightened, expressive realism. Their 'struggle to remake reality on canvas'[3] suggested extreme and often highly successful new ways of endowing the image with a direct, visceral power. And, like the abstract expressionists, they provided a heroic mode for the artist, far removed from the studio- and community-based blandness of the recent past. The new British expressionists derived their imagery from the deracinated types who wandered the Soho flats and clubs they inhabited. Their commitment was to reality, distorted perhaps, intensified certainly, but reality none the less. 'My object in painting pictures', Lucian Freud wrote in 1954, 'is to try and move the senses by giving an intensification of reality . . . Painters who deny themselves the representation of life and limit their language to purely abstract forms are depriving themselves of the possibility of providing more than an aesthetic emotion.'[4]

The expressionists inspired a generation of '1950s realists', such as Leon Kossoff and John Bratby, who derived from their example a new faith in the idea of figuration. The visual arts and literature are seldom precisely parallel, but the ideology of realism with its hard, no-nonsense empiricism was for this period common to both. The visual arts, however, were as usual more prone to the theoretical justification and, for many, this was provided through the decade by the socialist underpinning of neo-realism as defined by the Marxist critic John Berger writing in the *New Statesman*.

Against this, abstraction took on the role of the standard-bearer of the modern as opposed to the merely real. In *Nine Abstract Artists*, an influential book published in 1954, Lawrence Alloway represented abstraction as a specific reaction against the apparent softness of much of British art, a style he found claustrophobic:

'Both the loyal men and the dreamy boys developed an imagery of landscape which implied a kind of dark, meditative patriotism. The sceptered isle became an armoured womb . . . On the whole British non-figurative art stands apart from the prevailing British style which continues to be a form of nature romanticism. Even the post-war generation of sculptors is predominantly romantic with its emphasis on sensation and metamorphosis.'[5]

Abstraction, in contrast, was at the leading edge of human experience:

'The abstract painter submits himself entirely to the unknown. He believes that today the true language of colour and form is obscured and rendered ineffective by being put to the service of representation. [And Alloway quotes the painter Roger Hilton as saying:] In the last resort a painter is a seeker after truth. Abstract art is the result of an attempt to make pictures more real, an attempt to come nearer to the essence of painting; the truth which makes of it an art rather than a craft.'[6]

Alloway does not attempt to construct the critical scaffolding which Greenberg was later to erect against the edifice of abstraction, but he does share the abstract expressionists' active view of the artist. For Alloway, the painter is obliged not to sit passively before a scene and record it upon the canvas, he is to be a 'seeker after truth', he is to pursue the 'essence of painting' – above all, he is to be an artist. There are important undercurrents beneath his words. In one sense it is clear that, like Bacon and Freud, he had found something excessively small, modest and unambitious to react against. Alloway specifically characterizes this as romanticism, the pastoralism of Piper and Betjeman and the whole generation of 1940s romantics. In contrast, he offers a hard, visionary modernism which goes some way to reviving the modernist mood of the 1920s, specifically in architecture. Indeed Alloway played an important part in the architectural developments dealt with in the next section, 'Functionally, Englishly', but, unlike Bacon and the expressionists, Alloway's rejection of timidity provokes a Platonic striving towards purity and abstraction.

Alloway's role provided a critical continuity between the ambitions of 1930s modernism and post-war abstraction as it emerged from the artists' colony at St Ives in Cornwall. Naum Gabo, Barbara Hepworth and Ben Nicholson had all moved there, making it a centre for both constructivism and abstraction and, for some, the very image of the bland, dissociated modernism from which they were trying to escape. Frances Spalding characterized the St Ives School:

'What united these artists was a commitment to the town and the surrounding landscape and an astringent pursuit of abstraction. They formed an avant-garde, locally inspired but becoming internationally renowned, producing an art which placed more emphasis on the artist's feeling and encounter with his or her materials than on external referents, and which therefore offers a parallel with American Abstract Expressionism.'7

Nevertheless, St Ives was also a rural landscape with all the usual traditional overtones. Indeed, Peter Lanyon, one of the leading figures of the group, always insisted that he was a landscape painter; certainly there was more full-blooded abstraction among other artists in the group. But St Ives is most clearly associated with painting that borders on abstraction rather than entirely embracing it. A degree of figuration seemed to be needed to provide the hint of content.

Mainstream British abstraction's sense of attempting to build on an existing tradition, a recognizable place for the activity of painting in the world, is perhaps what prepared the ground for the impact of the Americans. The very rigour and completeness of the abstract expressionists' severance from previous conceptions of the role of the canvas subverted British worries about the 'content' of a work of art. It is significant, for example, that the St Ives artist Alan Davie was deeply influenced by Jackson Pollock's early use of mythological imagery. Davie stayed with that 'content' rather than follow the influence through to the heroic American conclusion in which all such imagery was eradicated in favour of a new mythology of the existential truth of the canvas itself.

The St Ives artist who succeeded in evolving a style and viewpoint resilient enough to withstand the Americans' impact was Roger Hilton. Born in 1911, Hilton had studied at the Slade and in Paris; he had been a prisoner of war. He taught after the war and, as a painter, turned to abstraction in about 1950; he was associated with St Ives from 1956. His character was too emotional to accept either the constructivist tendencies at St Ives or the critical basis of abstract expressionism. He spoke of the abstract artist as 'a man swinging out into the void; his only props his colours, his shapes and their space-creating powers'.8 Indeed, Hilton discovered his own method in the idea of space, albeit radically redefined:

'I have moved away from the sort of so-called non-figurative painting where lines and colours are flying about in an illusory space; from pictures which still had depth or from pictures which had space *in* them; from spatial pictures in short to space-creating pictures. The effect is to be felt outside rather than inside the picture: the picture is not primarily an image, but a space-creating mechanism.'[9]

It is difficult to be sure what precisely is meant by such language; clearly no artist is obliged to be able to explain himself. But the general point of fleeing from illusionistic space combined with the vivid, potent drama of Hilton's paintings themselves indicate that he had in many respects achieved his own version of abstract expressionism well before the Americans arrived. In Hilton's work the paint meets the canvas with a rare certainty.

The struggle of British abstraction against the American invasion was most directly embodied, however, in Patrick Heron's reaction. Heron was born in 1920, studied at the Slade in the 1930s and was a conscientious objector during the war. In 1944-5 he worked at St Ives as an assistant at the Bernard Leach pottery and subsequently as an art critic. Until the Tate exhibition, his paintings displayed a figurative style derived primarily from Matisse. He moved to abstraction after 1956, though always maintaining that 'there is no such thing as non-figuration. The best abstraction breathes reality; it is redolent of forms in space, of sunlight and air.'[10]

This position of modified abstraction led him away from his initial overwhelmed awe when confronted by the Americans. He came to dislike their extremity and to regard the 'creative emptiness' he once so admired as sterility. The dominance of the intellect in abstract expressionism had to be balanced by more traditional artistic components such as taste and intuition. He thus retained the St Ives instinct to preserve a line from abstraction back to reality, to hold on to the idea of content as external to the mere event on the canvas.

Meanwhile, in a political correlative of this artistic threat, the USA was making her power clear on a grander scale. On 26 July 1956 President Nasser of Egypt announced the nationalization of the Suez Canal. The move provoked a protest note from Britain: it was 'a serious threat to the freedom of navigation on a waterway of vital national importance'. After a summer of diplomacy the Israeli Army invaded Egyptian territory in the Sinai Desert in October. Britain and

France issued an ultimatum that the canal zone must be cleared. An air offensive followed and then paratroop and commando landings.

This was no Korea. Britain and France were condemned by the United Nations. In Parliament the Labour opposition was in uproar. The Americans were angry and detected foul play: 'No matter what the justifications were,' wrote the *Spectator*, 'it is generally believed, outside Britain and France, that Britain and France were bent on aggression. Worse than that, the rumour has spread widely that this was a put-up job, designed to circumvent the United Nations and to secure Britain again in full possession of the Canal.'[11]

The miscalculation was gigantic. Britain had defied the worldwide mechanisms of peaceful negotiation and embarked on a military action made unwinnable by her diplomatic folly. Worse, she appeared to have been involved in some shady double-dealing with Israel. Worst of all, she had alienated the Americans. 'On Britain's and America's ability to trust each other,' mused *The Times*, 'even in disagreement, the peace of the world depends.'[12]

Britain was forced to back down by American economic pressure. The episode came to symbolize the end of Imperial pretension. It was a moment of enforced realization that we were not the power we once had been, able to subdue ill-governed, lesser nations. Suez seemed to endorse both Jimmy Porter's despair and the sense of shrinkage in the works of the Movement. Finally, of course, it drove home the political and economic power of the USA, the hard 'reality' behind her sudden imaginative ascendancy.

Functionally, Englishly

For Alloway and the abstract expressionists, abstraction revitalized the concept of the modern. It offered a method of progress that neither delved back into the past nor accepted the continued dominance of Parisian modernism. It affirmed the modernist desire for continuous innovation as well as its heroic, radical style. It also implicitly rejected any dilution of the initial modernist fervour.

In Britain, of course, such dilutions were commonplace: softened, 'anglicized' modernism had occurred most visibly and, for a new generation, most irritatingly in architecture. The reconstructive mood of the late 1940s had produced an enthusiasm for the modern in building, but in the heavily modified form of the Festival of Britain style. For architects, this was a huge climb-down from the visionary convictions of the first modernists: Le Corbusier had written of radiant cities, Mies van der Rohe had signalled a new era with buildings of an inhuman purity and precision while Walter Gropius had aimed to aestheticize industry. These had been grand projects in which the programme seemed to have dictated, with absolute directness, the style. As if in some great rationalist redefinition of the world, every corner and wall appeared to be supported by a social, political and aesthetic theory.

At the Festival of Britain, though, the rationalism seemed to have been replaced by a fussy prettiness, the architectural correlative of the landscape romanticism Alloway loathed in British painting. Robert Maxwell described the feeling produced in young architects by this shrinkage of ambition:

'To the younger generation of architects – those whose contributions to British architecture would not be realized until the sixties – the style of the festival of Britain seemed at best sentimental, at worst effete. It lacked seriousness. It was bland, and it was parochial. Modern architecture had been sold short in Britain.'[1]

Alloway was again to play an important role in the reaction. He was a dominant member of a group that from 1950 took to meeting at the Institute of Contemporary Arts in London. Other members included the architects Peter and Alison Smithson, the artists Richard Hamilton and Eduardo Paolozzi and the critic Reyner Banham. From 1952 they were to call themselves the Independent Group. Between them they evolved, in architecture, the style of brutalism and, in painting and sculpture, the style of pop.

Banham called brutalism 'a violent and sustained polemic on style'[2] and the Smithsons placed themselves in 'the direct line development of the Modern Movement'.[3] Its name had a variety of associations: it evoked Le Corbusier's description of architecture as the transformation of '*des matières brutes*', a definition from very early in his career, but it also suggested his later 'brutal' handling of concrete, leaving it coarse, pock-marked and still bearing the moulded pattern of the wooden shuttering. The idea of brutality was also taken to be an affirmation of the role of the architect. The Festival layout had succumbed to the English picturesque tradition; architectural empiricism which dealt with the site as found and arrived at specific solutions in response to specific local conditions. To the brutalists this reduced the hard, visionary, rationalizing role of the architect and implicitly denied his godlike function as a transformer of the fabric of the world.

In fact, in Banham's account,[3] the brutalists were not the hardliners; during the 1950s softened modernism was being pursued with a Stalinist rigour. It became known as both the New Humanism and the New Empiricism and was heavily influenced by developments in Swedish domestic architecture. At the London County Council, the style was imposed by rules that all buildings of less than four storeys were domestic and therefore must have a pitched roof – higher buildings were to have their roof lines decided by group discussion.

Such pettiness and diminution of the role of the artist were intolerable. The Smithsons had responded with their school at Hunstanton, designed in the 1940s but not completed until 1954 owing to a steel shortage. It is now known as the first clear statement of brutalist intentions, though its predominant glass and steel imagery is far removed from the concrete of most of the movement's later manifestations. Hunstanton was superficially Miesian in style, but Mies would

have found intolerable the ruthless exposure of its working and structure. Its lines were clear, hard and geometrical, refusing to take on
the amiable curves and variations of the Festival style. Against its
largely horizontal composition, it contrasted a single cool vertical in
the form of a black steel water-tower.

The concrete forms of mainstream brutalism came from Le Corbusier, almost entirely from the impact of his Marseilles building, L'Unité
d'Habitation, which was constructed between 1946 and 1952. This is
a nine-storey block, 185 feet high, 420 feet long and 60 feet wide,
intended to house 1,600 people. It is raised on concrete legs or *pilotis*
and is surrounded by twelve acres of parkland. There is a shopping
street on the fifth floor and an extraordinary playground on the roof
intended for children but in reality resembling more a sculpture court,
a virtuoso display of Le Corbusier's infinite capacity to create resonant
and potent forms.

The building is frequently seen as the realization of Le Corbusier's
early dreams of a radiant city in which flats would be raised into the
air, freeing the ground for open space and separating traffic from
people. But that much had long been incorporated into the existing
orthodoxy of modern architectural thought and was to be incorporated
over the post-war years into many British cities. What was significantly
new about L'Unité was its texture and its relationship to the immediate
surroundings. Le Corbusier used raw concrete, incised and moulded
by the marks of wooden shuttering. The building was not radiant in
the manner suggested by his earlier, purist manner; it was thickly
sculpted, encrusted with the expression of its own manufacture. Its
slab-like form stood in its landscape, monumental and massive, a
decisive and unignorable intervention.

Sigfrid Giedion, the hard-line modernists' most revered historian,
wrote of L'Unité as a social gesture: 'In this building it depends on
the individual inhabitant whether he prefers to remain a lost number
in a huge building or will participate in collective activities that can
rouse him out of the melancholic isolation which is the common form
of existence in every large city.'[4]

L'Unité provided an image of something so decisively and
uncompromisingly new that it was imitated up and down the country
by architects and local authorities still in thrall to hard-modernist

reconstructive ideals. It provided the ideal response to the loathed, unarchitectural 'Swedishness' which, in the wake of the Festival, had become the New Town vernacular. At Roehampton in south London the two styles met head on: the Alton East Estate, built between 1952 and 1955, with its balconied towers and terraced houses embodied all the reconstructionist aspirations towards a gentle urban landscape of light, air and modest building ambitions; Alton West, in contrast, built between 1955 and 1959, incorporates Unité-style blocks, rationally organized as a rebuke to the picturesque East and as an assertion of uncompromised newness.

From the late 1950s until about 1964 brutalism became the dominant modern architectural style. Its hard concrete forms, relieved only by deeply articulated glass and steel elements, took over from the mild-mannered eclecticism of New Town 'Swedishness'. Its reign as a definable style was thus short-lived, but the word itself expanded to cover a much wider architectural range. In the popular imagination every big glass, steel or concrete building of the period became associated with brutalism, as did the radical and insensitive rebuilding of many British towns in the name of 'development'. The hard, antipicturesque ambitions of brutalism caught the mood of a brief period when, as Lionel Esher put it, 'everything was getting bigger – roads, car parks, lorries, multiple stores, office buildings, airports, hospitals, telephone exchanges. By the mid-sixties the context and scale of the first generation New Towns looked suburban.'[5]

Brutalism was thus anti-Little England. Its responses were those of architects and critics who could see little of value in the English tradition and who, like so many before them, had turned to the continent to find their grand gestures and all-encompassing rationalizations. Yet the most persuasive, influential and coherent enemy of brutalism actually came from the continent; to him, however, Europe was not the place of the liberated and unfettered modern, but a landscape so recently seized by Nazism. Britain had not been occupied, her character remained intact and that character *meant* something.

This defender of the faith of nationality was the Leipzig-born academic Nikolaus Pevsner. From 1949 until 1955 he was Slade Professor of Fine Art and a Fellow of St John's College, Cambridge.

He was already well into his massive catalogue *The Buildings of England*, a work that defined the architectural inheritance and taste of a generation.

Pevsner's first specific defence of the English picturesque appeared in the *Architectural Review* in 1954, but his Reith Lectures, broadcast in October and November 1955 and published in book form as *The Englishness of English Art*, broadened and elaborated the case. In many ways this short, somewhat elliptical book covers much of what Pevsner was trying to do with the entire *Building of England* series. He was defending the quality of the English visual tradition against the despair of Roger Fry and his successors, and he was stressing the potential for the continuity of that tradition in the programme of post-war rebuilding.

He begins whimsically with discourses on the English preference for monosyllables – the word 'chop' compared with its Italian equivalent '*costoletta*' – and with a defence of the whole idea of attempting to isolate national characteristics in art. He is writing, he says, a geography rather than a history of art. Then, via Hogarth, Reynolds, Blake and Constable as well as his formidably encyclopedic knowledge of English architecture, he goes on to trace typically English preoccupations with linearity, verticality and compartmentalism and the peculiar national habit of architectural revivalism. 'It is no accident', he wrote, 'that this architectural historicism started in England; for in England there existed, as we have seen a disposition in favour of narrative, and the thatched old English cottages as against the Italianate villas tell a story by their very costumes. Their effect is evocative, not strictly aesthetic.'[6]

He goes on to link the idea of the picturesque, in contrast to the hard, formal, rationalist planning of the continent, to the idea of liberty, of freedom from tyranny. It is an important polemical point with peace just ten years old and it is the moment at which he introduces the real inspiration of the book and of its tone: 'We are in need of a policy of healthy, attractive, acceptable urban planning. There is an English national planning theory in existence which need only be recognized and developed.' This theory is the picturesque, the sensitivity to place and occasion: 'If one wants to plan for the City of London, one must be sensitive to the visual character of the city.

The same exactly would apply to Cambridge, or to a small town with much character such as Blandford, or with little character such as Slough.'[7] And finally: 'If English planners forget about the straight axes and the artificially symmetrical façades of the academy, and design functionally and Englishly, they will succeed.'[8]

Pevsner goes on to praise the Festival of Britain, Sir William Holford's 'brilliant' plans for the precincts of St Paul's, and Harlow and Stevenage New Towns.

The book presents a uniquely convincing and optimistic analysis in the middle of the increasingly fashionable 1950s conviction that British cultural history had nothing to offer – it was destined to go the way of the Empire, to be dissolved and dispersed in the face of larger, more cosmopolitan demands. Pevsner saw the modern, modified by the English, as an entirely viable and potentially successful combination. The book's political edge came from it being the testament of an immigrant who had found something wholesome and continuous in the English tradition. But this did not make it an academic version of an Ealing film, for Pevsner was as devotedly modern as anybody else. Much of his criticism elsewhere is as rigidly determinist as the most hard-line French rationalist. Rather he was offering a way of being modern *and* English. Instead of escaping into a dream of the landscape and the double-hammerbeam church roofs of East Anglia, Pevsner suggested we should connect our modern planning to that dream – the Angel Choir of Lincoln Cathedral could be seen as an entirely legitimate precursor of Harlow New Town.

Pevsner's benign, gentle and persuasive vision became lost in the savage architectural polemics that ensued. As early as 1959 the first sign emerged that the whole idea of planning – brutalist, modern or even Pevsnerian – had become suspect. Ian Nairn writing in *Encounter*, observed: 'On a larger scale the city should be a place for everyone – tarts as well as good girls, spivs as well as model husbands and honest men. The city is the place of infinite choice, and what more important choice than that between good and evil or convention and freedom?'[9]

The organic vision of the city as layer upon layer of history, contingent and unpredictable, was beginning to supplant the whole ideology of the plan. Against this, even Pevsner's gentle picturesque appeared crude and insensitive to the demands of 'real' citizens. As evidence in the case for the defenders of the entirely contingent city, the concept of a visionary, planned environment ran into the dreadful reality of the works of scores of talentless 'Corb and Mies' devotees as well as the ludicrous ambitions of government and local authorities. Ruthless development was replaced by blind, paralysing conservation. The very word 'modern' when applied to architecture was to become pejorative and even the word 'plan' was, miraculously quickly, to become set in historical amber along with ration books and the Dome of Discovery.

Information Information

The other style to emerge from the Independent Group at the ICA was pop. It represented an improbably extreme contrast to brutalism in architecture. Where brutalism aimed for an orthodoxy, pop wanted a chaotic plurality; where brutalism aspired to a raw purity, pop aspired to its own corruption by every passing fragment of experience; by 1964 brutalism had lived and died, pop is still with us. Yet brutalism and pop shared something of the same inspiration, most obviously a commitment to the celebration of urban experience. The Smithsons wanted their buildings to announce that people were at work, to be realizations of the activity of the city. Pop derived its vocabulary from the fleeting-sense impressions of the city and from the resonance of its ephemera.

In 1953 the Independent Group staged an exhibition at the ICA called *Parallel of Life and Art*. It was later associated with brutalism, but its contents suggested other developments as well. A carefully contrived anti-art air pervaded the whole exercise. Magazine and newspaper images were incorporated, a gesture which, in the climate of the time seemed to be a reaction against both abstraction and traditional figuration, and to imply that these fragments, not the contrived forms of abstract painting, were the 'real' world. They were what Eduardo Paolozzi called 'the sublime of everyday life'.[1]

The exhibition included a statement of purpose:

'Technical inventions such as the photographic enlarger, aerial photography and the high speed flash have given us new tools with which to expand our field of vision beyond the limits imposed on previous generations. Their products feed our newspapers, our periodicals and our files, being continually before our eyes; thus we have become familiar with material and aspects of material hitherto inaccessible. Today the painter, for example, may find beneath the microscope a visual world that excites his senses far more than does the ordinary world of streets, trees and faces. But his work will necessarily seem obscure to the observer who does not take into account the impact on him of these new visual discoveries.'[2]

Uncertain and clumsy as the explanation may have been, this was the start of a vital and entirely distinctive post-war artistic approach, one foreshadowed by dada, surrealism and the works of Marcel Duchamp in the 1920s. Those artists had used assemblies of the random objects of experience, but had done so within a very specific 'art' context. Duchamp's urinal, for example, which he signed with a pseudonym and exhibited in a gallery, was not a piece that could be said to be 'about' urinals: it was, rather, about the environment in which Duchamp chose to place it. Equally, the random associations of surrealism were intended to provoke a sense of discontinuity prior to the revelation of 'something else', be it the pervasive nature of bourgeois reality or a transcendental otherness. The focus was thus not on the object but on what it might embody. But pop represents a more obviously technical development; it shifts the emphasis away from the art and towards the objects available for the artist's attention. Crudely, it preferred urban to rural imagery but, more important, it chose to assemble, rather than to transform, this imagery. Where Sutherland would have evolved metamorphosed natural forms, Richard Hamilton, the most celebrated artist of the first wave of pop, would simply juxtapose magazine images.

The ICA statement began the process by pointing out that technology had provided many more things to see. Contemplating the landscape was not entirely discarded; rather it was pointed out that you could equally well, these days, contemplate from the air or through a microscope. Technology had also made the creation and dissemination of a quite staggering variety of images into a commonplace, everyday experience.

Yet not until 1956, with the *This is Tomorrow* exhibition at the Whitechapel Gallery, was the rather vague polemic of the earlier exhibition refined to produce the clear style and radical posture of pop. The poster and catalogue illustration for the exhibition was Richard Hamilton's collage *Just what is it that makes today's homes so different, so appealing?*

Hamilton, born in 1922, had emerged from a combination of the advertising industry, evening classes in art and the Royal Academy Schools as well as an important and subsequently influential period as an engineering draughtsman. He went back to the Royal Academy after the war only to be expelled, and then to study at the Slade where he met Nigel Henderson, another member of the Independent Group. His collage shows a domestic interior: a woman is cleaning the stairs with a vacuum cleaner; another reclines almost naked on a sofa, an image apparently derived from cheap pornography. In the foreground a muscle-man poses with a huge lollipop bearing the word 'Pop'. There is a tape recorder on the floor, an immense tin of ham on the coffee table, and the cover from a romantic comic has been blown up to form a picture on the wall. Outside, a cinema is showing Al Jolson in *The Jazz Singer*. The ceiling of the room is formed by a photograph of the earth taken from a research rocket, and an aerial photograph of a crowded beach forms the rug.

Hamilton's raw materials were not new. Other Independent Group members such as Paolozzi, John McHale and Nigel Henderson had been collecting and assembling commercial imagery from comics and magazines for some years. But *Just what is it* suddenly focused the whole obsession and became an icon for the entire movement. The collage formed a traditional illusory space – an interior. It suggested, however wildly, a narrative of a real domestic existence. The black arrow containing the words 'ordinary cleaners reach only this far' pointing at the vacuum cleaner hose gives the whole picture the demonstrative, message-delivering style of an advertising poster. It is a picture both replete with content in the sense of a mass of decipherable and recognizable imagery and yet utterly devoid of content in that the imagery is taken out of context and placed within a frame at a wry, ironic distance. It is, nevertheless, celebratory; for, above all, pop aspired to a kind of innocence that attempted to rediscover a direct, transmissible delight in the variety of the world. Yet the innocence both attracted and alarmed the critic Adrian Stokes:

'I remember the flood of happiness I felt when it was represented that pop art showed affection, warm contact, with the urban environment. I mean an affection inspiring the terms of art, recording deep rather than contingent, impressions. But my own conclusion was that we remain homeless in our culture. Art, as valiant as ever, cannot claim it for our home yet seeks to reconcile us with this environment in terms of any astounding if unresolved affiliation that can be made.'[3]

Despite the difficulty, complexity and tentative quality of much of his writing, Stokes had always been capable of grasping the central preoccupations of his time. Before the war his art history, with its distinction between the carving and modelling traditions, had provided an important but largely unacknowledged critical framework for the sculpture of Hepworth and Moore as well as for the whole of 1930s modernism. His response to pop is important because it demonstrates both the recognition of its importance and the desire to draw it into the humane fold of the previous artistic orthodoxy. It becomes, in his analysis, an attempt via 'astounding if unresolved' connections to return us to a culture from which we have been severed.

Stokes's detection of the deracination of pop imagery was clear-sighted but his somewhat conventional attempt to cast a humane net of traditional artistic values over the shocks of that imagery was at odds with pop's own desire to harden and update the role of the artist. Hamilton, for example, listed the preoccupations which had determined the contents of his collage: 'Man, Woman, Humanity, History, Food, Newspapers, Cinema, TV, Telephone, Comics (picture information), Words (textual information), Tape recording (aural information), Cars, Domestic appliances, Space. The image should, therefore, be thought of as tabular as well as pictorial.'[4]

This is a true pop tone of voice. It is tough, lacking in the humane anguish of the previous generation or, indeed, in any metaphysical pretensions. The list says simply what is in the picture and ends with the statement that the picture itself is a list. It is devoid of any 'painterly' interest. Hamilton's technique was collage combined with some intervention by retouching, but solely to reinforce the sense that we were being given only received rather than created images. Finally and crucially we were being given language. The emphasis was on the elements of the picture as units of information. Its surface was dotted with words, even its title serving to insert a further intervening layer of ironic distance.

The significance of this lay in its reversal of the usual preoccupations of twentieth-century painting. Dada and surrealism before the war had failed to take root in Britain other than as elements of modernism or, as in the case of Moore, as stylistic alternatives rather than unarguable programmes. Painterly, mainstream modernism in the shadow of Picasso and Matisse had been the orthodoxy. This tradition tended to downgrade the importance of the subject matter of the painting. A tendency of immense and complex cultural significance lay at the heart of the modernist revolution. Art, in the service of the prevailing discipline of Christianity, would formerly assume that its images were of intrinsic, transcendental significance. Images from the Bible or of the saints carried with them a received system of meanings, however much they might be elaborated or varied by individual artists. The loss of such a system meant either that new meanings had to be found or that interest would shift from the thing represented to the means of representation. In surrealism the first approach led to the glorification of a mythology of the unconscious with its own alternative system of meanings. In mainstream modernism the second approach led to the emphasis on form and on the nature of the painted surface. This reduced the significance of the particular content of any painting. So in cubism we have guitars, tables, newspapers and so on, all of which have only fleeting importance in themselves. A painting was not a decoration for a church or a palace but a painting, no more and no less. Subject matter had been rendered deliberately contingent as a pretext for formal effects. This could not be more vividly demonstrated than by Henry Moore's delight on discovering the reclining figure and the way in which it could relieve him of the whole category of problems relating to content.

Bacon's expressionism and his realist contemporaries had, to some extent, disrupted this orthodoxy by their isolation of an evidently significant subject within the frame of the painting. This threw out the idea of a landscape or interior which merely 'happened' to be framed by the picture in favour of a determination to focus emotional and nervous energy within the picture. Bacon's celebrated series of screaming popes in which he used and distorted Velázquez's portrait of Pope Innocent X reflected the need to restore the subject to the centre of the artistic experience. But there was an atavistic element to the enterprise. In attempting to escape the anaemia and blandness they detected in late modernism, the artists felt they had somehow to pre-date it, to reassert the 'old-fashioned' values of paint itself.

Pop, however, was an attempt to move forward; rather than express-ive extremity, it adopted a dead-pan or ironic pose. It did not wish to assault, as Bacon did, the nervous system, rather it aimed to provoke the suave pleasures of the intellect and the senses and to unite us with the city and its technology. Its fragmentary imagery was placed before us as significant information, which the new urban self could interpret as it pleased.

If Hamilton was the synthesizer of this idea, Eduardo Paolozzi was its cataloguer. Born in 1924, he had studied at Edinburgh and the Slade and lived in Paris for two years until 1949. He was at the first meeting of the Independent Group, at which he delivered a lecture with no words. It consisted solely of projected images of comics, advertisements and horror films. In the 1950s he produced brilliant and chilling bronzes in which fragments of machinery and circuitry were cast into distantly human or animal figures. In his notes for a lecture delivered at the ICA in 1958, he partly explained the process:

'Here is a list of objects which are used in my work, that is to say, pressed into a slab of clay in different formations. This forms an exact impression (in the negative of course) and from this a store of design sheets can be built up. They range from extremely mechanical shapes to resembling pieces of bark.

METAMORPHOSIS OF RUBBISH
Dismembered lock
Toy frog
Rubber dragon
Toy camera
Assorted wheels and electrical parts
Clock parts
Broken cog
Bent fork
etc. etc.'[5]

The objects are both insignificant – they just happen to be around –

and significant in that they are chosen for our contemplation. The idea of the list itself was a pop obsession. It was dead-pan, it suggested the artist's role as an unselective accumulator of the facts of experience. Even when Hamilton wanted to attribute some values to the pop project, he resorted to a list. In a letter to the Smithsons in January 1957 he wrote:

'Pop art is:
Popular (designed for a mass audience)
Transient (short-term solution)
Expendable (easily forgotten)
Low cost
Mass produced
Young (aimed at youth)
Witty
Sexy
Gimmicky
Glamorous
Big business.

This is just the beginning. Perhaps the first part of our task is the analysis of Pop Art and the production of a table. I find I am not yet sure about the "sincerity" of Pop Art. It is not a characteristic of all but it is of some – at least a pseudo-sincerity is. Maybe we have to subdivide Pop Art its various categories and decide into which category each of the subdivisions of our projects fit. What do you think?'[6]

Talk of projects and categories indicates the progressive, impersonal style Hamilton and his contemporaries adopted. Embracing technology both as imagery and in the making of their art – most notably the use of silk-screen printing – seemed to provide a new impetus, a bustling sense of things to do. There was also the awareness of a new audience, incorporated in the very name of the movement, who would respond to the idea of an art based on the familiar ephemera of urban life. The success of this idea became clear enough in the popular cultural manifestations of the 1960s, for at the heart of pop was a denial of the old distinctions between high and low art. Its glorification of 'B' movies and magazine iconography was a deliberate sneer at the former hierarchies of significance. The oil, bronze and stone images of fine art were revealed as comically powerless when confronted by the visual feast provided by technology and mass communications.

The inevitable question of pop's 'seriousness' in this context would become irrelevant since the old categories of seriousness were revealed as vacuous. In this sense pop's inspiration had something in common with the other forms of 1950s dissent. But its most public role was to act as a bridge between that dissent and the efflorescence of mass culture in the 1960s. 'Serious' pop music and the 'alternative' society were born of a similar conviction that old cultural distinctions were worthless and had to be replaced by a new acceptance of the totality of modern experience. The imagery of Hamilton and Paolozzi was embraced by a far wider audience than Bacon's or Sutherland's precisely because it found an accessible means of affirming that the old, oppressive culture was in its death throes.

In its place was an endless plurality for pop was about inclusion, the incorporation of a vast new range of material into the repertoire of art. In the images from comics and horror movies the artists saw intense emotion distanced by stylization. In using them, they suggested that art was no longer about such sensations. Instead there was to be a harder, more classical distance which, in its turn, promised a more perfect integration with technology and the city. In the last analysis this mythology of integration and inclusion resulted in the full artistic flowering of pop in the USA in the work of Andy Warhol. The USA, as Peter Conrad has said, was the one country that could still create myths after the industrial revolution,[7] so perhaps she was the one country in which pop could take on the mythic status of its ambitions.

Pop's journey was, therefore, circular. In 1959 *Encounter* said: 'The most important new concept in American art is that "everything" can be art and that art can be "everything" '.[8] This would have struck Hamilton, Paolozzi and their colleagues with a degree of irony, considering the ten years they had spent working out the implications of precisely that insight. But, in any case, the USA had always lurked behind the pop imagination. American domestic design and car styling seemed to imply an organic, coherent place for machinery in contrast to the British insistence on fitting it into traditional forms – the polished wooden dashboard of a car, for example. Where we still displayed an inclination to lay our driving instruments symmetrically, the Americans produced sculpted forms expressive of the newness of the technology itself. Out of such trivia pop imagined a fantasy USA of urban celebration in which machinery would provide an impersonal sensuality and in which the self would no longer be torn by the existential crises of a jaded Europe.

Pop aspired, above all, to the cleanliness of this fantastic continent as a corrective to the grubby, muddy qualities of Europe. It wanted the unsullied spaces realized most perfectly in American architecture.

'The steel framework [wrote Peter Conrad] freed building from the need to grow by accumulating weight, which confirmed architecture's enslavement to gravity. Steel buildings cast off this pile-like ponderousness and could be light and graceful as well as hubristically tall. Buildings used to be wet, grubby and primeval. Up to the present the mud hut has been clearly traceable in modern building. Cement, mortar, the dried brick are all mud at one remove. Technology dries building out, makes it cleanly mechanical not soilingly organic.'[9]

Pop was the art of the dry.

Nagging Humanism

Pop longed for an integration, a wholeness, that would overcome the alienation of man in a world of machines. Its lists celebrated inclusiveness and an assault on previous hierarchies of acceptable imagery. In years to come this celebration disintegrated into the long, youthful carnival of the 1960s; it took on mystical overtones. What began as 'anything can be art' became 'anything goes' or 'if it feels good, do it', injunctions that were in turn justified by a religion of self-liberation.

It was a religion anticipated by the curious figure of Aldous Huxley with his experimental uses of the drugs mescaline and LSD, later to become the magical elixirs of youth. This relic of pre-war literary society had abandoned his role of pessimistic social prophet – most popularly exemplified by his novel *Brave New World*, published in 1932 – and left for the USA, there to engage with the task of uniting technology and his own unruly mysticism.

'As a private individual, the scientist inhabits the many-faceted world in which the rest of the human race does its living and dying [he wrote in *Literature and Science*, an essay published in 1963]. But as a professional chemist, say, a professional physicist or physiologist, he is the inhabitant of a radically different universe – not the universe of given appearances but the world of inferred fine structures, not the experienced world of unique events and diverse qualities, but the world of quantified regularities. Knowledge is power and, by a seeming paradox, it is through their knowledge of what happens in this unexperienced world of abstractions and inferences that scientists and technologists have acquired their enormous and growing power to control, direct and modify the world of manifold appearances in which human beings are privileged and condemned to live.'[1]

More succinctly he added: 'The new facts about nightingales are a challenge from which it would be pusillanimous to shrink.'[2]

In Huxley's novel *Island*, published in 1962, Will Farnaby, a journalist, discovers the island of Pala with its unique social and political system. The emphasis there is on knowing yourself. One of its inhabitants explains:

'You're not going to believe it,' said Dr Robert. 'The real thing isn't a proposition; it's a state of being. We don't teach our children creeds or get them worked up over emotionally charged symbols. When it's time for them to learn the deepest truths of religion, we set them to climb a precipice and then give them four hundred milligrams of revelation. Two first-hand experiences of reality, from which any reasonably intelligent boy or girl can derive a very good idea of what's what.'[3]

Huxley observed his own death, in California in 1963, from the vantage point of a large dose of LSD. It was a conclusion that perhaps vindicated Angus Wilson's view, expressed in 1955, that Huxley had 'never valued his life in adult terms'.[4] But, in Huxley's move from pre-war literary stardom to West Coast desert mysticism, determined to derive impersonal romance from the glamour of technology, could be traced one narrative of transformed values from the mess of the past to a pure, shimmering future. His emphasis on the different world seen by the scientist and on the distinction between a man like any other and the observer of the 'inferred fine structures' distantly echoes the earliest manifestos of pop. Yet there is none of pop's suave irony about his mysticism; science may supplant the poetry of nightingales, but only to replace it with something equally mysterious and evocative.

Among most of the pre-war generation, however, both science and the USA represented powerful and distinct threats. Both seemed apocalyptic and depersonalizing. Bertrand Russell, the great liberal defender of the scientific imagination, may have advocated a humanist acceptance of technology, but he could not tolerate the USA, the supreme exemplar of the integrated machine. Where once he had detected a certain exciting radicalism, now he saw only barbarism and terror. With the Cuban missile crisis in 1962 the final technological nightmare came closer than ever to realization. It stimulated Russell's loathing of the USA to a comic climax. He sent two telegrams to the respective leaders.

To Kennedy he cabled: 'Your action desperate. Threat to human survival. No conceivable justification. Civilized man condemns it. We will not have mass murder. Ultimatum means war. I do not speak for power but plead for civilized man. End this madness.' To Khrushchev: 'May I humbly appeal for your further help in lowering the temperature despite the worsening situation. Your continued forbearance is our great hope. With my high regards and sincere thanks.'[5]

Russell clearly did not share the dream of an integrated USA. But he continued to indulge the myth of science. In 1959 he issued this carefully hedged, *ex cathedra* statement: 'Science is at no moment quite right, but it is seldom quite wrong, and has, as a rule, a better chance of being right than the theories of the unscientific. It is, therefore, rational to accept it hypothetically.'[6]

Without the hedging this was, in fact, the popular orthodoxy. But the hedging, the element of doubt, was what could always protect the humanist from the worst implications of his faith. In Val Guest's 1955 film *The Quatermass Experiment* – derived from a television series – the dedicated scientist is responsible for unleashing a monster on the world, a fungus which takes over people's bodies and thrives on their blood. Quatermass, the scientist, then helps destroy it by an electric charge passed through scaffolding on the façade of Westminster Abbey, a poignant image. But, having completed the task, he then dashes back to his lab to start again, ignoring the doubts of lesser mortals. The Faustian myth had resurfaced, as hubristic as an American skyscraper. The implication of Quatermass's determination was that the cause of science, conceived as the continuous advancement of the frontier of knowledge into the territory of ignorance, had an objective value far beyond any risks involved. The effort was wholly impersonal and quite inevitable.

This sense of an overwhelming imperative is an important one. In Osborne and Pinter the eerie littleness of lives and the complete mismatch between people's preoccupations and the sort of world that seemed to surround them produced dramas of negation. The ritual of the personal seemed irrelevant or absurd, patently falling short of either the scale or the complexity of the forces beyond the stage. Science was such a force, as were nuclear weapons, the two superpowers and, in Pinter, a fragmented language. All produced, in an earlier generation of literati, a kind of vertigo.

'Mankind is confronted by vaster dangers, more bewildering problems then ever before,' wrote John Lehmann, a poet and publisher who had been part of the old literary world of the Woolfs and the Sitwells. 'The assumption behind the confident machine civilizations of the West are being questioned in the light of the obvious, the appalling failure of that civilization to fulfil its promises and justify the untold human sacrifice and effort that has gone into its century and a half of industrial expansion and competition.'[7]

The tone is that of the disillusioned progressive. There had been a belief that industry and technology would make the world better; in reality it seemed only to have made it bigger. It had become a threatening place to live, full of huge, looming shadows, all intent upon eliminating the individual. It was the message, delivered with a somewhat lighter touch, in Nigel Dennis's 1955 novel *Cards of Identity*. In a style of curious theatrical pastiche, Dennis describes the activities of a club that specializes in adopting and providing new identities for others. The operation is performed secretly and without the victim's permission. The point is obvious enough: the human personality, the bedrock of humanist ethics, had become transient and without an anchorage in the real world. Dennis's dandyish approach to this subject produces an odd, hybrid tone, derived in part from Lewis Carroll, which was to anticipate many later developments:

'Thus, as the days moved on, with the judge receding ever further into the previous weeks, one had the eerie feeling not that time was standing still – that would have been intolerable – but that it was growing younger in proportion as it became older, and that the judge, far from proceeding to a verdict, was struggling to a prediction . . . What made this habit even prettier was the fact that his language was likewise a struggle to go backwards: he set the speech of his boyhood in the context of archaic dignity, as if this were the only way he could express his shock and disappointment at being alive at all today.'[8]

The tone of satire and smart playfulness was to appear again in Joe Orton and Tom Stoppard. But, elsewhere in the novel, there is a more direct, less formalized air of anxiety:

'Exactly. And it's that spirit that's been destroyed. One comes home with the keys and finds all the locks have been changed. All the initials have gone from inside the bowler hats. All the value's gone out of the currency. There's no meaning in the church bells, no punch left in the hyphens or surnames. I don't like it at all. If I don't get an identity soon I shall start looking as helpless and vacant as everyone else.'[9]

This anxiety about some kind of impending dissolution – in a spiritual desert, a nuclear explosion or a bureaucratic nightmare - became the common currency of the age. Auden summarized it in a review of Hannah Arendt's *The Human Condition* (1959):

'Nobody, I fancy feels "happy" about the age in which we live or the future which even the living may know before they die. At all times in history men have felt anxious about their own fate or the fate of their class or community, but there has seldom been a time, I believe, when the present and the future of the whole human endeavour on this earth have seemed questionable to so many people.'[10]

That something was wrong seemed to be agreed by almost everybody. Why it was so and what conclusions to draw from this sense of desolation varied. In 1960 the art critic John Berger derived his political morality from the sensation: 'If a talented artist cannot see or think beyond the decadence of the culture to which he belongs, if the situation is as extreme as ours, his talent will only reveal negatively but unusually vividly the nature and extent of the decadence. His talent will reveal, in other words, how it itself has been wasted.'[11]

Kingsley Amis, apparently taking over Cyril Connolly's role of national expresser of cultural despair, took a similar view from a different angle: 'That the past ten years have been the worst, falsest, most cynical, most apathetic, most commercialized, most Americanized, richest in cultural decline of any in Britain's history is the theme pounded out by a double mixed orchestrally-accompanied choir of lone voices.'[12] And Herbert Read: 'The arts fight a losing battle in our technological civilization and I see no hope for them.'[13]

The terminal quality of so much thinking about the human condition began to produce a reaction. Perhaps philosophy could construct an escape from the predicament. Dorothea Krook in *Three*

Traditions of Moral Thought, a book which closely paralleled the thinking of Iris Murdoch, outlined a literary and non-scientific response to the bland cul-de-sac apparently represented by analytical philosophy. She first defined the problem, revealingly from a religious rather than humanist point of view:

'The prophetic aspect, however, will not be lost on the religious mind. For such a mind will long since have come to see the contemporary world as a world in travail, perishing from the lack of a saving faith, and all the destroying evils of the time as symptoms of the universal suffering and signs of the need for a universal redemption. Nothing will be too little or too great to find a place in its encompassing vision of a world hovering on the edge of the abyss. A book-of-the-month called *The Outsider*, testifying to the extinction of human feeling in representative modern men: a film called *The Prisoner*, bearing witness to the systematic bestiality which in so many places has become the norm of the relation of man to man; the plays of Tennessee Williams, recording the convulsive nausea of a man of crude but strong sensibility at the mean, shabby falsities – the incorrigible phoneyness – of the values dominating his culture; such phenomena, to the religious mind will not be less significant as symptoms of a world ripe for destruction than the helplessness of the historic churches to give either doctrinal or pastoral guidance to the masses of their faithless faithful; the fear and imbecility governing the conduct of international affairs; the shallow scepticism dominating the academies of the western world; the corruption of independent feeling and judgement by the techniques of modern propaganda; the ever-growing scale and magnitude of the commercial debasement of values in the popular forms of entertainment. And these will not less potently induce a sense of the helplessness and desolation of modern man than will the growing stock-piles of nuclear weapons, by which the rulers of the world may within the life-span of this generation effect the physical annihilation of all life on this planet.'[14]

The Prisoner was a 1955 British film set in a totalitarian state in which a cardinal is brainwashed, and *The Outsider* was Colin Wilson's description of the alienation suffered by men of genius. Published in

1956, it was immensely fashionable thanks to its popularization of existentialism in its most romantic-heroic mode.

Krook's summary of despondency of the age described a more specific, less aesthetic vacuum than that perceived by the Movement or the new dramatists. It involved the sense of a moral failure from which stemmed all the apparently uncontrollable evils of the world. Russell's urbanity on the subject of science or the celebrations of pop could only fuel this anxiety. It was the crisis of humanism: its progressive, secular values had replaced religion, but only to create a world of terrifying inhumanity. Amid all the activity, all the changes, the thread of some key plot had been lost.

Of course, there is a family resemblance between all this and the grand moans of the previous generation. Connolly's lost prevailing myth, the organic culture of Leavis or Eliot's loss of a national destiny had all sprung from similar perceptions. There were new elements, however: the now unignorable collapse of Britain as a world power; the USA's flicking aside of our military pretensions over Suez; the successful establishment of a welfare state and, through the 1950s, a marked increase in affluence, neither of which seemed to have been accompanied by any revived sense of reconstructive direction – the 'certain lassitude' identified by Iris Murdoch. Materialism appeared to be delivering the goods, but their dissemination seemed to encourage either apocalyptic despair or, in the case of Malcolm Muggeridge, a certain squeamishness:

'The New Towns rise, as do the television aerials, dreaming spires; the streams flow, pellucid, through the comprehensive schools; the BBC lifts up our hearts in the morning, and bids us good night in the evening. We wait for Godot, we shall have strip-tease wherever we go. Give us this day our Daily Express, each week our Dimbleby. God is mathematics, crieth our preacher. In the name of Algebra, the Son, Trigonometry, the Father, and Thermodynamics, the Holy Ghost, Amen.'[15]

Through it all there was the nagging, humanist suspicion that the affluent, urban civilization represented some kind of dangerous abandonment of values. Behind Muggeridge's bland and clumsy journalistic conceit is a nervy anxiety: another list – compiling them seemed to be a mania in the 1950s – intended to be containing and ironic but in reality the author is drowning. There is a frenzy about the choice of items and, over the science, he clearly has no control at all.

Muggeridge's problem was that he was trying to define the apparent malaise in purely social terms and, as a result, managed to sound merely like a fastidious dandy, picking his way through the rubble. Equally, much of the rest of the apocalyptic grumbling of the period can be dismissed as modishness, rather arid fodder for the odd article. But the important point was that such a posture was required at all. There seemed to be a need for a detached persona, dissociated from the material, a mandarin voice to dismiss the feeble excesses of the world. But the underlying tone in this voice is that of panic; different forms of life, different worlds seemed to have sprung up, uncontainable within the old, pre-war categories.

Typically Angus Wilson again defined this change most precisely. In 1963 he published *The Wild Garden*, which was based on lectures given in California in 1960. In the work he identified this growing sense of a discontinuity in the culture as an important element in his own literary procedures.

First, he established his own distance from the introversions of modernist fictions, most obviously from James Joyce: 'I have not capitulated to the temptation to gain a new hearing for my childhood loneliness in my novels.'[16] He goes on to say that, immediately after the war, he became aware that a 'mild social revolution' had taken place in England overnight, though the novelists had not yet noticed it – 'the very small-scale rentier and professional group to which my family belonged had no place in Labour's England.'[17] In this context he explains the heroes of his novels:

'The only quality that they have in common is the concealment from themselves of their ignorance of the shape of their own lives, a concealment which has to be subtle because it must deceive a habit of rigorous self-inquiry and a trained observation of the shapes of the lives of other people. They are practising the final hypocrises of the educated and the worldly.'[18]

Wilson had detected in the new world what amounted to a technical

problem for the novelist. The categories of meaning and culture that
had previously defined the writer's terms and his characters – their
cards of identity – had softly and silently vanished away. The Snark
had been a Boojum. Wilson's response was to turn that very fading
into the fabric of his fiction, into the artistic problem of portraying
ignorance among articulate and intelligent people.

Enchanted Precinct

Anthony Powell's was a radically different approach to the same problem: how to write fiction against a socially transformed background. Powell, born in 1905, had written five pre-war novels which had earned him a reputation as a comic satirist of London life. The war appeared to inspire an enormous leap in his ambitions. In 1951 *A Question of Upbringing* was published as the first volume in what became a twelve-novel cycle entitled *A Dance to the Music of Time*. The cycle was concluded in 1975 with *Hearing Secret Harmonies*.

Despite the novelty of the scale of Powell's post-war ambitions, he retained the context of his pre-war novels. For this remains the fiction of an upper-class *demi-monde*. Where other novelists of the 1950s felt the need to escape from the literary society of London into embittered, provincial reaction, Powell stood by his metropolitan cast. His postwar innovation was sheer length and, resulting from that, the implication that a legitimate fictional form could be found in the multiplicity of character and detail.

The oddity of the enterprise in the post-war climate has produced some inevitable critical pigeon-holing. The cycle could only be an epic and was, of course, 'a history of our times'. It is palpably neither. The narrowness of the focus, the fragility of the narrative interest and the extraordinary slowness of the pace all signal that Powell could have had neither epic nor history in mind. He did, however, evoke one classical precedent – the Poussin painting after which the sequence was named.

The critic Frank Kermode summarized the initial effect of Powell's cast of characters and the style with which he manipulates them: 'For a while one saw people in a new way; they behaved like acrobats in a slow-motion film. The absurdity of these people was suddenly enriched when one imaginatively slowed down their behaviour.'[1] Powell's characters execute their dance with, at times, painful slowness. They seem trapped in a medium heavier and more resistant than air.

The books are loaded with observation, with context, with digression and with analysis and yet it all springs from the mind of the first-person narrator, Nicholas Jenkins, who bears the narrative burden of the whole cycle.

Given this colossal restriction of point of view, Powell could have lightened his burden by cheating slightly with Jenkins. He could have artificially broadened his vision or given him a more definite and consistent role throughout the series. Either would have simplified enormously the technical problems of shifting his unwieldy cast about the stage. Instead, he allows Jenkins's mind simply to wander vaguely and verbosely where it may, as in this passage from *A Buyer's Market:*

'As I reached the outskirts of Shepherd Market, at that period scarcely touched by rebuilding, I regained once more some small sense of exultation, enjoyed whenever crossing the perimeter of that sinister little village, that I lived within this enchanted precinct, inconvenient at moments, as a locality: noisy and uncomfortable; stuffy, depressing and unsavoury; yet the ancient house still retained some vestige of the dignity of another age; while the inhabitants, many of them existing precariously on their bridge earnings, or hire of their bodies, were – as more than one novelist had, even in those days, already remarked – not without their own seedy glory.'[2]

In such fragments can be found the key to the whole enterprise. There is, first, the sense of modesty about feeling – 'some small sense of exultation' – or about poetic claims: 'not without their own seedy glory'. The observations have an apparent randomness: why, suddenly, do we have Jenkins's thoughts about his home? There is the conservatism – 'the dignity of another age' – as well as the consciousness that this is all set in the context of a certain lateness, a sense that produces a constant, weary rhythm: 'as more than one novelist had, even in those days, already remarked'. Finally, the prose itself is heavily punctuated, meandering, prone to lists and undemonstratively dandyish.

The most immediate effect of all this is to undermine any temptation to read the narrative as too directly historical. Powell's focus is narrow, a small section of wealthy, idle society is all he ever uses, so a historical reading would mean loading his characters with considerable symbolic and representative weight; in any case the prose works against this.

There is too much accumulation of detail and speculation around his characters for them to be read simply as embodying social or historic truths; they appear, instead, contingent and increasingly indecipherable. Critical incidents that arise appear enfolded on or to grow out of character in a way that would make it seem heavy-handed to extrapolate them further into the rationale of history. Powell, in a certain sense, has seen the possibility of such an interpretation first and hedged his bets. An indication of this knowingness is the way Jenkins himself, as an aspiring writer, is made actually to confront the whole problem:

'I began to brood on the complexity of writing a novel about English life, a subject difficult enough to handle with authenticity even of a crudely naturalistic sort, even more to convey the inner truth of the things observed. Those South Americans sitting opposite, coming from a Continent I had never visited, regarding which I possessed only the most superficial scraps of information, seemed in some respects easier to conceive in terms of a novel than most of the English people sitting round the room. Intricacies of social life made English habits unyielding to simplification, while understatement and irony – in which all classes of this island converse – upset the normal emphasis of reported speech.'[3]

One might well object that such a task has been performed before: what is new about Jenkins's problem? The South Americans are one clue; for the purposes of art a certain exotic distance, a degree of ignorance makes life easier: nearer to home there is too much to take in. Furthermore, Jenkins is not given to conclusions; he remains puzzled throughout. The motives for his selectivity and the meaning of his point of view will, therefore, remain perpetually shrouded in the same puzzlement. Nothing could be more characteristic of the books than Jenkins's repeated use of phrases like 'for some reason', indicating his baffled passivity, his eternal modesty about any possible significance.

At heart the problem is one of distance and authority. Powell is endeavouring to write, as it were, a 'real' novel, one that fits a certain conservative view of the role of fiction. The accumulated detail and observation are an almost grotesquely inflated form of the baggage of the novel medium itself; as a form it is bourgeois, acquisitive and materialistic. Within this landscape the characters move in the gelatinous air. From a distance, they bear a predictable burden of motives; but, in close-up, they remain irreducibly mysterious. There is no authority to give them sense, as the Catholicism does in Evelyn Waugh's ambitious chronicle *Brideshead Revisited*. And, in that absence, the whole idea of the novel as a record of events becomes fraught with difficulty.

In this context it is possible to return to Angus Wilson's *The Wild Garden:* 'Everyone says as a commonplace,' he wrote, 'that a novel is an extended metaphor, but too few, perhaps, insist that the metaphor is everything, the extension only the means of expression.'[4]

The very idea of length in a novel implies a kind of scientific determination to catalogue the nuances, associations and meanings of the central conceit. It is the form of the Enlightenment, deriving its conviction from the view that the world is susceptible to rational analysis. The metaphor is its hypothesis, the extension its experimental confirmation. With Powell, however, the process seems to be coming to a halt. The slowness and Jenkins's bafflement combine to suggest that this is a very late effort in the history of the novel. So much has been done before and yet failed or become irrelevant. All that endures is one more metaphor: the dance.

The sequence begins with the sight of workmen gathered around a brazier in the snow: 'For some reason,' muses Jenkins, 'the sight of snow descending on fire always makes me think of the ancient world.'[5] The thought turns the men into figures in a classical landscape: dancers representing the seasons, turned outward in a ring round the fire: 'The image of Time brought thoughts of mortality: of human beings, facing outward like the Seasons, moving hand in hand in intricate measure: stepping slowly, methodically, sometimes a trifle awkwardly, in evolutions that take recognisable shape: or breaking into seemingly meaningless gyrations.'[6]

The cycle ends with Jenkins staring at a bonfire when, 'for some reason', a long passage from Burton's *Anatomy of Melancholy* springs into his mind. Then, finally, the classical imagery returns with a noise from a nearby quarry becoming 'the distant pounding of centaur's hoofs dying away, as the last note of their conch trumpeted out over hyperborean seas'.And at last: 'Even the formal measure of the Seasons seemed suspended in the wintry silence.'[7]

In winter and in silence the metaphor, the book, is finally isolated as the one meaning, the one strand of consistent significance in all this. The characters in their dance have come to a halt, frozen in stiff postures like figures in some medieval fresco. This is not an image of Renaissance humanism; these are emblematic rather than completed, rounded humans. At this point Powell finally takes on the style of a mannerist author, a late flowering of a fictional style. His dance has become a mannered version of the idea of the novel itself. Just as Pinter's words detach themselves from their meaning to be used as threatening or cajoling noises, so Powell's metaphor is finally all that survives of his characters. The manner was all. The big difference is that Powell's final stasis carries with it the consolation of classical balance – the cool, completed composition of a Nicolas Poussin.

Far removed as this may seem from Kingsley Amis's beer-drinking Jim Dixon and 'the less deceived' Movement practitioners, an important connection can be made. This lies in the idea of the self in the novel: somehow this has been lost and these writers feel obliged to recover it. Dixon's internalized loathings are made into a viable self by their confirmation in the outer world. Jenkins discovers a final stasis, some kind of foundation of identity, in the contemplation of the strange abstraction of the dance of his contemporaries; he does not require the initial movement away from the class-based novels of the 1930s, only an extension of their inspiration. But the problem with both Amis and Powell is that they begin from a situation in which the self has been reduced, rendered almost inactive by the lateness of the hour. Only from that point can they begin their process of resuscitation.

Right Line

From one perspective Powell's achievement may appear a monument of artistic control. Never for a moment does he deviate from his progression to the classical stillness of his ending, in which we see the whole book before us: not as a dynamic narrative, but rather as a single image which is both lucid and mysterious. Yet, from another perspective, it can seem like an enfeebled, pallid exercise, a bloodless acceptance of defeat and a refusal to make the novel a working space in which the great moral and intellectual battles of the hour can be fought.

William Golding would probably take this latter view. Born in Cornwall in 1911 and educated at Marlborough Grammar School and Oxford, he worked in the theatre and as a teacher before joining the Royal Navy during the war. Afterwards he took to writing and teaching. He had published a collection of poems in 1935, but his first novel, *Lord of the Flies*, did not appear until 1954, to be followed in successive years by *The Inheritors* and *Pincher Martin*. Consciously or unconsciously, the books were aimed at restoring the entire moral programme of the fictional form. Their extraordinary vigour is neither that of realism nor of symbolism, but of a visionary moralist. Their traditionally solid qualities of narrative drive, descriptive power and factual precision stand in stark contrast to the calm musings of Powell; qualities that, presumably, account for the extraordinary success of *Lord of the Flies*, within a few years of its publication, as the representative modern novel for schools up and down the land. It gave teachers something to talk about – its complexities refer boldly outward to the world, not wiltingly inward toward the book.

With these three books Golding signalled his determination to use the novel as a means to an end: the fabrication of a myth, a significant narrative, with the material at hand – his own prose and the language as he finds it. The myth in question is the reverse of the Edwardian ideal of progress. Angus Wilson gave us deracinated progressives such as the architect Hubert Rose in *Hemlock and After:* 'a curiously lonely figure in his Edwardian tight trousers and brocade waistcoat, swaying in so ungainly a manner amidst the vast stretches of steel and glass'.[1] But Golding gives us the futile strivings of Pincher Martin, clinging to the rock where a shipwreck has left him and howling at the seagulls: 'I'm damned if I'll die!' Martin is materialistic man stripped of his society and its trappings. He is the bare, mythical creature at war with nature and the elements:

'He was struggling in every direction, he was the centre of the writhing and kicking knot of his own body. There was no up or down, no light and no air. He felt his mouth open of itself and the shrieked word burst out.

"Help!" '[2]

The deliberately and shockingly crude twist of the book's ending reveals, however, that this struggle will not be for survival on this earth. Martin had been dead all along. Golding is not concerned with nuances; Martin was being judged. I the end he would not release his grip on his worthless life and that was to be his final crime.

Lord of the Flies used the same central metaphor of shipwreck and isolation. In this case a group of boys is stranded upon a real island rather than just a rock. The device is used to expose the mythological systems which, by implication, lie not so very deep beneath the surface of the orderings and conventions of society. The boys establish their religion, their conflicts and their social order in unconscious mimicry of primitive, tribal systems. In *The Inheritors* we are actually shown those societies in formation as Neanderthal man is supplanted by his larger-brained successors. On the one hand Golding is overthrowing the romantic tradition of childhood innocence, on the other he is recreating a genuinely primordial innocence among his Neanderthals; his concerns are always very literally pursued.

This directness and simplicity are, however, frequently concealed by the intensity and conviction with which Golding throws himself and his readers into the parables he invents. Martin's rock, the boys' island and the prehistoric landscape are never allowed to become merely schematic or allegorical backdrops. They are realized with the conviction of an author who believes in the novel as fiction and in the importance of the self-sustaining qualities of that fiction. We must believe in the trials suffered by his characters if we are to be moved by their significance. This frequently produces a surface complexity in which the precision and quantity of the physical detailing seem to overwhelm the underlying moral direction. The effect becomes more pronounced in later works like *The Spire* (1964), in which this surface complexity is compounded by Golding's determination to plunge us as deeply as possible into the subjectivity of the central character, even at the expense of narrative clarity – yet, perversely, we are still outside him: 'He was laughing, chin up, and shaking his head. God the Father was exploding in his face with a glory of sunlight through painted glass, a glory that moved with his movements to consume and exalt Abraham and Isaac and then God again.'[3]

Interior and exterior are merged. Golding is writing in the third person, but his prose takes on Dean Jocelin's ecstasy. The words are rhapsodic, exalted and driven by the author's determination that we shall partake of his myth as a physical reality.

The complexity arises, then, from the lack of the kind of narrative distance usually associated with the employment of the third person. We must grope our way back to the essential myth through the experience itself. The fiction is intended to be overwhelmingly real and then to become, so to speak, even more real as we penetrate its mysteries. Reading it is intended to be as revelatory as the experience it describes.

In a brief piece of journalism entitled 'The Hot Gates', in a volume of the same title, Golding wrote of a visit to Greece and to the spot where Leonidas and his handful of Spartans held off the Persian invaders, a military triumph traditionally said to have paved the way for the Athenian Golden Age. The article is remarkably close to the novels in the clarity and certainty of his physical descriptions: 'I put out my hand to steady myself on a rock, and snatched it back again, for a lizard lay there in the only patch of sunlight. I edged away, kicked loose a stone, disturbed another with my shoulder so that a rivulet of dust went smoking down under the bushes.'[4] And it is like the novels in the directness and simplicity of its intentions:

'I knew that something real happened here. It is not just that the human spirit reacts directly and beyond all argument to a story of sacrifice and courage, as a wine glass must vibrate to the sound of a violin. It is also because, way back and at the hundredth remove, that company stood in the right line of history. A little of Leonidas lies in the fact that I can go where I like and write what I like. He contributed to set us free.'[5]

The insight is almost guide-bookish in its simplicity and, with its moral certainty – 'the right line of history' – and its humanist conclusiveness, it is far removed from the awestruck contemplation of the mysteries of the past in David Jones's story about the boy, the stile and the Battle of Naseby. Golding shows an unfashionable, unmodern faith in what is out there: in the existence of a self set against the background of history and the world; in the existence, above all, of a 'right line'. His achievement has been to find a convincing fictional form for that simplicity by allowing his language to become embedded in the actual experience of his myth.

In his novels the rocks, the sea, the world are illuminated by the significance of the underlying myth. A rock is made real by its presence within a purpose just as, in a Christian universe, every tree evokes the Cross, all blue evokes Mary and all white the Passion. For Golding's myth is intended to be what Frank Kermode has called one of 'total and satisfactory explanation',[6] As such Golding's intention is to cut across the doubts of recent artistic history and to appeal to an earlier literature, indeed society, in which we were at one with the world.

It was a project that aroused some distaste among the intellectuals who adhered to the prevailing analytical mode of the age. 'The truth is that Mr Golding', Goronwy Rees wrote in a review of his 1959 novel *Free Fall*, 'has set himself a problem in metaphysics, it is at the very least doubtful whether fiction is the best medium for solving its problems. Indeed there are moments when one wishes that Mr Golding could be converted to the view that philosophy is a therapeutic method for getting rid of such problems as these.'[7]

This is a confused but potentially important point. Rees is putting the logical positivist's view of all metaphysical matters: they are meaningless and philosophy exists to point this out. In this view Golding's whole project of constructing a metaphysical novel is a self-deceiving waste of time; but the point is that he is doing so as a reaction against the type of novel produced by the very tradition of which Rees seemed to be so enamoured. The existential or positivist self of much of modern fiction seemed to have become shrunken, barely existing at all. Instead Golding wants a self engaged upon a cosmic drama of salvation and damnation; but this drama is taken for granted, it is the driving force behind the novel. Golding is not arguing with the positivists, he is ignoring them. His novels are not about the struggle to create a metaphysic, its existence is taken for granted.

The effect is somehow medieval, though not in the frozen, hieratic sense of Powell. Where his characters attained the ideal stasis of a holy fresco, Golding's have an active, exemplary quality. His is an attempt to restore the stable relationship between the image and its meaning as it was before the long process of severance which took place through the Renaissance and the Enlightenment. But it is an instinctive response – that of a man determined to write novels without the attendant self-consciousness that activity usually seemed to require amid the analysis, existentialism and liberal anguish of the 1950s.

Tiny Spark

Golding thus addressed himself to his audience over the heads of those engaged with the intellectual problems of the age. He instinctively rejected disabling self-consciousness in favour of a willed, muscular recreation of the great dramas of human salvation. Iris Murdoch, who appeared on the literary scene at the same time, sensed the same difficulties with the reduced view of human character as realized in the contemporary novel. Her response, however, was a good deal more subtle. As a philosopher, the 'intellectual problems of the age' were her meat and drink, and in their unravelling and reinterpretation she found the inspiration for her fiction.

Murdoch was born in 1919, in Dublin, and educated at Badminton and Oxford. After working in the civil service she began to lecture in philosophy. She had, meanwhile, written a number of unpublished novels. Her first published book appeared in 1953. It was a long essay on Sartre which, remarkably clearly, defined her own artistic ambitions:

'The novelist proper is, in his way, a sort of phenomenologist. He has always implicitly understood, what the philosopher has grasped less clearly, that human reason is not a single unitary gadget the nature of which could be discovered once for all. The novelist has had his eye fixed on what we do, and not on what we ought to do or must be presumed to do. He has as a natural gift that blessed freedom from rationalism which the academic thinker achieves, if at all, by a precarious discipline.[1]

[...]

'Sartre's great inexact equations [the book concludes] inspire us to reflect. His passion to possess a big theoretical machine and to gear it on to the details of practical activity compares favourably with the indifference of those who are complacently content to let history get on without them. His inability to write a great novel is a tragic symptom of a situation which afflicts us all. We know that the real lesson to be taught is that the human person is precious and unique; but we seem unable to let it forth except in terms of ideology and abstraction.'[2]

Her first novel, *Under the Net*, appeared the following year. Thanks to its loose, eventful narrative and Bohemian ambience, it was promptly and roughly pigeon-holed by many critics alongside the various easily identified products of the Movement, anger and realism. Subsequent novels, appearing almost annually, revealed how astonishingly wide of the mark this critical judgement had been. The title of the first should have been the clue: it was a reference to Ludwig Wittgenstein's *Tractatus Logico-Philosophicus*, in which the net is used as an image of the form in which systems of thought attempt to cast reality. This was scarcely the stuff of Movement aesthetics. In the ideas of the enlightenment – Wittgenstein uses Isaac Newton as an example – the world is ultimately knowable so long as we have a sufficiently precise system with which to understand it, a grid upon which to plot its every element. The grid is the net and the implication of the title is that the enlightenment view is wrong, there is something under the net. It is there that the novelist discovers her 'blessed freedom'. It was the territory Murdoch has described and inhabited ever since in her fictional career.

The importance of her approach is that she confronts the whole problem of art via the problem of the self. She is content neither with the impersonal acceptance of contemporary imagery which had emerged in pop nor with a religious or mystical leap backwards into earlier systems of forms and meanings. Her position emerges most clearly in her 1970 essay *The Sovereignty of Good*, a central document in any intellectual history of the period, not simply because of its philosophical content but because of the way it attempted to restore the significance of art.

Murdoch begins by taking on her fellow philosopher Stuart Hampshire. Five years older than Murdoch, he succeeded A. J. Ayer as Grote Professor of Mind and Logic at London University and then moved to Princeton; from 1970 he was Warden of Wadham College, Oxford. He could be taken to embody a specific philosophical orthodoxy. Murdoch needed his philosophy to represent a particular view of man, but her intention was not solely philosophical: 'This "man" ... is familiar to us for another reason: he is the hero of almost every contemporary novel.'[3]

The man in question has one obligation: to move towards total knowledge of his situation. His morals must arise from a clear knowledge of himself and his possibilities. Reality can be variously interpreted by such men while thought or dream can exist only as shadows of actions or, perhaps, have no substance at all. The man exists in the movement of his overtly choosing will. This is existential man, susceptible and transparent to the analysis of behaviourist psychology and whose inner life can only feed off his outer. He was a product of a certain philosophical history. In the immediate past he was the offspring of Sartre and the existentialists. But, equally, he emerged from one view of Wittgenstein's legacy and, prior to that, from the revolution in enlightenment thought achieved by Kant.

'Wittgenstein has created a void into which neo-Kantianism, existentialism, utilitarianism have made haste to enter,'[4] Murdoch explained. The point was that he was a thinker who was easily interpreted for particular purposes. His philosophy divided into two parts: the early version depended upon the picture theory of language – words form pictures of the world; and the later abandons this in favour of the acceptance of a more open view. But in both cases language was formally absolute. It was our world; we cannot peer round it or beyond it because its limits are the limits of our world. From that point he stood back, adhering even in his later philosophy to the last line of the *Tractatus*: 'Whereof one cannot speak, thereof one must be silent.' Hence the void – was Wittgenstein saying there was nothing else, or simply that we could not talk of it?

He was taken to endorse the specifically modern view of the isolated will, always finally susceptible to analysis. We can, in the end, know a man completely as an interior constructed from the sum of his exteriors. He was accessible to science, an adequate net could be constructed:

'Stripped of the exiguous metaphysical background which Kant was prepared to allow him, this man is with us still, free, independent, lonely, powerful, rational, responsible, brave, the hero of so many

novels and books of moral philosophy. The *raison d'être* of this attractive but misleading creature is not far to see. He is the offspring of
the age of science, confidently rational and yet increasingly aware of
his alienation from the material universe which his discoveries reveal.'[5]

This man's crisis, the mainspring of the action in the novels in which
he appears, lies in the certainty of the scientific faith which created
him but also in its abject failure to reconnect him to the world.
However perfect his existential posture, finally it can do no more
than make him fully aware of this alienation. But for Murdoch this
demonstrates only the scale of philosophy's failure in providing a more
complex, integrated view of the self: 'What is at stake here is the
liberation of morality, and of philosophy as a study of human nature,
from the domination of science . . . Philosophy in the past has played
the game of science partly because it thought it was science.'[6]

Apart from her argument with Hampshire, this represented most
exactly Murdoch's response to the concluding line of Ayer's *Language,
Truth and Logic:* 'What we must recognise is that it is necessary for a
philosopher to become a scientist, in this sense, if he is to make any
material contribution towards the growth of knowledge.'

Murdoch now moves on to her affirmation:

'Words are the most subtle symbols which we possess and our human
fabric depends on them. The living and radical nature of our language
is something which we forget at our peril. It is totally misleading to
speak, for instance, of "two cultures", one literary-humane and the
other scientific, as if the two were of equal status. There is only one
culture, of which science, so interesting and so dangerous, is now an
important part. But the most essential and fundamental aspect of our
culture is the study of literature, since this is an education in how to
picture and understand human situations. We are men and we are
moral agents before we are scientists, and the place of science in
human life must be discussed in *words*. This is why it is and always
will be more important to know about Shakespeare than to know
about any scientist; and if there is a "Shakespeare of science" his
name is Aristotle.'[7]

In referring to 'two cultures' Murdoch is evoking the argument over

C. P. Snow's Rede Lecture of 1959 on *The Two Cultures and the Scientific Revolution*. Snow postulated a rift between the sciences and the humanities, and F. R. Leavis waxed indignant at the idea. In referring to it at all, Murdoch may be implicitly acknowledging that her own notion of the centrality of literature and that of Leavis could easily be confused as different ways of saying the same thing. The main difference is that hers lacks the dim, romantic vision of some ancient organic community as well as the disastrously partisan nature of some of Leavis's adherences: 'a small mind, brooding and vengeful,' Geoffrey Grigson had concluded, 'and a frequent barbarity of taste'.[8] Instead, she appeals more to her central insight that science itself is subordinate to language and the highest form of language is literature. In addition her defence of literature is from the point of view of practitioner rather than critic. Where Leavis seemed to be defending the rights of an academic industry, she is explaining her own artistic methods and inspiration.

The philosophical point is that, in defining their man, Hampshire, Ayer and the novelists are ignoring the evidence of the 'very tiny spark of insight' of art, a spark with 'as it were, a metaphysical position but not metaphysical form'. That spark signals that man, far from being the isolated will, takes his place against a background of concepts which have an existence beyond his own; among these concepts that of 'good' is sovereign.

In saying this, Murdoch is also rushing into the post-Wittgenstein-ian void; but she is evidently doing so to balance those who have rushed in to fill only the analytical side. Wittgenstein also left a hole which metaphysics could fill, if not through language then through art. As she says in *Sartre*: 'If we leave theory and look about us all that seems certain is that art may break any rule.'[9]

Murdoch is thus attempting to use the great twentieth-century philosophical 'given' – the centrality of language – against its primary exponents. They are guilty of what she called in an earlier *Encounter* essay 'dryness'. So far as she is concerned they use a facile reading of Wittgenstein to root out all the moister, human aspects as well as the metaphysical spark. They do so in the name of science, in the name of its hard primitivism which, in their analysis, is the only human activity left that can hold out any hope of the possibility of a movement towards truth. But such truth is a phenomenon of language like any other. Science is as completely entrapped in language as is anything else. To select its criteria as somehow nearer to the absolute is arbitrary, a choice determined by inclination and by temperament, rather than by the hard, analytical gaze.

In artistic terms it is this choice which produced post-Kantian man: the isolated, self-creating hero whose moral universe is born and dies with him. To Murdoch this is a wholly inadequate view of human personality, and its apparently unchallengeable place in literature is another illusion of language. Words – protean and mysterious, 'the most subtle symbols we possess' – indicate not the ultimately knowable nature of man but his position as the supremely unknowable. The Murdoch man is not merely complex, he is infinite as is language itself.

The importance of this essay is that it creates a convincing alternative to either religion, hard science or cosmic gloom. The loss of God, of a 'prevailing myth', of a final order need not lead us to the blank finality of valueless, causeless knowledge. It leads us instead to seek a different vision in which to encompass man; as the irreducible given as opposed to the last term in an analytical series. Rather than forcing us to remove all texture and meaning from experience, he opens up new possibilities. Values – above all, good – persist without God, meanwhile language, with its mythologies and connotations, exists as evidence of the metaphysical spark.

Finally it is art which provides the supreme distillation of this vision: 'Far from being a playful diversion of the human race, [it] is the place of its most fundamental insight, and the centre to which the most uncertain steps of metaphysics must constantly return.'[10]

To see art as a 'place' is a highly characteristic conceit, similar to her frequent references to the form of the novel as a 'space'. It indicates her imaginative need to open out the context in which she writes, to escape from the claustrophobic atmosphere of the type of fiction she had no wish to create.

Many have felt such an imaginative pressure before, but it is rare, especially in Britain, for a literary project to be expressed with such a comprehensive philosophical scaffolding. In the context of post-war culture it can be viewed only as a profoundly dissident posture. Its implication is that we do not, in fact, live in a late, desiccated culture, starved of the possibility of expression. Rather we are at the beginning of a new period in which art can claim a new centrality and in which a new vision of human personality can be forged.

Artistically this provided Murdoch with the foundations of her novels. They are not 'philosophical' in the sense of providing debates or embodying ideas and systems. These are present to an extent but are usually subordinated to the fictional process, and are better seen as infused with a point of view that has been philosophically arrived at. This view had opened out the implications of her fiction and provided her with the opportunity to produce a rhetoric which would have been unthinkable in tone and manner to many of her contemporaries:

'Events stream past us like these crowds and the face of each is seen only for a minute. What is urgent is not urgent forever but only ephemerally. All work and all love, the search for wealth and fame, the search for truth, life itself, are made up of moments which pass and become nothing. Yet, through this shaft of nothings we drive onward with that miraculous vitality that creates our precarious habitations in the past and the future. So we live; a spirit that broods and hovers over the continual death of time, the lost meaning, the unrecaptured moment, the unremembered face, until the final chop chop that ends all our moments and plunges that spirit back into the void from which it came.'[11]

Although this is from her earliest published novel, it is possible to see the dangers of Murdoch's new fictional open spaces. The sentence beginning 'What is urgent' would have been much better had she not added 'but only ephemerally' as its rhythmically weak tail. This tendency to allow the elaborations of feeling and meaning simply to pour into the books resulted in her immensely long later works, much of whose length seems frequently to lack adequate justification. The failing arises, however, from the celebration of an art form that she seems to feel she has rediscovered. Above all, her elaborations are justified in the name of character. In Murdoch's books character is revitalized as an element in the novelist's armoury. At their worst this makes them prone to endless speculations on motive and feeling but, at their best, they become highly dynamic and convincing realizations of her preoccupations.

Beyond her aim to renew the novel from the starting point of a more complex view of self lies the question of her actual fictional technique and its contribution to the art. In some senses her books can be seen as 'traditional' novels in that they consist of consecutive narratives designed to illuminate character and they provide fictional realizations of intellectual, political and moral ideas. Clearly this is the product of her own conviction of the importance of literature and its continuities. Many of the formal doubts of her contemporaries are, in any case, excluded by her own inclusive vision of character and the role of the author as impersonal and without the moral right to exercise power over or to reduce the stature of her characters.

Murdoch herself has written of the distinction between the big sprawling fictions of the past and the hard, crystalline modern product. The two clearly imply opposing views of the world: the former didactic, illustrative and inclusive, sprawling because the material and moral complexity of the world is taken to be the business of the novel, the latter is a distilled, contracted experience, its tautness suggesting a singularity of view and a focus on the importance of the way of seeing rather than what is seen. It is crystalline because it has grown itself around its own significant form, it does not reach out uncontrollably into the world.

Instinctively Murdoch dislikes the crystalline novel as its structure implies the very reduction of the self which she found so repellent. The controlling forces of her earlier novels thus tended to relax to allow the endless elaborations of the later books. But, perhaps most important of all, was the way this inclusiveness in her work seemed to permit several layers of reality to exist side by side. In her determination to exploit the 'space' of the novel, she permits her narratives to proceed through a variety of different modes: realistic, symbolic, discursive and so on. The effect is that we are never quite in the 'real' world, though, equally, we never quite cut ourselves off from its existence. The relationship between the abstract and the concrete is never stable, neither is our distance from the characters, who seem to come and go, sometimes with great clarity, sometimes indistinctly and at a distance. Take, for example, a passage from *The Good Apprentice*, published in 1985:

'It occurred to Edward for a moment suddenly to think, *perhaps Jesse does not exist at all?* Perhaps he's someone whom they invented or something they just believed in, like God? Or perhaps the word in their language isn't a proper name but means something quite different? He looked across the thick heavily scored work bench at Ilona who was wearing a leather apron and playing with the soldering iron. She smiled at him. The moment passed. He looked at her small brown hands, at the numerous tools in their neat rows, at the glittering barbaric baubles. He said, "I think you're marvellous, I can't think how you do it." He thought her bedroom must be just above this room. "Ilona there's such a strange place upon the hill, in that wood, a sort of long glade with a pillar in it." '[12]

An extraordinary number of elements of plot, psychology, theology, philosophy, descriptive detail and symbolism are touched upon in this brief extract. The inclusive style has been refined to a curious intensity, a passionate need to miss nothing of the significance of each moment. This loving attention to her characters occasionally stretches the prose to a breaking point where it slips into a gushing style, indistinguishable from the most cynical romantic fiction. But for the rest of the time it sustains a world that is instantly recognizable, a landscape of infinite significance created from the imaginative need to reject the shrunken image of modern man.

Whereof Thereof

Behind Murdoch's thought, and indeed behind a whole range of post-war British thought both philosophical and artistic, stood the awkward and enigmatic figure of Ludwig Wittgenstein, who died of cancer in his doctor's house in Cambridge in April 1951. Enigmatic to the end, the last words he spoke were: 'Tell them I've had a wonderful life.'

An Austrian, born in 1889, Wittgenstein was one of nine children of a prominent industrialist. Three of his four brothers committed suicide; the fourth lost an arm in the First World War and later made his name as a one-armed concert pianist. Wittgenstein came to England in 1908 to study engineering at Manchester, but became interested in the less practical field of the theoretical foundations of mathematics. This made him aware of the work of the great logician Gottlob Frege, whom he contacted. Frege advised Wittgenstein to study under Bertrand Russell at Cambridge. He did so, but the process was interrupted by the First World War, when he enlisted in the Austrian army. In that brief period at Cambridge, however, Wittgenstein had impressed and actually intimidated both Russell and G. E. Moore, the other outstanding figure in British philosophy, with the ferocity and brilliance of his arguments.

By 1919 Wittgenstein had completed a short book which was to be published in England in 1921 under the title *Tractatus Logico-Philosophicus*. With this he was convinced he had solved all the outstanding problems of philosophy, so he abandoned the subject to take up teaching in Austria. He subsequently became a gardener and, briefly, an architect before once more taking an interest in philosophy. He returned to Cambridge in 1929, submitting the *Tractatus* as his Ph.D. thesis. Moore, in his role as an examiner, commented: 'It is my personal opinion that Mr Wittgenstein's thesis is a work of genius; but, be that as it may, it is certainly well up to the standard required for the Cambridge degree of Doctor of Philosophy.'[1]

Apart from periods of absence, Wittgenstein worked and taught at

Cambridge for the remainder of his life. He did not publish another book in his lifetime, though on two occasions he had clearly been intending to. The reason he returned to philosophy was that he had become aware of what he considered to be errors in the *Tractatus*. Disentangling these errors occupied the remainder of his life. Indeed, he considered publishing the *Tractatus* as a preface to *Philosophical Investigations*, finally published posthumously in 1953, to demonstrate the extent of his change of heart.

The relationship between art and philosophy may sometimes be non-existent and they can never be simple. Art is the subject of the present work, philosophy only when important connections can be made. With Ayer and Murdoch those connections are obvious: their views of philosophy are closely linked to specific cultural conflicts, most clearly that between the positivist-scientific and metaphysical forms of imagination. Wittgenstein's role, however, is by no means as clear; in part this is because he produced two equally powerful but conflicting philosophies, in part due to the extraordinary and complex appeal of the man's personality and style of thought. In the future *Philosophical Investigations* may well come to be regarded as the central work published in this period in Britain. Certainly the significance of the vision that informs the book is awesome. 'That vision', wrote Roger Scruton, 'is a haunting and eloquent one, and to have seen its force is to have glimpsed, in Wittgenstein's philosophy of mind, a path out of the desert of empiricist and utilitarian thought.'[2]

I have touched upon Wittgenstein's thought in previous sections, but a more general summary is necessary. His primary perception was that problems of philosophy were problems of language. In the *Tractatus* he suggested that the only meaningful use of language was as a statement of fact. Mathematics and logic were no more than tautological systems which told us nothing new about the world, while metaphysical or ethical statements could have no meaning since they implicitly referred to a reality outside the world, i.e. outside language. They could therefore be neither true nor false, simply nonsensical. Behind this broad outline there were discussions of immense importance to philosophers, though they were frequently couched in language so oracular and condensed that they appeared to be designed to infuriate rather than enlighten. But the key theoretical basis of the book was the picture theory of language, which suggested that language contained within itself a system for making pictures of the empirical world. This element proved the book's undoing both for many of his followers and for Wittgenstein himself.

Shorn of its contentious picture theory, the book's influence was immense. Its apparent affirmation of natural science as the only possible form of knowledge, its assault on metaphysics and its fierce reduction of the role of philosophy to a process which would enable statements to be clarified all dazzled a generation of philosophers. The Vienna Circle of positivists was founded upon these principles and Ayer's *Language, Truth and Logic* sprang almost entirely from an attempt to codify these beliefs:

'I was entirely persuaded [Ayer wrote some years later] that the true propositions of logic and pure mathematics were tautologies or equations, in either case "saying nothing", that there was no such thing as natural necessity, that metaphysics was strictly nonsensical and that there remained no function for philosophy but the practice of analysis, preferably directed upon the theories and concepts of science.'[3]

Analytical philosophy became the orthodoxy of a generation in England. Its forthright statements provided an attractive, debunking mode for popularization and echoed a certain Englishness of attitude, a kind of commonsense scepticism, mistrustful of continental theory, which was to find echoes in the hard-headed posturing of the Movement. Its very Englishness indeed resulted in its association with the whole ideology of Little England. In a 1956 *Encounter* article Irving Kristol lamented the insularity of this form of national thought. A month later came the response from a professional philosopher: 'For the facts are that "philosophy" is no longer what it is taken for, it cannot be a total, streamlined response to the real world (whatever that may be). Philosophy and philosophers have changed, and you cannot change them back by calling the men in question complacent.'[5]

That was the manifesto of the British mainstream: philosophy was no longer about the 'big' questions, it was an activity aimed at deciphering propositions about the world. To the layman it simply seemed to have stepped backwards into an academic playground of hair-splitting, nit-picking and word games.

The difficulty was, as Ayer was also to note, that the *Tractatus* was booby-trapped. There was, for example, the remark that 'we feel that even when all possible scientific questions have been answered, the problems of life remain completely untouched' and: 'The solution of the riddle of life in space and time lies *outside* space and time.' In addition there were the resonant closing words: 'Whereof one cannot speak, thereof one must be silent.' To the Vienna Circle this did not need saying; there was nothing of which one could not speak. But there was *something* to be silent about: 'My work', Wittgenstein said in a letter, 'consists of two parts: the one presented here plus all that I have *not* written. And it is precisely this second part that is the important one.'[6]

This produced the, to the positivists, infuriating view of the *Tractatus* as 'important nonsense'. It attempted to step outside language in order to define its limits, an evidently impossible task. His way round this was to say that language could show rather than mean in these contexts which, in any case, were only the contortions produced by generations of philosophy, large parts of which were now demonstrably nonsense. But, in the end, Wittgenstein's ideal reader would master the *Tractatus*, realize the extent to which it was nonsensical and have no further need of it, or of the anguish of philosophy. So, from the beginning, Wittgenstein was separated by a huge philosophical divide from the very philosophers he had inspired. This divide widened with the long series of notes, written by both Wittgenstein and his students, after his return to Cambridge, and finally by *Philosophical Investigations* itself.

The central element of this work is the abandonment of the picture theory as a disastrously facile view of the workings of language, in favour of the acceptance of its infinite complexities and the importance of understanding words *in use*. Wittgenstein Two, as Russell was to call this philosophy, was radically different in style from Wittgenstein One. The title of the book suggests the first difference: these are investigations, tentative and exploratory. We are no longer at the end of philosophy, we may be at the beginning. Even so, a weary preface, written in 1945, concluded: 'I should have liked to produce a good book. This has not come about, but the time is past in which I could improve it.'[7] The book is fragmentary; it poses rather than answers questions. Its prose is note-like, groping and wondering: 'For how can I go so far as to try to use language to get between pain and its expression?[8] Above all, it accepts the multiplicity of language's uses and its centrality – 'to imagine a language means to imagine a form of life'.[9]

Russell had no time for this. To him it appeared that Wittgenstein had abandoned the entire philosophical project in favour of an interminable game of tinkering with sentences. Russell was a progressive, he believed in the forward movement of the Western tradition and in its continuity as well as in the significance of its efforts to help us to understand the world. But Wittgenstein no longer seemed interested in the world, only in language. He had moved away from the central problem of most preceding philosophy, that of knowledge, in favour of the investigation of the problem of meaning. For Russell this was open-ended and issueless, but for others it suggested that philosophy could almost start again, the romance of its quest had been restored. Language could dissolve the knots in our mind that separated us from the world; we could climb the ladder of argument and, on reaching the top, look back to discover the ladder had vanished. Wittgenstein spoke of people who would suddenly find themselves at peace with the world but unable to explain why – the knots had been dissolved.

Thus late Wittgenstein seems closer to Murdoch than to Ayer, though the booby-traps in *Tractatus* suggest he had been there all along. He had eradicated the false metaphysics of picture theory from his work, but had opened out the possibilities for a continued philosophical project far beyond anything in the *Tractatus*. He still could not go beyond what he believed to be possible in language, but the nature of the language itself was revealed to be infinitely subtle in its applications.

Wittgenstein Two removes science from the pedestal on which the *Tractatus* appeared to have placed it. Ayer described the change in his thought:

'Wittgenstein increasingly came to see science as inimical to philosophy. To put it more accurately, he thought that the prestige of science misled philosophers into fabricating explanations, whereas what was needed was an assortment of careful descriptions. He also blamed it for their failure to distinguish between empirical and conceptual questions.'10

However, the idea of restoring ourselves to the world, our philosophical problems dissolved, sounds uncomfortably like the unity of the mystics, a unity considered entirely meaningless by most of Wittgenstein's followers. The whole tenor of his thought, which had always tended towards the oracular, seemed to be moving away from the clarity and precision required of philosophy.

Few artists are likely to be influenced or, indeed, to understand the detailed, technical side of Wittgenstein's work. For philosophers, for example, the most important part of the *Investigations* may well be his onslaught on the idea of private languages. But the impact of both that book and the *Tractatus* on a more general audience is the result as much of their literary qualities as of their philosophical importance. They are documents of great beauty which portray an extraordinary mind on a unique quest.

Wittgenstein seemed to be struggling in the opposite direction to the rest of philosophy. He was a philosopher by instinct; left to its own devices, his brain philosophized. To turn it off after long seminars at Cambridge he would watch trashy movies from the front row of the cinema. His struggle was to attain the world from a position of theory, to undo the knots which his mind instinctively constructed. It was as though the ordinary, the everyday, was the one thing he found the most difficult.

In a memoir of Wittgenstein at Cambridge, F. R. Leavis recalled an incident when they hired a canoe on a summer evening and paddled upriver. They then walked across some fields and heard a fair in the distance. Wittgenstein wanted to go but Leavis refused on the grounds that they had to return the canoe and the boatman was waiting for them. They did so. Wittgenstein paid the man without tipping him. Leavis, embarrassed by this and by the resentment it caused, paid a tip. Wittgenstein protested but Leavis pointed out that the man had been kept waiting at the boathouse just for them. 'I always associate the man with the boathouse,' Wittgenstein replied, to which Leavis retorted: 'You may, but you know that he is separable and has a life apart from it.'11

Wittgenstein's abstract model of the world did not coincide with its reality. He was a man cut off from the world by his own genius for philosophy, his work was the struggle to re-establish himself in that world. Philosophy was, in the last analysis, his enemy.

Whispering Gallery

Wittgenstein had another enemy: a fellow Austrian who had also settled in England and whose thought was to have a far more direct and identifiable influence on post-war British thinking about the nature of art, Karl Popper. Such were his differences with Wittgenstein that they almost led to violence. On 25 October 1946 in the rooms of R. B. Braithwaite in King's College, Cambridge, Popper read a paper on the issue of whether there was such a thing as a philosophical problem capable of being solved. He believed there was, whereas Wittgenstein, believing in philosophy as an activity rather than a mechanism for providing solutions, did not. The argument was so furious that it concluded with Wittgenstein picking up a poker as if to attack Popper.

The near-victim of this attack had just arrived in England. Born in Vienna in 1902, he came under his assailant's influence to the extent of being associated for a while with the Vienna Circle. On Hitler's rise to power he moved to New Zealand and subsequently, in 1946, to England. In 1949 he became Professor of Logic and Scientific Method at the London School of Economics.

In common with the other members of the Circle, Popper's thought centred upon the idea of science; specifically, he was concerned with the scientific method. The traditional view of this was that the scientist assembled information about the world which he would then use as the basis of a theory. This was the inductive method in which the scientist is pictured as a neutral, objective collector of material. It is the Baconian picture and is the implicit backdrop to many arguments about the objective, impersonal nature of science. To Popper it was false in almost every respect; indeed, he came to deny the very existence of induction. For him the whole procedure was incredible. Collecting a mere random assemblage of information, as though the human mind were a kind of bucket, did not accord with the way scientists actually worked. The reality was that they *first* produced a hypothesis which they then tested against experience. In fact, even to begin the scientific process some hypothesis, however crude and mistaken, was essential. The procedure was then one of checking and correcting this initial hypothesis until a provisionally final hypothesis was attained.

Even this state of affairs could ever be regarded as only temporary. Indeed any statement about the world, to qualify as scientific rather than metaphysical, must be falsifiable. 'God is Love' is not scientific because it is not falsifiable; $E = mc^2$ is, however, because later experimentation and observation may confirm or deny it. Scientific method is, therefore, both for the individual researcher and for the history of science, a pattern of modified hypotheses. The survival of each is contingent upon its ability to accord with the known facts. Thus Newton's mechanics 'worked' until Einstein, whose relativity may similarly function until the next comparably general hypothesis.

On the face of it this suggests that knowledge is eternally condemned to be provisional, constructed upon the shifting sands of past knowledge and seemingly never moving any nearer to reality or truth. Popper's style of thought, however, is intrinsically optimistic and positive. He finds the concept 'truth' to be an essential force behind his conception of science. It may never be attained, but the process can continue only on the basis that it is somehow the object of the exercise. This moves a purely scientific theory into a wider field. Popper is evidently dealing with the mechanism by which we know the world. He views the mind not as a bucket but as a searchlight. The human role is progressive, illuminating, active and, supremely, it is human: our every notion of the world is built on previous notions.

'What we should do [Popper wrote], I suggest, is to give up the idea of ultimate sources of knowledge, and admit that all knowledge is human; that it is mixed with our errors, our prejudices, our dreams, and our hopes; that all we can do is to grope for truth even though it be beyond our reach. We may admit that our groping is often inspired, but we must be on our guard against the belief, however deeply felt, that our inspiration carries any authority, divine or otherwise. If we thus admit there is no authority beyond the reach of criticism to be found within the whole province of our knowledge, however far it may have penetrated into the unknown, then we can retain, without danger, the idea that truth is beyond human authority. And we must retain it.

'For without this idea there can be no objective standards of inquiry; no criticism of our conjectures; no groping for the unknown; no quest for knowledge.'[1]

This is a potent and inspired defence of the idea of the optimistic and progressive nature of human knowledge. It stood in stark and deliberate contrast to the anti-scientific and nihilistic tendencies that had become the intellectual vernacular of the late 1950s. The idea of truth as an abstraction beyond all our strivings has some similarity with Iris Murdoch's anti-existentialist view of the eternal moral verities, and its definition here is far removed from mainstream positivism. It provided a focus for human knowledge, a magnet that drew all its elements, like iron filings, into a single pattern. It was a view that implied a positive role for man in moving himself forward, in breaking down the barriers of the unknown. It approved his divine discontent, his eternal restlessness in forming ideas about the world and then testing them against reality.

It was a vision that was applied with spectacular success to art by Ernst Gombrich, whose *Art and Illusion: A Study in the Psychology of Pictorial Representation* was published in 1960. His earlier work, *The Story of Art*, appeared in 1950, but that had been a guide aimed at accessibility rather than a strictly theoretical exercise. Yet, straightforward as it was, it had raised a problem: why did visual art have a history at all? Why did different people at different times arrive at wholly different ways of representing the same thing? If we look at a man or a landscape, do we not all see much the same man or landscape?

The answer came in *Art and Illusion*; images are ambiguous, they seldom bear the simple relationship to reality which we allow ourselves to believe. They depend on convention, indeed a whole history of conventions without which they would frequently be incomprehensible. The ancient Egyptian paintings of men were intended not to look like but to be a substitute for a man. From that point on, however, art history became a process of producing images that *did* look like the world. Unfortunately, what the world looked like turned out to be fleeting and ambiguous, so artists created schemata: methods of representation which from time to time were accepted as looking 'like' the world. The individual artists would attempt a schema and then correct it until arriving at something acceptable. Similarly, succeeding generations would start from a previous schema. It is a precise parallel of Popper's scientific process – the schema simply replaces the hypothesis.

In this interpretation the period of medieval art saw the image again returned to its earlier role, prior to the restless movement towards representation; the classical progression was temporarily halted. With the Renaissance, the whole process began again.

'To the medieval artist', Gombrich explained, 'the schema is the image, to the post-medieval artist it is the starting point for correction.' This schema-correction process has continued into our time: 'It is this constant search, this sacred discontent, which constitutes the leaven of the Western mind since the Renaissance in our art no less than our science.'[2]

So every picture is primarily a response to preceding pictures, in a regression which we must perhaps accept as infinite. Gombrich says elsewhere that language may have originated in an initial act of imitation; for example, hunger may have been expressed by the sound of eating. From then on sounds built on sounds to form language, a self-sustaining entity that defines our entire consciousness. Similarly, images of animals may have started on cave walls as substitutes for the desired prey and then become a self-sustaining system of image-making, the system of art itself. 'For that strange precinct we call "art" ', Gombrich wrote in his essay 'Meditations on a Hobby Horse', 'is like a hall of mirrors or a whispering gallery. Each form conjures up a thousand memories and after-images. No sooner is an image presented as art than, by this very act, a new frame of reference is created which it cannot escape.'[3]

There is a history of art because that is all art is – a history: image feeds upon image, schema upon schema. Whether Popper's notion of a truth, quite separate from but having to aspire to all this activity, makes as much sense in art as it does in science is uncertain. Art is in any case a systematic fiction; it does not aspire to certainty in the way science does. However accurate a painting may be, according to the prevailing schema, it remains a painting. Gombrich's history of art does not appear to be a progress in one direction; it is a hall, not a corridor, of mirrors in which the images are reflected back and forth, apparently endlessly. The idea of 'truth to nature' that informs the writing of a critic such as Kenneth Clark is just another convention. We see what we have learned to see, nature and truth are both phantasms that are dissolving even as the brush touches the canvas.

The theory is profoundly anti-romantic and attacks the art-critical tradition of Clark and Ruskin. It echoes the thinking of early literary modernism in that it asserts the way in which art must deal with all previous art, just as T. S. Eliot's *The Waste Land* aspired to confront and embody all previous poetry. But Gombrich's expression of the position makes the artist seem more trapped; even if he chooses to close his eyes to the entire history of painting, the very fact that he can see at all grafts him on to the visual tradition. The impressionists' innocent eye or their supposedly scientific analysis of the objects of vision are so many fictions.

In defining this Gombrich knows that he is defining a serious problem for art, for he is separating art from the values with which it has in the past been associated. The moral significance attached to words like 'high' or 'low', 'light' or 'dark' is revealed as no more than 'a co-ordinate system erected by our culture'. Like David Jones, but without his despair or his religion, Gombrich sees us losing our imagery of significance:

'As we move away from the hierarchical society of the past, problems of symbols and values become, in fact, more acute. We have seen how strongly this type of society imprinted its frame of reference on the terms in which art was conceived. The "noble" and the "vulgar", the "high" and the "low", the "dignified" and the "common", are today not much more than pale, fading metaphors for what were once tangible realities. We need not mourn their passing away in order to realize that here an area of metaphor is passing out of our consciousness which, for centuries if not longer, gave man a symbol of value, however crude.'⁴

In 1968, in his book *Art and its Objects*, Richard Wollheim raised an important objection to Gombrich's thesis that artists could express themselves only with the use of a repertoire, a convention, that must in some way be understood by the spectator: his hypothesis about the world can be based only upon existing hypotheses. For Wollheim this failed to take into account the existence of the range of values being expressed, irrespective of the particular repertoire:

'And the answer is that, though it is a matter of decision or convention what is the specific range of elements that the artist appropriates as his repertoire and out of which on any given occasion he makes his selection, underlying this there is a basis in nature to the communication of emotion. For the elements that the artist appropriates are a subset of an ordered series of elements, such that to one end of the series we can assign one expressive value and to the other a contrary or "opposite" value: and the crucial point is that both the ordering relation that determines the series, e.g. "darker than" in the case of colours, "higher than" in the case of musical notes . . . and the correlation of the two ends of the series with specific inner states, are natural rather than conventional matters. It is because a move towards one end of the series rather than the other is, or is likely to be, unambiguous that, once we know what alternatives were open to the artist, we can immediately understand the significance of his choice between them.'[5]

In other words, for Wollheim the hall of mirrors has an exit. The artist may be doing no more than playing a game but the rules, however arbitrary, bear some relation to values and meanings outside the game.

Right or wrong, this is an important objection but it does not, as Wollheim acknowledges, in any way reduce the significance of Gombrich's central point that we can no longer pretend to stand before a work of art in all innocence. This was both a romantic view and that of the New Critics in literature, such as Leavis, who attempted to insist that the scrutiny of the text itself was all that was of significance: the work of art stood alone and inviolable.

With Gombrich and Wollheim the interaction between the spectator and the work became the interaction of the entire culture. Art is riddled with self-consciousness, both of itself as a work of art and of the conventions which allow it to function at all. It is soaked in history; or, perhaps more correctly, it *is* history.

PART THREE

Seeking Revenge

In May 1973 W. H. Auden wrote the poem 'No, Plato, No'. It concluded with the lines:

> yes, it well could be that my Flesh
> is praying for 'Him' to die
> so setting Her free to become
> irresponsible Matter.[1]

On Friday 28 September 1973 he declined supper after a poetry reading given in Vienna to the Austrian Society of Literature and was driven back to his hotel. During the night he suffered a heart attack and was found dead the next morning by his lover, Chester Kallman.

In October 1964 T. S. Eliot collapsed at his home and was rushed to hospital. The doctors held out little hope, but he survived long enough to return home once more, shouting 'hurrah! hurrah! hurrah!' as he was carried over the threshold. He lapsed into a coma after Christmas, regaining consciousness once to speak his wife's name – Valerie. He died on 4 January.

Evelyn Waugh died on Easter Day, 10 April 1966. He had a sudden heart attack at his home, Combe Florey in Somerset, after attending mass.

The deaths were emblems of a passing world. Through the 1940s and the 1950s the culture seemed to have been struggling with the legacy of these men and their formidable contemporaries. The image of their authority was sustained, even as distinctive post-war voices began to emerge in the 1950s, by some blurred awareness of a great and recent past. The 'new', as it appeared, still had an 'old' with which to struggle.

There were large-scale, less specialized correlatives of this. Winston Churchill died and was buried, in January 1965, with a ceremony that rivalled the coronation as a set-piece celebration of post-war national consciousness. The cranes in London's docks bowed, in anticipation of their own demise, when his river-borne coffin sailed by. At the funeral service the American 'Battle Hymn of the Republic' was sung. 'Britain without Churchill' was the headline on the next edition of the *Spectator*, as though nothing could remain unchanged by his passing.

Some change *was* in the air. Most notably the long, slow escape from the grip of austerity seemed to have at last come to an end, accompanied by a dawning realization among politicians that affluence was expected by the electorate. In 1954 R. A. Butler, then Chancellor of the Exchequer, spoke of doubling the standard of living over the next twenty-five years; in 1957 Harold Macmillan told the people of Britain that they had never had it so good; finally, in 1964 Harold Wilson led the Labour Party to an election victory with talk of the 'white heat of technological revolution'. This induced a sense, as in 1945, that the time had come to formulate a new national purpose.

'In recent years the country has lost its sense of purpose', said the election victory leader in the *New Statesman*, 'and, since the Conservatives were forced to abandon their half-hearted attempt to enter Europe, they have proved quite incapable of supplying one. Now, after a wasted year of electioneering, there is a universal desire to push aside the political slogans and to get on with the job of modernising Britain. The nation is waiting for the smack of firm government.'[2]

Affluence and its maintenance had become the primary political obsession, expressed in the integration of technology into people's homes, in a new landscape of consumption and in a wide range of libertarian outpourings, most frequently in the name of youth. What had been an imaginary world to the pop artists of the 1950s, a world inclusive of all the dreams of technology and the modern city, seemed in the 1960s to be on the verge of realization.

Indeed the very phrase 'the sixties' has since taken on a rare and potent cultural resonance for a generation born after the war. Those who were eighteen in the latter half of 1963 had not lived through a single day of the war. Symbolically they were severed by a date from the old rituals of authority and discipline that had persisted, in spite of every attack, through the long years of the 1950s. Just as Wells's embittered passing immediately after the war had seemed to symbolize the last gasp of the rational, optimistic Edwardian adventure, so the death of Churchill, as well as the artistic greats, seemed to signal that the long shadows of the pre-war titans had finally been dispelled.

A generation woke up to find that most of the grown-ups were gone, and those remaining were powerless to maintain the illusion of value in the old dispensation.

HEADMASTER: Would it be impossibly naïve and old-fashioned of me to ask what it is you are trying to accomplish in this impudent charade?

FRANKLIN: You could say we are trying to shed the burden of the past.

HEADMASTER: Shed it? Why must we shed it? Why not shoulder it? Memories are not shackles, Franklin, they are garlands.

FRANKLIN: We're too tied to the past. We want to be free to look to the future. The future comes before the past.

HEADMASTER: Nonsense. The future comes after the past. Otherwise it couldn't be the future.[3]

The passage is from Alan Bennett's 1968 play *Forty Years On*. Later in the same play comes this speech: 'I can see that room now, full of talk and smoke and people. And what extraordinary people they were. Eliot was there, Auden, Spender and Isherwood, the old faithfuls and young hopefuls, but always there was someone who one never quite expected to see. I saw A. E. Housman there once, lured down from Cambridge by Dadie Rylands and the prospect of All-in Wrestling at Finsbury Park.'[4]

The tone is impatient and playfully destructive. There is a certain superfluity that has replaced the pared-down anguish of the 1950s playwrights. The language has become full of possibilities for simple fun while the past, devoid of that crushing weight it so recently seemed to possess, had become absurd. The great cultural figures were merely daft, their dignity liable to be subverted by the suggestion of a sexual peccadillo. Sexual jokes at the expense of the old establishment became part of the 1960s vernacular. The collapse of the Conservative Government's authority in the years immediately prior to 1964 had been accelerated in 1963 by the Profumo scandal, which provided the lurid spectacle of a government minister pressured into a colossal, and rapidly exposed lie by his involvement with a bizarre cast of prostitutes, spies, and a West Indian jazz singer called 'Lucky' Gordon. 'There is clear evidence of a sordid underworld network,' Harold Wilson said in the House of Commons, capturing the gleeful public sense of a pompous establishment foundering on its weakness for the low life.

The point now was that the world was so obviously *different*. Authority was laughable, and money and fun were to be had. This produced a straightforward sense of liberation. 'All the "reforms" of the late fifties and sixties', Arthur Marwick wrote, 'marked a retreat from the social controls imposed in the Victorian era by evangelicalism and non-conformity'[5] These reforms and their accompanying mythology of liberation represented a new version of Utopia. Where the previous post-war version had stressed social justice, this stressed personal freedom. Philip Larkin found the new version as easily corroded by the acid of the undeceived Movement gaze as the old. The first stanza of his poem 'High Windows' reads:

> When I see a couple of kids
> And guess he's fucking her and she's
> Taking pills or wearing a diaphragm,
> I know this is paradise.[6]

In general, the issue of freedom from the arbitrary controls of the past did have a new imaginative power for a certain type of artist. Lindsay Anderson was born in 1923 in India, was educated at Cheltenham and Oxford and worked in the Intelligence Corps during the war. During the 1950s he was involved with cinema publications and with making short films; from 1956 to 1959 he was the key figure in the Free Cinema movement. Anderson's description of its activities, written in 1959, anticipate the aggressive, liberationist aesthetics of the 1960s: 'In making these films and presenting these programmes, we have tried to make a stand for independent, creative film-making in a world where the pressures of conformism and commercialism are becoming more powerful every day. We will not abandon these convictions, nor the attempt to put them into practice.'[7]

In 1963 Anderson made his first feature film, *This Sporting Life*, based on David Storey's novel about a miner who becomes a rugby star. Anderson accepted the trappings of realism in the novel but the intensity of his direction led the film to veer towards expressionism in spite of itself. But in 1968 *If* provided Anderson with a script that released both his aggression and his cinematic imagination.

Like Bennett's play it was set in a school. In the 1960s the public school became an irresistible image for anybody intent upon analysing the malaise of the old British establishment. But there is no simple fun in *If*; it concerns three boys who regard with loathing and distaste the school's attempts to make them play the game. The school's systems of authority are shown to be cold and brutal. The teachers make ineffectual, liberal gestures but the house prefects – the 'whips' – impose sadistic punishment, lust after pretty younger boys and demand insanely passionate allegiance to the institution of the 'house'.

Our sympathy is thus naturally enlisted for the three rebels. Yet they seem to be psychopaths: they gape admiringly at magazine pictures of armed soldiers cut out and pasted on the walls of their room along with the more usual nudes. Their real experience is that of the closed world of the school, but they imagine a world outside of violence and eroticism. This is their total existence – we are told nothing of their backgrounds – and one in which Travis, the leader of the three, takes voluptuous pleasure, in the sure knowledge that there will be no future to judge his conduct: 'The whole world will end soon,' he says, 'black, brittle bodies, peeling into ash.'

The image comes from the photo-journalism of the day. Mass communications had given Travis the conviction that intimations of the apocalypse lie all about him. They had invaded the world of the school, reducing its rituals of discipline to absurdity. The film slips into a more explicitly fantastic mode with a violent sexual scene in a café, occurring symbolically after Travis and his friend have escaped from the confines of the school and town on a motorbike. Finally Travis's own apocalypse arrives when, with his friends, he starts gunning down staff, boys and guests at the founder's day ceremony.

If is a characteristically 1960s fable about liberation and repression. It carefully encompasses telling contemporary details such as the head-master's determination to modernize and liberalize his school – an ambition that culminates in his death when he marches up to Travis and his heavily armed friends, crying, 'Boys! Boys! I understand you!' – but it does not provide any escape. The conflict between the self and society is shown as unresolvable: the boys are victims of strange and distorted sexual impulses while the teachers carry hopelessly inaccurate models of the world around in their heads. Society simply does not work, it can only end in a shoot-out.

The cold seriousness of *If*, however, was the exception. Similarly cold-hearted and clear-sighted views of the world tended to be expressed in the 1960s vernacular of comedy – gravity, after all, was the style of the discredited establishment. In this context the coldest, clearest-eyed comedian of them all was the playwright to whom Bennett's dialogue and structure owed so much: Joe Orton. His first major play, *Entertaining Mr Sloane*, appeared in 1964; three years later, aged thirty-four, he was battered to death by his lover Kenneth Halliwell.

In Orton the intellectual anguish of the humanist or the religious, all aesthetic pretension and all gentility were thinned into a disembodied comic skin that celebrated its own worthlessness. His immediate ancestors were perhaps the pop artists. They too had celebrated the fragmentary detritus of the world and, more significantly, they had demonstrated that art was a moving target. It could no longer be fixed within a frame, imprisoned inside the academy or sanctified by a self-elected priesthood. Its meanings were no longer self-evident, art could be anything. It was a development that thinkers like Herbert Read or novelists like Kingsley Amis found increasingly unpalatable.

In pop there remained the justification of seriousness, a base of solemnity: in Orton there was no such base. The necessity to destroy to expose the layers of lies that he perceived in all human conduct, was more powerful than any self-conscious desire to produce art. His biographer, John Lahr, prefaced the story of his brief life with a quotation from Gauguin: 'Life being what it is, one seeks revenge.'[8]

The certainty that nothing could be trusted, nothing was what it seemed and every abstraction was a lie, released Orton into a theatrical playground:

TRUSCOTT: You have before you a man who is quite a personage in his way – Truscott of the Yard. Have you ever heard of Truscott? The man who tracked down the limbless girl killer? Or was that sensation before your time?

HAL: Who would kill a limbless girl?

TRUSCOTT: She was the killer.

HAL: How did she do it if she was limbless?

TRUSCOTT: I'm not prepared to answer that question to anyone outside the profession. We don't want a carbon-copy murder on our hands. (*To McLeavy*) Do you realize what I'm doing here?

MCLEAVY: No your every action has been a mystery to me.

TRUSCOTT: That is as it should be. The process by which the police arrive at the solution to a mystery is, in itself, a mystery.[9]

The very idea of meaning is being assaulted. Truscott, a policeman, is a man who should, pre-eminently, possess social meaning. He represents authority, like the headmaster in *If*; but, in addition, his very vocation is the discovery of the truth. Yet this embodiment of social virtue is a madman. His idea of meaning is no more than an incoherent mass of newspaper clichés, a structure of deracinated verbiage with which he defines himself. His justification is nothing but an ever-receding series of mystifications of which the ultimate is that he *should* be a mystery, the better to perform his task.

The language – a vacuous demotic – bears some similarity to Pinter in its exploitation of routine banalities but, unlike Pinter, Orton is not content to let the phrases hang, revolving in the wind, losing meaning before our eyes. Rather he attacks the words, making them mean something in their own terms, but then turning the meaning ludicrously back on itself. Truscott ploughs on through his madness and inconsistency because he has no choice. Take away his corrupted language and he has nothing, even though that language has no sane reality to which it can cling. To Orton's characters only the forward movement of words counts, not their significance. Words combine and recombine, but they have become as arbitrary and self-contained as mathematical symbols.

In Orton's last play, *What the Butler Saw*, Dr Prentice's desire to conceal his attempt at an illicit affair from his wife drives him to ever greater heights of absurdity. It becomes clear to everybody that exposure would be infinitely less harmful than the horrific tangles into which concealment has led him, but he must go on. When the woman he has tried to seduce can take it no longer, she cries: 'We must tell the truth!' – Dr Prentice can only respond: 'That's a thoroughly defeatist attitude.'[10]

The truth is just another version, one variation of Prentice's mania. It has no further value, no moral weight; so its avoidance becomes a purely formal decision like any other. Orton's guile is revealed by the placing of the word 'defeatist'; its implications of moral rebuke are ironically set against a background of complete amorality. Prentice appeals to a value system that his every action undermines. The purpose of the whole project has been lost in the energy of its execution. Indeed the very idea of a purpose, however banal, becomes laughably presumptuous in the face of the torrent of meaninglessness which constantly overwhelms the characters. No attitude can save them.

Orton's drama was, in a sense, a demonic realization of the severance of meaning from the symbols of the past that had concerned Gombrich. Indeed, Gombrich was to define in the visual arts a type of aesthetic that seemed precisely to encompass Orton: 'This process implies, as I have tried to show, that a work of art comes to stand in a context where it is valued as much for what it rejects and negates as for what it is. In modern art these negations and negations of negations have reached a bewildering complexity . . .'[11]

Gombrich was alarmed at the possibility that art might never again embody values. There seemed to be a danger that all it could ever do from then on was work through a vast repertoire of available styles, producing infinite, empty variations. As the critic Andrew Kennedy observed, 'the choice of styles – the imaginary museum – seems to have become a permanent condition in our culture, in drama as well as in poetry and the novel'.[12] The lack of a single style or orthodoxy to contain the expressive energies of the age was the artistic consequence of the lack of a single meaning. In a world without foundations, all styles were equally valid. This implied a kind of knowingness in which the very idea of embodying values came to seem naïve; a state of affairs Gombrich himself had intellectually defined with his insight into the profound artificiality of all art, his hall of mirrors. But, as he had realized, the problem with this insight was that it suggested the kind of exhaustion of meaning and value expressed by Orton. It is one thing to perceive art as self-generating in a critical hypothesis, quite another to use it as a creative starting point. The very knowledge may condemn us to self-conscious inertia.

Yet in spite of it all Orton writes and what he writes is original; some development has occurred. He has played the old game by using, however anarchically, the forms of theatre. Gombrich found his own version of hope for continuance in the fact of this type of game. In what amounted to an attack on expressionism for wilfully breaking the rules at its own convenience, he put the case for the artist who elects to evolve his own variations within the rules. His sample game is one where the stamps on letters are used to communicate the feelings of the sender:

'What challenges the imagination is rather the game itself, the wealth of combinations adding up to sixpence which the reader is invited to explore. Perhaps those who get really absorbed in the game will try to fit their moods to interesting combinations rather than make the message fit the mood. Only those who do, I believe, may have the true artistic temperament – but that is a different story.'[13]

Orton is doing precisely this. For, endless as the self-denying progression of his content is, his form is positively conservative. His conventions are those of stage farce and comedy. Partly his reasons are straightforwardly subversive: by using the obvious imagery of policemen and infidelity, he can more clearly demonstrate their absurdity. But, more important, he needs the rules – without them his plays could have no reason to exist. The jokes exist to be funny and the plays exist to be dramatic. A modernist raid on the nature of form would simply get in the way. Orton needs his assault to be direct.

In effect, what Orton has stumbled on and Gombrich had defined was one variety of post-modernism, a much-abused term which had its heyday in the 1970s and 1980s. It has been used to define such a wide range of works in all the arts that it is almost impossible to be precise about its meaning. The need for it is more obvious: its use represents an attempt to create an orthodoxy which neither rejected modernism nor laboured under its shadow. It is intended to have a more liberating air than previous movements built solely on the impulse to reject the pretensions of modernism.

In the form I have just identified, it represents a kind of mannerism within which the forms of modernism have been transformed into one more style of the past. In this form it is characteristically playful and reluctant to adopt more than the most modest of ambitions – an obvious acceptance of the prevailing distaste for the large claims of the modernists. Its significance lies in its presentation of seemingly endless new possibilities to the artist. The modernist dead end, the radicalism that had frozen into a bleak orthodoxy in its worst manifestations, could be laughed at like anything else. It was just a style, no more and no less. Its grander claims were as absurd as those of Inspector Truscott, and as empty.

Orton's motives, however, were far from exclusively aesthetic. The conscious dynamic of his drama was his need to avenge himself on what he felt to be the intolerable restriction of the England of the *petit bourgeois*. As he wrote in his diary on seeing an attractive boy on a beach: 'England is intolerable. I'd be able to fuck that in an Arab country. I could take him home and stick my cock up him!'[14] This was the characteristic irritation felt by the libertarians of the 1960s. The restrictions of our national life produced in Orton an explosive desire artistically to tear down all systems of value and meaning or, in the more benign form of Alan Bennett's play, to laugh at them. In Lindsay Anderson a similar irritation produced a bleak vision of political paralysis in which society could not possibly work because the opposing tensions were ultimately irreconcilable.

Stylistically the urgency of the art demanded a very precise context. Orton's world is full of the language and paraphernalia of a very clearly observed society, equally Bennett's and Anderson's schools are well known and understood. The point is that these artists have highly specific intentions. They are not concerned with mythic generalities, pure forms or abstraction. They wish to act upon the world, so, first, they must be sure it is the world we all know, they need to be certain of its content.

Too Barren

The visual arts saw a parallel development. Pop had provided one means of liberation, but the determined and earnest projects of its founders seemed to have been overwhelmed by American abstract expressionism. From the 1956 Tate exhibition, this had coolly established itself as the international orthodoxy. The centre of the art world had moved from Paris to New York – either way, it was not London.

Sadly for the British innovators of the 1950s, the prevailing image of British painting remained one of timidity before the great foreign masters. In 1963 at the Whitechapel Gallery an exhibition of British painting in the 1960s drew complaints from the critic Max Kozloff that it was all too decorous and lacking in energy, the usual vocabulary when the USA is at the back of the mind.[1] But Kozloff also mentioned that, 'coming out of the Royal College of Art and represented most comprehensively by Ron Kitaj, is a scattering of painters interested in popular culture'. This was hardly a revolutionary interest given that pop had been around for almost a decade, but it indicated a certain weariness in the critic's mind with both abstract expressionism and its systematic critical underpinning as well as with the old modernist-Mediterranean style.

Furthermore, Kitaj was the right name to choose. He was born in Cleveland, Ohio, in 1932 and came to England in 1957. In 1960 he attended the Royal College of Art, where he met David Hockney, then twenty-three. A member of a Bradford working-class family, Hockney studied at the Bradford School of Art and from 1959 at the Royal College. In 1960 he saw a Picasso exhibition at the Tate and was overwhelmed by the master's versatility, his apparently effortless ability to employ a variety of styles and methods. This was clearly in sharp contrast to the single-minded abstract mood of the day. Hockney's own exhibition of 1962 was called *Demonstrations of Versatility* – a title asserting variety and plurality.

Both Kitaj and Hockney viewed the orthodoxy of abstraction with

189

suspicion: 'Everybody else was doing big abstract expressionist pictures,' Hockney was to write of that period, 'And I thought, well, that's what you've got to do.' But, after experimenting with the style, he gave up: 'It was too barren for me.'[2]

Hockney then took his problems to Kitaj: 'I'd talk to him about my interests; I was a keen vegetarian then, and interested in politics a bit, and he'd say to me Why don't you paint those subjects? And I thought, it's quite right; that's what I'm complaining about, I'm not doing anything that's from me. So that was the way I broke it. I began to paint those pictures.'[3]

Kitaj, an impatient and passionate figure with a distinctly literary imagination, was concerned to retrieve the idea of content for art. The theology of abstraction had become too vague, too inward-looking. His advice to Hockney offered a liberating simplicity: paint what you like. He was to be freed from intellectual and critical programmes; in the best 1960s style his own inclinations were to determine his content. This inclusiveness of all experience, however banal, had obvious affinities with pop, but it was an easier, more open, less austere programme than that evolved by Hamilton and the Smithsons. The impersonality of early pop was based on a cerebral rather than visceral response from the artist. For all its celebratory acceptance of the bric-à-brac of modern life, its products were dispassionate – Pinter rather than Orton. Equally its main preoccupations could be seen as static and inward-looking, the irony of its gaze could be interpreted as smugness. Their pictures, though full of the world, did not necessarily seem to be turned outwards to address it.

Hockney's first response to the possibility that his content could be exactly what he liked was gleefully literal:

'The idea came because I didn't have the courage to paint a real figure, so I thought, I have to make it clear, so I'll write "Gandhi" on this picture about Gandhi. I can remember people coming round and saying That's ridiculous, writing on pictures, you know, it's mad what you're doing. And I thought, well, it's better; I feel better; you feel as if something's coming out. And then Ron said Yes, that's much more interesting.'[4]

By writing on paintings Hockney was achieving a new kind of artistic space for himself. His paintings were at that stage, in execution at least, still in debt to the brushy mode of contemporary abstraction. But the words brought to them something of the poster-immediacy of pop. Above all, they stressed a directness of communication, a kind of innocence in contrast to the sophisticated justifications of abstraction. This innocence has been, through the years, a central element in Hockney's public persona. He has always been concerned to stress a certain literalness, a simplicity of intention, which claims only that a straightforward task is being undertaken. By writing on paintings he was saying, simply, that this showed they were paintings *of* something.

The sense of release he felt with the gesture is the correlative of Orton's joyous disembowellings of dramatic language. Both were escaping from an arid and puritanical modernism into a landscape of fun and naughtiness. Probably significantly, they both identified their homosexuality as part of their rejection of the artistic and moral codes they were being offered. But Hockney had none of Orton's aggression. His variety of post-modernism was a much gentler affair. Both his use of writing on pictures and many of his later innovations were inspired by early modernism – most obviously cubism – and he has never abandoned the idea of the pursuit of the new as an inevitable obligation for the artist. Yet the forms of modernism appear in his work as elements rather than the foundations of the whole enterprise; they have become fragments of just another style. Over the years Hockney has fitted even more snugly into the tradition of English romanticism in painting than overt romantics such as John Piper. The reason is that having established his own need for the content denied to him by abstraction he moved from daubed words on canvases to a form of content based entirely on his own artistic and public persona.

His remark 'I'm not doing anything that's from me' signalled the beginning of his transformation into a compulsive autobiographer. In 1963 he began to paint a series of domestic scenes as well as images of his travels. The abstract brushwork was replaced by harder, clearer shapes as his confidence in the figurative grew. Drawing became a central element of his art, and with it came the restoration of the idea of the painter as recorder and organizer of experience rather than metaphysical voyager in colour and form. The famous surfaces of his swimming pools and the various methods he used for representing a water surface were attempts to make pictures work directly as representation. He chose the closest thing to an abstract image in the world and then found a system of painting it as figuratively as possible.

This produced an accessible 'readable' art that, with his dyed blond hair and gold lamé jackets, made him a hero of popular culture alongside the Beatles, fashion models and all the other familiar paraphernalia of the 1960s. In this too his career showed parallels with Orton's, whose drama was for a time associated with the 'zany', offbeat style of the hour – just before his death there were plans for him to write the script for the next Beatles film.

Especially in the case of Hockney, one side-effect of all this was to draw the idea of the 'artistic' back from the edge of the avant-garde. The literalness with which he painted and drew from the inspiration of his life and his travels suggested a precise and comforting role for art. Significantly much of his work was illustration – for books, plays and operas – as if in acknowledgement of the role of art as accompaniment, part of a system external to itself. This made him a conservative force, re-establishing the ideals of craftsmanship and a more stable sense of content in art.

Kitaj, Hockney's old mentor, developed in a radically different direction. The hunger for content which he shared with Hockney was combined with a compulsively literary imagination: his exhibition catalogues are dense with footnotes listing his source material; his paintings are replete with a variety of narrative and argumentative elements. Whereas for Hockney the idea of restoring content came as a revelation of a method of painting that would allow him to establish a harmony between his life and his art, for Kitaj content was a matter of the utmost urgency: 'Collaging seems banal to me now,' he has said. 'I am saying that I cannot conceive any more of art as some kind of game without rules as Duchamp did or *art as such* as Greenberg terms it. Both these modern aspects of art will make themselves felt but I want much more for the thing. Dissipation in youth and a redemption in ageing – not untried before.'[5]

Like Hockney, Kitaj wanders the world playing the traditional role of the artist pursuing his one task of looking, but his attitude is considerably more aggressive. He is not content passively to delight in what he sees, he wishes to reorganize it: 'I think the last revolution was when the idea was introduced that you didn't *have* to depict people and things in the visible world anymore. *That* idea is my definition of Modernism.'[6]

This is an appeal to an earlier, purer ideal of modernism in which the work of art creates its own rules and is no longer subservient to the order of the real world. Kitaj frequently refers to T. S. Eliot, an artist whose early work similarly attempted to reorder experience as though depicting not the experienced but the experience. As John Ashbery has said: 'Such is Kitaj, the chronicler not of our "strange moment" but of how it feels to be living it.'[7]

His work is more alien and uncomfortable than Hockney's and is suffused with an insistent moral sense. A bleak commentary implicitly accompanies paintings like *Juan de la Cruz* (1967) or *The Ohio Gang* (1964) with their imagery of violation and corruption as well as their strong, though not easily definable, narrative element. With *If Not, Not* (1976) Kitaj's urge to encompass some kind of inclusive visionary vista prompted him to devise a Breugelesque space in which fragmentary dramas are enacted beneath a cliff topped by the entrance to Auschwitz.

The urgency with which Kitaj perceived the need for content in his paintings drove him to strive for a form of modern epic. As an artist he is something of a rarity in that he combines a formidable technique and a sophisticated awareness of form with a determination to make that form work to an external end – he feels he must make his paintings *do* something, they must interact with history on an epic scale.

Speaking of the Nazi massacre of the Jews and the conflict in the Middle East, he said:

'I intend to confront these impossible things in an art because some day when I'm chased limping down a road looking back at a burning city, I want the slight satisfaction that I couldn't make an art that didn't confess human frailty, fear, mediocrity, and the banality of evil as clear presences in art life.'[8] [And:] 'Some day there will be painters whose skills and imagination will be *seen to be done* by many, many people unversed in the half-baked philosophical double-talk in which our very difficult twentieth century is smothered.'[9]

Where Orton found content in the very absence of content and Hockney in re-creating a languid artistic persona, Kitaj finds it in the attempt to return art, urgent and involved, to life, albeit to a specifically modern and fragmented life. His conviction that art was once, somehow, a more potent medium, unadulterated by 'philosophical double-talk' is perhaps just another form of the atavism which so frequently afflicts so many contemporary artists. But its importance lies in the impatience it expresses, an impatience with the apparent difficulty of producing art that was both modern and in some way morally active. A similar impatience was expressed in Lindsay Anderson's writings and his film *If*, with their determination to engage with all history.

Kitaj and Hockney were accompanied by a whole generation of what might be described as 'painterly' pop artists such as Allen Jones, Derek Boshier, Peter Phillips, Joe Tilson and Peter Blake. As a group they created the utterly distinctive flat, bright iconography of the age with varying degrees of ironic distance and commitment, though none was quite to share the terrible urgency of Kitaj's vision. In a sense this may have been because this later pop generation was inspired by the perception of a joke. All were in some way reacting against the arid cul-de-sac of post-war avant-garde modernism, and Hockney and Kitaj were specifically appealing to what might be termed 'classical' modernism in the works of Picasso and Eliot. The joke was that, on the one hand, modern art had been pursuing projects of immense pretension, using the styles and forms of revolutionary movements of the past; on the other, society appeared to be becoming ridiculously cosy, affluent and undemanding. The critic Edward Lucie-Smith pointed out the fact that there was something faintly grotesque about the triumph of the avant-garde in 1960s Britain. The conditions, he pointed out, did not match those of the USSR of futurism or the Europe of dada: 'it seems as if the urgent gestures of protest and revolt are being directed at something which no longer deserves them, and which ought not, therefore, to provoke such actions.'[10]

Meanwhile, the revolt against abstract expressionism and its formidable underpinning from Clement Greenberg was to be given its own critical underpinning in the work of Richard Wollheim. Just as he had defined what he believed to be flaws in Gombrich's system of conventions, so now he came to assault the single-minded purity of Greenberg's aesthetics. Greenberg had insisted that the 'truth' of a painting was its surface:

'But [Wollheim wrote] from this it does not follow that a painting produced in conformity with this theory will insist upon the fact that it has a surface. Yet this is sometimes thought to follow both by critics and by artists; and consequential distortions are produced both in critics – so that, for instance, it is thought good enough to say of a painting that it insists upon the facts of its surface – and in art itself – so that we are confronted by objects which seem to acquire value from this insistence.

'The confusion may be put briefly by saying that in a modern work there is an asserted surface, but this does not mean that the assertion of the surface forms part of the picture's content.'[11]

This was an assault on the dread purity, truth and critical asceticism that had formed the abstract orthodoxy which the pop artists felt had separated the academy of art from life as lived. It had also created the feeling that painting was an occupation of fanatical simplifications:

'To talk of the use of surface and to contrast this with the fact of the surface, and to identify the former rather than the latter as the characteristic preoccupation of modern art, attributes to modern art a complexity of concern that it cannot renounce. For it is only if we assume such complexity that there is any sense in which we can think of the surface as being used. Use, we must ask, for what? And the answer to this has to lie in that complexity of concern. The point, I must emphasise, would not be worth making were it not for the widespread confusion which equates the autonomy of modern art with its single-mindedness, even with its simple-mindedness. To talk of the autonomy of art is to say something about where its concerns derive from, it is to say nothing about their complexity or variety.'[12]

Wollheim was not attacking abstract expressionism itself – indeed he regarded some of its products as the finest paintings of the age – rather he was attacking the reductive and exclusive nature of the critical theory that attempted to justify it. As a critic he was thus performing the same task as the artists who had moved so decisively back to figuration.

In rejecting dry avant-gardism, Hockney, Kitaj and their contemporaries were attempting to find an inclusive way of making pictures. Instead of responding to the problems of representation by abandoning them as not worth solving and taking up abstraction, they accepted the terms of the problems as the condition of their art. This context made the Gombrich crisis of self-consciousness seem no less alarmingly terminal. He would say that art history was simply a mountain of interdependent conventions rather than a tropism towards a more 'real' form of representation; accepting that, these artists would attempt to restore the linkage between those conventions and the world. They would play the game, which after all is what everybody else in the 1960s was trying to do.

Acid Dances

Hockney's innocent persona and all the directness of second-generation pop imagery were thus a reaction against what was perceived to be over-sophistication. To the public, the late modernist avant-garde seemed to have taken all the worst aspects of early modernism's formal concerns and used them to exclude any possibility of a more accessible, more 'human' content. It was as though art had been hijacked by a coterie which insisted on denying that title to the activities of others.

Pop art, in reaction, was liberal and inclusive; its pictures were bright, celebratory and optimistic. Nevertheless, it retained its roots in fine art, its forays into popular culture being self-consciously intended to bring new images back to the academy whence the artists had come. It retained, in addition, a hard professional sheen, a polished surface that drew attention to its professionalism and technique. It was always a highly 'finished' art.

The 'innocence' of its intentions was, in this sense, only skin deep. Elsewhere, however, the ideology of innocence, accessibility and of art for all had become the foundation of a movement. Pop culture shared its name with pop art but little else. It was founded on a newly affluent generation who were being more widely and systematically educated than any previously. It embraced a variety of exotic political and philosophical dogmas, all centred on vague notions either of spiritual liberation or political revolution. As a phenomenon it was largely limited to the educational institutions from which it sprang, though later apologists have tried to link it with worldwide political developments. Its main significance in this context, however, lies in its determination to annex and popularize the idea of art. Creativity became the touchstone of human value. On the one hand the entertainments of the newly affluent young were to be ennobled – popular music became 'progressive', significant and worthy of critical analysis – and, on the other, the traditional arts were to be democratized. So, as the equivalent of the pop festivals of the day, there was the Poetry International Festival at the Albert Hall in 1965. The American 'beat' poet Allen Ginsberg was the star and seven thousand people turned up to listen to four hours of poetry.

'All our separate audiences had come to one place at the same time [Jeff Nuttall wrote of the occasion], to witness an atmosphere of pot, impromptu solo acid dances, of incredible barbaric colour, of face and body painting, of flowers and flowers and flowers, of a common dreaminess in which all was permissive and benign ... There was a frisson for us all to savour as there had been at the first Aldermaston, and the Underground was suddenly there on the surface, in open ground with a following of thousands.'[1]

Towards the end, Ginsberg finally appeared to read. As he did so, an 'officer-class voice' was heard to cry: 'Can we have some real poetry now, sir?' Under the circumstances it was a good joke. Nuttall and his contemporaries wanted art, but they wanted free, unfettered outpourings that would evade any hierarchy in which one form of expression was more 'real', in the sense of conforming to standards, than any other. From now on 'reality' was that which came most naturally and with the least preparation.

Art, meanwhile, was one item in the long catalogue of liberationist-dionysiac essentials: 'The effect of culture', Nuttall wrote, 'has never been so direct and widespread as it is among the international class of disaffiliated young people, the provotariat. Consequently art itself has seldom been closer to its violent and orgiastic roots.'[2]

Art was a part of the heady cocktail of drugs, sex and revolutionary politics. Its role was either surgical, in cutting open the old order and exposing and removing its malignancies, or celebratory, a liberated howl of the new self, a self defined by its permanent and rapturous flux: 'We must reject the conventional fiction of "unchanging human nature",' Alexander Trocchi wrote, 'there is in fact no such permanence anywhere. There is only *becoming* . . .'[3]

William Blake was their hero. His life and art were taken to embody a romantic, visionary mythology. He was above all, a man, of childlike innocence of vision. For the idea of simplicity, of infantile spontaneity, in art as in all things, was central to this new radicalism. The idea that this movement sprang from 'the underground' as though in symbolic birth, that it somehow represented a paring down of man to his essentials as well as its curiously sentimental view of nature as evinced by Nuttall's 'of flowers and flowers and flowers' all suggested the possibility of an earlier, happier state. The retrieval of this condition appeared to offer the hope of some kind of international, mystic unity.

The infantilism and the innocence of the mystic were for a brief time taken into the slang of youth. The child's view formed the aesthetic basis of the Liverpool poets who emerged in the mid-1960s alongside the Liverpool pop groups. One of the most celebrated court cases of the era was the prosecution of *Oz* magazine for obscenity in its 'School Kids' issue. This was the hippie pose; for its adherents it evoked a world before 'the Bomb' had raised the possibility of sudden extinction. It was thus anti-scientific or, perhaps more accurately, anti-technological; though the technology of, for example, drugs was clearly acceptable as one route to self-liberation. Indeed, the self was to be pampered at all costs, for hippie politics were egocentric; they took it for granted that indulgence of the self was a moral and political act, a gesture of global significance.

'In so many ways it is now clear [Robert Nisbet wrote in 1972] this is what the culture of the 1950s and the 1960s was about: the self. Whether in radicalism, in literature, in the performing arts, in philosophy, psychology, music and art, not to mention sociology . . . the self, the autonomous self, the performing self, the contemplated self, *above all* the contemplated self – triumphed. It became of mounting concern as the 50s passed into the 60s to seek to strip the self of layers of socially-conferred role and identity in much the same way that on the stage intimacies of the body were stripped and exposed to the glare of the footlights.'[4]

The point about such an analysis is that it reveals the way the hippie programme enforced on both its adherents and its critics a curiously homogeneous view of the culture: Trocchi, Nuttall and Ginsberg would say the culture was in crisis and it was accepted. There seemed to be one issue and one conflict – between the radicals and the rest. The terms may frequently have been questioned but the importance of the analysis, the view that it represented some essential truth, was widely accepted. In part this is a result of both the vehemence and the resources available to the radicals. It was, after all, not simply a question of poetry readings, there were also flamboyantly dissident theatrical performances such as Peter Brook's *US*, about the Vietnam war, of which Frank Kermode wrote:

'As it is, the sole reason I can think of for urging anybody to see *US* is that it has some bearing on the strange crisis into which not our world but our theatre has somehow argued itself . . . It is useless to scream at us that the reason why we cannot distinguish between these "facts" and more comfortable fictions is that we own minis and wall-to-wall carpeting.'[5]

The 'strange crisis' was brought on by the way the hippie-political analysis seemed to succeed in polarizing the world into those for and those against revolutionary liberation. In part this was encouraged by the extraordinary vogue for youth that appeared in the 1960s. 'The young' became a political and social force whose views and prejudices were taken to be of immense significance. The decade had, after all, begun with an unusually youthful president of the USA: Kennedy. When he was assassinated in 1963, his age preoccupied the writers of the tributes: 'Here was a man', said a *Times* leader, 'only forty-six years old, boyish in looks, young in heart, eager and vigorous in spirit.'[6] Potentially, *The Times* thought, he was the first leader of the post-war generation. In the event, his death came to be seen as a terrible disaster visited specifically upon the young: the young, liberal, American dream had been destroyed.

Kennedy's career was taken to indicate that youthful idealism could be incorporated into mainstream politics. Afterwards, however, the idea was abandoned. Young politics came to mean something altogether too radical, yet none the less important. In establishing this position the young were helped by the existence of at least one external issue of unarguable significance: Vietnam. For the first time a war was brought into our homes by television and it was, undeniably, horrible and futile. Its imagery – the burnt bodies of which Travis dreamed in *If* – seemed absolute, an end to all arguments. The clean, bright technology of the American war machine was seen beside its effects: dirty, broken people. The radicals could also make much of the fact that we were implicated. The Prime Minister, Harold Wilson, supported American policy in South East Asia, so there did *seem* to be some connection between our minis and wall-to-wall carpets and the unending suffering of the Vietnamese. The innocent unity of the hippie dreams had its parallel in the international unity of guilt brought home to us by mass communications.

The success of the hippie issue, simply as an issue, thus thrived on the undermined confidence of its critics. The humanist-liberal modernists, who previously had carried the torch of a disciplined art that was the culmination of the Western traditions, found in the last analysis that they could only agree: Vietnam *was* horrible; the bomb existed; how could we pretend there was anything but a crisis demanding the most extreme response? And that response, from the hippies at least, was an extreme mystical tenderness which, carefully interpreted, could contain much respectability.

In 1968 David Holbrook wrote:

'What our society lacks is opportunities for us to complete our processes of growth, in terms of *being* by human contact, by love and sympathy, by creativity and modes of the "feminine element". Our society attaches the problem of identity to *doing* and *becoming*: to acquisitiveness, prowess, having and making, rather than to emotional richness, inner satisfaction, and inward peace. It therefore attaches identity to false male doing rather than to the female element of being I AM. It was this, I believe, that D. H. Lawrence saw; and it may even be what the hippies are groping towards.'[7]

Radical thinking was, in effect, calling the humanist bluff. Holbrook's 'may even be' was a phrase born of an uneasy sensation that perhaps the ground really was shifting under his feet, that perhaps the old bases of liberal judgement really were trivial. This would mean that the anguish and elitism attached to art were about to be exposed as unnecessary.

'At long long last "standards" went to the wind,'[8] Nuttall wrote of the proliferation of poetry magazines. Standards were the prison bars which had held humanism back from its true apotheosis – an undifferentiated orgy of self. The problem was that this orgy was all too easily revealed as having its own rigorous orthodoxy, a coercive system that recognized only the true path. Not surprisingly, among the artistic radicals of an earlier generation, this inspired a degree of unease.

'The society in which we live [Arnold Wesker said in a lecture at Birmingham] belongs to the Beatles not to Prokofiev. No matter how much you know that the depths stirred in you by a Prokofiev violin concerto are more profound than those stirred by a Beatle lament yet you cannot say this. You cannot say this because the moment you state your preference you immediately challenge the personality of the person whose preference you do not share. Especially for the younger generation who manifest their taste as a means of telling us what kind of people they are. And dare we say to all those lovely, arrogant young faces that after a while their music bores us, that the thoughts and emotion evoked by the music are shallow?'[9]

The childlike association of taste with personality, the elision of moral and aesthetic values, the general hippie impulse to draw everything together into one muddled but thrilling synthesis clearly threatened the existence of any hierarchies of quality. Yet equally the 'young faces' seemed to be everywhere and in control. They had taken over Alan Bennett's and Lindsay Anderson's public schools, but only the latter – and Wesker in the passage quoted – had detected the extent to which their regime was to be as arid, as issueless, as that of their former masters.

The mainstream hippie programme was parochial, juvenile and contradictory. Its curious blend of mysticism, politics and hedonism formed a quagmire of its own devising in which, inevitably, it drowned. Yet its attempt to requisition the idea of art to its cause represented a characteristic reaction of the age. It was a refusal of the ascetic pretensions of art in favour of something looser, more enjoyable and capacious enough to include all the popular manifestations of an age of mass culture. The definition of this type of art, however, leant heavily on a somewhat naïve and old-fashioned sentimentalism, complete with floral imagery, millenarian aspirations and a belief in a prelapsarian condition of innocence to which the righteous could aspire. This sentimentality was frequently concealed behind a bravura display of hard-headedness, but it is detectable as a kind of blind faith, even behind the thinking of the most devotedly avant-garde.

These, for example, are the words of Sean Kenny, the theatre designer:

'The ideal theatre is no kind of theatre. That is, no theatre in the sense of architectural or physical definitions ... I think to design a theatre today is simply to allow a space big enough for something to take place in ... I think the ideal theatre would be as big as you can get – cover the whole site with an aircraft hangar, as tall as you can afford, as wide as you can afford, as long as you can afford. And inside that you allow theatre to happen.'[10]

Kenny's space is the image of the liberationist ambitions of the age. It is empty yet replete with possibilities. It is big, an artificial universe made possible by inevitable economic growth and the benign application of technology. Finally it is undetermined; there are no 'architectural or physical definitions' to define or limit the possibilities of action. Liberated man would wander into this unencumbered space and create.

The Edge

The large-scale, celebratory adaptations of the arts by the 'underground' or the 'alternative society' were inspired by the sense that the old order was played out, it was time to change to something more open and free. The negative had a clear, answering positive: the world could be made better.

But the same negative insight could have far darker conclusions. What if the human psyche were irreparably damaged? What if the twentieth century and all its attendant woes had severed us far more completely from our human identity than we could possibly imagine? This bleak view was, in essence, that of A. Alvarez, a critic who evolved a theory based on the relationship between art and extreme experience: 'The movement of the modern arts', he wrote, 'has been to press deeper and deeper into the subterranean world of psychic isolation, to live out in the arts the personal extremism of breakdown, paranoia and depression . . .'[1]

For Alvarez there existed only the damage. Despair and suicide were the natural destinies of any modern artists. In the face of a world bereft of meaning, he was obliged to tunnel into himself and there confront the worst. Art constituted a 'living out' of this process and the supreme virtues of the artist were courage and clear-eyed sincerity to the last.

A familiar impatience lay behind this posture – the impatience of a man who wanted to make the arts do and mean something, but who could see nothing but limitation in the landscape of Little England. In poetry, in particular, the careful refusal of ambition and the provincialism of the Movement would tend to outrage a man of Alvarez's temperament. As if to drive the point home, the Movement had been followed by another determinedly low-profile group, possessed of a yet more self-effacing Englishness, and known, unamazingly, as 'the Group'. It was centred on Philip Hobsbaum at Cambridge, while its thinking was entirely dominated by the example of F. R. Leavis. The

Group stressed analysis and the clear, unsullied connection of language and feeling. Apart from Hobsbaum himself, its membership included George MacBeth, Peter Porter, Edward Lucie-Smith and Peter Redgrove. Its aspirations were wider than those of the Movement and its verse more ambitious, nevertheless it stood as yet another image of the marginal nature of the activity of poetry in a landscape that seemed to be changing uncontrollably and without regard to Leavisite critical formulations.

Redgrove, in particular, pushed Group discipline to the limit:

> Humming water holds the high stars
> Meteors fall through the great fat icicles.
> Spiders at rest from skinny leg-work
> Lean heads forward on shaggy lead-laces.[2]

Clearly this was language aspiring to be free of provincial considerations. And, indeed, MacBeth and Redgrove were included in the celebrated anthology *The New Poetry*, published in 1962, which Alvarez edited and used as a platform for his views on the necessary extremity of art.

Alvarez made it clear that the anthology was personal. It did not claim to be comprehensive, only to 'represent what I think is the most significant work of the British poets who began to come into their own in the fifties'.[3] His introduction was subtitled 'Beyond the Gentility Principle', and it adopted a tone of sceptical derision at the activities of the literary establishment. 'The reaction to Auden took the form of anti-intellectualism. He was thought to be too clever and not sufficiently emotional for the extreme circumstances of the forties. The war brought with it a taste for high, if obscure, rhetoric. The log-rolling thirties were followed by the drum-rolling forties . . .'[4] and so on. Alvarez then moves on to assault the Movement, most effectively by constructing a poem of his own out of lines taken from a number of different Movement poets to demonstrate the deadening unity of tone. 'This', he remarks, 'is the third negative feed-back: an attempt to show that the poet is not a strange creature inspired; on the contrary, he is just like the man next door – in fact he probably *is* the man next door.'[5]

Alvarez's own critical injunctions, in contrast, are more demanding:

'What, I suggest, has happened in the last half century is that we are gradually being made to realize that all our lives, even those of the most genteel and enislanded, are influenced profoundly by forces which have nothing to do with gentility, decency or politeness. Theologians would call these forces of evil, psychologists, perhaps, libido. Either way, they are the forces of disintegration which destroy the old standards of civilization. Their public faces are those of two world wars, of the concentration camps, of genocide and of the threat of nuclear war.'[6]

For Alvarez, a 'literary racket' and the complacency of the British had held our art back from its rightful place in the mainstream of his anguished version of modernism. Like the hippies, intoxicated by the horror of Vietnam, he could not avert his gaze from the great catastrophes of the century. They demanded an answering extremity from the artist.

Ted Hughes, Peter Redgrove's contemporary at Cambridge, turned this vision of a broken, terrifying world into a new and immensely popular poetic orthodoxy. Hughes was born in Yorkshire in 1930. In 1956, while at Pembroke College, Cambridge, he met and married the American poet Sylvia Plath. His first collection, *The Hawk in the Rain*, appeared in 1957. Plath, meanwhile, published her own first collection, *The Colossus*, in 1960 and *The Bell Jar*, a novel, in 1963. In that same year she committed suicide; a posthumous collection, *Ariel*, was published in 1965. Between them they were to have an almost incalculable effect on the British understanding of poetry. Indeed, each of them – Hughes the anguished contemplator of nature and Plath the woman hovering at the edge of sanity – came to represent a poetic type, perfect exemplars of the Alvarez thesis.

Hughes's first collection included a far wider range of stylistic influences than any of his later work, and the general tenor of these influences clearly announced that he would have no patience with Movement timidity. His poetic antecedents seemed to be Hopkins, Lawrence and Dylan Thomas rather than Hardy, and his subject

matter was not a blank, featureless landscape but a crushing, dangerous universe:

> A leaf's otherness,
> The whaled monstered sea-bottom, eagled peaks
> And stars that hang over hurtling endlessness,
> With manslaughtering shocks
>
> Are let in on his sense:
> So many a one has dared to be struck dead
> Peeping through his fingers at the world's ends,
> Or at an ant's head.[7]

Hughes's 'nature' is mechanical and pitiless. Thrushes on his lawn
are 'more coiled steel than living' and a snowdrop 'pursues her
ends/Brutal as the stars of this month.' In this world the 'I' of the
poems takes on a stunned, silent, observing role:

> A hoist up and I could lean over
> The upper edge of the high half-door,
> My left foot ledged on the hinge, and look in at the byre's
> Blaze of darkness: a sudden shut-eyed look
> Backward into the head.
> Blackness is depth
> Beyond star.[8]

The moment of a sudden intrusion of the world into the poet's
consciousness – in this case the sight of a bull – is placed alongside
the physical detail of the occasion. The process of looking over the
door is the dramatic holding of the breath prior to the delivery of the
insight. This is followed by the sensation of helpless otherness and
the anguish at the lack of any possible human connection: 'But the
square of sky where I hung, shouting, waving,/Was nothing to him;
nothing of our light/Found any reflection in him.'[9]

Over and over again Hughes's poetry documents this perceived gulf
between man and the world, this sense of humanist vertigo at the black
depths that have opened beneath our feet. Inevitably the inspiration led
him in the direction of myth:

'Any form of violence [he wrote] – any form of vehement activity –

invokes the bigger energy, the elemental power circuit of the Universe. Once the contact has been made it becomes difficult to control. Something from beyond ordinary human activity enters. When the wise men know how to create rituals and dogmas, the energy can be contained. When the old rituals and dogmas have lost credit and disintegrated, and no new ones have been formed, the energy cannot be contained, and so its effect is destructive – and that is the position with us. And that is why force of any kind frightens our rationalistic, humanist style of outlook. In the old world God and divine power were invoked at any cost – life seemed worthless without them. In the present world we dare not invoke them – we wouldn't know how to use them or stop them destroying us.'[10]

In essence this is a rather noisier version of Cyril Connolly's lack of a 'prevailing myth': the sense that, after religion, nothing can reconnect us to the world. Hughes's earlier verse dramatizes that sense, its success is to be judged by the accuracy with which we experience the dreadful otherness. But with *Crow*, published in 1970, he attempted something more. This is a fragmentary epic whose hero is a violent, intelligent bird, a survivor in an impossible landscape where 'God went on sleeping./Crow went on laughing.'[11] Even when awake God cannot function. His commands to Crow produce convulsions, more violence and hideous perversions of his wishes. This is a fable; for all their horror its scenes have a curious cartoon-like quality. We are being distanced from the mere contemplation of our severance from nature, we are being asked to contemplate a myth. It is a myth in the absence of all other myths, a myth of survival. It is presented in broken incantations, lurid catechisms and brief dramatizations. The intention is to reconnect us to the world through the intermediary of the terrible figure of Crow who, at least, can function, who does not feel the vertigo of the lost humanist.

The problem with Hughes's poetry is its persistently one-dimensional quality. In his determination to realize his vision, the verse becomes secondary, like make-up applied to the 'baddy' in a children's play to make him more frightening. There is thus a persistent sense of immaturity. Hughes appears to be living out nineteenth-century intellectual dramas of the loss of faith and values in the face of technology and evolution. His cry is that first instinctive one at the realization of the smallness of man in the universe or, more accurately, the cry of humanist anguish at the discovery that man's values cannot be found in the world.

The same anguish suffuses the poetry of Sylvia Plath but its realization in language is more complex, even if her poetic resources were never as fully developed as those of Hughes. Occasionally, however, in the earlier work it would be hard to tell the difference:

> Sand abraded the milkless lip.
> Cried then for the father's blood
> Who set wasp, wolf and shark to work,
> Engineered the gannet's beak.[12]

Gradually, a sinister, murmuring personal note began to intrude:

> This is a dark house, very big.
> I made it myself,
> Cell by cell from a quiet corner,
> Chewing at the grey paper,
> Oozing the glue drops.
> Whistling, wiggling my ears,
> Thinking of something else.[13]

Again the image is of an alien nature, but the voice is being emitted by the nature, not the observer, and there is a queasy precision about the language which is more than merely cosmetic. In *Ariel* this distinct externalization of the voice takes on the theatrical mode of a soliloquy: 'I'm no more your mother/Than the cloud that distils a mirror to reflect its own slow/Effacement at the wind's hand.'[14]

She also adopts nursery rhyme rhythms and taunting litanies that detail her own suicide attempts, but most of all she creates an increasingly cold and refined language to contain the psychotic stress which was finally to overwhelm her:

> The moon has nothing to be sad about,
> Staring from her hood of bone.
>
> She is used to this sort of thing.
> Her blacks crackle and drag.[15]

Alvarez called this later work her *real* poems. For him the poems in *The Colossus* were 'using her art to keep the disturbance, out of which she made her verse, at a distance'.[16] But for him the disturbance and the art had to be one:

'When Sylvia Plath died I wrote an epitaph on her in *The Observer*, at the end of which I said, "The loss to literature is inestimable." But someone pointed out to me that this wasn't quite true. The achievement of her final style is to make poetry and death inseparable. The one could not exist without the other. And this is right. In a curious way, the poems read as though they were written posthumously. It needed not only great intelligence and insight to handle the material of them, it also took a kind of bravery. Poetry of this order is a murderous art.'[17]

Happily, this bizarre and ghoulish episode in the history of criticism already looks extraordinarily dated. Plath can be seen to have had a sporadically brilliant poetic talent which, sadly, could never develop into mature art. In the event, she left behind a potent version of the romantic legend of the artist who died for her art. The final significance of both her and Hughes's work lies in the way they both attempted to evolve a poetic of the utterly personal, an impulse that, in spite of what Alvarez claimed, was in complete opposition to the primary inspiration of modernism. In the attempt, Hughes produced a drama of the confrontation of the shrunken humanist 'I' and its own failure to cope with the elementary 'givens' of a hundred years ago: the advance of science and the failure of religion. In Plath the same 'I' gradually disintegrated until every word was an axe, every poppy a bloodied mouth and every box a coffin.

The lure of myth and the need to produce a 'larger', more urgent poetry was felt elsewhere in the 1960s. Basil Bunting published his long poem *Briggflatts* in 1966. It is a literary curiosity in that it asserts the strong, regional identity of Bunting's Northumbrian background, yet does so through the means of Poundian modernism. But perhaps the most successful, and certainly now the most highly regarded of the decade's new poets, was Geoffrey Hill. Born in 1932, he published his first collection, *For the Unfallen*, in 1959 and subsequently *King Log* and *Mercian Hymns* in 1969 and 1971. Some of his broad themes as well as his repeated, and excessive, use of stark, physical effects he shares with Hughes: 'The second day I stood and saw/The osprey plunge with triggered claw,/Feathered blood along the shore,/To lay the living sinew bare.'[18]

Hill's verse is more supple and his preoccupation with myth as mediator in the world is more complex. Like Bunting, he also is heavily in debt to the tone of Ezra Pound: 'Ten years without you. For so it happens./Days make their steady progress, a routine/That is merciful and attracts nobody.'[19]

Mercian Hymns though, established the characteristic Hill tone, including myth and history in a curiously quizzical and ambiguous way that suggested a landscape still fleetingly possessed of ancient meanings:

> We gaped at the car-park of 'The Stag's Head' where a
> bonfire of beer-crates and holly-boughs whistled
> above the tar. And the chef stood there, a king in
> his new-risen hat, sealing his brisk largesse with
> 'any mustard?'[20]

Even more characteristic is the distinct tone of his meditations on religion:

> for the last rites of truth, whatever they are,
> or the Last Judgment which is much the same,
> or Mercy, even, with her tears and fire,
> he commends us to nothing, leaves a name
>
> for the burial-detail to gather up
> with rank and number, personal effects,
> the next-of-kin and a few other facts;
> his arm over his face as though in sleep.[21]

In Hill some of the difficulties of composing poetry in the climate of the day are confronted. His style is far from the trauma and psychosis of Hughes and Plath but, equally, it often seems constricted by its occasion, somehow restrained. It betrays the curious and continuing post-war crisis from which British poetry seems to suffer – an inability to find a firm footing either in the new or the old. Myth and contemporary psychosis were the attempts of the day to create an imaginative stability. In the end, however, they both seem to represent a marginal notion of the art, an acceptance of defeat in the face of the problem of the language now.

It Mystifies

The hippie liberationists' yearning for unity, though frequently vague and infantile, was an aspiration they shared with many others in the 1960s. Just as in the years immediately after the war there had been a vogue for books outlining grand historical and cultural syntheses, so in this period there was a fashion for sweeping summations. Often these came under the heading of 'alternative' explanations, an expression either of their political nature or of some magical or pseudo-scientific content. But the impulse was not confined to the margins: a combination of mass communications and the expansion of the higher educational system had created both the means and the demand for a way into culture, a democratization that was not necessarily accompanied by the threat of anarchy. Rather it seemed to offer a means of shoring up the shaky edifice of the West and its history.

Kenneth Clark's television series and book *Civilization* was the most spectacularly successful example. It was a romantic view of cultural history as a succession of geniuses, fruitfully interacting with the moving spirit and conditions of their age. Clark was no theorist, but he had the capacity to produce smooth and convincing descriptions of the changes from one age to the next. Even more seductive, these descriptions were couched in the prose of the educated connoisseur for whom the values of culture could not seriously be in question.

'There seems to be no reason why suddenly out of the dark, narrow streets there arose these light, sunny arcades with their round arches "running races in their mirth" under their straight cornices [he wrote of the Renaissance]. By their rhythms and proportions and their open, welcoming character they totally contradict the dark, Gothic style that preceded, and, to some extent, still surrounds them. What has happened? The answer is contained in one sentence by the Greek philosopher Protagoras, "Man is the measure of all things." '[1]

The content and the style were those of the humane liberal, and

213

presupposed a fraternity of reason for whom the values of the culture were absolute. Clark might observe that we happen to have the Sistine Chapel and the papal apartments because of the accident of an enlightened Pope in Julius II, indeed he might include acknowledgements of that very enlightenment in his summary of the intellectual climate of the Renaissance, but the works were isolated in their magnificence, free of such mundane considerations. They were products of genius, and genius romantically transcended all contingencies.

Yet surprisingly there was a pessimistic sub-text to *Civilization*. It became explicit in the final programme when Clark confronted his own age and admitted to a terrible uncertainty, which arose from his conviction that science, in its twentieth-century incarnation, had drained human imaginative energy away from art:

'For example [he said], Edison, whose inventions did as much as any to add to our material convenience, wasn't what we would call a scientist at all, but a supreme "do-it-yourself" man – the successor of Benjamin Franklin. But from the time of Einstein, Niels Bohr and the Cavendish Laboratory, science no longer existed to serve human needs but in its own right. When scientists could use a mathematical idea to transform matter they had achieved the same quasi-magical relationship with the material world as artists. Look at Karsh's photograph of Einstein. Where have we seen that face before? The aged Rembrandt.'[2]

Science, for Clark, had usurped the imaginative role of art. This disqualified him – a liberal heir of enlightened humanism – from maintaining for the present the role he had performed for the past. Indeed it seemed to disqualify every artist:

'For example, artists, who have been very little influenced by social systems, have always responded instinctively to latent assumptions about the shape of the universe. The incomprehensibility of our new cosmos seems to me, ultimately, to be the reason for the chaos of modern art. I know next to nothing about science, but I've spent my life in trying to learn about art, and I am completely baffled by what is taking place today.[3]

[And finally:] ' . . . good people have convictions, rather too many of them. The trouble is that there is still no centre. The moral and intellectual failure of Marxism has left us with no alternative to heroic materialism, and that isn't enough. One may be optimistic, but one can't exactly be joyful at the prospect before us.'[4]

So this extraordinary, massive picture-book and layman's guide turns out to be an uncomprehending gesture of humanist and romantic despair. The present does not seem able to produce the kind of society capable of sustaining the long procession of geniuses: 'There they are,' says Clark, 'you can't dismiss them.' His gentlemanly connoisseur's interpretation of the past still stands, but the future is anybody's guess.

The grand, falling cadence of Clark's concluding anxiety was a version of the growing conviction within the culture – manifested in a different form in Ted Hughes's invocation of a primitive, religious society – that certainty and harmony lay only in the past. He was broadcasting and writing at a time when the optimism of reconstruction and the belief in the possibilities of the modern had been superseded by conservation as well as the fear of anarchy and of cultural dissolution. The conviction that things had been good once but there was no certainty they would be good again became the contemporary version of the fear of the future once expressed by Mass Observation's 'working man'. By some, however, it could be seen as a hopelessly passive view; for them, the malaise Clark had detected could be diagnosed and treated, all that was required was a somewhat tougher view of history.

That view was Marxism. Its primary evangelist, at least in the art schools, was John Berger. Born in 1926 and educated at Chelsea School of Art and the Central School of Art, he had made his name in the 1950s with his reviews in the *New Statesman* in defence of neo-realism and his insistence on the need for art to serve social ends. His influence, especially in art education, was enormous. Clark may have had popular impact, but Berger provided the critical orthodoxy for the art students.

He also produced a television series and a book – both appeared almost as correctives to *Civilization* – *Ways of Seeing*, which appeared in book form in 1972. It was a Marxist critique utterly opposed to Clark's pantheon of towering geniuses: 'In the end, the art of the past is being mystified because a privileged minority is striving to invent a history which can retrospectively justify the role of the ruling classes, and such a justification can no longer make sense in modern terms. And so, inevitably, it mystifies.'[5]

Berger then turned to consideration of the Leonardo da Vinci cartoon *The Virgin and Child with St Anne and St John*, which made news because of a huge American bid to buy it and take it out of England:

'Now it hangs in a room by itself. The room is like a chapel. The drawing is behind bullet-proof perspex. It has acquired a new kind of impressiveness. Not because of what it shows – not because of the meaning of its image. It has become impressive, mysterious, because of its market value.

'The bogus religiosity which now surrounds original works of art, and which is ultimately dependent upon their market value, has become the substitute for what paintings lost when the camera made them reproducible. Its function is nostalgic. It is the final empty claim for the continuing values of an oligarchic, undemocratic culture. If the image is no longer unique and exclusive, the art object, the thing, must be made mysteriously so.'[6]

Berger's materialism was not new. The analysis of art as part of the fabric of bourgeois mystifications had been a familiar element of all Marxist criticism. Its new-found potency, however, derived in part from the clarity and polemical force of Berger's style, but mainly from the way it seemed to bring together a variety of impulses. The Marxist sense that society is somehow so profoundly wrong, so stricken with injustice and contradiction, that it must be a transitional phase before the onset of something better, clearly relates to the assumption of a depraved establishment that lay behind other forms of 'alternative' thought as well as in the 1960s image of the corrupt and absurd public school. In addition, Berger seemed to affirm the view that this corruption was coming to a head – the inflated price of a drawing was taken as evidence of terminal rot within the system. For the artist, the penalty of living in such a system was the commitment to a troubled awareness of form and to the role of the dissident, a man cast out by his own awakening historical self-consciousness. This is an important redefinition of Clark's ideal genius, not as a man sailing in the clouds, far above the petty concerns of his age, but as a representative figure torn by the contradictions of his task.

'From the tradition a kind of stereotype of "the great artist" has emerged. This great artist is a man whose life-time is consumed by a struggle: partly against material circumstances, partly against incomprehension, partly against himself. He is imagined as a kind of Jacob wrestling with an Angel . . . In no other culture has the artist been thought of in this way. Why then in this culture? We have already referred to the exigencies of the open market. But the struggle was not only to live. Each time a painter realized he was dissatisfied with the limited role of painting as a celebration of the material prosperity and of the status that accompanied it, he inevitably found himself struggling with the very language of his own art as understood by the tradition of his calling.'[7]

In this analysis the romantic idea of the artist as a man in constant – and previously mysterious – struggle arose because of his realization that he was being asked to do so little. He was battling against the impotence of the materials at hand to do anything but glorify the prevailing economic order. For Berger the artistic material that best expressed this impotence was oil paint, whose subtleties and sensuality provided the ideal means of realizing the ideology of possession. Significantly Berger uses Blake, the hippie hero, as an example at this point. He was an artist who seldom used oil, preferring instead materials that would 'make his figures lose substance, to become transparent and indeterminate one from the other, to defy gravity, to be present but intangible, to glow without a definable surface, not to be reducible to objects'.[8]

Berger and Clark in effect nourished each other. Both subscribed to a romantic ideal of the artist as supreme exemplar and focusing lens of the forces of his age, both saw the time as being ripe for a single, grand, cultural summary and yet both saw their age as being deeply flawed – Clark in the impoverishment of the arts by science's invasion of their imaginative territory, and Berger in its decadent bourgeois defence of art's inherent, pseudo-mystical value. But their perceptions of society's problems came from art: both remained within the confines of a high-art ghetto, far removed from festivities such as the poetry reading at the Albert Hall.

Germaine Greer, though an academic, produced a much more influential cultural synthesis from an entirely different starting point. *The Female Eunuch* was published in 1970. Greer, an Australian, was at the time teaching in the English Department at Warwick University as well as supporting and contributing to a number of 'underground' magazines such as *Oz* and *Suck*. The latter connections are evident in the style of the book's five dedications, with their evocations of life on the margin: 'It is for Kasoundra, who makes magic out of skins and skeins and pens, who is never still, never unaware, riding her strange destiny in the wilderness of New York, loyal and bitter, as strong as a rope of steel and as soft as a sigh.'[9] Similarly, a good deal of the book's vehement, prescriptive quality owes much to the earnest, arrogant proselytizing of the underground: 'If you think you are emancipated, you might consider the idea of tasting your menstrual blood – if it makes you sick, you've a long way to go, baby.'[10]

Greer's diagnosis and prescriptions were a good deal tougher and more precise than anything that had come from the rest of the underground. Society was flawed for her too, but this time the systematic, blind and unthinking oppression of women was to blame. Humanity was brutalized and corrupted by tragic discontinuities between the sexes. The first feminist wave, the suffragettes, had fought this through existing political institutions but Greer's second wave wanted to overthrow those institutions: 'The sight of women talking together has always made men uneasy; nowadays it means rank subversion. "Right on!"'[11]

With a combination of scholarship and visionary conviction, Greer then proceeds to produce a polemical dissection of the nature of society and its sexual politics. Her style seemed deliberately aimed at subverting the virtue of supposed 'objectivity' of male scholarship – it was adjectival, opinionated and relentless. Above all, it assumed that some momentous change was taking place in which the nature of human life would be fundamentally altered. For example, she speaks of feminine modes of thought, assisted by the machine culture, as potentially able to take over the world:

'The take-over by computers of much vertical thinking has placed more and more emphasis on the creative propensities of human thought. The sudden increase in political passion in the last decade, especially among the generation which has absorbed most of its education in this undifferentiated form, bears witness to a reintegration of thought and feeling happening on a wide scale. In the circumstances any such peculiarity of the female mind could well become a strength.'[12]

The 'reintegration of thought and feeling' evokes the millenarian wishful thinking of the underground, but it also reveals the instinct of the age for vast generalization, aimed at encompassing and rendering comprehensible every possible development. Greer is subsuming all the conflicts that had been defined by others – between feeling and dry philosophy, between socialism and capitalism, between art and science – into one conflict between the male and female influences in society. The effect of this simplification is to concentrate the mind on the 'real' issue, it allows us to see 'through' the illusions of the world. Inevitably this conviction – that there is one overriding reality behind all the exigencies of the world – takes on religious overtones:

'The love of fellows is based upon understanding and therefore upon communication. It was love that taught us to speak, and death that laid its finger on our lips. All literature, however vituperative, is an act of love, and all forms of electronic communication attest the possibility of understanding. Their actual power in girdling the global village has not been properly understood yet. Beyond the arguments of statisticians and politicians and other professional cynics and death makers, the eyes of a Biafran child have an unmistakable message. But while electronic media feed our love for our own kind, the circumstances of our lives substitute propinquity for passion.'[13]

The Biafran child was the disseminated image of suffering; it was reminiscent of the burnt bodies of Travis's apocalyptic visions in *If.* With the images of Vietnam, it provided Greer and many others with an unarguable absolute of innocent suffering caused by a great evil in which we were all implicated. Guilt was everywhere at that time. The conviction that great cultural and political summaries were possible was accompanied by the belief that everything was connected: the fitted carpets and the napalm that burned the Vietnamese peasants. Society was grossly flawed by some original sin in which we all shared, but the times were changing rapidly, a new Jerusalem was being constructed. The very fact that we could see, nightly on television news, the sufferings of the Biafrans or the Vietnamese and that technology was girdling the earth would transform the nature of the human soul. The hour was late, we must stand up and be counted.

'The old process must be broken,' concluded Greer, 'not made new. Bitter women will call you to rebellion, but you have too much to do. What *will* you do?'[14]

Unspoken Nets

The practical, active demands in *The Female Eunuch* were yet at odds with the vaguely hippie-like mysticism at the heart of the work: Greer's dream of reintegration. Equally, Berger's Marxism had a disconcertingly open-ended quality: it inspired a pervasive sense of dissatisfaction, but it was unclear how this could be taken any further other than into the grim landscape of ideologically determined art. But there was no doubt that such large-scale cultural thinking suggested an absolutely precise role for art: as part of the mechanism of social change. In doing so it implicitly threw the question of form back into the melting pot, but at least content was potentially stable. Marxism or feminist revolution was there to fill the moral, aesthetic and religious voids. Here was something to write, paint or compose *about*.

In the academies, however, a more systematic form of aesthetic radicalism had taken root. It was broadly related to the grand ambitions and revolutionary posturing of the 1960s, but its intellectual pedigree was far more intimidating and its impact more lasting and profound.

Structuralism can be related to the twentieth-century preoccupation with the nature of language: with the form rather than with the subject of discourse. In essence it is inspired by the insight that the world consists not of discrete objects but of relations:

'Our sensibility (or range of possible experiences, or capacity to conceptualise) has its limits and its *structure* [explained Ernest Gellner], and these limits and the principles which generate them, though we may not be able to observe them directly, we can hope to reconstruct from the range of material found within any one mind or work or language or culture.'[1]

The universe of traditional science consisted of a mass of *things*. Human knowledge advanced into this realm, the known gradually annexing the unknown. This meant that it could aspire to completion, when all things and their interactions had been observed and catalogued. Such a catalogue, in describing the things of the universe, would describe the entire universe.

In a variety of fields this view was potentially challenged by modern thought. In physics, quantum mechanics and the uncertainty principle made it clear that our knowledge could never be complete. The very act of observation transformed the reality we wished to describe. Meanwhile, psychoanalysis turned the entire scientific project inward while modernism in the arts undermined the stability of the objective world-picture. All this tended to draw attention to the observer rather than the observed. The truth of the world could be seen to reside less and less in a universe of matter *out there*, rather it must be definable only in the relationship between the observer and the observed, between *out there* and *in here*. More fully, it could be said that the observed did not exist at all: the only reality was the system of relationships through which we constructed it. Nothing could exist by itself, only by its relationship to other things, by its position in a structure.

Thus the only possible objects of study are these structures, which must contain all that we can know, and their investigation must one day reveal the 'permanent structures of the mind itself'.[2] Language is of course the primary structure, and structuralism was most successful in linguistics and literary criticism.

The history of modern structuralism is generally taken to begin with the Swiss linguist Ferdinand de Saussure (1857–1913). His ideas were crystallized in a series of lectures delivered at Geneva between 1907 and 1911, which were published in 1915, on the basis of notes taken by students, as *Cours de linguistique générale*. In this he outlined a view of language as a system of arbitrarily determined signs: there was no 'real' relationship between the word 'table' and the object it described, the one was merely assigned to the other. Such a sign could be understood only by its place in the structure of language as a whole. Language thus became a field, a network of relations, rather than simply a vast mound of words. We do not possess, create or invent this field, we inhabit it; it exists outside us. Saussure then made his celebrated distinction between *langue*, the whole system of language, and *parole* – the particular utterances arising from that system. On this distinction hinged the whole anti-empirical thrust of structuralism: *parole*, the empirical manifestation of language, was only half the story; the rest was the vast, unspoken net of *langue*. 'One way of approaching the fashionable doctrine of *structuralisme*', wrote Gellner, 'is to see that it is a *denial* of the empiricist theory of mind, of this echo or after-taste theory of human ideas.'[3]

Finally, even history was a victim of Saussure's analysis. He distinguished between diachronic and synchronic study of language: the first considered its historical development and is customarily described by the term 'philology'; the second considered language at one particular moment and is generally called 'linguistics'. Since the present system could be seen to contain within its fabric all its previous incarnations, linguistics rather than philology was given pride of place.

The same preoccupations were developed in a purely literary critical context by Russian formalist critics, such as Roman Jakobson, whose work was aimed at decoding systems of narrative and expression which were distinctively literary. With Claude Lévi-Strauss, structuralism invaded the realm of anthropology but finally, and most importantly for these present purposes, it became – with the related study of semiotics and in the writings of Roland Barthes – an elaborate and seemingly unchallengeable critical orthodoxy.

The importance of this orthodoxy lies, first, in its assault on its immediate predecessors and, second, in the implications of its own style and methods. The preceding orthodoxy, at least in Britain and the USA, was that of the New Criticism. For years this had been the prevailing ideology behind the teaching of literature and, indeed, behind the growth of literature as a subject of academic study. It is difficult to generalize about its theoretical position as it was inspired by an attitude rather than a programme, but its personnel were clear enough: critics such as F. R. Leavis, I. A. Richards, T. S. Eliot, William Empson, Yvor Winters and Cleanth Brooks. In the universities it dominated the teaching of several generations of students, and its critical approach determined the nature of literature in schools. However diverse the opinions of its practitioners, they were agreed on its primary aim: to establish the abiding importance of literary studies and their viability as an academic discipline.

Its emphasis was on the close reading of a text on its own terms. Wider references – to the author's biography, to the old tradition of literary history – were seen as either secondary or irrelevant to the thematic analysis of the text itself. Its tool was practical criticism and its goal was the formation of judgements that would create a hierarchy of significance. It was empirical in inclination and moralistic in intent.

The New Criticism, however, never quite constituted a coherent school of thought. Possibly this arose from the sheer oddity of its central demand that a work of art should be approached in some kind of condition of innocence, a pristine purity of perception. As Richard Wollheim remarked, 'it is hard to attach much sense to such an extreme demand'. But it is clear that this critical purism could be linked to the modernist rejection of the vagaries of late romanticism in favour of something harder and clearer. It was an act of cleansing, a gesture against the metaphysical clutter that had adhered to literary studies. Yet, in the work of its most influential practitioner, Leavis, the New Criticism was to develop vagaries of its own as he fought to maintain its moral and social justifications. His shoring up of the virtues of close critical scrutiny and 'evaluation' led him into a distinctly romantic view of society and history, far removed from the hard, clear light of the original modernist inspiration.

By Barthes's time, structuralism and semiotics could not have represented a more different view of literature and the world. Semiotics – the science of signs – had developed out of structuralism, a method of interpreting the world as a system of signs. Like words, these bore an arbitrary relation to the objects of perception, so their understanding could be achieved only through a study of their relationships. For practitioners like Barthes, semiotics provided a kind of vast, structuralist playground in which systems of 'signification' from fashion to food could be analysed indefinitely. Barthes's languid delectation of his subject matter inspired a proliferation of writing supposedly aimed at decoding the world. From literature it spread through journalism in the form of fashionable 'style' writing, which aspired to endow the ephemera of culture with urgent significance.

The central point of this radical form of analysis for the purposes of its conflict with the New Criticism was that it dismissed almost all previous claims that had been made for the literary text itself. The work of art, the text, was simply another code to be deciphered; its existence in the world was an expression of its relationship to myriad other such codes. It did not represent a culturally set-apart object to be approached with all the purity and innocence we could muster, rather it was an object of artifice, demanding the utmost in worldly sophistication from its audience. Even more shocking for the old establishment was structuralism's dismissal of the idea of the unique authorial self. The text was another *parole* derived from the pervasive *langue*; to speak of it being written by some uniquely significant individual was misleading. It was more true to see the author as being 'written' by the text.

The most devastating expression of this position came in Barthes's book *S/Z*, in which he analysed the Balzac short story 'Sarrasine'. He proceeded by breaking down every element in the story into one of five codes: the hermeneutic, the code of semes or signifiers, the symbolic code, the proairetic code and the 'cultural' code. The effect was akin to dipping the story in a bath of acid. Any sense of 'realism' was dissolved to reappear as simply a system of distorting and manipulating devices. The truth of Balzac's method was not that it represented a window on the world, rather that it represented a structure the contemplation of which could only show us its own workings. To speak of a single, creating genius with a definite creative intention had become absurd.

The whole process became yet more radical with post-structuralism and the works of men such as Jacques Derrida and Jacques Lacan. This produced the critical method known as 'deconstruction' in which every text was automatically assumed to undermine itself and the critic's task was to 'deconstruct' it for the purpose of revealing the entire process. Lacan, a psychoanalyst, saw the whole landscape of *langue* as analogous to the Freudian notion of the subconscious: both had form without substance.

Post-structuralism was a logical enough outcome. Structuralism claimed to have revealed the arbitrary nature of all signs and the overriding importance only of their relationships, but it still depended on the fixed position of the observer, the critic, whose assumptions and psychology would necessarily colour any of his interpretations. It depended on the idea of meaning. Post-structuralism attempted to remove even this fixed point to leave the world a shifting, impersonal mass of systems. Meaning, in this context, was simply a polite fiction. In reality, it could only ever be perpetually deferred.

Neither programme could mean anything to the humanists and empiricists of the New Criticism. Structuralism presented the world and literature as a mass of arbitrary signs drawn into systems of our own creation, beyond which we could not see and the study of which tended only inwards, to reveal the patterns of our own mind. The processes of literature and those of criticism were much the same in this view, and any idea that either the critic or the artist were, in any sense, interpreting the world for our benefit was absurd.

'Barthes's importance for literary criticism, then, [George Wasserman wrote] consists less in his individual literary pronouncements than in the example of his practice in which we see no criticism manages to escape the problematics that it exists to make plain. In perhaps no other critic are we made more aware that the critical act is an act of writing, guided not by the meaning of the object, but by the desire of the subject, and involved, therefore, in the fate of all the writing in the world.'[4]

Writing was an expression of desire. For Barthes it was an erotic act, barren in that it could not escape the systems, but infinitely fertile in the variations of the methods which it could penetrate those systems.

Culturally, the contrast between the New Criticism and structuralism represented the latest flowering of an old opposition. On the one hand was the Anglo-Saxon tradition, empirical and mistrustful of systems and theories. It was ever open to the appeal of common sense, and took as its starting point the central importance of 'the humanities' within the culture. Indeed, the work of Leavis was underpinned by the conviction that the study of literature took precedence over all other studies. On the other hand, structuralism was predominantly French. It was rationalist in the extreme and it believed that the world consisted of nothing but systems. Common sense could only be a bizarre concept and there were no means of establishing that one activity was more important than another, or indeed that one work was 'greater' than another. The ruthlessness of the approach contrasted with the British faith in literature as such, a faith that George Steiner felt sprang from an excessively narrow education system:

'For even this deeply responsible "classical" tradition of textual under-standing will be almost intractable to those whose training for literature has been essentially monoglot, and to those who have grown up in a climate of sensibility largely untouched by Kant, by Hegel, by Marx. It is just in this situation that planned parochialism may strike one as the last refuge of professional bankruptcy.'[5]

In the final extremity of post-structuralism there was little you could say about the ideology at all, precisely because of the inclusive circularity of its methods. Clearly, however, it was anti-humanist in that it discarded the ethical as an element of critical insight. But, most important, it was scientific in intent. Its constant recourse to elaborate categories and lists of codes betrays this central impulse towards a method as tough as science was perceived to be. Texts or signs were studied like organisms under a microscope or particles in an acceler-ator – not special in themselves but simply as samples from a universal structure.

The importance of this scientific parallel to structuralists themselves is revealed by the image used by critic and novelist David Lodge to explain the impact it had upon critical thought:

'Literary criticism is at present in a state of crisis which is partly a consequence of its own success. One might compare the situation to that of physics after Einstein and Heisenberg: the discipline has made huge intellectual advances, but in the process has become incompre-hensible to the layman – and indeed to any professionals educated in an older, more humane tradition.'[6]

Compare this to Kenneth Clark's admission of ignorance before the edifice of science. Clark could not contain science within his imaginative framework, though he thought he could see the signifi-cance of its achievements: it appeared to represent the ending of the humane study of art as a source of human knowledge. But the structuralists were attempting to force an aesthetic posture into a scientific mould. Behind Lodge's words one can hear the wishful thinking, the longing for a discipline as hermetic and impersonal as those of relativity and quantum mechanics. More brazenly this em-phasis inspired a form of scientific triumphalism. Edmund Leach, an anthropologist who had done much to bring the works of Lévi-Strauss to a British audience, delivered the Reith Lectures in 1968: 'Men have become like gods,' he said. 'Isn't it time to recognise our divinity? . . . the family with its narrow privacy and tawdry secrets is the source of all our discontents.'[7]

The old, closed, dark 'human' world could be swept aside by the new scientific deities. The aspiring science of structuralism was thus, in the arts or in anthropology, tougher minded than anything that had gone before. The New Criticism's roots were perceived to be embedded in romanticism, in the idea of an organic society and of organic form. It took what structuralists would call a diachronic view of art, a view that focused empirically on each manifestation and traced its historical antecedents to form a tradition. From this springs Leavis's 'great tradition' of the English novel or Eliot's view of tradition as the map in which the individual talent locates and defines itself. In contrast the structuralist effort was synchronic and its roots lay in the classical study of rhetoric, which treated language as a subject in itself rather than as a window on the world. Having been born in reaction to the vagueness of late romantic literary thought, the New Criticism thus found itself usurped by a movement making even harder, more rigorous, more classicist claims.

The critic Jonathan Culler summarized the difference: 'The synchronic study of language is an attempt to reconstruct the system as a functional whole, to determine, shall we say, what is involved in knowing English at any given time: whereas diachronic study of language is an attempt to trace the historical evolution of its elements through various stages.'[8]

So the structuralist is anti-history; for him it is another code embedded in the central system of language. The same applies to categories of meaning: a single meaning – a religious or moral sub-text – is simply another code. What is at issue is the nature of meaning itself, how it is encoded and transmitted, not the investigation of a single meaning supposedly intended by an author. All of which leads to the final and, for many, the most unpalatable consequence of structuralism: the abolition, together with the idea of the author, of the idea of the 'subject'. Since Descartes Western thought has focused on the self as the active principle behind the process of endowing the world with meaning; but if the system which the self is obliged to inhabit is the prime generator of meaning, the centrality of the self, the subject, becomes another polite fiction:

'But once the conscious subject is deprived of its role as a source of meaning [Jonathan Culler wrote] – once the meaning is explained in terms of conventional systems which may escape the grasp of the conscious subject – the self can no longer be identified with consciousness. It is "dissolved" as its functions are taken up by a variety of interpersonal systems that operate through it. The human sciences, which began by making man an object of knowledge, find, as their work advances, that "man" disappears under structural analysis.'[9]

The analysis of structure destroys all illusions of solidity. We are born into structures which pre-date us and will survive our death. Even the reduced existential individual, self-creating and self-moralizing, is dissolved in the acid bath of analysis. This same hard, visionary dissolution was expressed by Peter Ackroyd in his 1976 essay *Notes for a New Culture* as a specific corrective to what he identified as a persistent English refusal to face up to the implications of modernism:

'How is this modernism to be best expressed [he asked]? Perhaps it can be described as a sense of freedom. We no longer invest created forms with our own significance and, in parallel, we no longer seek to interpret our own lives in the factitious terms of art. Artistic forms are no longer to be conceived of as paradigmatic or mimetic. Our lives return to their own space, outside interpretation and extrinsic to any concern for significance or end. I might put this differently by suggesting that it is the ability of literature to explore the problems and ambiguities of a formal absoluteness which we will never experience. For these forms seem to proclaim the death of Man.'[10]

Yet structuralism was not the only linguistic system that threatened the stable role of the humanities in our culture. In the USA the linguist Noam Chomsky had proposed a 'generative grammar' in which 'deep structure' rules of grammar would produce all the possible sentences within a language. His work began from the mental operations which produced language and was thus intrinsically more dynamic in approach than structuralism with its primarily aesthetic emphasis. Where the structuralists would produce endless lists and diagrams, Chomsky seemed to be dealing more directly with the operations of the mind. The two approaches were not actually incompatible, but it was clear that structuralist linguistics had not cornered the market in rigour.

Chomsky's insights were linked to a more profound problem for structuralists: the post-structuralists' rejection of their effort as being insufficiently radical – for, however scientific structuralism might pretend to be, it remained centred upon the analysing self. Chomsky's view of the individual as possessing 'linguistic competence', an ability to generate new sentences from the resources of the grammar, and the classical structuralist view of him as a set of systems to be decoded, both represented serious compromises. They avoided the central truth laid down by Saussure: the arbitrary nature of the sign itself. The connection between signifier and signified was an accident of the culture. Any degrading of this arbitrariness was bad faith, a submission to a repressive ideology. For thinkers like Derrida and Julia Kristeva, the effort should be made to abandon the entire 'metaphysics of presence' whereby signs, signifiers and signified could ever be made stable and complete. Instead, the nature of the systems themselves should be adopted – protean, impersonal and wholly beyond our control. The post-structuralist aspired to a condition of permanent change. For Culler, however, this represented a submission to 'the myth of the innocence of becoming', the view that 'continual change, as an end in itself, is freedom, and that it liberates one from the demands that could be made of any particular state of the system'.[11]

The ideological condition of post-structuralism bears obvious similarities to the less articulate aspirations towards ultimate freedom heard elsewhere in the 1960s. Indeed, much of the attraction of this type of hard, radical theorizing can be seen to be its value as a weapon against the authoritarian armies of the recent past. Structuralism's tough rejection of humanist vagaries parallels the hippie rejection of order and the glorification of a condition of perpetual becoming, the Marxist rejection of bourgeois values and even Orton's rejection of morals and meaning. For Ackroyd it became a rejection of the loathed insularity of Little England. Structuralists themselves tended to interpret their movement in the widest possible context, at one with political and social developments throughout the world. Indeed such an interpretation lay in the very nature of structuralism because of its own insistence on the completeness of its explanation.

'The attitudes implicit in New Criticism itself [Terence Hawkes wrote] may, in turn, be said to have been influential on the "real foundations". How many, one wonders, of the civil servants, the teachers, the journalists who generate the climate of opinion that ultimately shapes the actions of politicians and generals, derive at least some elements in their total view of life from experiences whose essence is literary? Mass literacy, and an education system firmly based on it, has tended in twentieth century Europe and America to establish and reinforce an equation between literature and life that would have astonished any preceding age. When that equation comes, through the mediation of literary criticism, to acquire positive prescriptive force in respect of morality, politics, even economics, and when its presuppositions find themselves transmitted at large and unquestioned throughout an all-embracing system of education, then it seems reasonable to expect that "crises" in one area will find themselves mirrored in another.

'Eventually, the sense of crisis proves to be the agency which gener-ates the need for change. When liberal humanism in America and Western Europe encountered the series of debilitating post-war crises of conscience that ran from Algeria to Suez to Vietnam, the criticism which sustained that humanism, and which was sustained by it, was similarly shaken. In short the students who rejected liberal politics in the nineteen-sixties as a mystified game, rejected liberal (so-called "practical") criticism as part of the same package. It seemed no less of a game: literally ludicrous.'[12]

It was all one: the fitted carpet and the napalm. You could not take one part of the package and reject the rest. Structuralism revealed the world as a seamless, interacting system of systems. It had become, in the universities, the single most sustained and systematic response to humanism. Its role as a literary-critical tool could not be contained. The belief that the world was no more than a system of relations meant that there were no discrete parts that could be isolated for the purpose of study. Literary criticism was one with Suez. The attraction is obvious. Here was an orthodoxy without limits. Like eighteenth-century science it seemed to be a form of knowledge within which, finally, all would be encompassed. On the way the analytical and deconstructive processes could produce an infinity of delights. The supremely hedonistic Barthes had already shown the way with his brief, glittering essays on striptease, cars or anything else that caught his eye. Furthermore, the very nature of the structuralist effort created a hermetic liturgy, a novel and exotic vocabulary of phonemes, lexias, grammatology and actantial models, which seemed to offer to the elect the comforts of both religion and science: both salvation and understanding.

In spite of the success of this onslaught, however, the mainstream Anglo-American view resisted. Susan Sontag, for example, admired Barthes enormously, but her terms are interesting:

'For all his contributions to the would-be science of signs and structures, Barthes's endeavour was the quintessentially literary one: the writer organizing under a series of doctrinal auspices, the theory of his own mind. And when the current closure of his reputation by the labels of semiology and structuralism crumbles, as it must, Barthes will appear, I think, as a rather traditional *promeneur solitaire*, and as a greater writer than even his most fervent admirers now claim.'[13]

So, freed of the modish intellectual category in which he placed himself, Barthes will be restored to the very literary tradition which he had so eloquently attempted to deconstruct.

Meanwhile, in England the clash between structuralism and the old humanist study of literature erupted publicly in 1981. An assistant lecturer at Cambridge University, Colin MacCabe, was denied a permanent post. He was a structuralist in opposition to the old orthodoxy of the Cambridge English School as codified by critics like I. A. Richards and Leavis. The socialist Raymond Williams made a quiet appeal for a plurality of approach, but MacCabe left and humanism prevailed.

The artist, amid all this, could be forgiven for believing the critics were muscling in on his territory. The art critic Edward Lucie-Smith voiced the standard complaint of the old humanist-modernist and pleaded for intellectual leadership to be taken back from the critics and put in the hands of the artists:

'There is at the moment in the English art world, as in the world of the United States, a tendency for people to make themselves into amateur scientists. A lecture on linguistics will arouse the enthusiastic attention of the art public to a greater extent than a talk about some aspect of the visual arts. This betrays an impatience with what the artists themselves are providing, a loss of faith which is, I think, without parallel. It will be interesting to see if the artists, so long the leaders of the modern movement, the very vanguard of the avant-garde, will be able to reassert the claim to primacy which seems to be rapidly slipping away from them.'[14]

Prancing Mortals

The artist appeared to be losing the initiative. The ambitions and pretensions of the critical theorists suggested that analysis was taking over the task of art. Beneath the hard gaze of structuralism, to be an artist was of no more significance than to be a writer of advertising copy or a railway worker.

Critical theory thus had something of the same impact as analytical philosophy: it was seen as cold, inhuman, anti-imaginative and reductive. It threatened to trap the artist in a net of ideas and analysis which would make action all but impossible, and induced a paralysing self-consciousness. One was constantly catching oneself in the act, de-constructing the moment of creation. This seemed – again like analytical philosophy – to confine the excitement of the structuralist enterprise to the converted. From the outside, it appeared remote and its relentless circularity suggested that the history of ideas was becoming exhausted, futile. Meanwhile, those who still longed for the old emotional and humane satisfactions of art were being soft-headed.

Yet, in itself, this sense of the exhaustion of ideas could be seen to affirm the mannerist mode of the age. Artistic forms and styles had become playgrounds, stripped of significance beyond themselves. Equally, ideas, reason itself, seemed to be turning away from the warm sanity of humanism. Man, having made himself the measure of all things during the Renaissance and the Enlightenment, now found he was the measure of nothing, at best a by-product of his own systems.

This produced a kind of vertigo, a sick fascination with the abyss created by the death of Man as an object of knowledge and study. In Tom Stoppard's plays there is a constant attempt to ground the drama in this abyss, to start again on new territory. In his 1967 radio play *Albert's Bridge*, his hero leads a team of men engaged on the continual painting of a bridge. Four of them can manage the task in two years. That is precisely how long the paint lasts so, at the end of the period, all four must start again. But a new paint that lasts eight years is produced; if Albert now works alone, he will be continually employed. Being a philosophy graduate, it is a job he loves: it is whole, logical, self-justifying. In the event, he does not finish the painting in the allotted time and an army of painters is sent in to help him. They march on to the bridge in step and the pounding rhythm of their feet causes the entire structure to collapse. Albert has been fatally drawn by the attractions of an impersonal mathematical mechanism that finally proves disastrously defective.

As an image the play leans heavily on the work of Samuel Beckett, an Irish playwright who had been a disciple of James Joyce before the war. Possessed of immense learning and an austere and bleak personality, he had defended the literary innovations of his mentor and the radical ambitions of modernism against what he saw as the pointless propagation of the old myth of expression: 'What is the good of passing from one untenable position to another, of seeking justification always on the same plane?'[1] For Beckett the work of art's role in the world was exhausted; its repertoire of devices and stratagems had been revealed as a history of delusion. All that was left was the artist's incomprehensible obligation to paint, write or whatever and the mystery of the artistic occasion: 'All that should concern us is the acute and increasing anxiety of the relation itself, as though shadowed more and more darkly by a sense of invalidity, of inadequacy, of existence at the expense of all that it excludes, all that it blinds to.'[2]

Beckett's own art began with short stories and poems and, in 1938, the novel *Murphy*, a virtuoso assault on the dialogue, narrative and characterization of conventional fiction. After the war he began writing in French and making his own translations into English. This method produced the play *Waiting for Godot*, first staged in England in 1955. Its success and its influence were enormous. With it and with successive plays Beckett established a dramatic language – comic and coldly beautiful – that influenced to some extent almost every succeeding British playwright. His novels, meanwhile, tightened their focus on the smaller and smaller residues of consciousness, his characters spinning endless monologues out of increasingly extreme and incomprehensible situations and against the background of featureless yet universal landscapes:

'It was on a road remarkably bare, I mean without hedges or ditches or any kind of edge, in the country, for cows were chewing in enormous fields, lying and standing in the evening silence. Perhaps I'm inventing a little, perhaps embellishing, but on the whole that's the way it was. They chew, swallow, then after a short pause effortlessly bring up the next mouthful. A neck muscle stirs and the jaws begin to grind again.'[3]

Activity in the world has no meaning, it is merely repetitive, hypnotic. Equally, the Beckett character constantly resorts to futile, closed systems: the order in which biscuits should be eaten or the distribution of pebbles in a tramp's pockets. The systems may be mathematical, they form a mechanism for producing endless combinations, yet they only appear to tell us something new about the world. In philosophical terms they represent an a priori system of truths, that is, one independent of experience. They are like the justifications of Orton's Inspector Truscott: impressive but somehow heroically missing the point.

Yet the incessant rhythm of such explicatory mechanisms does, at least, appear to tell us we are alive. They have an exhilarating, comic quality, which Stoppard employs: Albert's incessant painting of the bridge is one such mechanism, but Stoppard's imagination, unlike Beckett's, is satiric. The a priori games provide materials for lampoons, for the traditional comedy that arises from the discontinuity between reason and the world. Where Beckett's plays shone with the hard, aggressive patina of the avant-garde, Stoppard's shimmered with the gratifications of the well-made West End success.

In *Jumpers* (1972) Stoppard explicitly deals with the clash between abstract systems and reality by making analytical philosophy itself the subject of his play:

DOTTY: As I recall *you* talked animatedly for some time about language being the aniseed trail that draws the hounds of heaven when the metaphysical fox has gone to earth; he must have thought you were barmy.

GEORGE: (*hurt*) I resent that. My metaphor of the fox and the hounds was an allusion, as Russell well understood, to his Theory of Descriptions.

DOTTY: Your metaphor of the fox and the hounds with Bertie as
the League Against Cruel Sports and yourself as John Peel
was altogether lost on the poor man. He was far too busy trying
to telephone Mao Tse-Tung.

GEORGE: I was simply trying to bring his mind back to matters of
universal import and away from the day-to-day parochialism
of international politics.[4]

The language is artificial and absurd, the ludicrous extravagance of
the conceits reinforcing the sense in which abstract thought is not
only removed from the world, it actually appears deliberately to be at
odds with it. The brain has lost its contact with reality precisely
because it has discovered so many versions of reality: international
politics derived from newspaper headlines is one version, the Theory
of Descriptions another. As George remarks later in the same play:
'How the hell do *I* known what I find incredible? Credibility is an
expanding field . . . Sheer disbelief hardly registers on the face before
the head is nodding with all the wisdom of instant hindsight.'[5] There
is no stability upon which to construct a world view, even the self has
become unknowable behind its systems – so George cannot even
know the boundaries of his own credulity. Meanwhile any mechanisms
whereby morality might be validated have long been lost:

BONES: He thinks there's nothing *wrong* with killing people?

GEORGE: Well, put like that, of course . . . But *philosophically*, he
doesn't think it's actually, inherently wrong in itself, no.

BONES: (*amazed*) What sort of philosophy is that?

GEORGE: Mainstream I'd call it. Orthodox mainstream.[6]

To be intellectually orthodox is to be socially outrageous. The
habits of the mind have departed from the practice of the world and
the world is left to empty ritual and instinct: Clive James compared
this failure of concepts to match reality in Stoppard to the development
of modern physics: 'Similarly with Stoppard's dramatic equivalent of
the space-time continuum: it exists to be ungraspable, it creator having
discovered that no readily available conceptual scheme can possibly
be adequate to the complexity of experience. The chill which some
spectators feel at a Stoppard play is arriving from infinity.'[7]

Stoppard's satirical mode makes him a commentator on rather than a practitioner of all this. His comedy implies a base of sense from which the madness can be observed. Whereas Orton realized his vision of a baseless world in his drama, Stoppard recreated it. The comedy is deliberate and grounded within a viewpoint, yet it shares with Orton the fascination with the insane, freewheeling system – mathematics, philosophy or the concealment of adultery – which only appears to be concerned with the world. In reality it is self-perpetuating and contact with the world can only be grotesque or disastrous.

This form of immense creative self-consciousness clearly relates both to the structuralist conception of art as a self-referring system among other such systems, and to Gombrich's Popperian aesthetic, which sees every step forward as a hypothesis built upon a mountain of previous hypotheses. It tends to produce a conception of artistic 'truth' that requires, above all, an awareness of every aspect of artifice.

This context explains the 1960s success of Laurence Sterne's novel *Tristram Shandy*; it became virtually the set book of this kind of awareness. Published in 1759, almost at the dawn of the era defined as that of the modern novel, it parodied every conceivable fictional device of prose narrative. It attempted to tell the life story of a man; but, such is the complexity of the task, he is constantly overwhelmed by the need to digress and to examine its own progress. Art ties itself in knots of ever increasing complexity and self-consciousness, but succeeds only in exposing its own artificiality and failure. The act of writing defeats the logic of narrative. This self-consciousness is a development of the self-awareness of form that characterized modernism, whose sense of the centrality of form produced, most characteristically, a fascination with the elemental and the pure, a determination to strip away the expressive accretions of the Victorian age. Its products were intended to exist within themselves, without need of external justification: Beckett defended Joyce's *Finnegans Wake* on the grounds that it was not about anything, it was the thing itself. In the postmodernist climate of Britain in the 1960s, there was the same awareness of form but also a new desire to produce expanded forms that celebrated rather than suffered under the obligation to express.

Brigid Brophy, in the preface to her 1973 biography of Ronald Firbank, *Prancing Novelist*, made clear the positive elements of her own literary self-consciousness. She wished to refute the claim, frequently and fashionably made at the time, that fiction was dead. Firbank's work, for Brophy, demonstrated precisely the opposite:

'Fiction seems to me the victim of a prejudice or, more probably, an inhibition . . . The inhibition has produced false rationalisations and distorted perspectives, including the habit of mistaking the trappings (naturalism) of one particular type of novels (Victorian ones) for the essence of the whole genre.

'Firbank, to my mind, is the novelist who freed fiction from naturalism or, to be exact, freed it again in the 20th century.'[8]

The point was that the death of fiction was being advertised on the basis that its characteristic naturalism was inadequate to the conditions of the day. But naturalism had merely been characteristic of one phase of the history of the novel. Firbank's dazzling and innovative technique – his musical construction, his elaborately woven dialogue and so on – exposed naturalism as a rather limited fad, a passing fancy of the Victorians. Above all, it exposed objectivity as phoney: the modern novelist could no longer make any such claim, he was embroiled in his own fiction, as, indeed, was his fiction: 'It became the mark of 20th-centuryness in fiction that the role of the work or of the author or of both is now a constituent of the work itself.'[9]

In Transit, Brophy's 1969 novel, realized the point artistically. It concerns the impulse that prompts the writing of fiction in the first place and is set entirely in an airport lounge, a location in which people are stripped of the identity of place and find themselves in transit between personalities. The narrative is a mass of riddles, digressions and devices, all playing with the problems of fiction and its execution. It is a game but a serious one for, as in baroque architecture, the significance of the game lies not in its obvious meanings. A writhing line of masonry here or a cherub there exists in relation to the other, in the constantly improvised juxtaposition of parts.

Again in her Firbank biography Brophy quotes a medieval lyric to exemplify the method:

O Western wind, when wilt thou blow
That the small rain down can rain?
Christ that my love were in my arms,
And I in my bed again.[10]

The image of the wind and the rain is accidental to the lover's grief and it is precisely this discontinuity of the experience that makes the lyric so moving; art has juxtaposed the human and the contingent. The baroque game – that of Sterne, Firbank and Brophy – is always played with one eye on the clock as it ticks away our passage to death. To be alive is to experience a discontinuity between consciousness and oblivion. Very well then, the baroque artist will celebrate that discontinuity.

For the modern to reinvent a form of the baroque was clearly an important development. It implied that self-consciousness, an excess of knowledge, need not be paralysing. The perception that progress was an illusion – that one style succeeding another was not a movement forward, merely one more reflection in the hall of mirrors – did not have to mean that all activity would freeze to a minimalist halt: now the artist could prance like Brophy's Firbank.

The implication of such prancing was, of course, that he could escape the nets of critical theory. So, for the relentless categorizing structuralist, self-consciousness could present a problem. Art could no longer appear quite such a passive symptom. There was, for example, the analysis of Roman Jakobson, a formalist much admired by a variety of theorists and a central figure in the history of structural analysis. His view was that literature alternated between metaphoric and metonymic phases: the first was experimental and innovative, the second tended towards the conventional and the realistic. The modernist phase would be metaphoric, the anti-modernist phase of the 1930s and 1950s would be metonymic. The problem with such a theoretical rhythm, however, was that awareness of it threatened its consistency. David Lodge saw the difficulty:

'Prediction seems particularly hazardous at present, because it is difficult to say what the dominant literary mode *is* now, certainly in England, and perhaps in America, or to place it on the metaphor-metonymy axis. This may be a familiar problem of perspective, that we are too close to our own art to distinguish the important from the trivial. Or it could be that our liveliest writers, having consciously or intuitively grasped the structural principles of the literary system, have ganged up to cheat it: refusing to choose between a dominantly metaphoric or metonymic mode of writing, they deploy both, in extreme, contradictory, often absurd or parodic ways, within the same work or body of work.'[11]

In other words: an art that has lost its innocence of theory is unlikely to prostrate itself before the theorist in order to oblige him with consistency. The critical theorist, having drawn his own practice, in theory at least, closer and closer to that of the artist, finds only that the artist is prancing away from him, changing the rules of the game, refusing to inhabit the theorist's precious axes.

Weapons Systems

The landscape of the baroque self, however, was perhaps a little specialized. Reality games were all very well but they conveyed no urgency. In fiction in particular, they seemed to imply an abandonment of the novel's aggressive role as the condenser of the age's preoccupations. Experiment and innovation suggested the exhaustion of the attempt to return to the old visceral impact of meaning, of recreating the new, real landscapes. And there were new forms of impatience abroad.

'The marriage of reason and nightmare which has dominated the 20th century has given birth to an ever more ambiguous world. Across the communications landscape move the spectres of sinister technologies and the dreams that money can buy. Thermo-nuclear weapons systems and soft-drink commercials coexist in an overlit realm ruled by advertising and pseudo-events, science and pornography.'[1] J. G. Ballard wrote this in the introduction to the French edition of his 1973 novel *Crash*. The tone is that of a man who has *seen* something, not that of one struggling through paralysing self-consciousness to *write* something. What he has seen is a unified vision 'out there' which enables him to write. The vision may be warped, but the distortions generate the energy for the writing. He goes on:

'To document the uneasy pleasures of living within this glaucous paradise has more and more become the role of science fiction. I firmly believe that science fiction, far from being an unimportant minor offshoot, in fact represents the main literary tradition of the 20th century, and certainly its oldest − a tradition of imaginative response to science and technology that runs in an intact line through H. G. Wells, Aldous Huxley, the writers of modern American science fiction, to such present-day innovators as William Burroughs.'[2]

The attempt to speak up for an abandoned or discredited alternative tradition was typical of the age. Brophy had assaulted the traditional literary view of the novel with Firbank's anti-naturalism; the structuralists had attempted to undermine the New Criticism and replace its canon of excellence with one of their own; Hockney and Kitaj had rejected the rigid modernist orthodoxy that had led to abstraction, and so on. Similarly, Ballard is claiming for science fiction, previously regarded, at best, as a rather trivial sideshow or, at worst, as the orthodoxy of the most marginal pulp literature, the status of the one appropriate fictional mode of the age.

This rather specialized enclave of sci-fi had long been regarded with affection by many of his contemporaries. Kingsley Amis produced *New Maps of Hell: A Survey of Science Fiction* in 1961, but made only the most modest claims for the literary significance of the form: 'This is not the stage at which one names names, but at least a dozen current practitioners seem to me to have attained the status of the sound minor writer whose example brings into existence the figure of real standing.'[3]

Ballard's claims were much bigger and evidently inspired by a high degree of aesthetic urgency:

'Can he (*the writer*), any longer, make use of the techniques of the perspectives of the traditional 19th century novel, with its linear narrative, its measured chronology, its consular characters grandly inhabiting their domains within an ample time and space?'[4] [he asks in the introduction to *Crash*; and, finally, in his most revealing passage:] 'I feel that, in a sense, the writer knows nothing any longer. He has no moral stance. He offers the reader the content of his own head, he offers a set of options and imaginative alternatives. His role is that of the scientist, whether on safari or in his laboratory, faced with a completely unknown terrain or subject. All he can do is devise various hypotheses and test them against the facts.'[5]

These themes – the lateness and decadence of the cultural hour, the lure of science and the image of the artist deprived of his context – are familiar enough throughout our period. But Ballard's is a new type of synthesis; he writes as though writing itself had awoken from a dream, only to find itself in a nightmare. The dream was that of the ordered characters and narratives of the nineteenth-century novel, their time certain and their spaces capacious; the nightmare is that of the real modern world. This is not simply a confusing world, as in Stoppard, in which the reason has run wild; it is utterly different from the one in which we fell asleep. Science and technology both seduce and repel; either way they are entirely unfamiliar.

Indeed, the landscape is so strange that Ballard does not even pretend to analyse it. Instead he stares blankly at it, extrapolates what he sees into a near future and then forms it into plots that serve only to deepen and extend his one central image. The process makes him a kind of extreme realist: the world and its objects are of rare importance in his fictions; they provide the material of his imagery of seductive, apocalyptic disgust:

'Above him, the inverted motorcycle fell on to the car's roof. Its handlebars passed through the empty windwhield and decapitated the front-seat passenger. The front wheel and chromium fork assembly plunged through the roof, the whiplashing drive chain severing the cyclist's head as he swept past. The pieces of his disintegrating body rebounded off the rear wheel-housing of the car and passed over the ground in the haze of broken safety glass which fell like ice from the car, as if it had been defrosted after a long embalming.'[6]

The description of the action is precise because it is important. What *really* happens in such situations is given significance by the mechanized fantasy in which they are used. *Crash* has a narrator, named Ballard, who finds himself caught up in the bizarre erotic fantasies of Vaughan. These fantasies arise from the contemplation of the interaction between human flesh and the machine in a car crash. Vaughan photographs, observes and plans such crashes and mixes their details into his relentless sex-life. Ballard is drawn into the web of this 'hoodlum scientist', who finally dies attempting to cause a crash with the car of the film star, Elizabeth Taylor.

There are two keys to the success of the work: the character of Vaughan, and Ballard's prose. At first glance Vaughan is the familiar science-fictional device of the man possessed of an evil vision, but the components of that vision – the sickly sweet detailing of his sexuality and his cowboy way with technology – are new. Vaughan is dirty, erotic and his relationship with machines is that of the manic user, not that of the old humanist who could not come to terms with their unnaturalness. To Vaughan the machine is not abstract, something fundamentally different from his own organic nature; rather it exhibits grotesque similarities to which he is erotically drawn.

Ballard's prose is suitably unforgiving. His narrator analyses and comments, but only from within his increasing immersion in the obsession. The narrative is rapid, detailed and determined: 'I edged the Lincoln forward a few feet. Behind me lay a block of darkness and silence, a condensed universe. Vaughan's hand moved across a surface.'[7]

The prose mimics the sense of nightmare – occasionally suggesting exits, but only to the howling void beyond. In *Concrete Island* (1974) he uses the most conventional of plot devices, a man trapped alone on an island, as if he were about to rewrite *Robinson Crusoe* or *Pincher Martin*. But the island is a fragment of land at a motorway junction from which the hero's injuries, inevitably from a motor accident, prevent him escaping. Throughout, however, it remains ambiguous whether he really wants to free himself. In any case, by the end the ritual of escape has been emptied of significance; it becomes simply one more thing that he does. Ballard's explicit justification for the whole operation is that his tales are 'cautionary'; they are 'a warning against that brutal, erotic and overlit realm that beckons more and more persuasively to us from the margins of the technological landscape'.[8] This suggests a highly conventional posture – the novelist as social prophet whose visions may draw us back from the brink of catastrophe – one that is contradicted both by his own declaration that the modern writer has lost his moral stance and by the sheer energy and exuberance with which he goes about his creations. Ballard is clearly deriving much satisfaction from his diseased visions.

Nevertheless, it is significant that Ballard needs to present a defence of the form itself in this moral context. He seems to require his books to be exemplary: without such a role they might cease to have any reason to exist or, more important, he might lose control of his invariably tight and well-made structures. Remove the idea of the book as cautionary fable and he might be obliged to allow his creations to follow those of the American science-fiction writer William Burroughs, where the logic of the lost, discontinuous, technological self is pursued into formlessness, into a rambling, contingently structured dream.

Born in 1930, Ballard began his writing career in 1956, as a member of a group of science-fiction writers called 'New Wave', with a short story in *New Worlds*. This magazine became the centre of the attempt to make science fiction more respectable, under the editorship, from 1964 to 1971, of Michael Moorcock, whose own fiction is related to Ballard's in its implicit impatience with the apparent smallness of the ambitions of other contemporary fiction. The difference is that, where Ballard's imagination tends towards the hermetic and the obsessed, Moorcock's is expansive and exploratory. His novels, in particular the extraordinary 'Jerry Cornelius' tetralogy, are attempts to engage fiction with history on a large scale. Science fiction provides the framework of devices such as time travel and disordered and unpredictable plotting, as well as catering for the reader's underlying fascination with technology. But the framework is not intended to provide the usual cheap thrills of the genre, rather it is used to liberate Moorcock from the conventional problems of the novel. It allows him to roam freely from one preoccupation to another and its very fictiveness prevents these preoccupations ever driving him out of the novel and into a type of journalism.

In this passage from *The Condition of Muzak*, the hero, Jerry Cornelius, is musing upon contemporary history while living in the over-grown roof garden of the Derry & Toms department store in Kensington:

'The image of a Britain become a nation of William Morris wood-carvers and Chestertonian beer-swillers drove him deeper into his jungle and caused him to abandon his books. He was only prepared to retreat so far. He was forced to admit, however, that the seventies were proving an intense disappointment to him. He felt bitter about missed opportunities, the caution of his own allies, the sheer funk of his enemies. In the fifties life had been so appalling that he had been forced to flee into the future, perhaps even help create that future, but by the sixties, when the future had arrived, he had been content at last to live in the present until, due in his view to a conspiracy amongst those who feared the threat of freedom, the present (and consequently the future) had been betrayed. As a result he had sought the past for consolation, for an adequate mythology to explain the world to him, and here he did, lost in his art nouveau jungle, his art deco caverns, treading the dangerous quicksands of nostalgia and yearning for times that seemed simpler only because he did not belong to them and which, as they became familiar, seemed even more complex than the world he had loved for its very variety and potential. Thus he fled still further, into a word where vegetation alone flourished and only the most primitive of sentient life chose to exist. He was thinking of giving up time-travel altogether.'[9]

There is here a certain largeness and ease about the prose which indicate that Moorcock feels free to treat the novel as an inclusive form, one actively capable of debate and argument. Furthermore, in the character of Cornelius, the fictional self is enlarged to take on a sort of heroic unity. He is not anguished or agonized in the manner of some late humanist anti-hero, rather he aspires to an imaginative completeness:

'You tried to maintain the old order. Your friend Beesley wanted to turn it against itself, to destroy it altogether. But Cornelius enjoyed it for its own sake. Aesthetically. He had no interest in its moral significance or its utilization. Computers and jets and rockets and lasers and the rest were simply familiar elements of his natural environment. He didn't judge them or question them, any more than you or I would judge or question a tree or a hill. He picked his cars, his weapons, his gadgets, in the same way that he picked his clothes – for the private meanings, for what they looked like. He enjoyed their functions, too, of course, but function was a secondary consideration. There are easier cars to drive than Duesenbergs, easier, faster, cheaper planes to fly than experimental Dorniers.'[10]

Moorcock and Ballard were in many respects to be the precursors of an opening-out of the possibilities of fiction that was to occur in the 1980s. The urban obsessions of Ballard and the large historical sense of Moorcock were to find echoes in the writing of Martin Amis, Peter Ackroyd and Timothy Mo. It was no accident that this impatient enlarging of the landscape of fiction had emerged from science fiction, from a dazed awareness of the potent imaginative nature of science and technology.

Cool Gadgets

The driving force behind the creativity of both Ballard and Moorcock was the sense that fiction needed to encompass entirely new forms of human organization. From their perspective, the human organism was losing its old footings: time and space were being reorganized by technology and the urban vision had taken over completely from the rural. Standing back and commenting on this in the old mandarin mode was no longer enough, it needed to be assimilated.

Clearly any such assimilation would tend to overthrow the old, humane conflicts of town versus country, science versus art and so on. In their place would be a sort of integration – a key idea of the time, expressed in a variety of forms from fringe religion to Germaine Greer and the radical architectural work of Buckminster Fuller. This integration could be detected, of course, in the aspirations of structuralism; but, equally, it appeared to be infecting the philosophy of science. In 1971 essay Stephen Toulmin perceived it as an important move away from the general idea of modernism. 'Whatever its origins,' he wrote, 'the effects of this early 20th century "modernism" were clear enough. All the way across the field, from logic and mathematics to the human sciences and the fine arts, the essential tasks of intellectual and artistic activity were redefined in static, structural, a-historical, non-representational and wherever possible mathematical terms.'[1]

That model of thought was divisive and rigid. In the 1960s it was replaced by a more organic view, concerned to involve the dynamics of change, concerned above all to integrate:

'Now we suddenly find ourselves faced with a new humanism. This shows itself in a preoccupation with the concrete and the historical, in a fresh determination to grasp the dynamics of change, in a sense of the complex interactions between different aspects of human life and nature, and a novel concern with "function": not in the quasi-physiological sense of early 20th century functionalist anthropology or the functional architecture of the 1920s, but in an evolutionary sense, focused on the "adaptiveness" of science, technology and the arts to the changing needs and conditions of human existence.'²

This might be described as the organic aspiration that lay behind much of the highly coloured activity of the 1960s. In this context it is seen as anti-modernist in that it rejects the austerity that had come to be associated with modernism in favour of a generous, and frequently rather vague, inclusiveness. For Toulmin it suggested an entirely new methodology of science and, therefore, of knowledge: 'The problem of conceptual change became inescapable the moment philosophers recognised that the rationality of any natural science involves something more than the logical coherence of the propositions forming its current intellectual cross-section.'³

All this 'adaptiveness' and integration is perhaps the bright side of Ballard's dark vision. It suggests that technology and humans must work more intimately together; science must be humanized and moralized rather than allowed to slump into the black erotic nightmare of *Crash*. Such an optimistic view clearly links to the creative view of science fostered by Karl Popper, who rejected Baconian induction as an entirely inaccurate version of the scientific method, preferring the speculative, imaginative leap, the testable hypothesis which preceded the evidence. In a 1969 lecture entitled 'Science and Literature' Peter Medawar, a disciple of Popper, argued that this vision of science overturned the old romantic contradiction between reason and imagination:

'All advance of scientific understanding, at every level, begins with a speculative adventure, an imaginative preconception of *what might have been true* – a preconception which always and necessarily goes a little way (sometimes a long way) beyond anything which we have logical or factual authority to believe in. It is the invention of a Possible World, out of a tiny fraction of that world. The conjecture is then exposed to criticism to find out whether or not that imagined world is anything like the real one.'⁴

Medawar's point is that the Popperian redefinition overcomes the old antagonisms of the 'two cultures':

'Our traditional views about imagination and criticism in literature and in science are based upon the literary propaganda of the romantic poets and the erroneous opinions of the inductivist philosophers. Imagination is the energising force of science as well as of poetry, but in science imagination and a critical evaluation of its products are integrally combined. To adopt a conciliatory attitude, let us say that science is that form of poetry . . . in which Reason and Imagination act together synergistically. This simple formal property . . . represents the most important methodological discovery of modern thought.'[5]

This all suggests that a new wholeness may be being born by the reunion of science and the imagination; the chasm between ourselves and our machines might prove to be a sentimental delusion sold to us by romantic propaganda. Again it is the obverse of Ballard, but, with him, such views share the sense that the urban landscape – the landscape of science – had taken over.

This amounts to an important intellectual version of what had been happening in popular culture. The 1960s were a period in which the city and its associations came to dominate the popular imagination. Nature had previously appeared as the repository of positive moral values, but now the urban and the artificial took on a new unapologetic vitality. Images of society became distinctly mannered and synthetic. The dreams of an integrated technological world of the 1950s brutalists and pop artists were realized in a new glorification of consumption and instant imagery: photographers took on a strange centrality in the culture.

'Accompanying the rise of the boutiquier went the rise of the photographer,' wrote, Arthur Marwick, the historian. 'Cameras were to art and advertising what washing machines were to domestic life: they fitted well into the international (the Germans were the great innovators) and, fairly, classless world of gadgetry. Where an upper-class figure, Antony Armstrong-Jones, led the way, he was quickly followed by two upwardly mobile products of the London working class, David Bailey and Terence Donovan.'[6]

It was not just a case of what Bailey and Donovan did, it was what they *were*. With their cameras they represented a natural harmony of man and machine and they provided images that reinforced the urban culture's view of itself. Bailey's dead-pan, angular and unambiguous portraits of people in indeterminate space suggested a timeless artificiality – humans without context. His photograph of the Kray twins, east London criminals, evokes something of the sickly, horrified fascination of Ballard's Vaughan. Dark-suited, tab-collared, Ronnie in front, Reggie behind, they stand there, alluring and repulsive, inhabiting a dream of themselves.

Indeed, the Krays took on a culturally exemplary quality. They represented a curious perversion of the dream of integration. In a book documenting their activities, John Pearson writes of one of them: 'The sort of crime he had carried on in Whitechapel could work just as well in the swinging London of the sixties: he would use the methods of old-style cockney villainy to blackmail, trick and terrify his way into his business, smart society, credit-dealing, large-scale fraud.'[7]

Pearson's list has something of the menace of Ballard's erotic litanies; but it also delineates a vision of a *connected* world, one in which society has been made homogeneous by the city and its fabric, in which the divisions of geography and class have been worn away to reveal the pitiless network of coercion beneath: the 'sordid underworld network' Harold Wilson had detected in the Profumo scandal.

Jonathan Raban saw the significance of the Krays as urban emblems in his 1974 book *Soft City*:

'I want to concentrate on the dimmer of the two, Ronnie Kray; a man whose grasp on reality was so slight and pathologically deranged that he was able to live out a crude, primary coloured fiction, twisting the city into the shape of a bad thriller. His story is an urban morality tale, and to understand it is to understand one of the deepest of all the wellsprings of city life: he shows how a style, cheaply come by in the emporium of the city, may completely supplant every forecastable reality, every determinable social pattern. He is a city man as wilful artist; and those of us who live in cities are perhaps a good deal closer to him than we like to think.'[8]

The idea of an artificial and integrated world was thus ambiguous.

The interacting systems of structuralism or Medawar's remarriage of reason and imagination offered a new wholeness of human knowledge – but the integrated, communicating city also made possible the lives of the Krays. It could become a black, structuralist image of a system operating without the intervention of man. It was created from the idea of communication, but the implications of that communication evoked a kind of dread.

Malcolm Bradbury, who played a critical godfatherly role to a new generation of fiction writers, suggested that something was being lost in the process:

'Not only, then, does the modern situation in communications weaken those features of a communal culture in which art was traditionally created and consumed; it also competes persistently with the artists for a view of reality.'9 [And:] 'Today, when we speak of culture, we increasingly come to mean the communications processes themselves, rather than the meanings and preferences they embody: which is one reason why the word itself becomes problematic.'10

Integration, communication, could thus become in itself a threat to the continuity of culture. The very seamlessness of the view of reality propagated by mechanisms such as television could usurp the role of the artist, while a fascination with the systems themselves could remove any interest in content in the traditional sense. Furthermore, the dread city of the imagination was made fact during the 1960s by a sudden and massive swing in attitudes away from the reconstructive changes to the urban fabric of the post-war years. The rebuilding programme with its Festival of Britain emphasis on the amiably contemporary had become 'The Rape of Worcester' and 'The Sack of Bath' as the grand redevelopment plans were suddenly seen in a different light. 'By the end of the sixties,' Lionel Esher wrote, 'slum clearance had begun to look like vandalism – the numbers game had ceased to signify.'11

The organic aspirations of the city were at their most consistently anti-modernist in architecture. The planned city was the opposite of the organic one and all the concrete 'improvements' were exposed as an assault on the human, the true. 'The roads are service roads,' Jonathan Raban wrote of the Millbrook housing estate in Southampton, 'they loop purposelessly around the estate in broad curves that conform to no contours. There is no street life on them; an occasional pram pushed by a windblown mother, a motorbiking yobbo or two, a dismal row of parked Ford Anglias, an ice-cream van playing *Greensleeves* at half-tempo, a mongrel snapping at its tail.[12]

The idea that an artistic vision could create a real new world foundered as Le Corbusier's dreams were badly translated into system building with its leaking roofs, broken lifts and, climactically, the collapse in 1968 of the Ronan Point block of flats. That same year the fourteen vast slab blocks of the Pruitt-Igoe development in St Louis were completed only to be demolished four years later. They had become a violent, uninhabitable, concrete desert.

Conservationism was born in opposition to the simplifying ideas of the planners. Architecture became hateful, representing a crude destruction of the organic fabric. With the defeat of the Covent Garden redevelopment scheme in London, the very idea of planning was overthrown. It was a development that can be seen to relate to Toulmin's benevolent analysis of the new humanism. Its historical dimension was expressed in a new determination to protect and restore old buildings. It was as though a new sense of the city as a communicating net were being extended backwards in time: the layered messages of the old would be exposed and preserved. The new, friendly city would be full of variation and surprise – not the monolithic shock of the skyscraper, rather the voyeuristic delight of gazing into a scrubbed and restored version of the past.

This was the organic, integrationist modification of the old rural-conservative versus urban-progressive conflict. Now the city, instead of being seen merely as a violent, alien contradiction of the values of the village in the fold of the hills, had become part of that same vision: cherishable and rehabilitated into the womb of the coherent past. A new English landscape was to be discovered in Georgian terraces and Victorian offices and shops.

Historically this development can be seen to have paralleled the slowly spreading realization in the 1960s that Britain was no longer a principal player on the world stage. It had taken some time.

'How far, and at what point, a majority of the British people had digested the fact that Britain was no longer a major world power [Arthur Marwick wrote] is difficult to determine: probably not till the 1960s, though, objectively, Suez is the watershed. In the imagery of newsreel, press, radio and television, Britain continued to be presented, along with France, as a "big" country.'[13]

Yet, equally, as the imagery of size had faded, a new national self-portrait had been painted in the 1960s, showing the country as somehow ingenious, lively and imaginative. We developed a role as a creator of popular culture. This involved a significant conceptual change: where the great power role had required an international view of culture – cosmopolitan architecture, great social plans and so on – this new role created a demand for all that was distinguishably English. Policemen's helmets and double-decker buses became icons of a national 'oddball' quality as did highly mannered and faintly surrealistic television programmes such as *The Avengers*. The paraphernalia of old England ceased to signify conservative solidity and became, instead, the furniture of a kind of dream, a correlative of the empty dream-space of a Bailey photograph and of the harsh black and white styling of the time.

Perhaps only in this dream could the new organic wholeness to which the age aspired be attained, for the period was in parenthesis. There were deaths – Auden and Eliot, for instance - which marked its boundaries, but there were also two apocalypses: in 1962 the Cuban missile crisis and the popularly accepted feeling that the world had been about to end; and in 1973 the first shock of the OPEC oil price increases, bringing the widespread conviction that the entire process of economic growth had come to an end, that the West's party was over. This shock fitted neatly with the conservationist instincts of the day; it seemed to tell us that the world and its past must not be trampled on by progress. It may have confirmed the 1960s organic aspiration but it also revealed the fragile foundations of its dreams of integration and of perpetual becoming, of its white-hot technology and cool gadgets.

PART FOUR

Scale Unknown

On 1 January 1973 Britain joined the Common Market; we became an economic region of the Europe whose unity, whose very existence, had been so difficult to imagine in 1945. That same year oil, previously the plentiful and cheap fuel of economic growth, became a political weapon as supplies to the West were cut and prices raised in the wake of the Arab-Israeli War in October. The two events symbolized complex transformations in the nature of the national identity. The first stressed that we were European, part of a federation whose ancient quarrels now looked quaint and old-fashioned in the context of the vast economic and military power of the USSR and the USA. It also implied that we were *merely* European, a state alongside other, equal states, rather than the cool, heroic saviour of civilization in its darkest hour. The oil shock exposed our vulnerability. The growth of the 1950s and 1960s was not as simple as it had seemed: the cars, the New Towns, the motorways all lost their appearance of solidity; they depended on an economic thread, easily severed by new forms of political will. Affluence had once inspired imaginations to doubt its value because there seemed to be some underlying spiritual or moral absence; now, as motorists queued for petrol, the doubts were justified, judgement day was imminent. Where once despair and foreboding had been no more than intellectual or artistic devices, now they entered the demotic.

Britain, in particular, did not seem likely to survive the crisis. In 1973 and 1974, the conviction grew that Britain was on the verge of becoming entirely ungovernable. In November 1973 a state of emergency was declared as a result of the miners' strike. On 13 December electricity supplies to industry and commerce were restricted to three days a week. At the general election in February 1974 the crisis finally brought down Edward Heath's Conservative Government. 'The world has changed dramatically since we last sought the support of the electorate,' said the Conservative manifesto.

Meanwhile, the geographical integrity of the country was being threatened. Welsh and Scottish separatism were in the ascendant, questioning the value of the union itself, and in 1974 there was a succession of increasingly effective IRA bombs.

The historian Arthur Marwick considered that, in many respects, the 1970s were a return to the 1930s, the 'devil's decade':

'Apart from a general sense of a worsening economy [he wrote] and declining living standards, the special doom-laden features which contemporary commentators singled out were the outbursts of militancy, violence and terrorism, the revelations of corruption in high places, and the break-up of the optimistic consensus which had, according to one point of view, successfully carried Britain through the difficult post-war years into the affluence of the sixties, or, according to another, had mischievously concealed the desperate realities of Britain's true predicament.'[1]

The 1970s were also to breed one entirely new form of anxiety: not on a national or even European scale, nor focusing simply on the possibility of a nuclear apocalypse, it sprang from the sense that the systems of the planet itself were in danger of collapse. These systems were seen as both natural and man-made. The oil crisis emphasized the fragility of the human organization, but it was also a reminder that earth's resources were finite. Radical conservationism was born from the vivid, frightening vision of the planet as a rapidly emptying fuel tank, being both depleted and polluted without regard to the future. The word conservation meant more than simply defending Georgian terraces against developers – though that was to be a part of the struggle – it was a question of life or death, of clean air, rivers and mountains.

This sense of an impending systems failure produced a strange recapitulation of the dread of 1945:

'Many spectres are haunting Europe today, [a columnist wrote in *Encounter* in January 1975] among them inflation, deflation, the threat of world economic depression, and the possibility of mass unemployment on a scale unknown since the 1930s . . . we live in a cemetery of disappointed hopes and cheated expectations, and as yet no one quite sees how we are going to make ourselves comfortable in it.'[2]

Where once mistrust of technology inspired a retreat into pastoralism, now it called for an effort on a heroic scale. It was not a case of protecting what we had, but of winning back territory. The gentle ideal of conservation had to take the offensive to match the scale of its opponents' operations in big business and government.

Meanwhile, also in 1973, the artist Michael Craig-Martin exhibited his work *An Oak Tree*. Craig-Martin was born in Dublin in 1941 and educated in the USA; but he moved to Britain in 1966, there to become closely associated with the conceptual art movement. *An Oak Tree* was a high point of conceptualism. It consisted of a glass of water on a shelf and a leaflet. The leaflet contained an interview with the artist in which he explains that the glass of water is, in fact, an oak tree.

The work evokes a painting by the Belgian surrealist artist René Magritte showing a pipe, painted with laborious realism, and, beneath, the words 'This is not a pipe.' Of course it is not, it is a painting. Craig-Martin, though, uses a real object, which could therefore be correctly labelled, but instead he insists that it is something else entirely.

In art anything is possible. If pigment on canvas can be taken to represent a landscape, why not a glass of water an oak tree? All art is fiction, a convention of lies. Modernism, in many of its guises, tried to pretend otherwise: there was, for example, Henry Moore's pursuit of 'truth to materials'. Modernist art debated the nature of its own form, revealing its means and its mechanisms and aspiring to tell the truth about itself, even if that should turn out to concern no more than its own nature. Magritte's joke was funny because it was true; but it was also circular, self-regarding. Craig-Martin's joke is funny because it is a lie: the glass of water is not an oak tree, yet art can say it is. Art transforms materials. To abandon this power, to strip away to the modernist essentials may be to abandon everything that art actually is.

In the post-modern landscape of 1973 the feeling was spreading that art and its fictions should be resurrected, that it should be allowed to speak again without stifling self-consciousness. Just as Hockney had once written on his paintings because he feared the vacancy of abstraction, so artists now began to long for an art that talked of something other than itself. 'One of the most striking characteristics of the art of the seventies', Edward Lucie-Smith wrote, 'has been the swing back towards content – that is, the work of art is seen as a means of conveying information, not simply as an exercise in style.'[3]

The contradiction was felt particularly keenly in sculpture. At the St Martin's School of Art in London a modernist orthodoxy of rigorous abstraction prevailed through the teaching of Anthony Caro and Philip King: an orthodoxy inevitably destined to produce disenchantment. 'The St Martin's sculpture forum would avoid every broader issue,' Bruce McLean recalled, 'discussing for hours the position of one piece of metal in relation to another . . . Twelve adult men with pipes would walk for hours around a sculpture and mumble!'[4]

McLean's implicit question is: What exactly were they walking around? A sculpture, a work of art, they would reply. The reply would have appealed to an old and increasingly mistrusted division between 'art' and 'life'. A work of art dwelled in a museum, indeed for the avant-garde that had frequently been the only thing that determined its status as a work of art. The men with pipes were, therefore, considering the metal object with a view to its suitability as a museum piece. McLean's broader issues were things that happened outside the museum gate; out there the nation, the continent and the planet seemed threatened by an elaborate process of violent collapse.

Lucie-Smith commented on the way this distinction was assaulted in the 1970s:

'What has been recognised by almost nobody is the blurring of the distinction between "high art", the art of the museum, and other forms of activity to which the word art may be applied. The art critic and art commentators of the 60s could conveniently operate within a very simple system. Things were either "art", anti-art or "non-art". The category to which they belonged was defined, not by examining what they looked like or were made of, but by interrogating the artist about his intentions. The declared intention of making art was enough to validate the work of art as such.'[5]

So part of Craig-Martin's *An Oak Tree* is the interview with the artist. Conceptualism rejected the impure filter of execution and adopted instead the direct statement of intention. Yet, equally, the statement asserted the imaginative autonomy of the artist and the art. But still *An Oak Tree* was a frozen moment, a moment of paralysis. The occasion of expression seemed to hang by a thread.

One way off this see-saw of intention and execution was Marxism, as propounded by John Berger. A work of art was a product of bourgeois triumphalism; it celebrated the dominance of the ruling class with its high price tag or its totemic isolation within a gallery. To the artist, however, that could seem as much of a dead end as the most arid late modernism. Knowing it, believing it, even offered no obvious way of deciding what to do next.

An acceptance of the fiction, of an art that addressed the imminently crumbling fabric of the world, however, did.

Doing Something

Sculpture is a very immediate event. Direct carving, as opposed to casting, represents an artistic intervention in the world, unmediated by any other mechanism – film, printing, performance or whatever. Painting largely shares this immediacy, but it is obliged always to deal with the problem of its two dimensions, an aesthetic task that must inevitably stand between itself and its statement. Imaginatively, at least, sculpture holds the promise of existing in the world as fully and directly as anything else, of being as true as anything can be.

In Britain in the 1970s and 1980s there was an efflorescence of sculpture based on this unarguable quality of the art. Inevitably this generation of artists lived under the shadow of Henry Moore, who had established the art as perhaps the only one in which post-war Britain was generally acknowledged to be a world leader. Yet, to a large extent, he had done so on the basis of an aesthetic that, at least from the late 1950s onwards, was definably pre-war. His mythic, huge, impersonal forms were linked with the grand icons of modernist art. They gazed across the ages, epic images at one with those of the past and, implicitly, of the future. If Moore had begun by attempting to free himself of the legacy of the Renaissance, he concluded by affirming its continuity.

Anthony Caro was born in 1924 in Surrey. He read engineering at Cambridge but, during his holidays, studied at the Farnham School of Art. After the war he devoted himself entirely to art and, in 1951, started work as an assistant at Moore's studio in Hertfordshire. His own sculpture in the 1950s showed a complex range of influences, though Moore was clearly predominant. He began teaching at St Martin's School in 1953. In 1959 he visited New York on a Ford Foundation travel scholarship, where he encountered a variety of artists but, most importantly, the sculptor David Smith, one of the many powerful figures responsible for the success of New York art in the 1950s. At once Caro decided he had been 'trapped by the sensuality of clay'.[1] Like Moore before him, he felt the time had come to liberate sculpture from the traditions of the Renaissance, and immediately expressed this liberation by abandoning traditional materials in favour of metal. Welding replaced modelling, full-blooded abstraction succeeded modified figuration.

On the face of it, this was a development with obvious parallels in painting. Just as many British painters, enmeshed in the complexities, indecisions and sheer range of possibilities of the post-war period, had been overwhelmed by the scale and grandeur of American abstract expressionism, so Caro now saw abstraction in metal as a release from the legacy of Moore and the British modernism of the 1930s. In sculpture, certainly in the hands of Caro, the effects were more far-reaching.

The central point was that Caro 'assembled' rather than carved or modelled his new sculptures, an impulse already seen in some of his 1950s work. Unlike Moore, he had then worked by building his clay upon an armature, a method that foreshadowed the idea of assembly. His early work also demonstrated a fascination with the sculpture's relationship with the ground. For Moore this relationship was with the base – most obviously in his reclining figures – but Caro was clearly aiming for something more direct, less hierarchical.

With his conversion to metal both these tendencies triumphed. He used industrial steel – tubes, I-beams, flanges and so on – which emphasized the unmodelled, assembled quality of the works and he abandoned the base or plinth entirely. The resulting sculptures were open, composed spatial incidents, which suggested an entirely different identity for sculpture in wholly new contexts. Moore, for all the vast variety of his innovations, had always maintained a connection with the traditional situations of sculpture: exterior public figures or interior, smaller pieces. Caro's pieces did not demand such clear social positions. They required, perhaps, only the potential neutrality of a gallery, the very social position with which Bruce McLean later lost patience.

In almost every sense Caro's work seems to represent a kind of balancing act. First, he rejects the traditionally expressive sculptural materials in favour of 'something really anonymous, just sheets maybe, which you cut a bit off'.[2] He then imposes a complex process of aesthetic ordering on the material – creating an occupied space with its own rules of composition – and thus counterbalances the anonymity of his materials. Equally, his work oscillates between apparently complete abstraction and a suggested figuration. His famous *Prairie* (1967) is painted yellow in apparent evocation of fields of corn and its slender tubes move delicately with any disturbance. Clearly something is being alluded to here, but not so definitely as to disturb the primarily abstract feel of the image. And, of course, the idea of balance suffuses the complex and delicate relationships of his sculptures to the ground. Finally, in historical terms, Caro's whole career represents a kind of pivotal moment, a moment when three-dimensional art took over from two- as the primary mode of the avant-garde. His sculptures have escaped from traditional space, claiming instead a more elaborate relationship with the physical presence of the observer. As such they anticipate the environmental works of the 1960s and 1970s as well as the whole idea of a work as an 'installation' within a gallery, rather than an object which merely happens, for the moment, to be exhibited there.

Caro was the primary inspiration of a group of sculptors all of whom, with the one exception of William Turnbull, were connected with St Martin's. They were called 'New Generation', after an exhibition of that name held in 1965 at the Whitechapel Art Gallery

'It strove after modernity [Frances Spalding wrote of the New Generation style], emulated modern building techniques and was strongly related to the architectural environment. The right angle is insistently present; even when the lines or planes lean, bend or curve, they do so in implied relation to the horizontal of the ground and the vertical of the wall. New Generation sculpture was in addition influenced by the current interest in "gestalt" psychology, which revolted against the atomistic approach in its concern with wholeness. In keeping with the ideas about "a good gestalt", much of this sculpture is immediately explicit: the forms can be perceived at a glance, understood from any angle.'[3]

The style was thus purist in intent, tending to isolate and distil impersonally universal forms. It related both to minimalism and conceptualism in its ambitions to refine itself as well as to tease the audience with cerebral games played with the observer-object relationship. As such, in the late 1960s it seemed, like other reductive forms of late modernism, to run out of steam and to be superseded by a wider, more public interpretation of the role of the artist.

Nevertheless, the effect of the post-war inheritance of Moore, Caro and the New Generation gave sculpture an unprecedented importance among the arts in this country. Even at the level of the perennially popular joke about the absurdity of modern art, it was generally sculpture – minimalist, exotic or merely baffling – which was portrayed as responsible for the most outrageous manifestations.

The reaction against the New Generation was akin to the rise of post-modernism in other arts. It sprang from an impatience with the mechanisms of abstraction, the idea of creating or imposing an order or harmony beyond that of the world itself. So, although Caro's assembled materials suggested a new openness to the found objects of the world, they were then, as it were, over-transformed into art. There was an implicit imperiousness about the sculptural gesture, a suggestion of the domination of matter. In contrast, environmental concerns, which were rapidly to become a kind of 1970s vernacular, demanded a greater respect for the world as found – for the detritus of civilization as much as for the objects of nature.

This emerged most vividly in the work of Mark Boyle and Joan Hills. In 1968 they collaborated on the celebrated *Journey to the Surface of the Earth*. This entailed blindfolded people throwing darts at a map; the artists then visited the places were the darts landed, where they recorded the contents, human or animal, plant or mineral, of a square of about two metres. The process was intended to be both random and objective. Both the site chosen and its contents were beyond the control of the artists; their role was simply to initiate the process and to carry it through. It was a complex gesture, which in purely aesthetic terms represented a reaction to the romanticism associated with abstraction and its mythologies. The forms of abstraction invite us to take the artist on trust, to accept his orderings, but with Boyle and Hills the artist's role becomes pure process. He subsumes his demands for order to the workings of chance and the world itself. The aesthetic presence of the final work does not determine the process; the object is simply there, a faithful recording of the world.

In addition, however, there is an underlying ecological polemic. Man has interfered with the world too much, here is an art that changes nothing of what it records. The chance element makes every part of the world equally precious and the painstaking realism of the process makes each part sacred. At the same time, the method carried scientific overtones with its objectivity and its requirement to gaze steadily simply at the world as found.

It was this which first emerged in the early work of Tony Cragg. He would assemble found objects from, for example, a beach and place them on a roughly drawn grid. The implication was that they would thus take on relationships as intense and meaningful as those of science. 'Using these little atoms', Mary Jane Jacob wrote of Cragg's work, 'like parts from which to form a whole, he has created a visual vocabulary that, like the language of science can be used to create models for thought from which we can learn to view the world differently.'[4]

Cragg's abstraction, however, rapidly gave way to figuration. He continued to use his mass of found objects – plastic and wooden fragments – but now he ordered them into recognizable images. In his *Britain Seen from the North* (1981) a huge map of Britain is laid horizontally and is observed from the Scottish end by a figure made of the same random fragments.

Bill Woodrow also used found objects but he transformed them even more elaborately. He would cut the outer wall of a washing machine and reform it into the shape of an electric guitar, a chainsaw or a bicycle. Michael Compton wrote of the polemic behind the work of Cragg and Woodrow:

'Both use that other kind of mass imagery that takes the form of consumer durables and packaging. It is an imagery which is equally the active product of professionals in a commercial system who are contriving to sell their products through a kind of fiction. Woodrow usually takes the skin of one styled product and turns it into a hand-crafted image from another, say a washing machine and a cowboy film. The wit of the transformation is often startling and the underlying sardonic and social comment clear.'[5]

Cutting and assembling had completely replaced carving and modelling in the sculptural mainstream. Stone and metal had lost their ascendancy in favour of a much more pluralistic acceptance of the world's materials into the repertoire of sculpture. The new skill was not the maintenance of the unity of a single object, but the creation of new unities from a multiplicity of objects. And the new unity tended to be rhetorical rather than purely aesthetic, an abstract discourse on the object's own occupation of space. For, inevitably, with these objects came associations: a washing machine cannot pretend to be as innocent as a block of stone, it is already made and endowed with meaning long before the sculptor touches it. Even rearranging one object as two in the manner of Woodrow cannot entirely remove this meaning, it merely adds new ones. The resulting collision is directly rhetorical: 'Through familiar objects in newly created forms, Woodrow tells us about the imbalances of our culture, the lack of synchronization between man and nature in our Western industrialized society, and the need for a new harmony between us and our world as symbolized by the many consumer goods that comprise it.'[6]

In Woodrow there are vigour and rawness, a type of violence characteristic of much of the sculpture of the age. His washing machine and guitar have a faintly offensive quality in the setting of a gallery, their jagged, scratched edges suggesting an impatience with any idea of 'finish'. They speak of an urgent need for content – in the event it appeared to be immediately at hand in the form of the characteristic 1970s anxiety about the viability of our civilization and the world.

The true hero of this anxious state, the artist who worked on a suitably grand scale to match the scale of the foreboding, was Richard Long. He was born in 1945 and emerged, almost inevitably, from the St Martin's School of Art, where he evolved his primary sculptural technique: walking. He walked back and forth in a straight line across a field until he had worn a visible track. He then photographed and exhibited the result as *A Line Made by Walking England 1967*. A year later he photographed a giant 'X' he had made in a field by cutting off the heads of flowers. The apparently excessive contrivance of such exercises vanishes before the works themselves. Far from being introverted, minimal gestures, they seem replete, brimming with subject matter. The line stands for all human intervention in the world as well as the line of a man's life. The world is changed by its presence, but lightly and benignly in obvious contrast to man's more disastrous interventions. This lightness of touch is of central import-ance to Long, and prompted him to repudiate his earlier associations with American land or earth art with its vast, abstract changes to the landscape.

'In the sixties [Long has said] there was a feeling that art need not be a production line of more objects to fill the world. My interest was in a more thoughtful view of art and nature, making art both visible and invisible, using ideas, walking stone, tracks, water, time etc. in a flexible way . . . It was the antithesis of so-called American "Land Art", where an artist needed money to be an artist, to buy real estate to claim possession of the land, and to wield machinery. True capitalist art. To walk in the Himalayas . . . is to touch the earth lightly . . . and has more personal physical commitment, than an artist who plans a large earthwork which is then made by bulldozers. I admire the spirit of the American Indian more than its contemporary land artists. I prefer to be a custodian of nature, not an exploiter of it. My position is that of the Greens. I want to do away with nuclear weapons, not make art that can withstand them.'[7]

This is an important statement, both for the light it casts on Long's work and for the mood it describes. Long is defining the delicacy of his own touch and his need for a kind of heroic gentleness but, in doing so, he is rejecting another kind of artistic heroism: the aggres-sive, romantic heroism of the American art movement that had seemed to colonize the art world since the late 1940s. From the work of Jackson Pollock and the criticism of Clement Greenberg onwards, the accepted orthodoxy was that the centre of the art world had moved across the Atlantic. This new American art was characterized by huge, grandiloquent scale, whether in the massive canvases of the abstract expressionists or in the land art against which Long was rebelling. In pop art it was the iconography of American popular culture in the forms of Mickey Mouse, Marilyn Monroe or the automobiles which dominated the dreams of integration and technology. The whole enter-prise was also, of course, accompanied by an active and powerful network of dealers. Meanwhile, at St Martin's, Caro's abstraction as well as his indebtedness to the American sculptor David Smith had, in effect, colluded in the continued imaginative dominance of America.

This American artistic ideal decayed rapidly in the 1970s. In 1977 at the Kassel Documenta in Germany it attained a kind of apotheosis: the American artist Walter de Maria spent $250,000, provided by an oil company, drilling a one-kilometre-deep hole in the ground, into which he inserted a brass rod. The work was entirely invisible, but the romantic American faith in the artist as somehow magically trustworthy meant that the project itself was justified. In response, the British artist Stuart Brisley dug his own hole nearby, built a wooden structure in it and lived there for two weeks. The extremity, visibility and the primitive overtones of his condition represented a calculated insult to the over-refined and expensive elaborations of the American.

American dominance had been imperialistic and, finally, oppressive. The critical orthodoxy, which formed the second wave of the American offensive, had come to seem dry and directionless. The emphasis on surface and on process appeared trivial in the face of a wounded world. As the technological confidence of the 1960s gave way to the uncertainty of the 1970s, the American art juggernaut faltered.

So, returning to Long's statement and to his work, it is clear they demonstrate a determination to make art *do* something. The words he employs – commitment, spirit, custodian and, of course, nature – all indicate a system of obligations and realities, whether spiritual or material, which stand outside the work of art and which he feels obliged to serve. He is the sworn opponent of McLean's mumbling men with their pipes.

The works he has produced have been a variety of stone circles and lines either in galleries or photographed at some remote site. Descriptions of the procedure, such as 'Long pointed stones scattered along a 15 day walk in Lappland [*sic*] 207 stones turned to point into the wind', appear in exhibitions as well as maps and photographs. That, of course, raises the question whether the virtually inaccessible work or the means of reporting it is the work of art itself; but it is also a procedure which stresses Long's own role as wandering artist. With that go more romantic and traditional overtones than are to be found in Cragg, Woodrow or Boyle and Hills. Indeed it is comparable, in a curious way, to David Hockney's carefully cultivated image. Both reduce the centrality of the artist while increasing that of the subject matter, and both free him from the studio and the interior of his own mind to wander the world and to look. In Hockney the context is urban, materialistic and highly 'artistic', in Long it is rural, spiritual and self-effacing. Both, however, accept the fiction, the glass of water that can be an oak tree, the transforming power of art.

Handsome Bastards

Walter de Maria's kilometre-long brass rod, invisible in its hole, and the impatient reaction it inspired had their correlatives in literature, where the grand ambitions of the 1960s also came to seem absurd in the 1970s and 1980s. Criticism – structuralism as well as the whole panoply of theoretical variations – had worked towards a politically and socially demystified 'scientific' vocabulary and introduced new methods of analysis that threatened to undermine the entire orthodoxy of literary studies. Equally, it had raised the spectre of a kind of artistic paralysis: the culture was threatening to grind to a halt under the burden of its own self-consciousness.

In Christopher Hampton's 1970 play *The Philanthropist: A Bourgeois Comedy* one character dismisses structural linguistics as a 'yet more complicated method of over-simplification' and Philip, the structuralist at the centre of the play, finally rejects his own work and the play itself by means of his favourite form of word-play, the anagram:

PHILIP: I thought of a new anagram today . . . 'imagine the theatre as real' . . . 'imagine the theatre as real' . . . it's an anagram for 'I hate thee, sterile anagram'.[1]

This is the territory of Tom Stoppard, of course, and such material has a particular affinity for the theatre – the presence of the real people providing an ironic, mocking contrast to the unreality of the contents of their minds. But it was in the novel that new forces emerged, dissatisfied with previous post-war orthodoxies. The novel provided the kind of capacious debating space in which the immediate issues could be confronted.

Malcolm Bradbury was born in 1932 and in 1970 became professor of American Studies at the University of East Anglia, where his teaching in creative writing exerted a fatherly critical influence on an entire generation of writers, encouraging them to move away from realism and towards experimentation. His own writing began with

273

three campus-satirical novels, all inheritors of the tradition stretching back to *Lucky Jim*, culminating in *The History Man* (1975). His hero, Dr Howard Kirk, a sociologist, is a manipulative, ambitious master of the whole range of intellectual chatter that had sprung up over the previous decade. He has absorbed without question every passing intellectual fad:

'Well, I trust everyone,' says Miss Callendar, 'but no one especially over everyone else. I suppose I don't believe in group virtue. It seems to me such an individual achievement. Which, I imagine, is why you teach sociology and I teach literature.' 'Ah yes,' says Howard, 'but how do you teach it?' 'Do you mean am I a structuralist or a Leavisite or psycho-linguistician or a formalist or a Christian existentialist or a phenomenologist?' 'Yes,' says Howard. 'Ah,' says Miss Callendar, 'well I'm none of them.' 'What do you do, then?' asks Howard. 'I read books and talk to people about them.'[2]

The very idea of literature as a speciality had been undermined by the complex net the theorists had attempted to cast over the world. All was structure, systems and signs; simply to read books and talk about them appeared impossibly naïve. Yet the extent to which all theories, even deconstruction in its most anarchic phases, could see only what they wanted to see made them eternally vulnerable to more urbane, rounded readings of the set texts. Thus the ubiquitous William Blake, is hurled by Kirk at the pragmatic Miss Callendar as a defence of the revolutionary struggle and a means of persuading her to go to bed with him:

'Here's a quotation from the Proverbs of Hell: "Sooner murder an infant in its cradle than nurse unacted desires." ' 'Yes,' says Miss Callendar, 'what's your question?' 'How you came to reverse it when we talked this morning?' 'Ah,' says Miss Callendar, 'I did it via the instrument of literary criticism.' 'This is your good critical intelligence,' says Howard. 'That's it,' says Miss Callendar, 'you see, I was offering a paraphrase of its implicit as opposed to its surface meaning. You see, read the lines carefully, and you'll find the fulcrum is a pun around the words "infant" and "nurse". The infant and the desires are the same. So it doesn't mean kill babies if you really have to. I means it's better to kill desires than nourish ones you can never satisfy.' 'I see,' says Howard, 'so that's what you people do over there in English. I've often wondered.'[3]

Bradbury's use of Blake is acute. The emblematic figure of the 1960s revolutionaries and anarchists is here rescued by Miss Callendar. What had been taken for a cry of liberation is revealed as an appeal for the sternest self-discipline. The wrong reading of the Blake quotation was inspired by the political need for a slogan; the right reading suggests a more discerning, more humane approach.

But this was commentary. Like Stoppard, Bradbury was standing back and writing about the conflict rather than evolving new aesthetic responses, and the problem here was the familiar post-war sense of the lateness of the hour. Almost more than any other art form, the novel seemed to have been subverted by twentieth-century artistic innovations. The vast experiments of Joyce and Proust threatened the professional sanity of their successors. Even Evelyn Waugh, who was so decisively to reject such modernist extravagances, detected that there was a sense in which his generation of novelists could only ever appear to literary history as minor. Meanwhile, critical theory had made its most devastating inroads into the landscape of fiction and the technique of narrative, leaving the critically aware novelist with a terrifying burden of self-consciousness.

In Britain the post-war years had seen a general retreat into an unambitious realism. This was frequently and often spectacularly challenged – by Murdoch and Golding, for example – but it remained the dominant literary convention up to the mid-1970s. Indeed it was, and to some extent still is, the basis of the teaching of modern literature in schools.

From the mid-1970s the general artistic significance of the novel was revitalized by the appearance of a new generation of writers who addressed the increasing problems of the form's limitations. It was a development that, yet again, carried with it post-modernist overtones in that it centred on the need to reactivate the form and to discover new context. In this context, the publication in 1973 of Martin Amis's first novel *The Rachel Papers* was an important moment. Amis, born in 1949, was the son of Kingsley, the author of *Lucky Jim*. To an

THE PLEASURES OF PEACE

extent, the son's first novel seems self-consciously to refer back to the
father's. It concerns a rather reckless, outcast young man and much
of its comedy derives from the jaundiced world view he adopts but,
where Jim Dixon was a hero who was primarily right, Charles Highway
appears to be fundamentally wrong.

The novel is Highway's first-person account of the state of his life
on the eve of his twentieth birthday. Highway is self-consciousness
personified: he perpetually observes every aspect of himself, from his
name – 'a rangy, well-travelled, big-cocked name' – to his figure:
'medium length, arseless, waistless'. Above all, he inhabits a world at
one remove from that of experience. He cannot feel or see anything
without watching, checking or recording the act of feeling or seeing:
'I recall turning at one point . . . to check on Gloria's face (just for
the files).'⁴ This act of recording contributes to the construction of
Highway's book: the Rachel Papers themselves. So all that happens
is seen through the need to compile that book. Highway's self-
consciousness is the very fabric of the novel, and the form of its
construction, its prose, always demands that he maintains his distance
from everything and everybody that crosses his path. The reader is
asked only to stand back and marvel at Highway's technique:

'Thus I maintained a tripartite sexual application in contrapuntal
patterns. This sort of thing: insert tongue, remove finger from ear;
withdraw tongue, stroke neck, trail pinkie of left hand along narrow
gash between her jersey and skirt (tastefully avoiding navel); kiss and
semi-lick throat and neck, "do" ear, and place hand unemphatically
on knee; stop "doing" ear and stroke hairline, bring mouth towards
her and hand up her leg at similar speeds; with mouth almost there,
hold her gaze for long second while hand takes off at aeroplane
trajectory from the runway of her thighs and lands . . . on her stomach
again just as mouths meet. That sort of thing.'⁵

The sexual act has become a contrived pastiche of spontaneity.
Highway knows it all and thinks it all while he is doing it; he cannot
turn off the words. He is trapped in the excited jazz solo – cool,
distant, ironic – of his own prose. And that prose, he is all too aware,
constantly runs ahead of anything resembling feeling, surprise or the

awareness of other people. 'Oh, hi. You still here?' he thinks at one point in bed when Rachel herself actually speaks.

His own sense of the problem appears as a vaguely gloomy but none the less self-satisfied acceptance: 'One of the troubles with being over-articulate, with having a vocabulary more refined than your emotions is that every turn in the conversation, every switch of posture, opens up an estate of verbal avenues with a myriad side-turnings and cul-de-sacs – and there are no signposts but your own sincerity and good taste, and I've never had much of either. All I know is that I can go down any one of them and be welcomed as a returning lord.'[6]

Highway's solo cannot be stopped, he cannot be brought up against the world because his language in its extremity, its flexibility and its self-regarding conviction is designed to subjugate, to possess everything it encounters. The one occasion on which he is silenced is by a stinging attack on his Oxford entrance essays during his interview for a place at the university. The academic takes apart the suave inconsistencies of his judgements and asks him 'just [to] read the poems and work out whether you like them'. But the Highway guard goes back up at once, the watchful solo restarts and he ends the novel with the words 'I refill my pen', still living through paper and ink.

The importance of this and of Amis's subsequent novels lies in their use of an entirely new language for fiction: that of a deracinated culture. It springs from journalism, slang and the hermetic world of post-hippie hedonism. Its distortions and hyperbole are partly those of satire, frequently against pornography, but mainly those of a language that is generating itself from within a kind of amoral stew: what one *Encounter* reviewer called 'a condition of radical cynicism'. The following passage comes from his second novel *Dead Babies*, or *Dark Secrets* as it was retitled in paperback. The book is macabre, dark and extreme; it is inhabited by the blank, deranged inheritors of 1960s excess. The loathsome, degraded figure of Keith is being discussed:

'Oh dear, poor little Keith.'
'Yeah, he's a mess, isn't he?'
'Like a sort of wrecky little doll.'
'Breath like a laser-beam,' mused Quentin.
'Or an oxy-acetylene burner.'

'Fat as a pig.'

'Smells like a compost-heap.'

'Or a dotard's mattress.'

'Be bald as an egg by the time he's twenty-five.'

'Or twenty-four.'

'Or twenty-three.'

'Or twenty-two.'

'He's that now.'

'At least.'

'Yes,' said Andy, 'it's amazing, when you come to think of it, that he's so cheerful.'

'Especially with us handsome bastards about the place.'

'Check.' Andy nodded, his eyes closed. 'Check.'[7]

In this nightmare there is no human connection between the success and the failure. Keith is physically repulsive, Andy and Quentin are not, but there is no revenge for Keith, no counterbalancing reward and no escape in his personality. He is, if anything, more depraved than the rest of the characters in the novel. With the loss of the moral and cultural dimension in the language, leaving it free to spin on in brilliant variations of slang, there has also vanished the protection the author could once extend to his characters. There is no mechanism that would allow the unstoppable rhythm of Amis's prose to pause and take pity. The characters are destined to be at the mercy of the words.

The self-consciousness in Amis is far from that in Brigid Brophy, for example. She allowed her novels to oscillate around the peculiar difficulties of the fictional process, whereas Amis accepts the fiction in the novel as a kind of a priori. Beyond that, his main concern is with the creation of a specifically modern, urban fiction whose self-consciousness is embedded in the knowing language of that environment. He finds the tools for art in the same landscape as J. G. Ballard: that of the paranoid city with its 'vampiric sky'. He finds its content in the terrible spectacle of a world severed from its culture and suffused with strange and threatening absolutes. 'Indeed they are remarkable artefacts,' he wrote of nuclear weapons in the introduction to his 1987 collection of short stories, *Einstein's Monsters*, and continued:

'They derive their power from an equation: when a pound of uranium-235 is fissioned, the "liberated mass" within its 1,132,000,000,000,000, 000,000,000 atoms is multiplied by the speed of light squared – with the explosive force, that is to say, of 186,000 miles per second times 186,000 miles per second. Their size, their power, has no theoretical limit. They are biblical in their anger. They are clearly the worst thing that has ever happened to the planet, and they are mass-produced, and inexpensive. In a way, their most extraordinary single characteristic is that they are man-made. They distort all life and subvert all freedoms. Somehow, they give us no choice. Not a soul on earth wants them, but here they all are.'[8]

Nuclear weapons finally gave Amis's cultural dread its apocalyptic dimension and, at the same time, inflated its central ambiguity. For there can be no doubt that he is revelling in the fragmentary freedoms of his deracinated language, in the variations of its slang, and that this celebration is fighting with a moral and organizing sense that wishes to subdue the monster, to bring it into line. Equally, in this passage, the big numbers and the scary facts are intoned with breathless fascination – but he wishes to horrify us, to reveal the whizz-bang excitement of science as an inhuman threat, as a fatally flawed language that has taken the fate of the earth out of our hands.

Nihilistic Recoil

F. R. Leavis died in 1978, aged eighty-three. He was one of the creators of the most potent and pervasive literary orthodoxy of its time, an orthodoxy based upon a cultural continuity. In reality, of course, it was only the severance of that continuity that had inspired its affirmation in the New Criticism. Nevertheless, in his later years Leavis clung closer and closer to his idea of a priesthood that would protect and guide the one true culture through its darkest hour. In 1975 he published *The Living Principle: English as a Discipline of Thought*:

'There's no redeeming the democratic mass university. The civilization it represents has, almost overnight, ceased to believe in its own assumptions and recoils nihilistically from itself. If you believe in humanity at all you will know that nothing today is more important than to keep alive the idea of the university-function – the essential university-function and what goes with it: the idea of an educated public. My preoccupation is to ensure that the living seed exists and that the life in it has the full pregnancy. Just how it will strike and take and develop, as it *must* if there is to be a human future, one can't foresee, change is certainly upon us, menacing and certainly drastic; to meet it, there must be opportunism – the opportunism that answers to a profound realization of the need.'[1]

The characteristically paranoid Leavis tone seemed to have been validated by a culture that had become unignorably different from the organic community of which he had once dreamed and upon which his entire, desperate aesthetic had been based. Now, in his final writings, he could see more clearly than ever before the whites of his enemies' eyes: 'I say nothing about the more expensive Sunday papers, where the élite, or coterie, of the literary world go about their business, nor about that (from the critical point of view) closely related phenomenon, *The Times Literary Supplement* – which, as I write, makes a point of testifying that Mr Amis is modern literature and the late W. H. Auden a major poet and a mind of world importance. There is no need here for a full account of our cultural plight.'[2]

What can save us is 'the living principle': 'Where there is an educated public the living principle will be a living presence and have some influence. Where it has, it will tell sometimes on writers (say) of *Times* leaders. Statesmen of all parties will, in such a civilisation, now and then find themselves recognising that if they continue to talk and act and bureaucratise on the blank assumption that rescuing Britain from its plight and curing its malady is a matter of ensuring a good percentage growth rate, a fair distribution and industrial peace, they will most certainly ensure a major human disaster.'[3]

It was the last cry of the humanist metaphysics that had come to terms with modernism, though never with the modern. For Leavis the university had become a correlative of the original grand modernist enterprise: holding together a potentially disintegrated culture in an act of imaginative will. The university was the last beacon in a darkening world whose reflected light could still glimmer elsewhere – in *Times* leaders – if permitted. The secular paradise was, in other words, still within reach but, again in a rather valedictory tone, another critic summarized more precisely and more sensitively the fact that the old continuity had definitively gone: the fact had to be confronted by literary criticism if it wished to survive.

'There are those who argue', Frank Kermode write in 1982, 'that the history of criticism is a history of error; but if we stay within that tradition, rather than seek to overthrow it, we shall have to say rather that it is a history of accommodations, of attempts to earn the privilege of access to that Kingdom of the larger existence which is in our time the secular surrogate of another Kingdom whose horizon is no longer within our range.'[4]

Writing in *Encounter*, John Harvey recalled one of Leavis's last public appearances before his death:

'He closed his last official lecture in Cambridge with an attack on the view that the good and the bad qualities of literature were some sort of moral absolute – a naïvety sometimes attributed to him. To clinch the point he quoted Santayana's observation on ethical absolutism to the effect that saying something is good in itself or bad in itself is like saying that whisky isn't intoxicating to me but stands there dead drunk in the bottle. Then he made some difficulty in switching off the light at the lectern, muttering *sotto voce*, "put out the light" and left.'[5]

Criticism might sustain a new culture, but it could not revive the old one. The new one, however, was difficult to define; it was easier to derive a creative impetus from a realization of the old, broken one. This was the background to Martin Amis's novels; but there it appeared transformed by the energetic contradictions of his own method. In British drama in the 1970s and 1980s the vision of the broken culture became the all-pervasive vernacular. Against this shattered background playwrights could evolve a variety of dramatic postures, for example the proletarian sentimentality and heroism of the character Iron from Nigel Williams's 1978 play *Class Enemy*: 'Lissen. I ain't got no fuckin' knowledge. I jus'ask don' I. Ask and ask and ask an' punch an' punch' an' I don' get no fuckin' nearer do I? Nuffink adds up nuffink makes sense not one thing means anyfing I jus' punch an' punch an' punch an' wot is there?'[6]

The speech almost summarizes the entire foundation from which the mainstream British theatrical orthodoxy sprang. The character is deadened by the anguish of ignorance, his language is broken and crude. Like so many anti-establishment dramas of the 1960s the play is set in a school, to dramatize society's failure to produce a transmissible culture.

In this play Williams was at one with what has come to be known as 'the second wave' of British dramatists. The first wave is taken to be the generation that emerged in the 1950s and early 1960s: Osborne, Pinter, Arden, Wesker and Orton. The second includes Edward Bond, Trevor Griffiths, David Hare, Howard Brenton and Caryl Churchill and, in purely chronological terms, could be said to include Stoppard, Simon Gray and Peter Shaffer. These three, however, do not stand in the mainstream of the second wave. This mainstream was defined entirely by an extraordinary unity of political purpose.

In part this unity can be explained by the degree to which the 1970s London theatre industry entered a period of sophisticated and relatively prosperous organization. The idea of fringe theatres, inspired by the American off-Broadway tradition, came to London in 1968 when Jim Haynes, founder of the Traverse Theatre in Edinburgh, started the Arts Lab and Charles Marowitz launched the Open Space. Both were products of the subversive mood of the day; but, equally, both discovered a sympathetic audience sufficiently large to justify, if not to pay for, their existence. Fringe theatres appeared all around London and provided previously undreamed-of opportunities for new playwrights. Where once there had been only the Royal Court, now there was any number of possibilities.

'In 1967 there was one independent socialist theatre group in Britain: Cartoon Archetypical Slogan Theatre,' David Edgar wrote in 1979. 'There are now at least 18 full time subsidized socialist groups, in addition to perhaps as many unsubsidized or local groups who propagate revolutionary socialist ideas.'[7]

At the other end of the scale the two national theatre companies - the National Theatre and the Royal Shakespeare Company – were progressing beyond the first phase of the struggle to establish themselves as permanent and unassailable entities. In 1976 the National moved into its first custom-built home on the South Bank and, after a long period of expansion, in 1982 the RSC moved into the Barbican Centre. With varying degrees of success, the provincial subsidized theatre network also entered a more secure, established phase.

The market for 'serious', that is, not primarily commercial, drama had thus expanded enormously and many new playwrights appeared to satisfy the demand. Yet in spite of the numbers, and perhaps because of the very nature of the Fringe, the type of drama produced was remarkably uniform. In essence it accepted the idea of a wounded culture, pessimistic and broken – 'the only thing that binds us together today is a profound unease,' said Howard Brenton – and applied the bandage of radical left-wing ideology. From the past this could be taken to spring from the pessimistic cultural generalizations of Osborne, the committed realism of Wesker and, further back, the ambitious, politically active theatre of Brecht; but the systematic nature of the politics was quite new in post-war British theatre. Meanwhile this drama found additional energy from the election, in 1979, of the radically right-wing Government of Margaret Thatcher. The sense of urban despair and blight that had become the demotic of the 1970s was to find dramatic focus in the 1980s in the mythology of 'Thatcher's Britain'.

'Their simplicity of aim,' John Spurling wrote in 1974 of the new playwrights, 'the fact that they are not trying to set up mirrors of human behaviour for all time but only to cope with relatively temporary issues, goes with an engagingly cavalier attitude towards the theatrical means at their disposal.'[8]

Little can be said about drama as bizarrely specialized as Trevor Griffiths's *The Party*, in which a professor and a Trotskyite organizer discuss the ethical issues involved in Marxist action. Evidently the intention is to force an appreciation of theatrical truth as the clear presentation of issues and ideas; beyond that the play can have significance possibly only to a student of Marxist theory. More dramatically, Howard Brenton exhibits the group style in perhaps the purest form. In his *Weapons of Happiness*, commissioned by the National Theatre, there is a sudden moment of violence which leaves Ralph Makepeace and Josef Frank on stage:

RALPH: Contact lens.

FRANK: I plead.

RALPH: If it comes on to snow I'll never find it. Frank!

FRANK: I plead

RALPH: Help me, man!

(JOSEF FRANK *shakes his head*.)

FRANK: I plead.

RALPH: For godsake, what's the matter with you?

FRANK: I plead guilty of being a war criminal. And of committing a whole number of grave crimes for the benefit of the US imperialists. To the detriment of the working people of Czechoslovakia and the whole peace camp. All the dogs of Europe.[9]

The sharp intensity of the violence, a man symbolically lost on stage and another preoccupied with apparently remote issues of international politics form a typical theatrical image of the age.

In many respects drama of this type is simply not asking to be judged as theatre, rather by its effectiveness. It was being written by a generation which regarded aesthetic considerations as entirely secondary to political function: a generation of graduates who had identified with the revolutionary aspirations that surfaced in the universities in 1968. 'May '68 disinherited my generation in two ways,' Brenton explained. 'First, it destroyed any remaining affection for the official culture. The situationists showed how all of them, the dead greats, are corpses on our backs – Goethe, Beethoven – how gigantic the fraud is. But it also, secondly, destroyed the notions of personal freedom, freak out and drug culture, anarchist notions of spontaneous freedom, anarchist political activity.'[10]

The idea of Western culture as a kind of vast confidence trick derives from the straight radical view that it was merely one of the many tools of oppression deployed by the ruling class. Yet, in a less programmatic sense, it echoes John Wain's analysis in the 1950s. In general the view is familiar enough; what is new in Brenton's interpretation is, first, the unarguable conviction and vehemence with which he upholds that view and, second, the way in which he speaks from a position of acquired wisdom. The uprisings of the 1960s had been local and ineffective; very well then, the revolutionary must devise more sophisticated weapons. Again, Brenton spoke of the gentler hippie-like souls who attempted to construct closed 'alternative' communities within society: 'The truth is that there is only one society – that you can't escape the world you live in. Reality is remorseless. No one can leave. If you're going to change the world, well, there's only one set of tools, and they're bloody and stained but realistic. I mean communist tools. Not pleasant. If only the gentle, dreamy, alternative society *had* worked.'[11]

The failure of the liberationist ideals of the 1960s also had technical implications for political drama. It was quite clear that the British proletariat were *not* politicized by the activities of the far left. This drove the dramatists into a long period of introspection both about the means by which they might reach 'the masses' and about the relevance of writing plays for performance to limited audiences in 'bourgeois' venues such as the National Theatre. The point was that this was a form of writing that began from a conception of the audience; the artist, therefore, sat down to write burdened with the technical demands of reaching and then politicizing an audience.

David Edgar caught the emphasis precisely: 'What is obviously needed is a way of transforming the techniques that have been developed in metropolitan theatres into forms that are formally and geographically accessible to audiences directly involved in the struggle against exploitation and oppression.'[12]

This demand that the audience be, as starkly as possible, affected produced two common stylistic features in the plays themselves: the tendency towards the epic and the suppression of psychology. Epic, according to Edward Bond,[13] arose from the collapse of Christianity. It had been a natural form to the Greeks because their gods had been superhuman; the Christian god was transcendent, he reduced the significance of the world and removed the basis of the epic ideal. The post-Christian world found its significance restored – 'beauty and truth have to become immanent in the world again – and epic once more become a possible form'.[14]

Psychology, meanwhile, was simply a bourgeois demand: 'The way we see the world depends on our political consciousness and our class situation. And there's absolutely no way of making sense of human experience apart from that,'[15] said Bond.

Brenton was more specific: 'I've always been against psychology in plays. I think that psychology is used like a wet blanket by many playwrights, and as a very easy explanation and I wanted to stop that dead in its tracks . . . One of the formal ways of doing that was to emphasize the role, the action.'[16]

All this resulted in grand dramas of alienation in which deliberately representative characters strode through history in order to make clear the political continuities. Chichester in Brenton's *Romans in Britain*, for example, says:

I keep on seeing the dead. A field in Ireland, a field in England.
And faces like wood. Charred wood, set in the ground. Staring at me.

The faces of our forefathers.

Their eyes are sockets of rain-water, flickering with gnats.
They stare at me in terror.

Because in my head there's a Roman spear. A Saxon axe.
A British Army machine-gun.

The weapons of Rome, invaders, Empire.[17]

The language is intended to suggest a man hypnotized by the revelation of his place in history, his oneness with the oppressors of the past. The revelation is complete and 'true'; it exists prior to the language, prior to the play. The effort of the writing, therefore, is solely to uncover and render vividly this truth.

The realization of that truth would prepare the way for a society unencumbered by the evils of this one. Trevor Griffiths described the intentions of one of his television plays: 'What I was trying to say was, "We have lost sight of human possibility, of the possibility of being human in the way in which society is now organising itself, through institutions, systems and structures." '[18]

This, finally, is the significance of this remarkably uniform and widespread form of drama. The burden of content is lifted entirely from the writer's shoulders. His content is an imaginary historical progression, which, he believes, he detects in everything he sees. Britain is a depressed, haunted, miserable place because this truth has been systematically concealed by a malevolent, capitalist ruling class. It is a land of sporadic, inexplicable violence and a land blind to the true nature of history.

This vision became a stylistic convention in drama, novels, films and television. It has affected even writers who did not share the political fervour of these playwrights. It entered the vernacular as yet another form of national despair in the tradition of Cyril Connolly's epic glooms, John Osborne's frenzied attacks and the general cultural pessimism of the 1970s. Yet only in this bizarre, driven generation of playwrights did it become so elaborately sustained by the very institutional forces they seemed so concerned to destroy.

Half English

Michael Moorcock's hero Jerry Cornelius, and indeed the left-wing playwrights, suffered from a familiar illusion of the 1970s: the belief in the conspiracy theory. In Cornelius's case, a certain sentimentality about the various liberations of the 1960s encouraged the belief that there had been a deliberate effort to stamp out the good times. The idea was abroad that there were malign forces, usually categorized as Fascist, who were afraid of what they had seen on the streets. So, always the supreme representative of his age, Cornelius had sought his 'adequate mythology' in the art nouveau jungle atop the art deco caverns of the Derry & Toms department store: the mythology, in other words, of the stylized past.

In the 1970s the past acquired a cultural presence of rare potency. At the most trivial level it emerged as a widespread decorative fascination with the Georgian, Regency, Victorian and Edwardian periods, which seemed to represent a more decorative, more stable way of life. Television re-creations of those periods became as frequent as soap operas or the news. The medium seemed to have discovered an appropriate convention in the unlikely form of the historical novel. The hypnotic particularity of television intensified the sensation that issues of class, honour, nationality and social custom had once existed as realities, as meticulously well defined as the flawlessly re-created costumes.

Crudely, therefore, the past seemed to work, to be consistent. The present, in contrast, appeared confused and threatening. It was a sense that affected many countries: nostalgia became a potent popular force in the USA, for example. In Britain, though, its particular poignancy arose from the feeling that, as a nation, we had lost our identity; the Empire had gone and we were being subsumed into Europe. The past was a time when we had national significance and its loss had produced, in the 1960s, what amounted to a playful revelling in insignificance: national icons, such as policemen's helmets or the

Union Jack, were transformed into popular emblems. In the 1970s came a need to contemplate again what had once been important as a way of holding at bay an overwhelming sense of unimportance.

The Empire, slowly demolished throughout the twentieth century, was taken, above all else, to incarnate that importance. Meditating on its decline became as distinct a literary mode as the television dramatization of novels of the past. Paul Scott's four novels known as *The Raj Quartet* appeared through the 1960s with the final part, *A Division of the Spoils*, being published in 1975. Significantly, one of the work's main incidents – the alleged rape of Daphne Manners by Hari Kumar in the Bibighar Gardens – echoed E. M. Forster's own liberal dissection of the imperial culture, *A Passage to India*. The image of miscegenation, violence and uncertainty was clearly irresistible as a means of encapsulating the ambiguity of empire. 'The relationship of Britain and India as Scott portrays it,' wrote David Rubin, 'is allegorized as a sexual embrace.'[1]

The slow, cumulative pace of Scott's work, its complex chronology and dramatis personae as well as its even meditative tone all indicate a painstaking and powerful determination to use the novel form as a surgeon's knife to open up the many resonances of colonialism. Throughout, it stresses the moral, social, political and psychological interconnectedness of every fragment of Scott's vast canvas and, at every step, the book echoes with a curious, almost indefinable significance:

' "And the officer who was best man at your sister's wedding," Bronowsky went on. "Captain Merrick. Have you had news of him? He interested me considerably. I thought him an unusual man."

'Spoken casually like that in these strange but civilized surroundings the familiar name, Merrick, had the same disconcerting effect as a sudden change in the intensity of the light. He found himself concentrating on certain essentials. The girl was a stranger, not Laura. The Merrick she and Bronowsky knew need not be his Merrick. But her manner had altered. The prominence of bone seemed more accentuated. This, perhaps, was imaginary. She said that it was to visit this Merrick in hospital that she had gone to Calcutta. This Merrick, her Merrick, had been wounded and a Captain Bingham killed. Her Merrick had tried to help someone called Teddie and had lost an arm. He had pulled Teddie out of a blazing truck while they were under fire. He was in for a decoration. Captain Bingham and Teddie must be one and the same man. She had gone to see her Merrick in hospital because her sister was anxious to find out if there was anything they could do.'[2]

In the imaginary landscape of India people seem unsure of one another's existence. Merrick's identity shifts and changes and the social hierarchy of names – Teddie or Captain Bingham – creates unexpected confusions. The cast appears to be subjected to some kind of huge mirage; they are trapped in baffled contemplation of others and of history. Such dreamlike uncertainty undermines the heroic imperial myth. People remain a mystery to one another in spite of their attempts to simplify their differences through the crude mechanisms of empire. And the mystery is, in effect, a justification for this use of the novel. History alone could not capture the fading, dreamlike condition of the Raj.

A similar sense of bafflement, though with comic overtones, suffuses J. G. Farrell's dissections of the end of empire. He too embarked on an enormous fictional project to cover the subject: it was as though the scope of the content, of the British Empire itself, demanded an equivalently large-scale response from the novelist. Farrell was, however, a more self-conscious artist than Scott and his perception of a culture, hopelessly unaware of its own place in history, is realized more precisely in the language of his novels. This lack of awareness is seen not as tragedy, but as farce. In this passage from Farrell's 1973 novel *The Siege of Krishnapur* Fleury, only seconds after narrowly escaping death at the hands of a Sepoy warrior, finds the padre at his side:

' "Think how apt fins are to water, wings to air, how well the earth suits its inhabitants!" exclaimed the Padre, suddenly appearing at Fleury's side as if conjured up by this reference to Heaven. "In everything on earth we see evidence of design. Turn from your blindness, I beg you in His name. Everything from fish's eye, to caterpillar's food, to bird's wing and gizzard, bears manifest evidence of the

Supreme Design. What other explanation can you find for them in your darkness?"

'Fleury stared at the Padre, too harrowed and exhausted to speak. Could it not be, he wondered vaguely, trembling on the brink of an idea that would have made him famous, that somehow or other the fish designed their own eyes?'[3]

The padre's intervention is grotesque, insane, yet even in extremity Fleury's mind responds. His response is radical and extraordinary, it could have made him famous, but the moment is lost to history and we are left only the conventional view of the clergyman. History, to Farrell, has become contingent farce yet, as in Scott, it is somehow connected; but connected by a distinctly post-modernist, self-conscious personality:

'Imagine a clock in a glass case; the hands move unruffled about their business, but at the same time we can see the workings of springs and wheels and cogs. That ordered life in Tanglin depended in the same way on the city below, and on the mainland beyond the Causeway, whose trading, mining and plantation concerns might represent wheels and cogs while their mute, gigantic labour force are the springs, steadily causing pressures to be transmitted from one part of the organism to another ... and not just at that time or just to Tanglin, of course, but much further in time and space: to you thousands of miles away, reading in bed or in a deckchair on the lawn, or to me as I sit writing at a table.'[4]

The interconnections of economic and mechanical forces, the pressures of wheels, cogs and springs are fictionally realized – but they *were* real once, as real as the facts of Farrell writing or his reader reading. The past in the historical novel is less fictional than the present in a contemporary one. It is made more true by virtue of its distance. John Spurling has written of Farrell's work: 'When J. G. Farrell, having written three novels with contemporary settings, turned to historical settings, it was no doubt largely because the passage of time puts inverted commas around issues which once seemed of vital importance and allows the novelist to observe human behaviour more coolly and clearly from a seat in the gods.'[5]

The distance in time is the correlative of Farrell's ironic distance. The importance of this is that it represents a 'harder' attitude to the past than that of the television series or, more important, than that of, for example, the poet David Jones. In Jones's essay on George Borrow, which I quoted in Part Two, 'Late Times', the past is evoked by a religious visionary. Jones believed that the connection with history is part of the sacramental system. It is an expression of the continuity of religious experience. For the secular novelist, however, it becomes an essential imaginative act; the strangeness of the past makes us aware of the unfathomable present. Equally it evokes pity, the pity for the continual human failure to do anything at all about the forces of history, however farcical. Farrell's *The Singapore Grip* contains the following description of the last moments of an old Chinese:

'In one cubicle, not much bigger than a large wardrobe, an elderly Chinese wharf-coolie lies awake beside a window covered with wire-netting. Beside him, close to his head, is the shrine for the worship of his ancestors with bunches of red and white candles strung together by their wicks. It was here beside him that his wife died and sometimes, in the early hours, she returns to be with him for a little while. But tonight she has not come and so, presently, he slips out of his cubicle and down the stairs, stepping over sleeping forms, to visit the privy outside. As he returns, stepping into the looming shadow of the tenement, there is a white flash and the darkness drains like a liquid out of everything he can see. The building seems to hang over him for a moment and then slowly dissolves, engulfing him. Later, when official estimates are made of this first raid on Singapore (sixty-one killed, one hundred and thirty-three injured), there will be no mention of this old man for the simple reason that he, in common with so many others, has left no trace of every having existed either in this part of the world or any other.'[6]

Farrell and Scott found a content for their novels in the issues 'in inverted commas' of the past. Equally, they discovered a pessimism in the face of the intractability of those issues. It was as though the urban despair of contemporary writers had leaked out to inhabit history. The incomprehensible, technological execution of the old Chinese is a clear enough anticipation of the many imagined deaths that were to occur in the shadow of nuclear weapons – the great externalizations of post-war pessimism. There is also a kind of hopelessness in the attempt to see the coolie as anything other than a number. Even when Farrell makes us feel his fate through the poignant detailing of the dead wife and the candles, it still evokes only immense helplessness rather than direct human sympathy. This finds its parallel in the death of Little Joe the crossing-sweeper in Dickens's *Bleak House*, with its anguished sense of the sheer weight of suffering in the world. Through newspapers and television, Farrell's audience was in daily contact with a whole world of random death, injustice and poverty. The helplessness was correspondingly more complete, a fact that perhaps accounts for the writing being correspondingly thinner.

So, alongside history as a form of artistic content, also emerged an alien world: that of the coolie in his tenement, a world obviously opposed to a Europe with its aspirations towards cultural and political cohesion and to a controllable centrality. This alien world played a part in the dissident 1960s view, when the Vietnam war provided an external meaning to the internal sense of discord within the culture. For the left, the war showed an imperialist power engaged in the subjugation of a peasant Third World population; it provided an imagery of technology attempting to crush a rural society. Jungle was defoliated by napalm and chemicals in the pursuit of a guerrilla army that was to prove unbeatable due to its seemingly magical powers of merging into the landscape and the population. It was the ideal horror story for the primitivists at the rock concerts or at the great Albert Hall poetry reading. The Communist Vietcong were like an avenging force of nature, beyond the reach of electronics, chemicals and high explosive; but, above all, they were alien, unfamiliar.

In addition the 'meaning' of the Vietnam war seemed to pre-empt debate in much the same way as environmental concerns seemed overwhelming in the 1970s. There was a sense in which mere passive contemplation of this absolute came to be all that was necessary. Just as David Bailey had once pointed his camera at his dead-pan models or celebrities without comment, so the recording of Vietnam became a process of silent observation. Television film showed American troops using Zippo cigarette lighters to set fire to peasant huts – no more needed to be said. To comment would be merely to reveal the crippling burden of Western culture that stood between us and the reality of the experience. Journalism thus took on immense cultural significance; it represented the idea of an honest form of communication that attempted to do without the predispositions of culture. In the form of the New Journalism, which emerged from the USA, it aspired to art; it abandoned overt selection and news values in favour of long reflections simply on what was happening. It aimed for objectivity by making plain its own subjectivity. The evidence was unarguable because it was perceived rather than analysed by the crude instrument of a Western, and therefore ignorant, mind. Journalism simply brought back the strange and terrible news from the lands we had once tried to own, from cultures we had assumed were secondary.

Vietnam and the Empire merged in the imagination to represent a terrible crime of which we had been found guilty. The imaginary journalist in alien lands, always romantically on the move and travelling light, both actually and psychologically, became a kind of literary ideal. Of course, this part had been played for years by Graham Greene, but the insistent pressure of his Catholicism and the tough, disciplined structuring of his novels disqualified him as a possessor of an entirely undeceived eye. All the strands, however, of empire, of the past, of alien lands and of the journalist came together in V. S. Naipaul.

Naipaul was born in 1932 to a Brahmin family in Trinidad; his father was a journalist. He came to England in 1950 to take up a place at University College, Oxford, and later settled here permanently, though from 1960 onwards, he travelled extensively. Central to any understanding of Naipaul is the fact that, apparently from the beginning, he had no intention of doing anything but write. The idea of writing and its significance lies at the heart of all his books. Despite the wide range of their settings and forms, they can all be viewed as meditations on the act of their own compositions. His four earliest novels, published between 1957 and 1961 and culminating in *A House for Mr Biswas*, were based on Trinidad life and show Naipaul refining and simplifying his fictional method. Through the 1960s his settings widened and took on a more cosmopolitan and political tone; most significantly, they showed the beginnings of an elision of the fictional and the journalistic. At the same time Naipaul was also producing books of travel and political journalism.

In 1971 he published *In a Free State*, a novel that deliberately avoided any suggestion of the form's traditional conclusiveness. Three separate stories are simply placed side by side and framed by a prologue and an epilogue 'from a journal'. The primary effect of this is to reduce the usual novelistic sense of an exemplary story rounded and completed by an authorial intention. The intention cannot, of course, be entirely eliminated; but the simple juxtaposition of the stories in a montage implicitly reduces its role and heightens the significance of the reader's response. This, in turn, encourages a sense of objectivity, of a journalistic determination to provide exemplary material without manipulation. The point is made most obviously by the journal framing the stories, which presents Naipaul himself as an inquiring, curious observer:

'The tramp was unfolding his magazine. He stopped and looked at the chocolate. But there was none for him. He unfolded his magazine. Then, unexpectedly, he began to destroy it. With nervous jigging hands he tore at a page, once, twice. He turned some pages, began to tear again; turned back, tore. Even with the raucousness around the Egyptian the sound of tearing paper couldn't be ignored. Was he tearing out pictures – sport, women, advertisements – that offended him? Was he hoarding toilet paper for Egypt?'[7]

In the journal the tramp exists as irreducibly exterior to the narrator; he is not fictionalized, his behaviour seems opaque, mysterious. In the stories, however, the fiction takes over. The first, 'One out of Many' is narrated by a servant whose master moves from Bombay to Washington. After some persuading he agrees to take the servant with him. The shock of the move and the wholly alien world he discovers in Washington lead to no revelation, only to a supreme resignation:

'I am a simple man who decided to act and see for himself, and it is as though I have had several lives. I do not wish to add to these. Some afternoons I walk to the circle with the fountain. I see the dancers but they are separated from me as by glass. Once, when there were rumours of new burnings, someone scrawled in white paint on the pavement outside my house: *Soul Brother*. I understand the words; but I feel, brother to what or to whom? I was once part of the flow, never thinking of myself as a presence. Then I looked in the mirror and decided to be free. All that my freedom has brought me is the knowledge that I have a face and have a body, that I must feed this body and clothe this body for a certain number of years. Then it will be over.'[8]

The human condition is terminal in every sense. As part of the Bombay masses, the servant had no individuality, only an identity conferred by the crowd. In Washington he discovers individuality, but in that he finds only a body with demands that must be met and then only death. Neither condition leads onward because there is nowhere to go. The servant's change of circumstances only reveals that no real change is possible.

In many respects, this radical scepticism finds its logical expression in Naipaul's journalism – in, for example, books like his *Among the Believers: An Islamic Journey*, published in 1981. Here he is confronted with the bizarre and frequently horrifying spectacle of a religion in the process of trying to interpret itself as a social order. At every level Naipaul – is an outsider in this world, which emerges, therefore, as exotic, but, at the same time, finally knowable as a product of the weaknesses and needs of its human inhabitants.

'The life that had come to Islam had not come from within. It had come from outside events and circumstances, the spread of the universal civilization. It was the late twentieth century that had made Islam revolutionary, given new meaning to old Islamic ideas of equality and union, shaken up static or retarded societies ... Behzad, the communist (to whom the Russian rather than the Iranian revolution was "the greatest turn in history"), was made by Islam more than he knew. And increasingly now in Islamic countries there would be the Behzads who, in an inversion of Islamic passion, would have a vision of a society cleansed and purified, a society of believers.'[9]

The tramp of *In a Free State* is finally knowable because he can be seen as the unwitting victim of his history and his condition. Similarly the great mystery of Islamic fundamentalism with all its rural simplifications is explainable by the interaction of the *realpolitik* of the late twentieth century and the mythologies of an ancient religion. The journalistic task is complete: the strange has been explained by the operations of a Third World mind steeped in the complex mixture of empiricism and rationalism that is Western culture.

Through all this, Naipaul is implicitly meditating on his own role - not simply his identity and history, but also his activity in writing all this down. In many respects, the books to this point suggest a book that has not yet been written, a book that would unify the novels and the journalism as well as the conflicting elements of his own biography. Any such unification, of course, is made difficult by the sceptical, undeceived quality of his own gaze. To write it requires a synthesis which, by its nature, would be untrustworthy. In the event, however, it was written.

The Enigma of Arrival, subtitled 'A novel in five sections', was published in 1987. It remains, for the moment, his masterpiece in that it achieves precisely the unification implied by his earlier work. In essence, it is an autobiography which sets out to explain and describe his life in a small cottage on an estate near Salisbury in Wiltshire. The primary content of the work is his life there, the landscape and the people with whom he lives. To begin with, this content seems to be organized around two themes: the unavoidable quality of change, even in the most apparently unchangeable of rural environments, and the process of Naipaul's own adjustment to living in the very England whose presence had been such a powerful imaginative component of his childhood:

'The history I carried with me, together with the self-awareness that had come with my education and ambition, had sent me into the world with a sense of glory dead; and in England had given me the rawest of stranger's nerves. Now ironically – or aptly – living in the grounds of this shrunken estate, going out for my walks, those nerves were soothed, and in the wild garden and orchard beside the water meadows I found a physical beauty perfectly suited to my temperament and answering, besides, every good idea I could have had, as a child in Trinidad, of the physical aspect of England.'[10]

Amid the immense accumulations of detail of his life in England

and the flashbacks to his origins, the real theme begins to emerge: how and what to write. Fiction, for example, has come to possess a kind of impossibility for him:

'That ability to project what I read on to Trinidad, the colonial, tropical, multi-racial world which was the only world I knew, that ability diminished as I grew older. It was partly as a result of my increasing knowledge, self-awareness, and my embarrassment at the working of my fantasy. It was also partly because of the writers. Very few had the universal child's eye of Dickens. And that gift of fantasy became inoperable as soon as I came to England in 1950. When I was surrounded by the reality, English literature ceased to be universal, since it ceased to be the subject of fantasy.'[11]

The process of discovering a form and a content becomes a process of reduction. The fantasies and posturing of his earliest work is steadily replaced by a colder and clearer determination to watch and observe without illusions: 'I had discovered in myself . . . a deep interest in others, a wish to visualize the details and routine of their lives, to see the world through their eyes; and with this interest there often came at some point a sense – almost a sixth sense – of what was uppermost in a person's thoughts.'[12]

Through this process of reduction, he works towards a revelation of what originally inspired the book. The title – the name given by Apollinaire to a painting by de Chirico – began as the title of another book, a novel based on the painting; but it comes to take on all the mysteries of seeing things for the first time, of being born into a real English landscape, of having an imagined land made real. In addition, it comes to stress that there *is* an enigma, an irreducible quality about human life. This had once been expressed in religion, in history, in the sacred places of childhood, but now 'every generation was to take us further away from those sanctities'. The world would be remade in the face of death of his sister – which occurs in this book – and of his brother, Shiva, to whom it is dedicated.

Quite apart from its self-evident beauty and sureness, the importance of *The Enigma of Arrival* lies in the way Naipaul has searched through the complexities of his own biography to discover a written unity. The long, precise descriptions of trees, fields, paths and people are not related to the whole in any traditional artistic sense. Rather, they are allowed to imbue the entire work with significance. The controlling hand of authorial intent is, in a supreme elevation of the journalistic impulse, removed to allow the world in. Naipaul is staring long and hard at his world and, finally, allowing it to make the book. Thus the 'meaning' of any incident exists prior to the book and is then discovered in the act of writing. In addition, the facts of Naipaul's story are drawn together so as to provide a kind of synthesis of a whole range of obsessions. He is an eternal alien, he has lived through the end of empire and he has wandered the world as a journalist, an observer. With *The Enigma of Arrival* the whole imperial episode and the long mystery of Britain's new national identity seem to have been brought home. It returns to an English landscape of villages, manor houses, cottages and churches made, at last, as irreducibly strange as the people who created it.

Not Frivolous

The worship of excess that had characterized the 1960s was nowhere more rapidly qualified in the 1970s than in poetry. The combination of vast, populist outpourings on the one hand and the terminal anguish of the A. Alvarez school on the other inevitably produced the uneasy feeling that more delicate life forms were in danger of being extinguished. Not, however, that the anguish could be abandoned, merely that it could be dealt with in a more responsible fashion.

'We move daily deeper [wrote the poet Alan Brownjohn in 1972] into a complex and alarming kind of technical, late capitalist civilization where the surfaces get smoother and the realities ever more violent, irrational and ruthless. One's first, instinctive response is to resort to the counter-irrationality of a counter-culture. But the only effective response, in the long term, will come from a rational, sceptical temperament which will calmly and wisely dismantle the machinery of horror and organise the commonwealth of decency.'[1]

Such an assertion, mildly and tentatively stated here, became a clamorous orthodoxy in the years that followed. By 1980 Peter Jones and Michael Schmidt were speculating that the poetry of the previous decade would come 'to denote a new and attentive approach to traditional formalism, no longer disabled by the strategic ironies of the 1950s; a period of "unillusion", when young writers began to find their way home from the euphoria and betrayed optimism that characterized much of the 1960s'.[2]

In fact the change was, initially at least, a critical one rather than a transformation in the audience's view of poetry. Ted Hughes retained his role as the popular image of the anguished poet 'wading bloody-toothed-and-clawed through the detritus of a collapsed civilization with a wry grin of satisfaction on his swarthy face'.[3] The sales of his books dwarfed those of most other poets and, thanks to school syllabuses, he had come to be *the* representative of contemporary poetry.

The critical temperature had fallen, though. Larkin enjoyed a revitalized reputation; his precise, crafted verse finding more sympathy in a less progressively minded decade. His poetic persona became a gloomy but significant part of the national identity, particularly after the publication in 1974 of his collection *High Windows*; its title poem expressed, perhaps, once and for all the glum dryness of the Movement, its determination to persist, undeceived and unamazed. From its first stanza evoking the sexual promiscuity of the days and the poet's remoteness from such delights, Larkin proceeds to a typically remote and inconclusive close:

> Rather than words comes the thought of high windows:
> The sun-comprehending glass,
> And beyond it, the deep blue air that shows
> Nothing, and is nowhere, and is endless.[4]

In addition, in the cooler climate, there was a general agreement that poets such as Geoffrey Hill, C. H. Sisson, Donald Davie and Charles Tomlinson represented a more convincing critical continuity than anything that had emerged in the 1960s. It was not that the names on the list had much in common, rather that they seemed to represent the kind of taut, fastidious seriousness that the age demanded. But, although Larkin once again found himself in tune with an uncertain and pessimistic age, this new seriousness tended to regard the Movement as a whole with a good deal of suspicion. Its systematic exclusion of so much from the content of poetry came to seem a wilfully extreme, almost fanatical effort: 'Today, looking back on the poets included in *New Lines*,' wrote Ian Hamilton, 'it seems difficult to conceive of aridity more notable than theirs.' He added: 'Efforts, in some of these poems, to extend a narrowly literary anti-romanticism into a general critique of what Conquest describes as "great systems of theoretical constructs" or "agglomerations of unconscious commands" now look fairly laborious and crude.'[5]

Meanwhile, C. H. Sisson attacked Larkin for aspiring to discard the 'myth-kitty', the range of arcane references so dear to modern poets, in favour of a certain purity, a plainness of speech: 'But of course it is only rhetoric, or nonsense,' wrote Sisson. 'A poem can have meaning only in terms of words other people use, and which we have from our ancestors. It is a part and not a whole or, if one allows it to be a whole, it can be so only in the sense in which individual people may be "wholes", members of a company.'[6] Sisson believed in plainness of diction too, but his poetic resources were infinitely larger and he had none of Larkin's aversion to intellect. In addition, his view of history was that of a classicist and an Anglican, a position that put him well outside any developing mainstream.

Other new voices, however, did not immediately appear, and at first there was no statement of intent to rival the popular impact of Alvarez's assertions in *The New Poetry*. After the excitements of the 1960s, poetry seemed to be returning to its natural role as the least regarded, most unpopular of the arts to be included, patronizingly, as a space-filler in the columns of the more serious magazines. Nevertheless, a new orthodoxy was developing. Its terms were diffuse and lacking in the polemical fervour of previous movements. Indeed, its definition and the acknowledgement that it existed at all did not appear until 1982 with the publication of the *Penguin Book of Contemporary British Poetry* edited by Blake Morrison, himself a historian of the Movement, and Andrew Motion. The book was produced specifically as a reaction to Alvarez's own Penguin anthology of 1962 and aimed to document a 'shift of sensibility' which had appeared in the writing of a number of new poets. 'It follows a stretch', wrote Morrison and Motion, 'occupying much of the 1960s and 70s, when very little – in England at any rate – seemed to be happening, when achievements in British poetry were overshadowed by those in drama and fiction, and when, despite the presence of strong individual writers, there was a lack of overall shape and direction.'[7]

They go on to define the qualities the new poets have in common:

'Typically, they show greater imaginative freedom and linguistic daring than the previous poetic generation. Free from the constraints of immediate post-war life, and notwithstanding the threats to their own culture, they have developed a degree of lucid and literary self-consciousness reminiscent of the modernists. This is not to imply that their work is frivolous or amoral. The point is rather that, as a way of making the familiar strange again, they have exchanged the received idea of the poet as the-person-next-door, or knowing insider, for the attitude of the anthropologist or alien invader or remembering exile.'[8]

The reaction here seems to be against the timidity and easy familiarity of the Movement or the Group; but it is a reaction combined with a certain cool, literary distance to distinguish it from the extravagances of the 1960s. The passing remark 'notwithstanding the threats to their own culture' evokes Alan Brownjohn's rallying cry to the 'rational, sceptical' types who would face disaster and rebuild the 'commonwealth of decency'.

The hero of the new orthodoxy was Seamus Heaney, born in 1939 and the most prominent member of a whole new generation of Irish poets, who formed an entire wing of the new movement, as defined by Motion and Morrison. Heaney was influenced initially by Philip Hobsbaum, an enthusiast of both the Movement and the Group, who had taught at Belfast in the early 1960s and subsequently by Hughes and, more powerfully, the American Robert Lowell. He was, for Motion and Morrison, 'the most important new poet of the last fifteen years'.[9]

Heaney's poetry is frequently very close to that of his predecessors. The opening lines of 'Death of a Naturalist' could be Lowell or they could be Hughes:

> All year the flax-dam festered in the heart
> Of the townland; green and heavy headed
> Flax had rotted there, weighted down by huge sods.[10]

The physicality and the threat are familiar enough, but the poem does not follow the usual progress to synthesized despair. Half-way through a new voice emerges: 'Here, every spring/I would fill jampotfuls of the jellied/Specks to range on window-sills at home.'[11] The autobiographical, domestic note modulates the existential queasiness. Heaney's position is more oblique than Hughes's: he is inserting drama, a variety of voices and perspectives into the movement of the verse. The crushed, anguished self, appalled by the prospect of meaningless nature, is replaced by a sudden breathing and identifiable presence: 'I sickened, turned, and ran.'

There is a distant, but nevertheless real, parallel here with Sisson's attack on Larkin. Sisson believed in history and had no patience with Larkin's attempt to thin his poetic moment to a single present, to remove the 'difficult' accretions of language. Equally, Heaney is reacting to the undramatic – and, indeed, unhistorical – self in Hughes. The moment of observation in Heaney, though frequently couched in excessively familiar language, is a more complex, oblique and thoughtful instant.

In addition, of course, Heaney and his contemporaries had the Troubles: the violence that began in 1969 between Catholics and Protestants in Northern Ireland. Inevitably, English critical assessment was coloured by the fact that here appeared to be poets with something that urgently needed writing about. The post-modernist instinct to discover something in the world, rather than simply in the art, could be satisfied by real bullets and real bombs. As further encouragement, the Troubles were the product of history at its most potent. Speaking of Heaney's 'Bog Poems', Morrison and Motion say they 'refract the experience of the contemporary Irish Troubles through the sufferings of a previous Northern civilization and its sacrificial victims'.[12]

In poetry, both the image and the Troubles emerge as threats, questions and assaults on the observing self which, as in the childhood memories, is drawn into the drama. The following extract is from 'Punishment', from the collection *North*, published in 1975, which established Heaney's position as the leading figure in the poetic mainstream.

> I almost love you
> but would have cast, I know,
> the stones of silence.
> I am the artful voyeur
>
> of your brain's exposed
> and darkened combs,
> your muscles' webbing
> and all your numbered bones:
>
> I who have stood dumb
> when your betraying sisters,
> cauled in tar,
> wept by the railings,

who would connive
in civilized outrage
yet understand the exact
and tribal, intimate revenge.[13]

Heaney offered both a sophisticated and disciplined development of a familiar tradition, as well as this intoxicating sense of a poetry engaged with visible and difficult politics. But he also offered an essentially foreign temperament which allowed him to distance himself from the influences from which he sprang. He has said that English poets like Hughes, Larkin and Geoffrey Hill are 'afflicted with a sense of history' and that they have reacted to a threat to the identity of England by becoming defensive about their land in the manner of a colonized nation. He added that 'English poets are being forced to explain not just the matter of England, but what is the matter with England.'[14]

The English, lacking such a perspective or such an issue, nevertheless succeeded in creating a kind of poetic renaissance of the type defined by Morrison and Motion. James Fenton provided the school with a cool, capacious, cosmopolitan and Audenesque style. He, in turn, christened the style of Craig Raine and Christopher Reid, two other members of the Morrison–Motion school, 'Martian' as a reference to their method of using startling images to evoke the sense of seeing something for the first time, without explanatory knowledge, as in Raine's 'A Martian Sends a Postcard Home':

> Mist is when the sky is tired of flight
> and rests its soft machine on ground:
>
> then the world is dim and bookish
> like engravings under tissue paper.[15]

Such effects did not impress Jones and Schmidt: 'Dr [Blake] Morrison recommends Raine's mixed metaphors as an aspect of alert vision. To us they seem more to display confusion or, worse, *mere* levity.'[16] – but there could be no doubt that the new orthodoxy, of which Raine was a primary representative, proved immensely successful. The message emanating from Morrison's and Motion's anthology was that here was a distinctly readable, at times playful, poetry that was once again engaged with politics and 'ordinary' life – in short, with the real. A double reaction is implied: first, to the drabness and gloom of the Movement and second, to the 'difficulty' of modernism. Both were prevailing views of the nature of modern poetry at the time and both were ripe for replacement with a more generous definition of the nature of poetic content.

'And though there are', wrote Morrison and Motion, 'as we have emphasized a number of different "schools" and tendencies at work in the anthology, and while all the poets have distinct and distinguished individual talents, what we are struck by powerfully is the sense of common purpose: to extend the imaginative franchise.'[17]

Exact Speech

The careful balancing act between the arid modern and the equally arid anti-modern, which Blake Morrison and Andrew Motion had performed with their anthology, found an extraordinarily close correlative in the development of architecture in the same period. The clumsy and large-scale housing and town-centre developments of the 1950s and 1960s were identified as combining both the inhuman ambitions of modernism and the drab, urban landscapes of the 1950s. A brief mannerist phase ensued in which the concrete, steel and glass of the modernist vernacular were modelled and sculpted in more deliberately expressive ways. This phase had been signalled as early as 1964 with James Stirling's and James Gowan's Engineering Building at Leicester University, as well as by Stirling's History Library at Cambridge (1968). By the 1970s even these freer forms had come to be identified with some kind of general failing in modern architecture.

The reaction – as with the Penguin poetry anthology – was to create some kind of balance of stylistic forces, which neither rejected modernism nor embraced its dogmas. In fact, 'post-modernism' first became a widely used term in architecture, precisely to define this balancing act. In practice, it came to stand for an extraordinary plurality of styles imposed randomly and somewhat chaotically upon buildings, usually in the name of 'brightening the place up a bit'. Clients found themselves in a similar position to the Victorian merchants who were able to specify either a Gothic or a Classical exterior to their building, irrespective of its interior scheme. With more sensitive treatment, however – for example, the houses by Jeremy Dixon in St Mark's Road, Kensington – the idea of liberation from the hard modernist orthodoxy began to look more substantial.

But one important and undesirable role for architecture in this period was as a political and cultural battleground. This arose less from anything that was built than from what was said, for architecture became the primary target of a radical attempt to redefine the nature of the culture. The balancing acts of the delicate sensibilities of the poets or architects attempting to distance themselves from the horrors of the recent past were both liberal, humanist attempts to sustain the continuity of the consensus: the warm, progressive beliefs of the post-war middle classes in equitable distribution and the gradual dismantling of ancient prejudices. But, through the 1970s, the conviction grew that it was a consensus that had failed: Britain was in economic decline; the idea that the country was 'ungovernable' persisted through years of strikes and economic crises. Phrases like 'the British disease' and 'the sick man of Europe' tripped off people's tongues almost without thought. 'No country', wrote Peter Jenkins in the *Guardian*, 'has yet made the journey from developed to underdeveloped. Britain could be the first to embark upon that route.'[1]

In part this was a national version of the international sense that the world was somehow critically damaged by progress and that the time of reckoning had come. But, more specifically, this sense of a British malaise arose from the interpretation of contemporary issues in terms of a national conviction that, in some profound sense, we simply could not cope. All this provided an extraordinary amount of ammunition for what came to be known as the New Right. Politically this movement found its ultimate realization in the Conservative election victory of 1979 which brought Margaret Thatcher to power. The implications of this victory and of Mrs Thatcher's personality have, over the ensuing years, been defined and redefined. But, so far as 1979 was concerned, its general meaning seemed clear enough, even if its intellectual foundations were uncertain:

'In Mrs Thatcher's case it was less clear whether she stood for a new ideology or whether she represented merely a set of values or instincts [wrote Alan Sked and Chris Cook]. She was by 1979 certainly identified with several – thrift, patriotism, self-help, hard work and responsibility to the family. Her watchwords were initiative, duty, independence. John Nott spoke for many when he identified these values with those of nineteenth century liberalism.'[2]

Thatcher was no intellectual and the theoretical basis of her political convictions – the monetarist economics of Milton Friedman – was to provide no particular consistency. What *was* consistent was her rejection of what had gone before and, in this, she found herself with more sustained and sophisticated intellectual and cultural backing than any previous British politician.

The 1979 Conservative election manifesto spoke of the 'liberty of people under the law'. It added: 'The most disturbing threat to our freedom and security is the growing disrespect for the rule of law,' and: 'The years of make-believe and false optimism are over. It is time for a new beginning.' The election leader in the *Daily Telegraph* focused on this feeling that the time had come to overthrow the post-war liberal consensus, which had led us to the brink of ruin: 'To Margaret Thatcher has fallen the task of alerting the people to imminent but unsensed catastrophe, while yet avoiding the shrill tones of a latter-day Cassandra, comparing ill with Mr Callaghan's *faux bonhomie* and reassurance. Could she have done otherwise?'[3]

The new political assertion was that Britain could be great again. The abandonment of 'greatness' after the war in favour of some vague dream of collective Utopia had failed. Better now to recreate the conditions of greatness as defined, in the imagination of the New Right, by the economic triumphs of the Victorians as well as their addiction to the simple virtues of family and home.

In 1982 this new greatness attained its most spectacular demonstration with the Falklands war. Korea had been the affirmation of the international consensus of democrats, Suez had marked the end of empire, the Falklands was to reverse them both. We regained the islands after an Argentinian invasion and, in doing so, we celebrated the continuity of our concern for our distant people. The sheer historical perfection of the image was such that opposition to the adventure was almost lost in its contemplation. But, when it did emerge, the terms were interesting. The *New Statesman*'s view was:

'The puzzle that the thing we call "Britain" presents to the world is that of a community of peoples perhaps as civilized, and humane of temper, as any who may be found – yet which is led, again and again, into enterprises which are self-defeating as they are dishonourable. The reason, of course, is that the thing we still have to call our government – the United Kingdom state – was never designed to rule a group of democratic, European individual nations such as the

English, the Scots, the Welsh and the Irish are capable of being. It was brought into existence to run, by bluff and cheap-skate contrivance, a shabby world-wide empire that was assembled by blunder, force and fraud in various proportions. Like an old magician, it knows no other trick, and so long as it has its dominion over us it will betray us – and make us pay the price of betrayal in our best blood.'[4]

So the Falklands was another crass, imperial adventure. But, now, such an adventure is seen to spring from the imperial nature embedded in Britain herself. The triumph of the right was driving the left into ever more extreme diagnoses. The simple fact was that what had gone before was being assaulted with extraordinary cunning and, in the case of the Falklands, luck. What had gone before was collectivization, the spreading of the power of the state, the dominating moral presence of government and, above all, the planning of people's lives and of the future. This was the ideology of the new liberalism and it was based on the assumption that most people would agree that, most of the time, the social developments since 1945 had been broadly correct. But, for the New Right, they were almost completely wrong. And, in artistic terms, the most glaring advertisements of their failure were to be found in their architecture.

Given that, by the early 1970s, conservationists as well as politicians had already promoted a popular antipathy to the buildings of the previous twenty years, this was a good populist cause for the New Right. It was also an intellectual battleground on which their enemies were desperately vulnerable. In 1977 and 1978 David Watkin published his books *Morality and Architecture* and *The Rise of Architectural History* and, in 1979, Roger Scruton published *The Aesthetics of Architecture*. The books attacked the critical foundations of modernist architecture. Specifically they aimed to undermine the 'historicism' of modernist critics like Pevsner and Giedion. This propagated the view that there was a spirit of the age that effectively demanded certain types of building, to build otherwise was a complete waste of time. For the New Right, this was thinly disguised Marxism. In addition, Scruton and Watkin attacked the assumption, found in a great deal of modernist architectural writing, that aesthetic values enjoyed some kind of automatic continuity with moral, social and political ones. 'The attempt to force the connection,' wrote Scruton, 'to translate the moral sense into aesthetic standards, without first recognising the sense of autonomy which aesthetic understanding must always preserve, that attempt is mere ideology, of no persuasive force.'[5]

Neither Scruton nor Watkin was primarily attacking modern architecture itself; rather they were concerned to expose the inadequacy of its theoretical base and to replace it with a foundation of classical aesthetic thought. Nevertheless, so far as the New Right was concerned, modernist buildings became the symbols of the appalling severance of the continuity of conservatism that had occurred in the twentieth century, or, more precisely and most damagingly for Britain, in the post-war years. For Scruton, the most brilliant and versatile of the New Right's intellectuals, the urgency of the task arose from his determined belief that the entire cultural and political complexion of the age should be changed. Just as Thatcher wished to root out socialism from the political life of the country, so Scruton wished to eliminate soft liberalism from the academic life. In particular he wanted to expose the woolly liberationist ideals of the 1960s:

'Now, the notion of an ideal freedom in which no history, society, or custom is presupposed – a freedom of the pure unencumbered Self – is of course one of the most powerful among received ideas. It has been appropriated not only by the advocates of "existential psychotherapy" and "authentic choice" but also by forward-looking clergymen, educationalists, and even certain sections of the Tory party. The incoherence of the idea has often been commented upon. One cannot sever a man from the historical forces which have shaped his identity – placing him in a world of endless random movement, with no sense of place, time, history or custom – one cannot do that and still expect him to have a "Self" to be "liberated", still expect him to be the kind of creature for whom freedom is a value and not a source of fear. The incoherence of the idea lies not so much in its conception of freedom, as in the naïve presuppositions about the "Self" on which it is based. The Self is a social product, and to remove all hardship and opposition, all need of fellowship and custom, is to bring about not self-freedom but self-dissipation. And in the megalomania of

Whitman and Ginsberg one sees, of course, not the liberation of the Self, but its dissolution into unmeaning fragments.'[6]

This is the very heart of New Right thinking. All the paraphernalia of socialism and liberation and, indeed, of a great deal of modern art had tended to reduce the self either to a tiny, expendable speck within the wider collective, or to some kind of gaseous substance floating in infinite space. But, in the harder reality of the New Right, the self was connected to and defined by society and history. It was a public entity with moral obligations and a definite place within its culture. The huge enterprise of structuralism and semiotics that had aimed to dissolve that self in a maze of systems was thus yet another prime target for Scruton. In this passage he attacks the Italian structuralist Umberto Eco:

'All he seeks in the abstruse regions of model theory is the rhetoric of technicality, the means of generating so much smoke for so long that the reader will begin to blame his own lack of perception, rather than the author's lack of illumination, for the fact that he has ceased to see. Therein lies the disease of semiosis. What is true of Eco is, so far as I can see, true of all the practitioners of his art. Perhaps it needs another Ben Jonson to reveal the complex motives behind all this. But we can be sure that, while there was a humane beginning to this madness, its "method" leaves humanity behind.'[7]

Previous British mistrust of continental theorizing had tended to produce only an instinctive rejection. The empiricist Englishman had long been convinced that French rationalism produced monsters and, because of the very nature of his empiricism, he scarcely needed to prove it. But Scruton is no empiricist; indeed, as I quoted elsewhere, he has written of the hope that Wittgenstein's philosophy of mind might find us a 'path out of the desert of empiricist and utilitarian thought'.[8] He is not content, therefore, simply to ignore the grand French *savants* like Derrida, Lacan, Foucault, and Althusser. He actually reads them and then takes them apart in the name of a cool neo-classicism, an appeal to an older, seemingly more lucid rationalism.

The implications of such thinking for the nation's view of itself were far-reaching. The liberal view of the recent political past was that it was a broadly good-natured, though accident-prone, progression in roughly the right direction. But such a view could be mere cosy indulgence. The truth might be that we had made the most colossal miscalculation, been implicated in an ill-judged attempt to separate us from our true history. In this context, the moral force of the Festival of Britain, the National Health Service, the Arts Council and all the other herbivorous growths of post-war liberalism were threatened; their claim to be unarguably good, helpful things was challenged. Indeed, under the corrosive gaze of this reassessment, even our conduct of the war turned out to be bungled. The historian Correlli Barnett published his book *The Audit of War* in 1986. Using unpublished government papers, he attempts to demonstrate that the apparent triumphs of wartime production were, in fact, illusions. We survived only because we were propped up by American money. British productivity and design almost never matched those of our enemies or our allies. Weak management and bloody-minded unions were as much a feature of wartime industry as they had been of the 1970s:

'And so it was [Barnett concludes] that, by the time they took the bunting down from the streets after VE-Day and turned from the war to the future, the British in their dreams and illusions and in their flinching from reality had already written the broad scenario for Britain's postwar descent to the place of fifth in the free world as an industrial power, with manufacturing output only two-fifths of West Germany's, and the place of fourteenth in the whole non-communist world in terms of annual GNP per head.

'As that descent took its course the illusions and the dreams of 1945 would fade one by one – the imperial and Commonwealth role, the world-power role, British industrial genius, and, at the last, New Jerusalem itself, a dream turned to a dank reality of a segregated, subliterate, unskilled, unhealthy and institutionalised proletariat hanging on the nipple of state maternalism.'[9]

In this closing paragraph Barnett, his voice almost rising to a howl of anguish as he outlines the ultimate nightmare of the New Right, is remarkably close to describing the same society that was being realized in the exclusively left-wing drama of the time: Nigel

Williams's character Iron in *Class Enemy* could be one of his proletarians, while Barnett's disgust and dismay at their condition could be emotions derived directly from the plays of Brenton or Hare. The New Right and the Old Left can thus be seen to share the imagery of a broken culture. The explanations and remedies are different; what they were determined to see in the world, the imaginary population and landscape of the kingdom, was the same.

But the left, especially in the theatre, had the artists, the right theorists and historians. Explanations for this have repeatedly been put forward and, indeed, there have been attempts to define dramatists, notably Stoppard, as right wing. The left's explanation tends to be that sensitive people think the way they do; the right's that to be right wing means to believe in the relative unimportance of politics as such, so to be apolitical means you are really right wing. The New Right could thus claim a good many supporters among those who did *not* stand up to be counted. One who did, however, and whose voice is among the most resonant of the explicitly political post-war artists is C. H. Sisson.

Sisson was born in Bristol in 1914. He worked in the civil service before the war and, after three years in the army, returned to Whitehall. The earliest poem he has preserved dates from 1944 and his first collection, *London Zoo*, did not appear until 1961. 'My beginnings', he has written, 'were altogether without facility, and when I was forced into verse it was through having something not altogether easy to say.'[10] What was 'not altogether easy' was the question of the identity of the observing 'I'. That first poem is entitled 'On a Troopship', and anticipates all the unnerving simplicity of syntax and rhythmic originality that were to mark his later work:

> Practising my integrity
> In awkward places,
> Walking till I walk easily
> Among uncomprehended faces
> Extracting the root
> Of the matter from the diverse engines
> That in an oath, a gesture or a song
> Inadequately approximate the human norm.[11]

314

The quiet voice, searching for a place, has no foundation for an understanding of the world, but it seems to be discovering one in the balance of the verse itself. Sisson, again, has said: 'The proof of the poem – any poem – is in its rhythm and that is why critical determination has in the end to await that unarguable perception.'[12]

In 1971 he published *English Poetry* 1900–1950, in which he outlined a broadly classicist and modernist view: pro-Ezra Pound and anti-W. B. Yeats. For Sisson, the achievements of twentieth-century poetry were the restoration of an exact form of speech and the recognition of a new, wider and more subtle realism. The fantastic, mythic orders willed into existence by Yeats had no part in this: 'The poets of the half-century, so far as they are genuine, have contributed to bringing the wayward big mouth of the public back to an exact speech which manages to correspond to the real movements of the mind and to reflect reality. Reality is more elusive than the more strident merchants of so-called fact would have us believe.'[13]

Inevitably, for a pessimist like Sisson, the development produced a corresponding reaction:

'Looking back over the half-century, as well as one can at this distance, one sees the real inventiveness was mainly before 1925. In this period poetry was corrected and improved by the canons of prose. By the thirties an ideological overlay has spoiled the outline. By the forties a twentieth century version of Lord Chesterfield's lesson in poetics is creeping back: "Prose, as you know, is the language of common conversation; it is what you and everybody speaks and writes – but poetry is a more noble and sublime way of expressing one's thoughts." The dog returns to his vomit.'[14]

Sisson's ideal is a classical plainness of speech, something he constantly had to struggle to achieve against his own technical facility. This plainness was pressed into the service of his politics (Tory), his religion (High Anglican) and into the protection and sustenance of the institutions of civilization. All contributed to finding and placing the self within the social and historical context Scruton had defined as being undermined by the forces of liberationism and socialism. But the essentially polemical nature of this position is not simply translated into persuasive verse, for Sisson's God is distant:

So speech is treasured, for the things is gives
Which I can not have, for I speak too plain
Yet not so plain as to be understood
It is confusion and a madman's tongue.
Where drops the reason, there is no one by.
Torture my mind: and so swim through the night
As envy cannot touch you, or myself
Sleep comes, and let her, warm at my side, like death.[15]

Sisson's poetry ranges from spare, pithy Augustan phrase-making to Wordsworthian romanticism and harsh satire against the modern world. But always the intention is to make the verse 'act' in the world as a way of reconnecting the culture.

Michael Schmidt wrote of his work: 'In effect his quest is for the integrated vision of the "first years" of our culture. He is clearing passages to the vital common past, building bridges. His "I" should not deceive us into imagining the poems are merely personal. His tools in the quest are rhythm, a mind that apprehends the manifold nature of his ideas and subject matter, and courage in the dark realms he is compelled to traverse.'[16]

Clearly, to see Sisson simply in terms of party politics, as a hero of the New Right, would be absurd and limiting. Nevertheless, his work does represent the imaginative resurfacing of the hard, classical impulse, the belief in historical continuity and the need to sustain it; and this impulse had resurfaced in the best and most informed of the theory of the New Right. Above all, he shared with the New Right theorists an aversion to the idea of progress. The belief that mankind was embarked on some long project of self-improvement was characteristic of the left and was manifested in the dogmatic determinism of modern architectural criticism. But, to the conservative, classical eye, little changes. Indeed Sisson's novel of 1975, *Christopher Homm*, begins with the death of its hero and ends with his birth, a mockery of any belief in movement forward in human affairs.

In Sisson there is also the powerful, classical, tragic sense. The religion, which should keep despair at bay, seems frequently a matter of will rather than of belief, a formal acknowledgement of the importance of Christ to the culture. Real, unrelieved darkness, meanwhile, is everywhere apparent. With his latest collection, *God Bless Karl Marx!* (1987), this tragic tone takes on a valedictory formality, still relieved by Augustan satire, but now homing in on a kind of statement which attains the ideal classical balance of the personal and the universal and yet which retains his immense gift for rhythmic control and innovation:

> The brightness that things had, at one time!
> When the curtain went up, everything was there,
> Brilliant, alive, coloured. These two bricks
> Recall it, but I cannot live again.[17]

Like Helium

oh the strange story of the quantum!
if I smile will she smile
no one smiles, your eyes
are like broken glass are
you unemployed?[1]

The conservatism, the implicit retreat, of the 1970s was a complex phenomenon. Crudely, it appeared as a kind of economic shock, the realization that the growth that had sustained the indulgences of the 1960s was reversible. Versions of this revelation accounted for the transformation of 1960s primitivism into a variety of anti-progressive movements from fringe religion, conservationism and vegetarianism to the hard classicism of Scruton or Sisson. Most familiarly, the impulse manifested itself as a rejection of the obviously modern by the mainstream practitioners of the various arts. In architecture, the radical new canon of modernism was attacked and replaced, by the academic critics at least, with an assertion of the continuity of classicism. In sculpture, gallery-bound abstraction was superseded by a more public, gestural style with an overwhelming consciousness of its own identity as part of the material of the earth. Theatre, now dominated by the demands of a subsidized circuit, discovered an aggressively political role. Painting, the art most subject to an international market and audience, tended to display a far greater plurality. Nevertheless, the 1981 Royal Academy exhibition *A New Spirit in Painting*, did attempt to define a single common development that was appearing in the work of an enormous range of different artists. 'The new concern with painting', said the catalogue, 'is related to a certain subjective vision, a vision that includes both an understanding of the artist himself as an individual engaged in a search for self-realisation and as an actor on the wider historical stage.'[2]

The dominating tendency seemed to be a greater awareness of the idea of an audience and a concern with the restoration of some form of traditional relationship with the artist as a social presence. In David Hockney, Richard Long or even in the architecture of Jeremy Dixon, the identity of the artist as an interpreter, an element in a social context, was rediscovered. Again, in the words of the Royal Academy catalogue, 'the subjective view, the creative imagination, has come back into its own and is evident in a new approach to painting'.[3] But no such tendencies are ever quite as uniform or complete as they seem. The implication of any dominating orthodoxy is that something has been dominated, and in no art was that more true than in literature. I have outlined the development of the mainstream of poetry in the period, which mainstream, broadly speaking, determined the work patronized by the leading publishing houses. From the Movement onwards, this development had deliberately turned its back on those of modernism, the very developments that C. H. Sisson had identified as the most significant of the century.

Yet even Sisson's work, in its tautness and frequent uncertainty, represents a kind of inability to cope with the legacy of the immediate past, of Pound, Eliot and Auden. In part this may be due to the fact that the legacy was deeply ambiguous. From the glittering solitude and self-sufficiency of the lines of *The Waste Land*, Eliot had progressed to the softer, more conventional music of the *Four Quartets* and he had accompanied the change with a critical assertion of the very cultural continuities he had once so vividly shown to be destroyed. Auden, too, having attained the superb rhetoric of *The Sea and the Mirror* retreated rapidly into infantile old age, cradled once again by the fogs of Oxford and old England. Pound alone had sustained the great enterprise; but the best work in the *Cantos* is concealed beneath piles of nonsensical rubble and, in any case, critics could safely dismiss the man as insane. So the legacy of the moderns was not modernism itself, but rather its rejection; and succeeding generations of poets took their cue from that later rejection, rather than from the earlier modernism.

There were, however, many dissident voices. Anne Cluysenaar, writing in 1972, detected in the provincial tone of British poetry a certain willed turning away from the horrors of the age, a kind of Georgian renaissance inspired by the sight of the trenches:

'British poetry, still insulated from the full continental shock, did need shaking up ten years ago, not because poets like Davie were unaware of the horrors of war (or, in due course, Stalinism); on the contrary, the moderate tone and scope of their poetry was consciously connected with suspicion of irrationally extreme impulses – but because they were, I believe, still suffering from a more or less severe form of psychic numbing.'[4] [She went on to find, in the ascendancy of Ted Hughes and Sylvia Plath, a certain immaturity:] 'The truth is that the literary world is like an adolescent struggling with a first intimate sense of death – unable to function maturely in the new existential context. In this respect at least, the scientist is fortunate to have early contact with a different culture. The shock is less severe and the terms are at hand with which to handle it.'[5]

The suggestion was that poets were simply not adapting to the twentieth century, rather they were expressing anxieties brought on by the developments of nineteenth-century science. It was a tendency also detected by David Holbrook in an anguished and polemical book, *Lost Bearings in English Poetry*, published in 1977:

'They may feel that "God is dead", and the universe bleak, so that the individual must conceive of himself as a mere organic functioning body-self which is no more than a bag of bones doomed to eventual decline and death, in a universe consisting of moving atoms controlled by the laws of physics and chemistry, changing only by chance and necessity, dominated by the laws of Evolution and the Second Law of Thermodynamics.'[6]

For Holbrook, too, this was an old-fashioned response and one that failed to take account of the real role of man as creator of the languages that would order the universe. Science was not the absolute it had once seemed to be, it was merely another language.

For some the problem lay far deeper: it was not simply that British literature was failing to understand its age, rather that it had failed to understand literature itself. In 1976 Peter Ackroyd published *Notes for a New Culture*, another polemic, but this time directed at the contemporary condition of English letters. Some basic features of the assault are shared with Holbrook and Cluysenaar: most notably a distaste for the Plath–Hughes orthodoxy and a conviction that it was fundamentally inadequate to the task of writing poetry. But Ackroyd's analysis focuses not on the moral and contemporary failings but on more ancient shortcomings in the national imagination: 'There has been a general transition within European culture which has either been misread or ignored, and I hope to bring this within view, but my central purpose has been to counter the general malaise of English literature and literary studies – by suggesting a spirit and a language of enquiry which will lend them a fresh access of strength.'[7]

Ackroyd's view was that there had been two distinct 'modernisms'. The first had occurred in the seventeenth century with the advent of the scientific imagination, and produced 'a novel self-consciousness' in which the imagination seemed to be embarking on an entirely new quest. The world was to be discovered through the medium of science, a medium which would supplant the medieval forms of knowledge that had previously shrouded the universe in darkness and incomprehension. With this was born the idea of the modern and a view of language as entirely transparent: there was man and there was the world and language existed to provide potentially perfect communication between the two.

Ackroyd's second modernism involved the long process of dismantling this dogma in the face of the growing realization of the opacity of language rather than its transparency. This appears as an entirely continental development, manifested in the works of Flaubert, de Sade, Nietzsche and Mallarmé, which laid the groundwork for the more familiar 'modernism' that cultural history now dates back to the later years of the nineteenth century. British nineteenth-century thought failed repeatedly to understand the wider implications of this development, and attempted instead to redefine it in terms of the native humanist and empirical traditions. As a result there was, in England, 'no literature but rather a continuing rhetoric of social truths'.[8]

The modernist discovery of the nature of language as absolute, the maker of our world rather than simply its interpreter, undermined the primacy of the scientific imagination. 'The world' was not a fixed entity outside ourselves to be gradually, and ultimately completely, understood; rather it was embodied within the language. Science was simply one version, one pattern on the fabric of language. Equally, the humanist effort to locate man in his world and to define values in that relationship was over; 'Man', in this humanist sense, was as dead as God. The humanist idea of the individual was simply a product of the autonomous, protean, formal absolute of language.

From this point Ackroyd could have taken several directions; most obviously he could have brought Wittgenstein into the picture. In the event, he brings himself to the present day in the entirely French landscape of Derrida and Lacan and in the elaborations of structuralism and post-structuralism. In this passage he concludes his assault on the British failure to progress beyond the first modernism:

'It is clear that, now, England is a dispirited nation. The social weakness runs very deep, and does not yet seem close to any definition let alone resolution. This analysis has, I hope, marked out certain features of this decline. I have attempted to define the impoverishment of our national culture and I hope to have demonstrated that, from the beginning of this century, it has rested on a false base. The "humanism" which the universities sustain, and which our realistic literature embodies, is the product of historical blindness. It has been associated with a sense of the "individual" and of the "community" which stays without definition, except in the works of some literary academics who appeal to a literary "tradition". But the actual facticity and autonomy of literature has not been recognised in this country, and so literary studies have been readily attached to such external pursuits as sociology and anthropology.'[9]

For Ackroyd, literature, by definition, was writing about nothing; the very autonomy of language had the double effect of placing literature, particularly poetry, at the highest level of intellectual significance, and yet, at the same time, denying it any of the ethical, social or political significance which had, in humanist literary studies, referred literature back to the world. The concluding structuralist landscape of the book should not be allowed to detract from the importance of its assertions and the form they took. The book is not primarily critical, it is preparatory, a ground-clearing operation intended to establish a new sense of creative freedom:

'We no longer invest created forms with our own significance and, in parallel, we no longer seek to interpret our own lives in the factitious terms of art. Artistic forms are no longer to be conceived of as paradigmatic or mimetic. Our lives return to their own space, outside interpretation and extrinsic to any concern for significance or end. I might put this differently by suggesting that it is the ability of literature to explore the problems and ambiguities of a formal absoluteness which we will never experience.'[10]

In part, this ground-clearing is a preparation for Ackroyd's own writing, but it also provided a justification for an entire generation of poets who had been virtually ignored in favour of the prevailing orthodoxies of the day. One such was Ackroyd himself, who had already provided one realization of his critical stance in a 1973 collection entitled *London Lickpenny*. It is from this collection that the quotation at the beginning of this section is taken. The poem, 'Among School Children', continues:

> What do these words mean? (a) love-cries
> (b) quantum (c) unemployed.
> Have you ever met anyone with eyes
> like broken glass? If you have write about it.
> If not, would you like to? Why?[11]

The explicitly 'poetic' form of the earlier lines is subverted by the sudden intrusion of the schoolroom and a pastiche of its crude demands of literature. But this, too, is subsumed into the poem itself to form a balance, devoid of statement, and to lead finally to a concluding – and poignantly meaningless – demand that evokes Ackroyd's view of humans as 'outside interpretation': 'Try to explain in your own words how/ the writer felt when he saw the girl/ with eyes like broken glass.'[12]

The heroes of Ackroyd's fully modern poetry were John Ashbery, Frank O'Hara and Kenneth Koch, three American poets closely associated with the dynamic world of the visual arts in New York in the 1950s. But there was also an English hero: J. H. Prynne, a Cambridge don and the most comprehensively gifted of living British poets. 'His poetic forms', Ackroyd wrote, 'offer a writing that calls into question our conventional response to what we think of as "poetic" and what we think of as non-poetic.'[13]

This, of course, is to define Prynne's work in terms very close to those in which Eliot's was defined at the time of *Prufrock* and *The Waste Land*. Poetry drew all the resources of the language as it existed, to act as a focusing lens that would brighten and purify the existence of words themselves. The point, however, was not that the task had been accomplished by Eliot once and for all but that it was continuous. Poetry was an activity that accompanied and concentrated the changing fabric of the language. This extract is taken from Prynne's 'Down where changed', published in 1979:

> A limit spark under water
> makes you see briefly
> how patience is wasted
>
> that deep sadness is a perk
> of the iron will; no sound
> catches the binding dark
>
> side of this relish, head-on
> in thermite lock. Each one
> bound to wait, the other
>
> blunders to see it and suffer
> the play at choking
> or not turning away.[14]

We are not being asked to derive 'meaning' from this lyric, or to attribute to it a specific insight, landscape or sensation. The place we are in is language itself; we are being asked to observe its movements and its identity, the tensions involved in its echoes from the worlds it creates and destroys. There is no poetic 'self' determining or limiting the operations of the language, rather there is simply the concentration of language on this particular occasion. Such poetry is not the language of crisis or of great, intense moments. It can happen at any time and include any content because it is a way of seeing rather than an excuse for statement. It is also capable of an entirely original and startling form of beauty, as demonstrated by Prynne's poem 'Crown':

The hours are taken slowly out of the
city and its upturned faces – a rising fountain
quite slim and unflowering as it
is drawn off. The arrangements of work
swell obscurely round the base of the
Interior Mountain, in the pale house with
its parody of stairs. The air is cold; a
pale sunlight is nothing within the con-
strictions of trust in the throat, in
the market-place.

And the question rises
like helium in its lightness, not held down
by any hands, followed by the faces dis-
owned by the shoes & overcoat settling in
behind the wheel and pulling the door shut.[15]

Prynne's role as a poet living in exile from the mainstream of British poetry publishing was shared by a number of his contemporaries who wrote poetry that would be adjudged correspondingly 'difficult' by the poetry establishment. Their work was published by a few small journals and presses. In 1987, however, a distinct effort was made to enlist these exiles in a defence of their own position, adopting the increasingly traditional strategy of publishing an anthology. Called *A Various Art*, its editors Andrew Crozier and Tim Longville made clear in the first sentence of their introduction their intention to answer those other anthologies edited respectively by Alvarez, and Morrison and Motion: 'This anthology represents our joint view of what is most interesting, valuable, and distinguished in the work of a generation of English poets now entering its maturity . . .'[16]

The editors go on to attack the 'redefinition of taste' that occurred in the 1950s and involved the suppression of large parts of the tradition of modern poetry:

'Poetry was seen as an art in relation to its own conventions – and a pusillanimous set of conventions at that. It was not to be ambitious, or to seek to articulate ambition through the complex deployment of its technical means; the verse line should not, by the pressure its energy or shape might exert in syntax, intervene in meaning; language was always to be grounded in the presence of a legitimating voice – and that voice took on an impersonally collective tone. To its owners' satisfaction the signs of art had been subsumed within a closed cultural programme.'[17]

To the generation of poets included in the anthology this presented a 'depthless version of the past', and 'to accept the version of English poetry then being sanctioned would be to become like a fly on a wall that had just been built'. So this generation, who began writing in the 1960s, turned to the more potent and ambitious example of American post-war art and to the poetic legacy of Pound and William Carlos Williams. Meanwhile, the mainstream continued with its constricted view of the nature of poetry: 'The poetry generally on offer is either provincial or parasitically metropolitan, and furnishes the pleasures of either a happy nostalgia or a frisson of daring and disgust.[18] This anthology, in contrast, though not offering a unified school, does at least offer a consistent degree of seriousness – 'a poetry deployed towards the complex and multiple experience in language of all of us'.

In truth, this consistency turns out to be more significant than the editors seem to acknowledge in their introduction. In the anthology itself it appears as a common determination to use words as freely as the best modern painters had succeeded in using paint or, perhaps a more appropriate comparison, as composers had used music. As in Prynne's work, a vast multiplicity of styles and types of language is freely drawn into poetry. The two extracts below are from Iain Sinclair's 'Lud Heat' and Douglas Oliver's 'In the Cave of Suicession', respectively:

> we can gaze
> with a whole body of lust
> across the table the libidinous plates
> the Upmann cigar & german wine
>   the lies
> shield a condition of secrecy
> that needs all his five-litre cunning
> & is the holiest mood he can summon
> in the heat of the matter between them.[19]

The beam is absorbed with laughter
of veils in confusion sombrely though
the dust of darkness in progress
   no-one waiting
only attacking the solitary inquiry
descending into the mountain to cut the thinnest figure.[20]

These are utterly distinct tones, entirely at odds with the voices accepted in the mainstream and infinitely more capable of accepting the multiple identities of language. The charge of 'difficulty' makes little sense once the initial step of accepting a new, more generous definition of the importance of poetry is taken. At times there is even a quite original form of 'simplicity', as in Veronica Forrest-Thomson's extraordinary meditation, 'Cordelia or "A poem should not mean, but be" ', which plays lightly, absurdly and almost dangerously with the usual poetic requirement of intensity and rhythm. It also includes this blissfully pristine statement of the autonomy of art, a statement as precise as Michael Craig-Martin's *Oak Tree*: 'The word you want is Dante./ He said he loved Beatrice. Whatever he did/ He didn't love Beatrice.'[21]

The poetry in *A Various Art*, most clearly Prynne's, does not depend on the post-war pendulum swings between myth and 'ordinary' life, or between extremity and provincialism. It depends upon language and all its possibilities – which are, of course, *all* possibilities – and, as such, it can travel as freely and widely through experience as have the other arts that have shown themselves less constricted by the prevailing orthodoxy of retreat. Prynne does not comment upon the fact that, for example, science has defined our culture; rather he evolves a poetry that includes that invasion and reveals its triumph as, in part, illusory. This extract is from 'The Glacial Question, Unsolved':

As
   the 50° isotherm retreats there is
   that secular weather laid down in pollen
   and the separable advances on Cromer (easterly)
   and on Gipping (mostly to the south).
   The striations are part of the heart's

desire, the parkland of what is coast
inwards from which, rather than the reverse.
And as the caps melted, the eustatic rise
in the sea-level curls round the clay, the
basal rise, what we hope to call 'land'.[22]

The poem is accompanied by references; but the books cited are not literary, they are scientific works. Poetry here – and at last – is reaching out and annexing new territory, claiming back the task of distilling and purifying the language, living up to its heritage.

Curved Lines

The dominant artistic form of the late 1970s and 1980s has been the novel. Many mundane reasons have been proffered for this sudden flowering of fiction, from the publicity successes of literary prizes to the changing structure of both the market and the publishing industry itself. It is impossible to know whether such reasons in fact, constitute causes or merely symptoms: either way what *is* clear is that they were accompanied by greater ambition and a wider imaginative framework in fiction. A new generation of writers appeared with a more varied range of influences and preoccupations, and, meanwhile, there was a resurgence of interest in the work of established artists like Iris Murdoch and William Golding.

Timothy Mo's immense 1986 novel, *An Insular Possession*, includes an appendix containing the supposed unfinished autobiography of one of the main characters. This passage appears: '... nor could the world of art long remain immune where the spheres of science and scholarship had already been affected, for the discovery of photography (which I have the temerity to observe was no accidental invention, just as the discovery of the Americans was inevitable, but a reflection itself of a changing view of the world) came as a pebble hurled into its still depths.'[1]

The primary narrative of the book, told through a variety of devices including newspaper extracts and letters, concerns the First Opium War in the 1830s and the establishment of the port of Hong Kong. It is, thus, a historical novel, but of a quite different kind from those of Paul Scott or J. G. Farrell, in which history was used to place issues in 'inverted commas'. The role of history here is far more complex and more intimately bound up with the role of fiction itself. First, Mo has adopted, both in this 'autobiography' and in the letters and newspaper cuttings, the language of the time. The authorial, narrative voice is distanced by this device and we are given not simply a different perspective but a different way of life. Second, he is using this distance to focus upon a moment of profound change – in this case the 'discovery of photography' – which, his character asserts, was not an accidental technological development, but rather a culturally determined expression of a new way of regarding the world. Finally, in the novel as a whole, Mo realizes this theme of change in an implicit contrast between the Western idea of narrative and the static tableau-like form of the Chinese 'novel'.

His novel is thus being used as a positive form of knowledge. Its multiplicity of effects are intended to create a wholly new understanding. Whereas conventional realism would provide an image of a supposedly identifiable world perceived through the language of the novel, this more inclusive, more ambitious, form suggests that the novel itself is capable of creating its own, unique reality. Such ambitions and, indeed, the scale and feeling of *An Insular Possession* are representative of the new wave of fiction writing. Mo shared with two other writers of this generation – Kazuo Ishiguro and Salman Rushdie – a half-foreign perspective on the form and a consequently more cosmopolitan determination to activate its broadest possible significance.

Critical, as opposed to economic, explanation for this resurgence of interest in fictional form had, in fact, long anticipated the event itself. One reason for this was the academic success of structuralism in the 1960s. The new discipline thrived on accumulated detail and the intricacies of narrative. So, taking their cue from Roland Barthes's study of Balzac, the structuralists focused primarily on fiction. The critic Frank Kermode became involved in the enterprise: 'My conclusion, then, is what the twentieth-century interest in the Novel, in its technical potentialities, made some writers especially conscious of what might be made of certain hitherto unregarded aspects of narrative texts; of what might be suggested as apprehensible beyond or *across* those texts. There are difficult questions I cannot raise here and one of them is the nature of rules we apply to discourse when we know it to be fictive.'[2]

Structuralism imposed an immense self-consciousness on fiction by insistently drawing attention to the devices with which it established itself as fiction. On top of that, it examined the reading process and the way readers accept the conventions of fiction and accept novels as, temporarily, 'true'. Clearly the practical danger of this, as with all structuralist thought, was that the self-consciousness would prove debilitating and it would become impossible even to begin to write a novel. At this point Kermode drew back, commenting that he found deconstructionism 'the most frightening manifestation of the newer criticism'[3] as it seemed to offer nothing more than an eternal analysis.

Two other critics, both of whom were also novelists, anticipated the development of a new fiction in the early and mid-1970s. Malcolm Bradbury and David Lodge both believed that there was a kind of aesthetic gap between realism and modernism, which new writers would feel obliged to fill.

'As, influenced by developments in human knowledge, particularly in the field of psychology [wrote Lodge in 1971], the writer pursues the reality of individual experience deeper and deeper into the subconscious or unconscious, the common perceptual world recedes and the concept of the unique person dissolves: the writer finds himself in a region of myths, dreams, symbols and archetypes that demand "fictional" rather than "empirical" modes for their expression. "The mimetic impulse towards the characterisation of the inner life dissolves inevitably into mythic and expressionistic patterns upon reaching the citadel of the psyche." On the other hand, if the writer persist in seeking to do justice to the common phenomenal world he finds himself, today, in competition with new media, such as tape and motion pictures, which can claim to do this more effectively.'[4]

The modernist novel had drifted into the dream landscape of James Joyce's *Finnegans Wake*, a book which could not conceivably have a successor. But, meanwhile, the realistic novel seemed wilfully to ignore the intellectual developments of the century and was, in any case, being superseded by film and television as the most vivid and direct form of narrative communication. Bradbury combined a similar insight with the post-war sense that 'style' was not an absolute: art could now draw on any style of the past, including modernism, without committing itself to one as a 'true' realization of the needs of the age. In 1980 he wrote: 'Any writer in the modern world is likely to feel the complex refractions surrounding him now, the pluralised images, the shattering weight of story, the seriality of production-systems which throw at us forces, assumptions, styles from any sources. There is an overwhelming multiplicity of goods, and a universality of signs; there is also a want of significance. It is not surprising that this is increasingly manifested to us as, in art, a style or perhaps an anti-style.'[5]

So the novel began to feel the presence of a familiar post-war force in British art. It was squeezed between the sense of an unrepeatable modernism and the littleness of the conventional anti-modernism forms. There was even the sense that, somehow, the Americans had managed to come up with a solution on a heroic scale as they had done once before with abstract expressionism. In the novel there were seemingly gigantic figures such as Norman Mailer, whose *The Naked and the Dead* and *An American Dream* showed a complete lack of the fictional nerves which seemed to afflict the British, or Truman Capote, who in 1966 had redefined fiction as reportage with *In Cold Blood* or Saul Bellow, who seemed to have discovered a fictional form to encompass the apocalypse. Even the French had had the excitement of the *nouveau roman*.

The creative effect of all this pressure began to gain momentum through the 1970s. The forerunners had been Michael Moorcock and J. G. Ballard but they had approached the problem of fiction from an entirely different angle; they had begun with an admiration for science fiction and gradually transformed this into a new, more potent fictional language in the case of Ballard and a larger, more inclusive style in Moorcock. Martin Amis seemed to combine both impulses. After *The Rachel Papers* his novels maintained the surface brilliance and concentration of the prose and combined it with more elaborate formal structures that finally opened out into *Money*, a *tour de force* in which his prose and his preoccupations seemed finally to achieve a perfect match. In addition, from the late 1970s Ian McEwan, once a pupil of Bradbury's, began to publish short stories and novels suffused with a rank and macabre atmosphere of decay but also possessed of a spare and curiously crystalline and shocking formality. His story 'Psychopolis' opens: 'Mary worked in and part-owned a feminist bookstore in Venice. I met her there lunchtime on my second day in Los Angeles. That same evening we were lovers, and not so long after that, friends. The following Friday I chained her by the foot to my bed for the whole weekend.'[6] Meanwhile, the larger-scale, grand, culturally inclusive form of the new novel appeared, so far as the new public was concerned, in 1981 with Salman Rushdie's *Midnight's Children*.

The effect of this efflorescence created a readiness in the novel-reading public to accept, indeed to demand, narrative innovation. The very definition of the literary novel was widened to include science fiction, historical novels and fantasy. The term 'magic realism' was borrowed from the South American novel to describe this sense in which fiction had become a far more varied form of entertainment. Yet this renaissance in the novel also produced a resurgence of traditional forms: the moral and religious comedy of character in A. N. Wilson and, in William Boyd's *A Good Man in Africa*, a colonial farce, heavily influenced by Evelyn Waugh.

The success of the new novel in creating a more receptive public even surfaced in film and television, the two forms which had seemed to threaten the novel's role as the primary narrative form. *The Draughtsman's Contract*, a film by Peter Greenaway, appeared in 1982. It was an elaborate, formal, 'puzzle' film, set at the end of the seventeenth century, and dealt with a change in the nature of perception. The draughtsman was a rational man, making drawings of a country house. He was a representative of what Peter Ackroyd would have called 'the first modernism'; he worked on the basis that the world could be made lucid by observation. But messages seem to be concealed within the house, sprites inhabit the garden and recurring shots of fruit suggest a changing, unstable world, subject to decay and inaccessible to the draughtsman's eye. The draughtsman wishes to see one story in the world, but it evades him. The fiction is far too complex, its successive levels prove only how little we can really see.

In 1984 Neil Jordan's film *The Company of Wolves* seemed to lean heavily on another development in the new novel: that which could, most accurately, be described as 'magic realism'. The film is anchored at the beginning and the end in the ordinary life of a family in a house in the country; the remainder of the narrative is conducted entirely through the imagery of childhood dream and fantasy, with its attendant horrors, sickly sweetness and half-glimpsed significance. Like a childhood story it has a strong, conventional narrative drive, but Jordan nowhere feels the need to reinforce this with suggestions of the meaning of all his imagery in the 'real' world. The fantasy is self-sustaining; its force is such that, although we awake from it, we are not tempted to question its 'reality'.

In television, the supreme expression of this new narrative freedom was Dennis Potter's *The Singing Detective*, broadcast in 1987 in six parts. In his television plays Potter could be said to have been, along with Murdoch and Ballard, one of the forerunners of the entire developments of narrative innovation. His plays increasingly abandoned the stilted demands of television realism in the pursuit of a strange and impassioned form of artistic biography. Born in 1935, he was stricken by psoriatic arthropathy in his early twenties. The disease, and the appallingly radical treatments it required, drove his writing inwards; images of disease, anguish and disgust gradually began to fill his plays, and he successively abandoned realistic narrative ordering for highly expressionistic forms, evocative of visions, delirium and religious revelation. Potter has said that he was never afraid of over-writing in the face of the amount of underwriting there was in the world.

With *The Singing Detective* he created a series of overlapping narratives – a man being treated for psoriasis in hospital, a detective thriller, a childhood trauma – which were connected in some senses by mechanical narrative devices but, more important, by a dramatization of the nature of fiction itself. The narratives enfold themselves around the issues of truth and lies, guilt and innocence and knowledge and ignorance. They take place in separate locations and at different times. The mass audience of television is expected to understand that there is an imaginative order more important than any mechanical plot. In fact, Potter's virtuosity went too far: the central sections of the serial frequently seemed artistically immobilized as he simply ran through a series of variations and interactions between the narratives. Nevertheless, for long periods, and especially at certain supremely successful moments of unification of the narratives, Potter succeeded in creating an intensity of which the television medium usually seems incapable. The following extract is from the published script of the serial. The hero Philip Marlow, as a boy, has suddenly reappeared, high in a tree, at a moment when, in the hospital, his older self is suffering the most extreme agonies of his disease and is unable to escape into his thriller fantasy – the story of *The Singing Detective*. The intended accent of the speech is that of the Forest of Dean where Potter himself was brought up.

'When I grow up I be going to be the first man to live for ever and ever. In my opinion, you don't have to die. Not unless you want to. Not me. (*Pause*) When I grow up I be going to leave the light on *all night*. I be! No matter bloody what (*Pause*) I be going to have *books*. I be going to have *books*. All over the – on shelves, mind. I be going to have a *shelf just for books*. (*Pause*) When I grow up I'm – (*Savagely*) I be going to have a *whole tin* of evaporated milk on a *whole* tin of peaches I be! I bloody be, mind! I bloody buggering damn buggering be! Oy. And I shall cus (*Pause*) I'm going to – I'll tell tha what – When I grow up I'm – When I grow up -

　(*He stops, distressed.*)

　Everything will be all right. When I grow up, *everything* – There'll be none of – there'll be no – Everything ool be *all right*. (*Tiny uncertain pause*) Won't it? Won't it, God? Hey? Thou's like me a bit – doosn't God? Eh? (*Longer pause*) When I – When I grow up, I be going to be – *a detective*.'[7]

In the event, he grows up to write detective stories, reliving which provides an escape into fantasy in the extremity of his illness. The boy's speech ties the narratives into one and explains the impulses of childish frustration that lie behind much of the older Marlow's conduct in the hospital; and, more important, behind his drive to create fictions.

Potter's technical innovations are driven by the need to intensify a personal condition and vision. Formally, he has much in common with a novelist like Brigid Brophy and the fictional self-consciousness of *In Transit*, but there is none of that baroque distance in Potter. He is explicitly concerned to externalize his mental state, to make an emblem of the struggle of his own self to invent fictions and to dramatize his own motives for doing so. In this sense his forms, though clearly related to developments in the novel and inspired by the same need to avoid both smug littleness and arid modernism, seem exclusive to him. It is as though, in using them, he exhausts them, renders them inoperable.

　In fact this could be said to be a danger for the new fiction as a whole. The newly aware audience would demand trickery in novels, newspaper reviews would be obliged to explicate devices which would then be found interesting or not. Indeed there are many cases where the novel seems to have become the victim of its own requirements for novelty. The fact that Potter's play was on television, establishing layered narrative in the demotic, increases the danger – new tricks would have to be found. The novel, instead of being a stable, capacious form, in which the sensitive spirits of the age could invent their characters and elaborate their preoccupations, would become almost indefinable even as fiction behind a fog of devices. The new novel was potentially the very opposite of the generous, encompassing space defined by Iris Murdoch.

One novel at the centre of the new wave seemed to incorporate many of its characteristics and yet to escape its most banal trickiness: Peter Ackroyd's *Hawksmoor*, published in 1985. Since *Notes for a New Culture*, Ackroyd had published two novels: *The Great Fire of London* and *The Last Testament of Oscar Wilde*. He has also written a biography of T. S. Eliot in which he developed his own convictions about the autonomy of art into a study of the human conditions that might result in its production. Above all, it aimed to portray the way the private torment of Eliot's life could be transformed into the entire drama of the age.

In the Oscar Wilde novel, Ackroyd had discovered an extraordinary gift for literary mimicry; it was written entirely in almost flawless Wildean prose. This gift was employed again in *Hawksmoor*, but this time he had also discovered a form which would fully realize his own literary preoccupations. The novel is set in the late seventeenth century at the time of the 'first modernism', the birth of the scientific imagination and its accompanying view of language as a transparent window on the world. The architect Christopher Wren embodies the new consciousness as he rebuilds London from the ruins of the Great Fire and with the memories of the plague still alive for most of its inhabitants. The fire destroyed much of the medieval city and the plague had created images of a darker, crueller universe than the one imagined by the new science. Wren's assistant was, in fact, Nicholas Hawksmoor, architect of a series of London churches that represent perhaps the strangest flowerings of the English Baroque. In the novel his name is changed to Dyer, the name Hawksmoor being reserved for the present-day scenes; these alternate with those set in the seventeenth century and narrated by Dyer. Ackroyd's Hawksmoor is a detective investigating a series of deaths which have occurred at various churches – all, in the event, designed by Dyer/Hawksmoor.

Dyer is a practitioner of the black arts. His mind is steeped in the medieval darkness of the plague. He feels nothing but contempt for the rationalizing Wren and he subversively designs his churches to satisfy cabalistic demands. His mind wanders in a remote, inhumane landscape. In this extract he watches the traditional moment when the mason's son lays the topmost stone on the spire of one of his churches:

'He gazed steadily at me for an Instant and I cryed, *Go on! Go on!*; and at this Moment, just as he was coming up to the spiry Turret, the timbers of the Scaffold, being insecurely plac'd or rotten, cracked asunder and the Boy missed his Footing and fell from the Tower. He did not cry out but his Face seem'd to carry an Expression of Surprize: Curved lines are more beautiful than Straight, I thought to myself, as he fell away from the main Fabrick and was like to have dropped ripe at my own Feet.'[8]

Meanwhile Hawksmoor, the detective, finds himself investigating crimes he is convinced are connected, but he cannot understand how. The landscape of London is inhabited by unreal presences, the world echoes with strange voices and seems, suddenly, inexplicable:

'The music of a popular song now came from the radio as Hawksmoor gazed out of the window; and he saw a door closing, a boy dropping a coin in the street, a woman turning her head, a man calling. For a moment he wondered why such things were occurring now: could it be that the world sprang up around him only as he invented it second by second and that, like a dream, it faded into the darkness from which it had come as soon as he moved forward? But then he understood that these things were real: they would never cease to occur and they would always be the same, as familiar and as ever-renewed as the tears which he had just seen on the woman's face.'[9]

Hawksmoor is a novel of ideas – in the passage above the old theory of eternal recapitulation seems to be dawning on the detective – but it has only one central idea: that our language is our world. Hawksmoor's modern world is thinner and more standardized than that of Dyer because his language is. And yet the echoes of Dyer's black, plague-ridden world are everywhere: visible in the masonry of his buildings; ancient traces in the language. Although the language of science superseded that of the medieval world it could never quite eradicate its legacy. Wren never knew of the occult schemes concealed in the plans of Dyer's churches. So the modern language turns out to be inhabited by the ghosts and demons of the past, it ties us to history. Indeed, since we are inhabitants of language rather than users, it places us in a single, contemporaneous history.

Hawksmoor is an extraordinary condensation of the preoccupations of the new novel that has emerged over the past decade; but it is also a brilliantly clear fictional realization of the primacy of language. It is a post-scientific novel in that it insists that science is no more than one variant of the common fabric of language. It can be compared to Gombrich's vision of art as a sum of its histories, a hall of mirrors in which each succeeding artist can only build on the mountain of past conventions. So, with Ackroyd, we can only live in the language as it is, a vast unknowable echo chamber, still inhabited by the voices of the past: 'Their words were my own but not my own.'[10]

This resurgence of interest in the complexities of narrative, specifically in the anti-realist layering of narrative, is a development that reaches far beyond the stylistic playground of the post-modern. Post-modernism, as most familiarly defined, tends towards mannerism, the use of styles emptied of content. Its inclusiveness is that of inhibited self-consciousness, but the inclusiveness of Potter and Ackroyd, as well as of many others among the new generation of novelists, is that of a new confidence in the capacity of the artistic medium. It is a movement towards the genuine engagement of art with the conditions of consciousness, a movement already achieved by J. H. Prynne.

Even in British architecture, the art most plagued by the demands of money, politics and stylistic fad, a form of narrative has emerged. Richard Rogers's Pompidou Centre and Lloyd's Building both suggest a form that can be 'readable' and imaginatively inclusive without simply resorting to 'recognizable' elements. Equally, Will Alsop has been teaching and producing an architectural style which relies on its own 'disarticulation', its ability to allow buildings to become complex, disconnected forms and yet to provide a continuous experience, a type of narrative. To be, in a word, inclusive: that is, to avoid the old swinging of the artistic pendulum between 'ordinary' life and extreme emotion, between nervous retreat and grand gesture, in order to allow the real, unfettered play of the imagination.

That, of course, is the best that art can ever achieve anywhere at any time. I hope that I have shown that it has occasionally done so in post-war Britain, in spite of the many creative and national failures of nerve I have been obliged to record.

In time, as I said, the years that have passed since the war will be reduced by certainties. But it is better to be here in *this* time before that happens; which is, of course, another way of saying it is better to be alive than dead. From here, we cannot judge how we shall be reduced by later generations. We can only be sure they must be wrong because they are not seeing it from here – from now.

Nor can we be sure of something else: whether we have a national culture at all. This may be an urgent, if unanswerable, question at a time when we are about to be finally and fully subsumed into Europe and after years of economic and political domination by the USA. Modernism seemed to signal the severance of all Western culture from its past, the disintegration of the climate of reason that had sustained it since the Renaissance. The many British efforts since then to retie the knot have proved significant only by their imaginative failure. The dead hands of a revived empiricism, a crude sentimentality of place, various bleak orthodoxies of despair as well as the quaint notion of an academic élite have all been laid upon my period and all have proved artistically sterile. The best work has come, instead, from the most fluid, least programmed imaginations that have proved capable of assimilating, rather than merely defeating, the enemies their age has bequeathed them: realism, political rhetoric and scientific triumphalism.

These distinctive successes could have been achieved only in post-war Britain. They were the wild flowers that sprang from its rubble. Defining them in terms of a national cultural continuity, however, is a task that may still have to be deferred; it may, in any case, not be worthy of undertaking. Accidents of geography should not be allowed to lay conditions upon the imagination. We may wish to know what precisely it is that connects us – uniquely us – to, say, Lincoln Cathedral, a masterpiece that all are agreed is supremely 'English'. But the connection is impossible to establish. We do not share the beliefs of its designers and we have to work hard even to understand their technical problems. The closer we look at Lincoln's vaulting or its Angel Choir, the clearer it becomes that the only connection of which we can be sure is that we inhabit the same island. Nikolaus Pevsner once brilliantly and movingly described subtle continuities, an Englishness of style – of linearity and disarticulated parts – that suggest there may be something that endures. But can we really detect or imagine within ourselves the content behind that style? Perhaps. Perhaps there is a line that would enable us to join hands with the builders of Lincoln's Angel Choir. One thing, however, our period should have proved beyond all doubt: it is curved.

Notes

PART ONE

Strange Light

1   *The Times*, 3 May 1945.
2   Ibid.
3   Ibid, 9 May 1945.
4   Charles Williams, *All Hallows' Eve*, Faber and Faber, 1945, p. 1.
5   Correlli Barnett, *The Audit of War*, Macmillan, 1987, p. 1.
6   Muriel Spark, *The Girls of Slender Means*, Penguin, 1966, p. 7.
7   Anthony West, *H. G. Wells: Aspects of a Life*, Penguin, 1985, p. 147.
8   H. G. Wells, *The Happy Turning: A Dream Life*, Heinemann, 1945, pp. 49–50.
9   H. G. Wells, *Journalism and Prophecy 1893–1946*, compiled and edited by W. Warren Wagar, Bodley Head, 1965, p. 316.
10 *The Times*, 3 May 1945.
11 Ibid, 8 August 1945.
12 *Horizon*, vol. XII, no. 69, September 1945, p. 149.
13 Arthur Marwick, *British Society Since 1945*, Pelican, 1987, p. 55.
14 Humphrey Jennings, *Pandaemonium*, Picador, 1987, p. xxxix.

Modest Windows

1   Kenneth Clark, *Landscape into Art*, John Murray, 1986, p. 230.
2   Rex Warner, *The Aerodrome*, Oxford University Press, 1983, p. 178.
3   Evelyn Waugh, *Helena*, Penguin, 1987, p. 13.
4   *The Essays, Articles and Reviews of Evelyn Waugh*, edited by Donat Gallagher, Methuen, 1983, p.312.
5   John Betjeman, 'Sunday Afternoon Service in St Enodoc Church, Cornwall', included in *Collected Poems*, John Murray, 1958, p. 132.
6   P. G. Wodehouse, *Full Moon*, Herbert Jenkins, 1947, p. 135.
7   This discussion of Ealing is heavily indebted to Charles Barr's *Ealing Studios*, Cameron and Tayleur in association with David and Charles, 1977.
8   Ibid, p. 130.
9   Ibid, p. 177.
10 Ibid, p. 61.
11 Ibid.
12 Lionel Esher, *A Broken Wave: The Rebuilding of Britain 1940–1980*, Allen Lane, 1981, p. 18.
13 Philip Larkin, *A Girl in Winter*, Faber and Faber, 1986, p. 96.
14 Ibid, p. 165.
15 Ibid, p. 183.

16 Kingsley Amis, *Collected Poems 1944–1979*, Penguin, 1980, p. 16.
17 William Cooper, *Scenes from Provincial Life*, Methuen, 1983, p. 75.
18 Ibid, p. 3.
19 T. S. Eliot, *Notes Towards the Definition of Culture*, Faber and Faber, 1983, p. 123–4.
20 Peter Ackroyd, *T. S. Eliot*, Hamish Hamilton, 1984, p. 273.
21 Ibid, p. 271.
22 T. S. Eliot, *Collected Poems 1909–1962*, Faber and Faber, 1983, p. 222.

School Building

1 Evelyn Waugh, *Brideshead Revisited*, Penguin, 1981, p. 42.
2 *Spectator*, no. 6098, 11 May 1945, p. 424.
3 W. H. Auden, *The English Auden: Poems, Essays and Dramatic Writings 1927–1939* edited by Edward Mendelson, Faber and Faber, 1986, p. 212.
4 Ibid, p. 211.
5 Evelyn Waugh, *Decline and Fall*, Penguin, 1975, p. 120.
6 F. R. Leavis, *New Bearings in English Poetry*, Penguin, 1967, p. 174.
7 Lionel Esher, *A Broken Wave: The Rebuilding of Britain 1940–1980*, Allen Lane, 1981, p. 45.
8 Arthur Marwick, *British Society Since 1945*, Pelican, 1987, p. 58.
9 Quoted in Anthony Jackson, *The Politics of Architecture*, The Architectural Press, 1970, p. 167.
10 *Horizon*, vol. XIII, no. 77, May 1946, p. 327.
11 Ibid, p. 329.
12 Ibid, vol. XV, no. 87, April 1947, p. 153.
13 *Spectator*, no. 6216, 15 August 1947, p. 198.
14 Angus Wilson, *The Wrong Set*, Secker and Warburg, 1949, p. 113.

Graceful Attitudes

1 Michael Roberts, *T. E. Hulme*, Carcanet, 1982, p. 204.
2 *The Essays, Articles and Reviews of Evelyn Waugh*, edited by Donat Gallagher, Methuen, 1983, p. 288.
3 Ibid, p. 277.
4 Ibid, p. 300.
5 Evelyn Waugh, *Helena*, Penguin, 1987, p. 79.
6 Ibid, pp. 144–5.
7 Graham Greene, *The Heart of the Matter*, Heinemann, 1948, p. 297.
8 Graham Greene, *The End of the Affair*, Heinemann, 1951, p. 56.
9 *The Collected Essays, Journalism and Letters of George Orwell. Volume IV. In Front of your Nose*, edited by Sonia Orwell and Ian Angus, 1945–50, Secker and Warburg, 1969, p. 441.

Dangerous Citizens

1 *Horizon*, vol. XII, no. 72, December 1945, p. 365.
2 *Spectator* no. 6111, 10 August 1945, p. 117.

3   *New Statesman* vol. XXX, no. 755, 11 August 1945, p. 85.
4   Ibid, vol. XXX, no. 757, 25 August 1945, p. 142.
5   From 'Ending as a Sage', in *Shaw: An Autobiography 1898–1950 Selected from His Writings*, edited by Stanley Weintraub, Max Reinhardt, 1971, p. 222.
6   L. L. Whyte, Scientific Thought in the Coming Decade, *Horizon*, vol. XVIII, no. 103, July 1948, p. 5.
7   Bertrand Russell, *The Impact of Science on Society*, Unwin Hyman, 1985, p. 53.
8   Ibid, p. 91.
9   Ibid, p. 102.
10 A. J. Ayer, *Language, Truth and Logic*, Victor Gollancz, 1950, p. 153.
11 George Orwell, *Nineteen Eighty-Four*, Penguin, 1987, p. 198.

Nightmare Shapes

1   Evelyn Waugh, *Unconditional Surrender*, Penguin, 1975, p. 59.
2   *Spectator*, no. 6095, 20 April 1945, p. 3503.
3   Ibid, no. 6096, 27 April 1945, p. 403.
4   *New Statesman*, vol. XXIX, no. 742, 12 May 1945, p. 279.
5   *Horizon*, vol. XII, no. 69, September 1945, p. 149.
6   *New Statesman*, vol, XXIX, no. 724, 6 January 1945, p. 11.
7   *Horizon*, vol XI, no. 63, March 1945, p. 211.
8   Ibid, vol. XII, no. 67, July 1945, p. 12.
9   *New Statesman*, vol. XXXIII, no. 828, 4 January 1947, p. 14.
10 *Horizon*, vol. XI, no. 65, May 1945, p. 296.
11 Jean-Paul Sartre, *What is Literature?*, Methuen, 1983, p. 124.
12 Herbert Read, *The Philosophy of Modern Art*, Faber and Faber, 1952, p. 46.
13 Ibid, p. 21.
14 Ibid, p. 107.
15 Ibid, p. 105.
16 *The Times*, 20 December 1945.
17 *New Statesman*, vol, XXXI, no. 776, 5 January 1946, p. 7.
18 *Apollo*, vol. XLIII, January 1946, p. 2.

Poignant Key

1   *Victor Pasmore*, with an introduction by Alan Bowness and Luigi Lamberini, Thames and Hudson, 1980.
2   Quoted in Frances Spalding, *British Art Since 1900*, Thames and Hudson, 1986, p. 108.
3   *The Critical Writings of Adrian Stokes Vol. III 1955–1967*, Thames and Hudson, 1978, p. 155.
4   Herbert Read, *The Philosophy of Modern Art*, Faber and Faber, 1952, p. 194.
5   Benedict Nicholson in the *New Statesman*, vol. XXXIV, no. 852, 12 July 1947, p. 29.
6   Kenneth Clark, *Landscape into Art*, John Murray, 1986, p. 73.
7   David Sylvester, *Interviews with Francis Bacon*, Thames and Hudson, 1975, pp. 28–9.
8   Ibid, p. 56.

9   Ibid, p. 12.

Reclining Figures

1   John Russell, *Henry Moore*, Allen Lane, The Penguin Press, 1968, p. 102.
2   Ibid, p. 28.
3   Quoted in Roger Berthoud, *The Life of Henry Moore*, Faber and Faber, 1987, p. 230.

A Mouth

1   *Horizon*, vol. XI, no. 61, January 1945, p. 17.
2   Ibid, vol. XX, no. 118, October 1949, p. 279.
3   Ibid, vol. XII, no. 67, July 1945, p. 72.
4   *The Collected Essays, Journalism and Letters of George Orwell Vol. IV. In Front of your Nose 1945–50*, edited by Sonia Orwell and Ian Angus, Secker and Warburg, 1969, p. 62.
5   W. H. Auden, 'In Memory of W. B. Yeats', in *Collected Poems*, Faber and Faber, 1976, p. 197.
6   Quoted in Humphrey Carpenter, *W. H. Auden: A Biography*, Unwin Hyman, 1983, p. 70.
7   W. H. Auden, 'Consider', in *Collected Poems*, Faber and Faber, 1976, p. 61.
8   Quoted in Ian Hamilton, *The Little Magazines: A Study of Six Editors*, Weidenfeld and Nicolson, 1976, p. 98.
9   Peter Conrad, *Imagining America*, Routledge and Kegan Paul, 1980, p. 199.
10 John Bayley, *The Romantic Survival*, Constable, 1957, p. 93.
11 F. R. Leavis, *The Common Pursuit*, Chatto and Windus, 1952, p. 294.
12 W. H. Auden, 'New Year Letter', in *Collected Poems*, Faber and Faber, 1976, p. 161.
13 Quoted in Humphrey Carpenter, *W. H. Auden: A Biography*, Unwin Hyman, 1983, pp. 313–14.
14 W. H. Auden, *For the Time Being: A Christmas Oratorio*, in *Collected Poems*, Faber and Faber, 1976, p. 269.
15 Ibid.
16 Ibid.
17 Ibid.
18 W. H. Auden, *The Sea and the Mirror*, in *Collected Poems*, Faber and Faber, 1976, p. 309.
19 Quoted in Humphrey Carpenter, *W. H. Auden: A Biography*, Unwin Hyman, 1983, p. 328.
20 W. H. Auden, *The Sea and the Mirror*, in *Collected Poems*, Faber and Faber, 1976, p. 309.
21 Ibid.
22 W. H. Auden, 'In Praise of Limestone', in *Collected Poems*, Faber and Faber, 1976, p. 414.

Unseen Lights

1 *New Statesman*, vol. XXXII, no. 808, 17 August 1946 p. 115.
2 H. G. Wells, *Tono-Bungay*, Pan, 1975, p. 325.
3 Ibid, p. 328.
4 Anthony West, *H. G. Wells: Aspects of a Life*, Penguin, 1985, p. 149.
5 *The Times*, 3 May 1951.
6 Ibid, 4 May 1951.
7 *Wyndham Lewis: An Anthology of his Prose*, edited with an introduction by E. W. F. Tomlin, Methuen, 1969, pp. 393–7.
8 Ezra Pound, Canto CXV, in *The Cantos*, Faber and Faber, 1987, p. 794.

PART TWO

Late Times

1 David Jones, *Epoch and Artist*, Faber and Faber, 1973, pp. 71–2.
2 David Jones, *The Anathemata*, Faber and Faber, 1972, p. 11.
3 Ibid, pp. 90–1.
4 David Jones, *Epoch and Artist*, Faber and Faber, 1973, p. 40.
5 Kenneth Clark, *Landscape into Art*, John Murray, 1986, p. 5.
6 David Jones, *The Anathemata*, Faber and Faber, 1972, p. 15.
7 *Encounter*, vol. 2, no. 2, February 1954, p. 69.
8 David Jones, *The Anathemata*, Faber and Faber, 1972, p. 24.
9 Ibid, p. 28.
10 David Jones, *Epoch and Artist*, Faber and Faber, 1973, p. 13.
11 Lawrence Durrell, *Justine*, Faber and Faber, 1984, p. 100.
12 Ibid, p. 194.

Small, Clear

1 *Spectator*, no. 6519, 5 June 1953, p. 718.
2 Ibid.
3 John Osborne, *Plays for England*, Faber and Faber, 1963, p. 75.
4 *Encounter*, no. 88, vol. 16, January 1961, p. 16.
5 Kingsley Amis, *Socialism and the Intellectuals*, Fabian Tract 304, 1957.
6 Ibid.
7 Arthur Marwick, *British Society Since 1945*, Pelican, 1987, p. 101.
8 *Spectator*, no. 6588, 1 October 1954, p. 399.
9 In an interview with the author.
10 Kingsley Amis, *Lucky Jim*, Penguin, 1975, p. 40.
11 Ibid, p. 39.
12 Ibid, p. 121.
13 Ibid, p. 26.
14 *Declaration*, edited by Tom Maschler, MacGibbon and Kee, 1957, p. 22.
15 Ibid, p. 94.
16 Kingsley Amis, *Lucky Jim*, Penguin, 1975, p. 215.
17 Philip Larkin, *Required Writing: Miscellaneous Pieces 1955–1982*, Faber and Faber, 1983, p. 79.

18 Philip Larkin, 'Church Going', in *The Less Deceived*, The Marvell Press, 1985, pp. 28–9.
19 Frank Kermode, *Puzzles and Epiphanies: Essays and Reviews 1958–61*, Routledge and Kegan Paul, 1963, p. 153.
20 *Encounter*, vol. 7, no. 4, October 1956, p. 74.
21 See Blake Morrison, *The Movement: English Poetry and Fiction of the 1950s*, Oxford University Press, 1980.
22 Robert Graves, *The Crowning Privilege*, Pelican, 1959, p. 135.
23 Ibid, p. 157.
24 Kingsley Amis, *Lucky Jim*, Penguin, 1975, p. 250.
25 Philip Larkin, *The Whitsun Weddings*, Faber and Faber, 1986, p. 23.
26 Angus Wilson, *The Wild Garden*, Secker and Warburg, 1963, p. 114.
27 *Encounter*, vol. 4, no. 4, April 1955, p. 12.

Very Nice

1 *The Plays of John Whiting*, Heinemann, 1957, p. 236.
2 John Osborne, *Look Back in Anger*, Faber and Faber, 1986, pp. 84–5.
3 Ibid, p. 10.
4 *The Times*, 14 October 1967.
5 *Encounter*, vol. 7, no. 2, August 1956, p. 71.
6 Harold Pinter, *The Birthday Party*, Methuen, 1976, p. 9.
7 Andrew Kennedy, *Six Dramatists in Search of a Language: Studies in Dramatic Language*, Cambridge University Press 1975, p. 167.
8 Harold Pinter, *The Birthday Party*, Methuen. 1976, p. 87.
9 Harold Pinter, *The Caretaker*, Methuen, 1960, p. 38.

Instantly Elated

1 Quoted in Frances Spalding, *British Art Since 1900*, Thames and Hudson, 1986, p. 185.
2 Christopher Isherwood, *The World in the Evening*, Methuen, 1954, p. 38.
3 Frances Spalding, *British Art Since 1900*, Thames and Hudson, 1986, p. 149.
4 *Encounter*, vol. 3, no. 10, July 1954, p. 23.
5 Lawrence Alloway, *Nine Abstract Artists: Their Work and Theory*, Alec Tiranti, 1954, p. 2.
6 Ibid, p. 30.
7 Frances Spalding, *British Art Since 1900*, Thames and Hudson, 1986, p. 172.
8 Ibid, p. 172.
9 Quoted in *British Art in the Twentieth Century*, Royal Academy of Arts, 1987, p. 291.
10 Ibid, p. 432.
11 *Spectator*, no. 6697, 2 November 1956, p. 595.
12 *The Times*, 2 November 1956.

NOTES

Functionally, Englishly

1 Robert Maxwell, *New British Architecture*, Thames and Hudson, 1972, p. 16.
2 Reyner Banham, *The New Brutalism: Ethic or Aesthetic?*, The Architectural Press, 1966, p. 11.
3 Ibid.
4 Sigfried Giedion, *Space, Time and Architecture*, 1954, Harvard, p. 536.
5 Lionel Esher, *A Broken Wave: The Rebuilding of Britain 1940–1980*, Allen Lane, 1981, p. 57.
6 Nikolaus Pevsner, *The Englishness of English Art*, Penguin, 1986, p. 48.
7 Ibid, p. 181.
8 Ibid, p. 188.
9 *Encounter*, no. 65, vol. 12, February 1959, p. 54.

Information Information

1 Quoted in Diane Kirkpatrick, *Eduardo Paolozzi*, Studio Vista, 1970, p. 11.
2 Ibid, p. 19.
3 *The Critical Writings of Adrian Stokes Vol. III 1955–1967*, Thames and Hudson, 1978, p. 289.
4 Richard Hamilton, *Collected Words*, Thames and Hudson, 1984, p. 24.
5 Diane Kirkpatrick, *Eduardo Paolozzi*, Studio Vista, 1970, pp. 120–1.
6 Richard Hamilton, *Collected Words*, Thames and Hudson, 1984, p. 28.
7 Peter Conrad, *Imagining America*, Routledge and Kegan Paul, 1980, p. 197.
8 *Encounter*, no. 67, vol. 12, April 1959, p. 52.
9 Peter Conrad, *Imagining America*, Routledge and Kegan Paul, 1980, p. 149.

Nagging Humanism

1 Aldous Huxley, *Literature and Science*, Chatto and Windus, 1963, p. 11.
2 Ibid, p. 98.
3 Aldous Huxley, *Island*, Chatto and Windus, 1962, p. 160.
4 *Encounter*, vol. 5, no. 1, July 1955, p. 73.
5 *Encounter*, vol. 20, no. 1, January 1963, p. 88.
6 *Encounter*, vol. 12, no. 1, January 1959 p. 4.
7 John Lehmann, *The Open Night*, Longman, 1952, p. 3.
8 Nigel Dennis, *Cards of Identity*, Weidenfeld and Nicolson, 1955, p. 101.
9 Ibid, p. 149.
10 *Encounter*, vol. 12, no. 6, June 1959, p. 72.
11 John Berger, *Permanent Red: Essays in Seeing*, Methuen, 1960, p. 70.
12 *Encounter*, vol. 15, no. 1, July 1960, p. 6.
13 Ibid, vol. 19, no. 4, October 1962, p. 27.
14 Dorothea Krook, *Three Traditions of Moral Thought*, Cambridge University Press, 1959, p. 296.
15 *Encounter*, vol. 21, no. 1, July 1963, p. 17.
16 Angus Wilson, *The Wild Garden*, Secker and Warburg, 1963, p. 15.
17 Ibid, p. 27.
18 Ibid, p. 30.

Enchanted Precinct

1 Frank Kermode, *Puzzles and Epiphanies: Essays and Reviews 1958–61*, Routledge and Kegan Paul, 1963, p. 127.
2 Anthony Powell, *A Buyer's Market*, Heinemann, 1955, p. 153.
3 Anthony Powell, *The Acceptance World*, Heinemann, 1955, p. 32.
4 Angus Wilson, *The Wild Garden*, Secker and Warburg, 1963, p. 150.
5 Anthony Powell, *A Question of Upbringing*, Flamingo, 1986, p. 5.
6 Ibid, p. 6.
7 Anthony Powell, *Hearing Secret Harmonies*, Flamingo, 1986, p. 252.

Right Line

1 Angus Wilson, *Hemlock and After*, Secker and Warburg, 1952, p. 233.
2 William Golding, *Pincher Martin*, Faber and Faber, 1984, p. 7.
3 William Golding, *The Spire*, Faber and Faber, 1983, p. 7.
4 William Golding, *The Hot Gates and other occasional pieces*, Faber and Faber, 1984, p. 19.
5 Ibid, p. 20.
6 Frank Kermode, *Puzzles and Epiphanies: Essays and Reviews 1958–61*, Routledge and Kegan Paul, 1963, p. 200.
7 *Encounter*, vol. 14, no. 1, January 1960, p. 84.

Tiny Spark

1 Iris Murdoch, *Sartre*, Fontana, 1968, pp. 9–10.
2 Ibid, pp. 119–20.
3 Iris Murdoch, *The Sovereignty of Good*, Routledge and Kegan Paul, 1970, p. 7.
4 Ibid, p. 15.
5 Ibid, p. 80.
6 Ibid, p. 27.
7 Ibid, p. 34.
8 *Encounter*, vol. 12, no. 4, April 1959, p. 68.
9 Iris Murdoch, *Sartre*, Fontana, 1968, p. 117.
10 Iris Murdoch, *The Sovereignty of Good*, Routledge and Kegan Paul, 1970, p. 73.
11 Iris Murdoch, *Under the Net*, Chatto and Windus, 1954, p. 245.
12 Iris Murdoch, *The Good Apprentice*, Penguin, 1986, p. 163.

Whereof Thereof

1 Quoted in A. J. Ayer, *Ludwig Wittgenstein*, Penguin, 1986, p. 7.
2 Roger Scruton, *The Politics of Culture and other essays*, Carcanet, 1981, pp. 23–4.
3 A. J. Ayer, *Ludwig Wittgenstein*, Penguin, 1986, pp. 130–1.
4 *Encounter*, vol. 7, no. 1, July 1956, p. 84.
5 *Encounter*, vol. 7, no. 2, August 1956, pp. 72–4.
6 A. J. Ayer, *Ludwig Wittgenstein*, Penguin, 1986, p. 31.
7 Ludwig Wittgenstein, *Philosophical Investigations*, Basil Blackwell, 1972, p. viii.
8 Ibid, p. 89.

9 Ibid, p. 8.
10 A. J. Ayer, *Ludwig Wittgenstein*, Penguin, 1986, p. 143.
11 *Recollections of Wittgenstein*, edited by Rush Rhees, Oxford University Press, 1984, pp. 57–8.

Whispering Gallery

1 *Encounter*, vol. 19, no. 3, September 1962, p. 57.
2 E. H. Gombrich, *Art and Illusion: A Study in the Psychology of Pictorial Representation*, Phaidon, 1980, p. 148.
3 E. H. Gombrich, *Meditations on a Hobby Horse and other essays on the theory of art*, Phaidon, 1963, p. 11.
4 Ibid, p. 27.
5 Richard Wollheim, *Art and its Objects*, Cambridge University Press, 1980, p. 59.

PART THREE
Seeking Revenge

1 W. H. Auden, *Collected Poems*, Faber and Faber, 1976, p. 669.
2 *New Statesman*, vol. LXVIII, no. 1754, 23 October 1964, p. 597.
3 Alan Bennett, *Forty Years On*, Faber and Faber, 1969, p. 52.
4 Ibid, p. 57.
5 Arthur Marwick, *British Society Since 1945*, Pelican, 1987, p. 145.
6 Philip Larkin, *High Windows*, Faber and Faber, 1985, p. 17.
7 Quoted in Elizabeth Sussex, *Lindsay Anderson*, Studio Vista, 1969, p. 32.
8 John Lahr, *Prick Up Your Ears: The Biography of Joe Orton*, Penguin, 1986.
9 Joe Orton, *Loot* in *The Complete Plays*, edited by John Lahr, Methuen, 1983, pp. 250–1.
10 Ibid, p. 400.
11 E. H. Gombrich, *Meditations on a Hobby Horse and other essays on the theory of art*, Phaidon, 1963, p. 29.
12 Andrew Kennedy, *Six Dramatists in Search of a Language: Studies in Dramatic Language*, Cambridge University Press, 1975, p. 232.
13 E. H. Gombrich, *Meditations on a Hobby Horse and other essays on the theory of art*, Phaidon, 1963, p. 69.
14 John Lahr, *Prick Up Your Ears: The Biography of Joe Orton*, Penguin, 1986, p. 16.

Too Barren

1 *Encounter*, vol. 22, no. 1, January 1964, p. 39.
2 David Hockney, *David Hockney*, Thames and Hudson, 1976, p. 41.
3 Ibid.
4 Ibid.
5 R. B. Kitaj, *Paintings, Drawings, Pastels*, Thames and Hudson, 1982, p. 39.
6 Ibid.
7 Ibid, p. 14.
8 Ibid, p. 43.
9 Ibid, p. 39.

10 Edward Lucie-Smith, *Thinking About Art: critical essays*, Calder and Boyars, 1968, p. 20.
11 Richard Wollheim, *On Art and the Mind*, Allen Lane, 1973, p. 118.
12 Ibid, p. 124.

Acid Dances

1 Jeff Nuttall, *Bomb Culture*, Paladin, 1970, pp. 182–3.
2 Ibid.
3 Quoted in ibid, p. 157.
4 *Encounter*, vol. 38, no. 3, March 1972, p. 55.
5 Ibid, vol. 27, no. 1, January 1967, p. 62.
6 *The Times*, 22 November 1963.
7 *Encounter*, vol. 31, no. 2, August 1968, p. 39.
8 Jeff Nuttall, *Bomb Culture*, Paladin, 1970, p. 162.
9 *Encounter*, vol. 27, no. 5, November 1966, p. 4.
10 Quoted in Ronald Hayman, *The Set-Up: An Anatomy of English Theatre Today*, Eyre Methuen, 1973, pp. 76–7.

The Edge

1 Quoted in David Holbrook, *Lost Bearings in English Poetry*, Vision, 1977, p. 101.
2 Peter Redgrove, 'The Half-Scissors', in *British Poetry since 1945*, edited by Edward Lucie-Smith, Penguin, 1986, p. 183.
3 *The New Poetry*, selected and introduced by A. Alvarez, Penguin, 1986, p. 17.
4 Ibid, p. 23.
5 Ibid, p. 25.
6 Ibid, p. 26.
7 Ted Hughes, 'Egg-Head', in *Selected Poems 1957–1981*, Faber and Faber, 1985, p. 23.
8 Ted Hughes, 'The Bull Moses', ibid, p. 45.
9 Ibid.
10 *Encounter*, vol. 59, no. 1, June 1982, p. 73.
11 Ted Hughes, 'Crow', in *Selected Poems 1957–1981*, Faber and Faber, 1985, p. 116.
12 Sylvia Plath, 'I Want, I Want', in *The Colossus*, Faber and Faber, 1968, p. 36.
13 Sylvia Plath, 'Poem for a Birthday', ibid, p. 81.
14 Sylvia Plath, 'Morning Song', in *Ariel*, Faber and Faber, 1965, p. 11.
15 Sylvia Plath, 'Edge', ibid, p. 85.
16 A. Alvarez, 'Sylvia Plath', in *The Art of Sylvia Plath*, edited by Charles Newman, Faber and Faber, 1970, p. 58.
17 Ibid, p. 67.
18 Geoffrey Hill, 'Genesis', in *Collected Poems*, Penguin, 1985, p. 15.
19 Geoffrey Hill, 'The Songbook of Sebastian Arrurruz', ibid, p. 92.
20 Geoffrey Hill, 'Mercian Hymns', ibid, p. 107.
21 Geoffrey Hill, 'The Mystery of the Charity of Charles Peguy', ibid, p. 195.

It Mystifies

1 Kenneth Clark, *Civilization*, BBC and John Murray, 1971, p. 89.
2 Ibid, p. 344.
3 Ibid, p. 345.
4 Ibid, p. 347.
5 John Berger, *Ways of Seeing*, BBC and Penguin, 1987, p. 11.
6 Ibid, p. 23.
7 Ibid, p. 110.
8 Ibid, p. 93.
9 Germaine Greer, *The Female Eunuch*, MacGibbon and Kee, 1971, p. 5.
10 Ibid, p. 51.
11 Ibid, p. 13.
12 Ibid, p. 108.
13 Ibid, p. 144.
14 Ibid, p. 331.

Unspoken Nets

1 *Times Literary Supplement*, 31 July 1981, p. 881.
2 Terence Hawkes, *Structuralism and Semiotics*, Methuen, 1986, p. 18.
3 *Times Literary Supplement*, 31 July 1981, p. 881.
4 George Wasserman, *Roland Barthes*, Twayne, 1981, p. 123.
5 *Times Literary Supplement*, 6 February 1981, p. 135.
6 David Lodge, *Working with Structuralism: Essays and Reviews on Nineteenth and Twentieth Century Literature*, Routledge and Kegan Paul, 1982, p. vii.
7 *Encounter*, vol. 30, no. 2, February 1968, p. 51.
8 Jonathan Culler, *Structuralist Poetics: Structuralism, Linguistics and the Study of Literature*, Routledge and Kegan Paul, 1975, p. 12.
9 Ibid, p. 28.
10 Peter Ackroyd, *Notes for a New Culture*, Vision, 1976, p. 147.
11 Jonathan Culler, *Structuralist Poetics: Structuralism, Linguistics and the Study of Literature*, Routledge and Kegan Paul, 1975, p. 251.
12 Terence Hawkes, *Structuralism and Semiotics*, Methuen, 1986, pp. 155–6.
13 Susan Sontag, 'Writing Itself: On Roland Barthes', in *A Susan Sontag Reader*, Penguin, 1982, p. 426.
14 *Encounter*, vol. 35, no. 3, September 1970, p. 65.

Prancing Mortals

1 Samuel Beckett, *Proust and Three Dialogues with Georges Duthuit*, John Calder, 1976, p. 110.
2 Ibid, p. 124.
3 Samuel Beckett, *Molloy*, Calder and Boyars, 1966, p. 9.
4 Tom Stoppard, *Jumpers*, Faber and Faber, 1986, p. 22.
5 Ibid, p. 29.
6 Ibid, p. 39.
7 *Encounter*, vol. 45, no. 5, November 1975, p. 68.

8 Brigid Brophy, *Prancing Novelist*, Macmillan, 1973, p. xiv.
9 Ibid, p. 6.
10 Ibid, p. 69.
11 David Lodge, *Working with Structuralism: Essays and Reviews on Nineteenth and Twentieth Century Literature*, Routledge and Kegan Paul, 1982, p. 74.

Weapons Systems

1 J. G. Ballard, *Crash*, Triad Panther, 1985, p. 5.
2 Ibid.
3 Kingsley Amis, *New Maps of Hell: A Survey of Science Fiction*, Victor Gollancz, 1961, p. 156.
4 J. G. Ballard, *Crash*, Triad Panther, 1985, p. 8.
5 Ibid, p. 9.
6 Ibid, p. 100.
7 Ibid, p. 123.
8 Ibid, p. 9.
9 Michael Moorcock, *The Condition of Muzak*, Fontana, 1978, p. 176.
10 Ibid, p. 183.

Cool Gadgets

1 *Encounter*, vol. 36, No. 1, January 1971, p. 56.
2 Ibid, p. 53.
3 Ibid, p. 56.
4 *Encounter*, vol. 32, no. 1, January 1969, p. 17.
5 Ibid, p. 18.
6 Arthur Marwick, *British Society Since 1945*, Pelican, 1987, p. 135.
7 John Pearson, *The Profession of Violence: The Rise and Fall of the Kray Twins*, Weidenfeld & Nicolson, 1972, p. 101.
8 Jonathon Raban, *Soft City*, Hamish Hamilton, 1974, p. 64.
9 Malcolm Bradbury, *The Social Context of Modern English Literature*, Basil Blackwell, 1971, p. 230.
10 Ibid, p. 243.
11 Lionel Esher, *A Broken Wave: The Rebuilding of Britain 1940–1980*, Allen Lane, 1981, p. 75.
12 Jonathan Raban, *Soft City*, Hamish Hamilton, 1974, p. 18.
13 Arthur Marwick, *British Society Since 1945*, Pelican, 1987, p. 106.

PART FOUR

Scale Unknown

1 Arthur Marwick, *British Society Since 1945*, Pelican, 1987, p. 188.
2 *Encounter*, vol. 44, no. 1, January 1975, p. 35.
3 Edward Lucie-Smith, *Art in the Seventies*, Phaidon, 1981, p. 92.
4 Quoted in *A Quiet Revolution: British Sculpture since 1945*, edited by Terry A. Neff, Thames and Hudson, 1987, p. 16.
5 Edward Lucie-Smith, *Art in the Seventies*, Phaidon, 1981, p. 8

Doing Something

1 Diane Waldman, *Anthony Caro*, Phaidon, 1982, p. 30.
2 Quoted in Edward Lucie-Smith, *Movements in Art since 1945*, Thames and Hudson, 1987, p. 228.
3 Frances Spalding, *British Art since 1900*, Thames and Hudson, 1986, p. 208.
4 Mary Jane Jacob, 'Tony Cragg: "First Order Experiences"', in *A Quiet Revolution: British Sculpture since 1945*, Thames and Hudson, 1987, p. 55.
5 Michael Crompton, *New Art at the Tate Gallery 1983*, Tate Gallery, 1983, p. 60.
6 Mary Jane Jacob, 'Bill Woodrow: Objects Reincarnated', in *A Quiet Revolution: British Sculpture since 1945* Thames and Hudson, 1987, p. 162.
7 Quoted in Graham Beal, 'Richard Long: "the simplicity of walking, the simplicity of stones"', ibid, p. 112.

Handsome Bastards

1 Christopher Hampton, *The Philanthropist: a bourgeois comedy*, Faber and Faber, 1970, p. 78.
2 Malcolm Bradbury, *The History Man*, Arena, 1987, p. 106.
3 Ibid, p. 143.
4 Martin Amis, *The Rachel Papers*, Panther, 1977, p. 24.
5 Ibid, pp. 100–1.
6 Ibid, p. 154.
7 Martin Amis, *Dark Secrets*, Panther, 1975, p. 27
8 Martin Amis, *Einstein's Monsters*, Jonathan Cape, 1987, p. 8.

Nihilistic Recoil

1 F. R. Leavis, *The Living Principle: English as a Discipline of Thought*, Chatto and Windus, 1975, p. 7.
2 Ibid, p. 12.
3 Ibid, p. 69.
4 Frank Kermode, *Essays on Fiction 1971–1982*, Routledge and Kegan Paul, 1983, pp. 31–2.
5 *Encounter*, vol. 52, No. 5, May 1979, p. 59.
6 Nigel Williams, *Class Enemy*, Methuen, 1983, p. 70.
7 *Theatre Quarterly*, vol. VIII, no. 32, Winter 1979, p. 25.
8 *Encounter*, vol. 44, no. 1, January 1975, p. 66.
9 Howard Brenton, *Weapons of Happiness*, in *The Plays of the Seventies*, Methuen, 1986, p. 97.
10 *Theatre Quarterly*, vol. V, no. 17, March – May 1975, p. 20.
11 Ibid, p. 10.
12 Ibid, vol. VIII, no. 32, Winter 1979, p. 32.
13 *Gambit*, vol. 9, no. 36, p. 38.
14 Ibid.
15 Ibid, p. 42.
16 *Theatre Quarterly*, vol. V, no. 17, March–May 1975, p. 8.
17 Howard Brenton, *Romans in Britain*, Methuen, 1982, pp. 97–8.

18   *Theatre Quarterly*, vol. VI, no. 22, Summer 1976, p. 44.

Half English

1   David Rubin, *After the Raj: British novels of India since 1947*, New England, 1986,
    p. 121.
2   Paul Scott, *A Division of the Spoils*, Granada, 1983, pp. 148–9.
3   J. G. Farrell, *The Siege of Krishnapur*, Book Club Associates, 1974, p. 161.
4   J. G. Farrell, *The Singapore Grip*, Fontana, 1981, p. 12.
5   John Spurling, 'As Does the Bishop', included in J. G. Farrell, *The Hill Station*,
    Weidenfeld and Nicolson, 1981, p. 141.
6   J. G. Farrell, *The Singapore Grip*, Fontana, 1981, pp. 217–18.
7   V. S. Naipaul, *In a Free State*, Penguin, 1982, p. 13.
8   Ibid, pp. 57–8.
9   V. S. Naipaul, *Among the Believers: An Islamic Journey*, Penguin, 1981, pp. 398–9.
10 V. S. Naipaul, *The Enigma of Arrival*, Penguin, 1987, p. 52.
11 Ibid, p. 155.
12 Ibid, p. 220.

Not Frivolous

1   Alan Brownjohn, 'A View of English Poetry in the Early Seventies', in *British
    Poetry since 1960*, edited by Michael Schmidt and Grevel Lindop, Carcanet, 1972,
    p. 249.
2   *British Poetry since 1970*, edited by Peter Jones and Michael Schmidt, Carcanet,
    1980, p. ix.
3   Robert Stuart, 'Ted Hughes', ibid, p. 76.
4   Philip Larkin, *High Windows*, Faber and Faber, 1985, p. 17.
5   Ian Hamilton, 'The Making of the Movement', in *British Poetry since 1960*, edited
    by Michael Schmidt and Grevel Lindop, Carcanet, 1972, pp. 72–3.
6   C. H. Sisson, 'Poetry and Myth', in *British Poetry since 1970*, edited by Peter
    Jones and Michael Schmidt, Carcanet, 1980, p. 172.
7   *The Penguin Book of Contemporary British Poetry*, edited by Blake Morrison and
    Andrew Motion, Penguin, 1982, p. 11.
8   Ibid, p. 12.
9   Ibid, p. 13.
10 Seamus Heaney, 'Death of a Naturalist', in *British Poetry since 1945*, edited by
    Edward Lucie-Smith, Penguin, 1985, p. 343.
11 Ibid.
12 *The Penguin Book of Contemporary British Poetry*, edited by Blake Morrison and
    Andrew Motion, Penguin, 1982, pp. 13–14.
13 Seamus Heaney, 'Punishment', in ibid, p. 29.
14 Seamus Heaney, 'Englands of the Mind', 1976 lecture quoted in Jeremy Hooker,
    The Presence of the Past: essays on modern British and American poetry, Poetry
    Wales Press, 1987, p. 11.
15 Craig Raine, 'A Martian Sends a Postcard Home', in *The Penguin Book of
    Contemporary British Poetry*, edited by Blake Morrison and Andrew Motion,
    Penguin, 1982, p. 169.

16 *British Poetry since* 1970, edited by Peter Jones and Michael Schmidt, Carcanet, 1970, p. xxix.
17 *The Penguin Book of Contemporary British Poetry*, edited by Blake Morrison and Andrew Motion, Penguin, 1982, p. 20.

Exact Speech

1   Quoted in Alan Sked and Chris Cook, *Post-War Britain*, Penguin, 1986, p. 327.
2   Ibid, p. 329.
3   *Daily Telegraph*, 2 May 1979, p. 18.
4   *New Statesman*, vol. 103, no. 2664, 9 April 1982, p. 3.
5   Roger Scruton, *The Aesthetic of Architecture*, Methuen, 1979, p. 253.
6   Roger Scruton, 'Buckminster Fuller', in *The Politics of Culture and other essays*, Carcanet, 1981, p. 155.
7   Roger Scruton, 'The Impossibility of Semiotics', ibid, pp. 42–3.
8   Roger Scruton, 'Sense and Sincerity', ibid, p. 24.
9   Correlli Barnett, *The Audit of War*, Macmillan, 1987, p. 304.
10 Quoted in Michael Schmidt, *50 Modern British Poets*, Heinemann/Barnes and Noble, 1979, p. 266.
11 C. H. Sisson, 'On a Troopship', in *In the Trojan Ditch*, Carcanet, 1974, p. 156.
12 Quoted in Michael Schmidt, *50 Modern British Poets*, Heinemann/Barnes and Noble, 1979, p. 269.
13 C. H. Sisson, *English Poetry 1900–1950*, Hart-Davis, 1971, p. 262.
14 Ibid.
15 C. H. Sisson, 'The Usk', in *In the Trojan Ditch*, Carcanet, 1974, p. 34.
16 Michael Schmidt, *50 Modern British Poets*, Heinemann/Barnes and Noble, 1979, p. 271.
17 C. H. Sisson, 'Toys', in *God Bless Karl Marx*, Carcanet, 1987, p. 38

Like Helium

1   Peter Ackroyd, 'Among School Children', in *The Diversions of Purley and other poems*, Hamish Hamilton, 1987, p. 9.
2   Christos M. Joachimides, *A New Spirit in Painting*, Royal Academy of Arts, 1981, p. 14.
3   Ibid.
4   Anne Cluysenaar, 'Post-culture: Pre-culture?', in *British Poetry since 1960*, edited by Michael Schmidt and Grevel Lindop, Carcanet, 1972, p. 215.
5   Ibid, p. 223.
6   David Holbrook, *Lost Bearings in English Poetry*, Vision, 1977, p. 17.
7   Peter Ackroyd, *Notes for a New Culture*, Vision, 1976, p. 9.
8   Ibid, pp. 33–4.
9   Ibid, p. 146.
10 Ibid, p. 147.
11 Peter Ackroyd, 'Among School Children', in *The Diversions of Purley and other poems*, Hamish Hamilton, 1987, p. 9.
12 Ibid.

13 Peter Ackroyd, *Notes for a New Culture*, Vision, 1976, p. 129.
14 J. H. Prynne, 'Down Where Changed', in *Poems*, Agneau 2, 1982, p. 306.
15 J. H. Prynne, 'Crown', ibid, pp. 115–16.
16 *A Various Art*, edited by Andrew Crozier and Tim Longville, Carcanet, 1987, p. 11.
17 Ibid, p. 12.
18 Ibid, p. 13.
19 Ibid, pp. 343–4.
20 Ibid, pp. 206–7.
21 Ibid, p. 121.
22 J. H. Prynne, 'The Glacial Question, Unsolved', in *Poems*, Agneau 2, 1982, pp. 64–6.

Curved Lines

1   Timothy Mo, *An Insular Possession*, Chatto and Windus, 1986, p. 589.
2   Frank Kermode, *Essays on Fiction 1971–82*, Routledge and Kegan Paul, 1983, p. 31.
3   Ibid, p. 5.
4   David Lodge, *The Novelist at the Crossroads and other essays on fiction and criticism*, Ark, 1986, p. 5.
5   *Encounter*, vol. 55, no. 1, July 1980, p. 36.
6   Ian McEwan, 'Psychopolis', in *In Between the Sheets*, Picador, 1979, p. 103.
7   Dennis Potter, *The Singing Detective*, Faber and Faber, 1986 p. 77.
8   Peter Ackroyd, *Hawksmoor*, Abacus, 1986, p. 25.
9   Ibid, p. 158.
10 Ibid, p. 217.

Bibliography

The following is a list of critical, analytical and biographical works to which I am directly indebted.

Peter Ackroyd, *Notes for a New Culture*, Vision, 1976.
– *Ezra Pound and His World*, Thames and Hudson, 1980.
– *T. S. Eliot*, Hamish Hamilton, 1984
Lawrence Alloway, *Nine Abstract Artists: Their Work and Theory*, Alec Tiranti, 1954.
A. Alvarez, *Under Pressure*, Penguin, 1965.
– (ed.), *The New Poetry*, Penguin, 1986.
Kingsley Amis, *New Maps of Hell: a survey of science fiction*, Victor Gollancz, 1961.
Mark Amory (ed.), *The Letters of Evelyn Waugh*, Weidenfeld and Nicolson, 1980.
Roy Armes, *A Critical History of the British Cinema*, Secker and Warburg, 1979.
W. H. Auden, *The Dyer's Hand and other essays*, Faber and Faber, 1963.
Martyn Auty and Nick Roddick (eds.), *British Cinema Now*, BFI, 1985.
A. J. Ayer, *Ludwig Wittgenstein*, Weidenfeld and Nicolson, 1985.
Reyner Banham, *The New Brutalism: Ethic or Aesthetic?*, The Architectural Press, 1966.
Correlli Barnett, *The Audit of War*, Macmillan, 1987.
Charles Barr, *Ealing Studios*, Cameron and Tayleur/David and Charles, 1977.
John Bayley, *The Romantic Survival*, Constable, 1957.
John Berger, *Permanent Red: Essays in Seeing*, Methuen, 1960.
– *The Moment of Cubism and other essays*, Weidenfeld and Nicolson, 1969.
– *Ways of Seeing*, Penguin/BBC, 1987.
Roger Berthoud, *Graham Sutherland: A Biography*, Faber and Faber, 1982.
– *The Life of Henry Moore*, Faber and Faber, 1987.
David Blamires, *David Jones: Artist and Writer*, Manchester University Press, 1971.
Alan Bowness and Luigi Lamberini, *Victor Pasmore*, Thames and Hudson, 1980.
Malcolm Bradbury, *The Social Context of Modern English Literature*, Basil Blackwell, 1971.
– (ed.), *The Novel Today: Contemporary Writers on Modern Fiction*, Fontana, 1977.
Brigid Brophy, *Don't Never Forget: Collected Views and Reviews*, Jonathan Cape, 1966.
– *Prancing Novelist*, Macmillan, 1973.
– *Baroque-'n'-Roll and Other Essays*, Hamish Hamilton, 1987.
A. S. Byatt, *Degrees of Freedom: The Novels of Iris Murdoch*, Chatto and Windus, 1965.
Humphrey Carpenter, *W. H. Auden: A Biography*, Allen and Unwin, 1981.
Kenneth Clark, *Civilization: A Personal View*, BBC/John Murray, 1969.
– *Moments of Vision*, John Murray, 1981.
– *Landscape into Art*, John Murray, 1986.
Michael Compton, *New Art at the Tate Gallery 1983*, Tate Gallery, 1983.

THE PLEASURES OF PEACE

Susan Compton (ed.), *British Art in the 20th Century: The Modern Movement*, Royal Academy of Arts/Prestel, 1987.

Peter Conrad, *Imagining America*, Routledge and Kegan Paul, 1980.

Andrew Crozier and Tim Longville (eds.), *A Various Art*, Carcanet, 1987.

Jonathan Culler, *Structuralist Poetics: Structuralism, Linguistics and the Study of Literature*, Routledge and Kegan Paul, 1975.

– *On Deconstruction: Theory and Criticism After Structuralism*, Routledge and Kegan Paul, 1983.

James Curran and Vincent Porter, *British Cinema History*, Weidenfeld and Nicolson, 1983.

Terry Eagleton, *Criticism and Ideology*, Verso, 1978.

– *Literary Theory: An Introduction*, Blackwell, 1983.

T. S. Eliot, *Notes Towards the Definition of Culture*, Faber and Faber, 1948.

Lionel Esher, *A Broken Wave: The Rebuilding of Britain 1940–1980*, Allen Lane, 1981.

William Golding, *The Hot Gates and other occasional pieces*, Faber and Faber, 1965.

E. H. Gombrich, *Meditations on a Hobby Horse and other essays on the theory of art*, Phaidon, 1963.

– *Art and Illusion: A Study in the Psychology of Pictorial Representation*, Phaidon, 1980.

Lawrence Gowing, *Lucian Freud*, Thames and Hudson, 1984.

Robert Graves, *The Crowning Privilege*, Pelican, 1959.

Graham Greene, *A Sort of Life*, The Bodley Head, 1971.

Germaine Greer, *The Female Eunuch*, MacGibbon and Kee, 1971.

Ian Hamilton, *The Little Magazines: A Study of Six Editors*, Weidenfeld and Nicolson, 1976.

Richard Hamilton, *Collected Words 1953–1982*, Thames and Hudson, 1983.

Terence Hawkes, *Structuralism and Semiotics*, Methuen, 1977.

Ronald Hayman, *The Set-Up: An Anatomy of English Theatre Today*, Eyre Methuen, 1973.

– *Leavis*, Heinemann, 1976.

Robert Hewison, *Under Siege: Literary Life in London 1939–45*, Weidenfeld and Nicolson, 1977.

– *In Anger: Culture in the Cold War*, Weidenfeld and Nicolson, 1981.

– *Too Much: Art and Society in the Sixties 1960–75*, Weidenfeld and Nicolson, 1986.

Roger Hilton, *Paintings and Drawings 1931–73*, Arts Council of Great Britain, 1974.

David Hockney, *David Hockney*, Thames and Hudson, 1976.

Richard Hoggart, *Auden: An Introductory Essay*, Chatto and Windus, 1951.

– *The Uses of Literacy*, Chatto and Windus, 1957.

David Holbrook, *Lost Bearings in English Poetry*, Vision, 1977.

Jeremy Hooker, *Poetry of Place: Essays and Reviews 1970–81*, Carcanet, 1982.

– *The Presence of the Past: Essays on Modern British and American Poetry*, Poetry Wales Press, 1987.

Aldous Huxley, *Literature and Science*, Chatto and Windus, 1963.

Anthony Jackson, *The Politics of Architecture*, The Architectural Press, 1970.

Humphrey Jennings, *Pandaemonium*, Picador, 1987.

Christos M. Joachimides and others, *A New Spirit in Painting*, Royal Academy of Arts, 1981.

David Jones, *Epoch and Artist*, Faber and Faber, 1959.

– *The Anathemata*, Faber and Faber, 1972.

Peter Jones and Michael Schmidt (eds.), *British Poetry since 1970*, Carcanet, 1980.

Andrew Kennedy, *Six Dramatists in Search of a Language: Studies in Dramatic Language*, Cambridge University Press, 1975.

Anthony Kenny, *Wittgenstein*, Penguin, 1973.

Frank Kermode, *Puzzles and Epiphanies: Essays and Reviews 1958–61*, Routledge and Kegan Paul, 1963.

– *Modern Essays*, Fontana, 1970.

– *Essays on Fiction 1971–82*, Routledge and Kegan Paul, 1983.

Diane Kirkpatrick, *Eduardo Paolozzi*, Studio Vista, 1970.

R. B. Kitaj, *Drawings, Paintings, Pastels*, Thames and Hudson, 1982.

Dorothea Krook, *Three Traditions of Moral Thought*, Cambridge University Press, 1959.

John Lahr, *Prick Up Your Ears: The Biography of Joe Orton*, Penguin, 1986.

Philip Larkin, *Required Writing: Miscellaneous Pieces 1955–1982*, Faber and Faber, 1983.

F. R. Leavis, *The Common Pursuit*, Chatto and Windus, 1952.

– *New Bearings in English Poetry*, Penguin, 1967.

– *The Living Principle: English as a Discipline of Thought*, Chatto and Windus, 1975.

John Lehmann, *The Open Night*, Longman, 1952.

Wyndham Lewis, *Enemy Salvoes: Selected Literary Criticism*, Vision, 1975.

David Lodge, *Working with Structuralism*, Routledge and Kegan Paul, 1981.

– *The Language of Fiction*, Routledge and Kegan Paul, 1984.

– *The Novelist at the Crossroads and other essays in fiction and criticism*, Ark, 1986.

Edward Lucie-Smith, *Thinking about Art: Critical Essays*, Calder and Boyars, 1968.

– *Art in the Seventies*, Phaidon/Oxford, 1981.

– *Movements in Art since 1945*, Thames and Hudson, 1984.

– (ed.) *British Poetry since 1945*, Penguin, 1986

Bryan Magee, *Men of Ideas: Some Creators of Contemporary Philosophy*, Oxford University Press, 1982.

– *Modern British Philosophy*, Oxford University Press, 1986.

J. L. Martin, Ben Nicholson and Naum Gabo (eds.), *Circle*, Faber and Faber, 1971.

Tom Maschler (ed.), *Declaration*, MacGibbon and Kee, 1957.

Arthur Marwick, *British Society Since 1945*, Pelican, 1987.

Robert Maxwell, *New British Architecture*, Thames and Hudson, 1972.

Peter Medawar, *The Limits of Science*, Oxford University Press, 1985.

Paul de Monchaux, Fenella Crichton and Kate Blacker (eds.), *The Sculpture Show*, Arts Council of Great Britain, 1983.

Blake Morrison, *The Movement: English Poetry and Fiction of the 1950s*, Oxford University Press, 1980.

Blake Morrison and Andrew Motion (eds.), *The Penguin Book of Contemporary British Poetry*, Penguin, 1982.

Iris Murdoch, *Sartre*, Fontana, 1968.

Peter Murray and Stephen Trombley (eds.), *Modern British Architecture since 1945*, RIBA, 1984.

Terry A. Neff (ed.), *A Quiet Revolution: British Sculpture since 1965*, Thames and Hudson, 1987.

Edward Neill, 'Modernism and Englishness: Reflections on Auden and Larkin', in *Essays and Studies 1983*, John Murray for the English Association.

Charles Newman (ed.), *The Art of Sylvia Plath*, Faber and Faber, 1970.

Jeff Nuttall, *Bomb Culture*, Paladin, 1970.

James Park, *Learning to Dream: The New British Cinema*, Faber and Faber, 1984.

John Pearson, *The Profession of Violence: the rise and fall of the Kray Twins*, Weidenfeld and Nicolson, 1972.

Nikolaus Pevsner, *The Englishness of English Art*, Penguin, 1986.

Karl Popper, *Unended Quest: An Intellectual Autobiography*, Fontana, 1976.

Jonathan Raban, *The Society of the Poem*, Harrap, 1971.

- *Soft City*, Hamish Hamilton, 1974.

Herbert Read, *The Meaning of Art*, Penguin, 1951.

- *The Philosophy of Modern Art*, Faber and Faber, 1952.

- *Henry Moore: A Study of His Life and Work*, Thames and Hudson, 1965.

Rush Rhees (ed.), *Recollections of Wittgenstein*, Oxford University Press, 1984.

J. M. Richard, *An Introduction to Modern Architecture*, Penguin, 1953.

Michael Roberts, *T. E. Hulme*, Carcanet, 1982.

David Rubin, *After the Raj: British Novels of India since 1947*, New England, 1986.

Bertrand Russell, *The Impact of Science on Society*, Unwin Hyman, 1985.

John Russell, *Henry Moore*, Allen Lane, 1968.

Michael Schmidt, *50 Modern British Poets*, Heinemann/Barnes and Noble, 1979.

Michael Schmidt and Grevel Lindop, *British Poetry since 1960*, Carcanet, 1972.

Roger Scruton, *The Aesthetic of Architecture*, Methuen, 1979.

- *The Meaning of Conservatism*, Macmillan, 1980.

- *The Politics of Culture and Other Essays*, Carcanet, 1981.

C. H. Sisson, *English Poetry 1900–1950*, Hart Davis, 1971.

- *Anglican Essays*, Carcanet, 1983.

Alan Sked and Chris Cook, *Post-War Britain*, Penguin, 1986.

Alison and Peter Smithson, *Without Rhetoric: An Architectural Aesthetic 1955–72*, Latimer New Dimensions, 1973.

Frances Spalding, *British Art since 1900*, Thames and Hudson, 1986.

Stephen Spender, *The Struggle of the Modern*, Hamish Hamilton, 1963.

John Spurling, *Graham Greene*, Methuen, 1983.

James Stirling, *Buildings and Projects 1950–74*, Thames and Hudson, 1975.

Adrian Stokes, *The Critical Writings of Adrian Stokes*, Thames and Hudson, 1978.

Elizabeth Sussex, *Lindsay Anderson*, Studio Vista, 1969.

David Sylvester, *Interviews with Francis Bacon*, Thames and Hudson, 1975.

John Russell Taylor, *Anger and After: A Guide to the New British Drama*, Methuen, 1962.

Lorenza Trucchi, *Francis Bacon*, Thames and Hudson, 1976.

Kenneth Tynan, *Tynan Right and Left*, Longman, 1967.

Diane Waldman, *Anthony Caro*, Phaidon, 1982.

Anthony West, *H. G. Wells: Aspects of a Life*, Penguin, 1985.

Angus Wilson, *The Wild Garden*, Secker and Warburg, 1963.

Richard Wollheim, *On Art and the Mind*, Allen Lane, 1973.

- *Art and its Objects*, Cambridge University Press, 1980.

Alan Young, *Dada and After: Extremist Modernism and English Literature*, Manchester University Press, 1981.

Index

361

INDEX